Words matter!
Donald Marks
aka dimitri markov.
2Feb25

BloodBird

Medical Fiction

by

Dimitri Markov

n.d.p. for DH Marks

1991
Revised 2018

The Dangerous Doctors Series
by **Dimitri Markov**
n.d.p. for DH Marks

- **BloodBird** - When the organ isn't the only thing transplanted
- **The Surrogate** - A young woman trapped in the greed and power of the IVF industry
- **Her Charm Was Contagious** – A dangerous doctor and a patient who just loved everyone to death
- **Vera Mortina** - When the patient is not the sick one
- **Transit States** - collected poetry of Donald Harvey Marks

Available as paperback on Amazon and ebook on Kindle.

About the author

Dimitri Markov is the writer's name for Donald Harvey Marks, a physician and writer of intense medical fiction on the theme of **Dangerous Doctors**. Markov (Marks) gets his too-near-to-real-live material by observing others in the greater healthcare field for their actions, beliefs, hopes, fears and fantasies. Markov employs his lifetime of medical experience to explore the ill-defined boundary between medical fact and medical fiction. His **Dangerous Doctors** series of medical fiction includes: Vera Mortina, Her Charm Was Contagious, BloodBird, and The Surrogate. These works tell the (fictional) stories of good doctors, nurses and various health care providers, and doctors who are dangerous because of their faults : anger, jealousy, insecurity, greed, and mental illness. Dangerous to patients, dangerous to themselves, and certainly dangerous to those doctors and nurses they work with every day. Themes

include *in vitro* fertilization, paranoia and insecurity of aging, commercialization of medical care, and the transplantation of consciousness. If you enjoy true-to-life medical fiction by Robin Cook, Michael Palmer, Patricia Cornwell, Carol Cassella, Kathy Reichs, and Arnaldur Indridason, and the writing style of Scott Turow, then you should be reading Dimitri Markov's **Dangerous Doctors** series. In that sense, it will probably be dangerous for you to relate to your own health care providers the same way again. Comments and correspondence are welcome at
DimitriMarkov52@gmail.com

Personal blog of the author at
https://dhmarks.blogspot.com/

Acknowledgement

I would very much like to thank all my readers for their valuable assistance in comments, punctuation, plot issues, and encouraging feedback.

Preface

All the characters and events in this book are of course just totally, totally fictitious. And how could it be otherwise? The author certainly would be very surprised nevertheless if readers do not relate to some circumstances in a more or less personal way or recognize certain character traits in their own acquaintances, particularly those in the health care fields.

Chapter 1

FirsThought Scientific, Inc.
Northwest of Neuse, North Carolina

Sunrise passed unnoticed, its dull orange essence remaining well-hidden from all life below. On this damp North Carolina morning, it seemed that all life's occurrences happened in an odd kind of time-delay, and long hours would pass before the fog could dissipate, slower and much later than usual. Until then, the entrapped moisture managed to grip the pungent odor of industrial pollution near its ground level origin, poisoning the morning's beauty. This late in the year, the chemical stench typically stayed sequestered near a small algae-choked pond, but on this day the pond force-fed its thick green sludge into the mouth of a small artificial creek which cruelly cut a jagged, toxic pattern through the heart of FirsThought Scientific.

Close by that creek, Karolena Kreisler, a thirty-two year old research physician, stood once again motionless, as if paralyzed by a physical ailment rather than by the spiritual indecision that gripped her as she starred searching for elusive answers through the murky gray fog obscuring the vast industrial reserve of FirsThought.

At five-three and one hundred fifteen pounds, Karolena had the lithe, compact body of an athlete. Her blond hair was cut short but feminine and matched her fair Central European complexion. Karolena's features were well-defined and strong rather than subtle, an image reinforced by her formal-appearing over-sized white lab coat with the red and black FirsThought Scientific logo embossed over the breast pocket.

Several pressing issues clouded Karolena's mind, making it difficult for her to concentrate. Short-term, she debated whether she should, in just a few hours, once again compromise her ethics by participating in a research project whose very nature she found increasingly questionable, her complicity implying tacit approval on her part. Long-term, her concerns went much much deeper, addressing her precious career at FirsThought. After a few minutes, seeing no use in making herself sick dwelling on matters beyond her control, Karolena slid the control on her sim-cigarette unit to the 'off' position, straightened her coat, then started out toward the Basic Research Building -- known to her fellow FirsThought insiders as Red One.

A medium-sized biotechnology company, FirsThought specialized in commercializing products for transplantation across and within species, and in developing new treatments for neuro-degenerative diseases. FirsThought was a joint venture between the

State of North Carolina, Winston County Medical Center -- WCMC in nearby Neuse and a small group of private investors.

Red One was one of the oldest structures at FirsThought, having been built only thirty years after the turn of the century. Six of its seventeen floors were buried well below ground, using technology which back then was thought to save energy and decrease radiation exposure. Each floor was devoted to a specialty area of research, and every inch of space in the myriad offices and cluttered laboratories and corridors was crammed to overflowing with scientific equipment in various states of repair. Competition for space was keen, the fighting for funding was on occasion brutal, and Karolena found the pace of research often exhilarating.

Once inside Red One, Karolena quickly entered the service elevator and called out her destination – level B-2, the animal facility -- to the elevator's AllSee – a voice recognition unit, among other things. AllSee units were everywhere, in every building, every city, and every country. There were several brands, but all basically were disembodied holographic faces which floated hauntingly in the air, could communicate, and were tied to the world wide net. For several moments, she shifted uncomfortably back and forth as the elevator doors struggled to close against misfitting metal and years of rust, before finally closing with a screech painful enough to make her cringe as the sound seemed to literally crawl up her back. Then, annoyingly, nothing happened. She knew that elevator technology was certainly over two hundred years old, and with proper maintenance she expected the elevators, like everything else, should function properly. Yet, Karolena was all too aware that was a big caveat, the essential one. Karolena had learned to wait, for waiting was indeed a reality these days. She reflected that, twenty, maybe twenty-five years ago all the stress everyone bore in their daily lives might have caused an epidemic of gigantic ulcers. Now suffering from ulcers was only medical history, but enduring mind-numbing waits unfortunately fell under current events.

While waiting for the elevator to move, Karolena stared with disgust at the foul notes etched into the discolored walls -- no one seemed to care enough any longer about the aesthetic quality of their environment to cover up the filth. The strong, acrid smell of animal urine and feces left over from the transport of animal cages in the same elevators used by people stung her nostrils, urging her to end this confined trip ASAP.

Flicking her pack o f sim-cigs, she knocked one loose - a newer, non carcinogenic flameless brand, and used her lips to pull it from the pack. The taste immediately was tart when she activated the unit, almost bitter, and she inhaled deeply, and then closed her eyes as a warm rush flowed into her lungs and the vapor medications traveled throughout her body, imparting a needed jolt of calm in so uncomfortable a situation. Seconds later, she exhaled clear, warm breath. Ah, now all was tolerable. The vapors in the sim-cig were in actuality a complex drug delivery system, carrying various mood modifiers released at user-controlled speeds and intensities and which were identified by the brand names each sim-cig bore: Summer Calm, Rouge Reliance, Forever Patience, Inner Confidence, High Availability, Persistence Pays, or her favorite – Deep Pleasure. She, like many of her acquaintances, used them almost like an addict, except that they were told the sim-cigs were definitely not physically addicting. For Karolena, she found the fast onset mode worked best.

After another long moment suspended motionless, the elevator suddenly started with a jerk and continued down, accompanied by a low whining sound and a palpable vibration, both of which she found most disquieting. Then, just as unexpectedly, the elevator slammed to a stop, forcing Karolena to quickly grab a side rail to keep stable. The elevator slowly slid sideways a few hundred feet, then stopped again. The doors took an eternity to open wide enough for her to exit safely.

Karolena's pace quickened as she walked along the long, echoing corridor smelling of animal urine and disinfectant until finally stopping in front of a dull gray anonymous door, this one labeled "Blütfink/Growth." The local AllSee politely greeted her, scanned her wrist ID bracelet and matched it to her stored face profile. The AllSee also sensed her annoyance, but detected no aggression or harmful intent. It chose not to engage Karolena in conversation and granted her entry clearance. The magnetic lock clicked open and Karolena could proceed inside the room.

Once inside, Karolena looked around disapprovingly at the small, dimly-lit room. The walls were painted a dull institutional gray, bare spots showed through at innumerable places, and disparate styles of light panels covered the walls and low ceiling. Security cameras, tied into the company's neural network optical recognition scanner, and from there to Plant Security, integrated nearly invisibly into several upper walls. Circular metal gratings embedded in the rough concrete floor accommodated the frequent automated washings of the animal cages. Yet it all looked so dirty that at times it was difficult for Karolena to accept that the area was also completely sterile.

"A prison," she mumbled to herself, shaking her head, "looks just like a prison." Still, despite the deteriorating facilities, she did enjoy her work, or at least had done so up to now. The sim-cigs certainly helped keep that so, she laughed to herself. But she knew that the research project she was principally involved in was important, it did give a sense of purpose and direction to her life, and she still looked forward to coming to work each day. Walking over to the first row of cages, Karolena pulled out the one labeled "G3a," and almost reached inside before stopping when she heard the click of the magnetic door lock. Not expecting anyone else there so soon, she turned quickly.

Dr. Rickhard Blütfink, a wiry man of medium build and thinning brown hair, entered, pushing an old metal cart filled with equipment. The cart rumbled and shook as it passed over one of the floor drains, giving Karolena the unnerving impression that something important was about to fall off. Blütfink, the Associate Director of Surgical Research at FirsThought, smiled widely upon seeing Karolena and gave a cheery greeting, laced with a slight German accent.

Blütfink, like Karolena, was an expatriate, an emigrant who had lived in Texas most of his life, having moved there as a child with his parents from Düsseldorf, Greater Germany after a plutonium spill had poisoned the land. After attending Medical School at The University of Texas Health Science Center, he completed his surgical residency almost twenty years ago, and joined FirsThought shortly thereafter, moving to North Carolina. Blütfink claimed to find the atmosphere at FirsThought intellectually stimulating and the work interesting and challenging, key factors that had attracted him here from Houston. Blütfink was twice married and twice divorced, without children, and at forty-five still looked young and intense. Cocky and opinionated, he liked to think he learned from his mistakes.

"Why, Karolena, what a pleasant surprise," Blütfink oozed, as the door slammed shut behind him with a thud. "Aren't you the hard worker."

"I just wanted to get a head start, Rickhard, that's all," she told him, while finishing adjusting the cages. An unwieldy collection of past baggage tended to keep their present conversations tense and brief, and neither had felt completely comfortable together in months. The pressure and doubt Karolena felt about her assignment today did little to help ease their being together, especially under such closed-in circumstances.

Karolena stared uncomfortably for a moment at the small portable incubator sitting on the cart, before carefully lifting it up and placing it onto the table top. The room's dimmed artificial light accentuated her thinnish face, as her distorted reflection flickered in the incubator unit's plastic hood, making her features appear to herself perhaps a bit stark and mean. Karolena noticed that her vision seemed a bit blurry, which had happened once before this week, and she wondered if she needed to get her vision checked. A slight sense of nausea rippled through her body, and she shivered briefly.

"Well, I appreciate your coming in early to get things set up. I depend a lot on you. We all do." Karolena blushed uncomfortably at the compliments, and looked away. Blütfink gestured to the cart, and then tried to explain, as if an excuse was needed, "I had to be here for the early morning delivery."

Karolena nodded to Blütfink, then glanced momentarily at the incubator unit, understanding all too well what delivery he was referring to. Actually confronted with the incubator, staring right at it, Karolena now realized she would soon have to again ‘look' at the fetus, and she wasn't sure she could deal with that, not just yet at least.

Blütfink, his voice still colored with traces of concern, stared at her a moment, seemingly puzzled about what to say next, before asking, "Are you all right?"

"Why, what's the matter?" she asked, standing a little straighter. Caring about her well-being had never been one of Blütfink's strong points, and she was surprised that he even bothered to ask. Yet, Karolena knew what he was getting at. Never one to successfully hide her feelings, or disguise well her physical state, Karolena was still disturbed that her inner feelings were all too obvious and too easily read. She strove to be stronger and self-reliant, like her father.

"You just look a little pale and tired to me, that's all," Blütfink replied, the concern in his voice sounding, for once, genuine.

"I'm okay, I guess." Karolena touched his shoulder lightly, and said, "Thanks for asking." Blütfink was right, though, she did feel more tired than usual, and more than she could reasonably explain. Conflicting thoughts of using another fetus as a research model had bothered Karolena terribly all last night, and she had slept poorly as a result. Remembering how worn she had looked when she awoke this morning, Karolena wondered if her recent difficulty sleeping had taken more of a toll than she had realized? Hadn't she already made an adequate effort to fix herself up this morning, to look presentable before venturing out, she wondered, as she quickly ran her fingers through her hair?

Although intellectually, Karolena supported a woman's right to have an abortion, still, she had seen too much detail too close up to simply brush off as unimportant the procedure or the ‘products of conception,' as the aborted fetus was called. With the population continuing to decrease just about everywhere, any child was worth keeping, she thought. Adoptions bid out at astronomical prices, so an actual aborted fetus, like the one confronting them today, was quite rare. Of course, Karolena also worried about the special handling of the tissue that was required on her part. She looked askance at Blütfink, but his mind appeared elsewhere, as too often was the case for him. The preparation and use of experimental human tissue was not a task Karolena wanted to entrust to just any research surgeon, especially someone without her particular viewpoint and sensitivity. But even more to the point, she was uneasy about the ethics of what she was doing, and she felt that, bit-by-bit, her working at FirsThought was compromising her own moral code. The immediate effects on her psyche were all too obvious. She feared what the long range effects on her would turn out to be.

In her own mind, perhaps almost as ethically or morally questionable as using a human fetus for research, was the actual design of today's transplant experiment -- it just appeared to her to be both completely unnecessary and completely inhumane. Karolena had on her own initiative spoken up and protested about these issues several times, but whenever she did, Blütfink in flowing but impersonal terms stressed "the importance to mankind" of their research project, and how "valued" he found her assistance. To a certain extent, she knew that he was right, and Karolena appreciated how important her research, their research on the future expanded use of organ transplantation was. More and more people were getting organs transplanted every day, just to stay alive. She got that. But Blütfink's reassuring words, though, seemed more a thinly disguised reminder that it was her job to simply assist in the research, and nothing more. As a FirsThought employee, Karolena felt obligated, perhaps even coerced, to support what at times could only be described as dreadful draconian experiments, and it was primarily this pressure to, prostitute-like, engage in an act she found personally objectionable that disturbed her most. Karolena resented having her opinions constantly ignored. At times, she wondered if she was the only ethical person at FirsThought.

"Good, I'm glad you're okay," Blütfink smiled pleasantly, although his smile appeared to Karolena to possess a subtle, forced nature to it. "I expect this experiment might take a lot longer to finish and I wanted to start on it first thing." He turned to continue preparing for the experiment, but, after looking more closely at Karolena, again asked, "Are you sure something isn't bothering you?"

"No," Karolena insisted, finding his reaction to her uncertain feelings somewhat condescending She wondering why Blütfink continued to ask her -- could he be so blind to her feelings as to not even sense, to not know? She reflected for a minute on just how shallow she over time had found Blütfink to really be. Superficial, yes, insensitive, yes, but totally unreachable and unreasonable, perhaps not. Regardless, despite her twisted trail of lost protests in the past, she now felt certain that her principles were worth another attempt, perhaps the last attempt. Karolena collected herself and, in as calm a manner as she was able to present, looked at the face she had once fondly touched and firmly told him, "Yes, there is something bothering me. It's your experimental design, Rickhard."

"Look," Blütfink groaned, staring at the ceiling for approval. "I don't really have the time or the interest in discussing all your misplaced misgivings again. I know how your feelings about this type of research seem to have changed over time, and I can understand that, and to a certain extent I feel that way too. I'm not heartless, you know. But can't we save that discussion for later, Karolena, okay?"

"No, it's not okay. I think, I really think" she felt compelled to go on, for her own sanity, “that we're making a mistake doing things this way." She gestured meekly over to the incubator, already regretting having made the attempt to change his seemingly unchangeable mind. Unfortunately, her initial assessment of Blütfink was correct. That did not surprise her; but what then, she wondered, was really her appraisal of her own self? Ultimately, didn't that matter the most? Knowing that answer, she finally told him, "And I'm not sure I want to participate in these bizarre experiments any longer, either."

"What do you mean?" Blütfink glared in her direction, putting down some instruments and taking a step closer to her.

"Simple. I think we should use another animal

model system. Don't you?" she asked, placing her hand reassuringly on his shoulder. Karolena feared he didn't want to change things, especially this far along, but she did, and that was what counted right now.

"We've been over that a hundred times already, Karolena. It's definitely an old issue, don't you think? Look, if you can't handle the work," he told her, his voice rising and gaining in tension, "just let me know, okay, and I'll try to get another surgeon in here who can. It will be difficult, and this is not at all a good time for a change, we both must realize that, I hope we do, but if I need to, I will." Neither his face nor his voice resounded in certainty.

His unkind remarks caught Karolena hard, like a slap to the face, and she stepped back. Undoubtedly Blütfink could replace her in the lab as seemingly effortlessly as he had replaced her in his personal life, although it might take some time. They both knew that. Everyone, she supposed, was replaceable. Still, she could perform the technical aspects as well as Blütfink, if he only knew.

As a German national, Karolena had her choice of higher educational institutions all over Europe; yet, over her father's objections, she had preferred to study at the University of Brussels. Her family's financial stability made cost considerations not relevant, and the intellectual milieu in Brussels was freer and more invigorating, although she never would have dared tell anyone she thought so. There, in the Belgian sector of Greater Germany, she had only recently completed the

European equivalent of a doctorate in transplant surgery. Early on, Karolena chose a research career, with its lower risk of blood-borne infections, over the actual daily practice of surgery. Her chronic liver inflammation, a curse that had been with her since her teens, would hardly tolerate an episode of infectious hepatitis or any other viral infection lurking in the world of contemporary medical practice. She already was more sensitive to toxins in the food and water than most people, and the fear of injuring her frail liver was constantly with her, and seemed to influence in one way or another her every act – from where she lived and worked, to what she ate and drank. The effects of toxic pollution were a major challenge to just about everyone's life these days.

Karolena seemed naturally skilled in surgery, and she had surprised her family and disappointed her acquaintances at the University of Brussels when she sought a research position in the states. Although it was general opinion that science in the US wasn't as advanced as it was back home in Western Europe, at least there was more academic freedom. Of even greater appeal to Karolena, the overall level of toxic contamination of the environment was much lower in the states, and, once she had secured her father's blessing and financial backing, she had made the move. She was reminded that it had been a while since hearing from her father, and she vowed to message him soon.

"Look, Karolena, please, if just for today, try and cooperate, will you? It's very important that this one experiment goes well."

"Why this one in particular?" Karolena asked. It was the very fact that this experiment seemed so indistinguishable to her from all its predecessors that also made it seem so very unnecessary.

"Oh, well I guess then you haven't heard," Blütfink frowned, collecting himself. "It seems," he paused with a heightened air of irritation, "that the powers that be, particularly Bob Wilder over at WCMC, want to kill funding for this project."

"Oh, Rickhard, that's, that's," Karolena searched for a word that would sound the least disingenuous, "that's just terrible." She found it odd that he was not even aware that she and Susan, Wilder's wife, were friends, and Susan filled her in about a lot that was going on at WCMC. Karolena saw no reason to make that public information.

"Apparently our work just hasn't generated the positive data they were looking for. These admin types, they've got no concept of just how long research like this can take," he complained, shaking his head. He looked around the room, gestured at all the equipment, and then rolled his eyes.

“No, I had no idea," she admitted, moving nearer to Blütfink and once again placing her hand on his arm to reassure him.

"I always try not to let my personal feelings get in the way, here or elsewhere, Karolena, but that's why I'm particularly nervous about the outcome of today's research." He crossed his arms, and then turned away from her. "We really need a winner here."

A small transport ''bot entered the room, placed something into the secure frig, and then left.

Karolena attempted to smile supportively, a difficult task to say the least, given her negative opinion of their work. For the moment, she would try to support their effort, but she realized that the issue was far from resolved.

Bringing her mind back to matters at hand, if only for the moment, Karolena shrugged, and busied herself connecting the incubator -- a four-foot long unit with a vague and unfortunate resemblance to a coffin -- to the electric and oxygen outlets on the wall. Her hand trembled slightly as she twisted the quick-disconnect lever, making her acutely aware of just how nervous she felt.

Financial pressures at FirsThought made everyone double task, surgical technicians were hard to come by, and Karolena, in addition to assisting Blütfink with surgery, often set up the Experimental Surgery operating room, prepared the animals, and administering some pre-op medications and anesthetics. Karolena also handled some of the details of post-operative care. She enjoyed working with animals, although not necessarily in this unwholesome way, and tried to use her position to insure that the animals suffered as little as possible during the procedures. But who, she quietly reflected, was looking out for her?

With Karolena occupied elsewhere, Blütfink donned a set of penetration-resistant gloves and lifted the cover of animal cage labeled G3a. Inside, the tan-colored kitten, who cowered in a ball in the corner of the cage opposite him, appeared to him to be healthy enough. The food consumption indicator showed it had been eating the dry brown cat chow at the expected rate, although the water level was down only 2 milliliters. A dented and crimped steel nipple, covered with animal gnaw markings, ran from the discolored plastic water bottle into the cage. "Good," Blütfink grumbled to himself. "It still looks healthy, but apparently it's not very thirsty."

Finished for the moment setting up the incubator, Karolena moved toward Blütfink and examined closely the indicator on the outside of the animal cage. She flicked the water bottle with her finger; the water inside showed no sign of the slimy green algae that might have given it a bad taste. Yet, knowing the sorry state of the environment they all lived in, Karolena was left wondering whether the cat had tasted some subtle crud in the local water supply. If so, perhaps she too had been drinking toxins, particularly ones that might further damage her already fragile liver. That possibility, which she was constantly on guard against, left her with a bad taste in her mouth, and she could only observe, "Well, Rickhard, considering how much solid food the kitten ate, I agree that it should have had more to drink. I wonder if the technicians are giving the animals fresh water every day like they're supposed to."

Blütfink shrugged and, returning his attention to the matter at hand, said, "Here, kitty, here kitty, kitty," before gently lifting the small kitten by the scruff of its neck, supporting its bottom with his hand, but managing to keep the frightened little animal at arm's length. The kitten stiffened and protectively dug its claws into the cage floor, trying to hold on, and let out a loud meow of protest, before crouching down.

Blütfink at first tried speaking to the kitten as softly as he was capable of, hoping to calm it down. Being remarkably unskilled in those areas, and certainly no more or less so with animals than with humans, his tact rapidly failed and he quickly became impatient as the cat squirmed away. Looking once again at his watch, Blütfink pinched the kitten's hind leg before forcefully pulling it up. Briskly stroking its fur, he quickly muttered, "nice kitty, nice kitty," as he made a forced cradle of sorts with his arm to hold it more securely. Once Blütfink appeared to have a firm grip on the kitten, he flipped the grated steel lid down onto the cage with a bang, noisily sliding the cage back into the holder, and in the process eliciting several loud meows of protest from other cats in the fifty-odd cages lining the walls.

"It's okay, nothing will happen," Blütfink lied to the kitten.

The stiff fabric of Blütfink's lab coat smelled of bleach and blood and hair from other animals, and seemed to warn the cat of unpleasant things to come. Not fooled, it fought back. Realizing he would be unable to calm the kitten, Blütfink told an unsuspecting Karolena, "Here. Take it," and nearly tossed the kitten to her.

Karolena too had a difficult time getting a secure

hold on the agitated kitten. Terrified, the kitten hissed loudly and sank a claw into Karolena's palm, instantly drawing blood through the glove she was wearing.

"Damn." Karolena cursed, pressing her cut hand against her coat. "So much for penetration-resistant gloves." Surprised and hurt, she almost dropped the kitten.

Blütfink quickly grabbed the anxious kitten back from Karolena. "I've got no time for nonsense like this." Blütfink forced the kitten's neck in a wooden brace on the lab table top, pinning the rest of its body down with the rear plastic cover of the animal dissection box.

"Easy, little kitty," Karolena said, while stroking its exposed head. "You too, Rick. Easy." She hated the way he treated animals, almost as a lower form of life, incapable of feelings and unworthy of love and respect; it was a wonder to her that he had any interpersonal skills with patients, let alone with her. Now, it seemed that the pressure to close down his precious little program was making him even more irritable.

"Let's just be sure to anesthetize the cat real well before the `surgery," Blütfink cautioned, looking askance at Karolena's injured hand. "And be sure to wash your hand. We sure-as-hell don't want to risk transmission of a feline virus from a cat scratch, especially these days."

Karolena looked momentarily at the scratch wound on her hand, which had quickly stopped bleeding, but now seemed to have developed a slight tingling sensation. Directing her attention back to the kitten,

Karolena plunged a syringe containing anesthetic into its hind leg muscle. Her heart went out to the helpless little cat, and she almost withdrew the needle from its struggling, writhing little body without injecting the drug. Then, trying to get a hold of herself, she pressed down on the plunger, realizing this was the best way, best for them both. Soon the cat quieted as the drug mercifully took effect. At least for the cat, suffering was over.

"You know, I'm always amazed at the strength of these small cats," Blütfink spoke mostly to himself, shaking his head as he uttered a nervous little chuckle, barely discernible above the lab's background noise.

Karolena peeled the damaged glove off her hand and pressed some antibiotic-impregnated gauze over the cut. "It only tried to protect itself. You can understand that, can't you?" She wondered if the kitten wasn't smarter than she, and could almost imagine the terror that cat must have felt, being caged up and then injected.

"You're sure touchy today, aren't you?" Blütfink commented as he grabbed Karolena's hand and roughly examined it. The bleeding had stopped, and he let go when she complained that his grip was hurting her. "I think you better wash the cut with antiseptic soap and water before continuing. Are you up to date on all your shots?"

Karolena nodded that she was current on her vaccinations, including one for feline viruses. She had been cut this way at least once before, and felt reassured that at least the animals in their facility were clean, or at least were cleaner, as far as the presence of viruses, than were animals out in the wild. She walked over to the sink and washed the cut with soap, dried her hands, and then returned.

In only a moment, the anesthesia had taken effect. Karolena lifted the now-limp kitten out of the containment box and gently placed it on a specially designed small animal surgery table, then moved it under a dissecting surgical scope.

Blütfink watched as Karolena methodically strapped down the cat's legs and neck. Having reached a natural point to pause in today's work, they left for the changing rooms, stripped their outer clothes, and put on clean paper and vinyl tops and pants, booties, face masks and hair covers. Standing side by side, without speaking, but separated by a hologram curtain, they sterilized their hands in a bath of translucently sparkling alpha rays at a radiation sink, then donned fresh sets of sterile gloves.

Once back in the procedure room, Blütfink turned to his dissecting instruments and pulled back the sterile draping towel. In the mean time, Karolena had already shaved fur off the kitten's lower abdomen with electric clippers, then went over the area more closely with a razor in preparation for the surgery. She could have used one of the surgical ‘bots, but had opted to do it herself.

"Good," Blütfink sighed, glancing at his watch several times, "it's about time to start, finally. Look, Karolena, I've got a million things to do, so, let's make this quick. Okay?"

Looking down indifferently at the limp kitten, Blütfink took the small tissue clamps Karolena handed him. He bit the clamp into the skin which overlay the area to be opened by incision, then applied a slight upward pressure to lift the skin off the kitten's intestines. Blütfink checked his watch again, and then glanced over at Karolena, whose hands were mimicking his moves. "Patience, Karolena. You'll have plenty of opportunity to do this tomorrow. Sometimes I just like to do it myself. It keeps me closer to my . . . to our work," he corrected himself, almost gratuitously.

Choosing not to reply -- what would be the use -- Karolena simply looked away. There were times when Blütfink seemed so superficial. How could she once have been intimate with him? The question was painful. She and Blütfink had actually known each other for several years before her moving to FirsThought. After having met at various scientific meetings, they had seen each other casually for a few years, and developed a distant video "friendship." Shortly after that, video calls morphed into hooking up via the AllSee, with holograms, which really seemed to enhance the experience. Karolena had few "ties" at home other than her father, and nearly jumped at the opportunity of a position at so prestigious a company as FirsThought, an opportunity she now realized must have been engineered by Blütfink for his own sordid purposes. And to think he was one of the reasons that prompted her to relocate to the states. She could be such an idiot.

Karolena remembered, with an uncomfortable

feeling now how Blütfink had conveniently befriended her shortly after her arrival in the states, supplying the safe harbor in a foreign land she needed to survive. Unfortunately, what little they had didn't last; Blütfink had another agenda, and, after months of a drifting and meaningless relationship, she had finally been forced out of frustration to tell Blütfink what had become painfully obvious to her -- that their own relationship wasn't working anymore and had become an uncomfortable burden. Amazing to her, and despite frequent arguments and diminishing intimacy, Blütfink had shown no sign of wanting to end their failing relationship. And why should he have, she wondered? After all, he had all the advantages and none of the inconveniences. Now, her remembrances of the short affair nearly sickened her -- she had been such a fool. Her eyes had been closed for too long. The thoughts pained her and made her feel sick to her stomach.

Finally, Karolena had needed to bluntly explain to Blütfink that it was time to separate. She knew it, he somehow couldn't see it, but that was his problem. Their last evening together had not gone well, and even now just thinking about those tense moments depressed Karolena and made her feel like a fool all over again. In those ensuing months, she had formed several good friendships, and had dated a few nice men, although nothing serious had developed so far, and she had carved out a promising and pleasant independent life of her own. She involuntarily shook her head, clearing her thoughts and forcing herself back to reality; her guard was now back up.

Facilities in the animal room were cramped, forcing Karolena to sit with her chair wedged close to Blütfink's at the dissecting table. Her leg by necessity exerted a very slight but intensely noticeable pressure against his, and the feeling distracted her, and made her remember how, it seemed just recently, Blütfink had reached out for her in the dark, gently placing his hand on her soft inner thigh. She remembered the solid shape of his hand, its thick texture, its warmth, the soft sounds he made when asleep, the particular minty scent of his after-shave, the scratch of his stubble on her shoulder in the morning. Then she remembered seeing the reaction on his face when he first noticed the scars on her abdomen, the results of a surgical wound infection improperly treated, and something she easily could have and should have had cosmetically corrected, but didn't. Her father advised her to never alter her body simply to please anyone else. That advice made a lot of sense to her. Although Blütfink never admitted staring at the scars, it was obvious to her that he did, one of many things he never discussed with her, or she with him.

After an uncomfortably quiet few minutes, Blütfink abruptly got up from the dissecting table and walked away. He filled a small black foam bucket with shaved ice from a floor unit, unlocked the secure refrigerator with his wrist ID and pulled out several vials of an experimental growth factor produced at FirsThought which would be tested today.

Growth factors -- complex, naturally-occurring proteins, themselves long strings of amino acids --

influence the ability of tissues to grow. Their healing applications lay in such diverse areas as wound care, organ transplantation and the new field of body shaping. The basic scientists at FirsThought had been working on a new synthesis procedure for years. Once they thought they had succeeded, Blütfink was asked to assay the growth hormone's effects on a living organism, hence today's experiment. It was an effort whose success was now made all the more urgent by the threatened budget cuts.

The growing environmental toxin problem had, early into the new century, made organ failure, particularly of livers, widespread, and the need to transplant livers as common a procedure as face lifts had once been. Transplantation was big business, or at least it could once again be if only more organs would be available for use, and it was still one of the most frequent surgeries performed. Only the continued shortage of retrovirus-negative donor livers limited the number of surgical procedures far below the demand. Transplants, though, were a major income-generating activity at WCMC, which, apparently through simple good fortune, seemed to be hampered just a bit less than surrounding hospitals by the continuous organ shortage. WCMC, through its directed financial support, wanted FirsThought to increase the transplantation rate by way of a biotech breakthrough on the supply side, hence their up to now enthusiastic support of Blütfink's research.

By the time Blütfink returned to the procedure table, Karolena had already cut through the kitten's thin skin, the lanky muscle layers, and the transparent abdominal lining -- the peritoneum --, and had isolated the right kidney, prompting Blütfink to comment to her, not at all gratuitously, "You know, you're remarkably well-trained."

Karolena smiled ironically at his remark, remembering having told him more than once that the fewer kittens she 'wasted' the better. Karolena understood well there was no intention of using any other organs from this kitten for today's experiment, or of allowing it to survive. As a result, she knew that Blütfink wouldn't care what effect the surgery had on the donor kitten, just as long as the procedure didn't take inordinately long, and didn't inconvenience him too much. Karolena was more than aware of his irritation at her insistence on going slowly, and reducing the animal's suffering. This conflicted with his desire to get things over with as soon as possible. He had always seemed to her to be in a hurry about something, and she often found being around him made her a little anxious. She had tried to recommend to him a sim-cig with anxiety vapor, but he denied have a problem with nervousness, and claimed that vapors made him cough.

Karolena turned to the portable incubator Blütfink had brought in earlier, and gently lifted the cover. Reaching in, she removed a small human fetus; it weighed approximately three pounds and was still breathing on its own, with chest movements that were barely flutters. It had its own pediatric nurse ‘bot, which hovered around intensely, and listened to everything they were saying. Without the intensive life support the fetus was receiving, though, it could never hope to survive. Karolena's hands shook perceptively as she carefully wrapped the fetus in a warming blanket and cradled it in her arm, quietly talking to it. "Do you want to look at him, Rick?" she asked, her voice faint, distant and audibly cracking.

"Don't be stupid, Karolena," he sneered, backing away. "How old is it anyway?"

Karolena flashed a displeased look at Blütfink, and then rubbed her sleeve across her forehead. "Well, from its early stage of development and the fact that it's breathing on its own, I'd say, oh, about thirty weeks old." Her voice cracked in between words now, and she felt more ashamed of herself than she ever had.

"Thirty weeks. Good, that's more than adequate, don't you think?"

"Yeah, I guess," Karolena said, a confused, sad, lost look enveloping her face. She swallowed hard, and cleared her throat.

Blütfink sighed, looked at her disapprovingly, and then asked, "Now what's the matter?"

"It's just that it's so hard to believe that no one from the mother's family wanted this baby." Karolena looked into the fetus's eyes, and stroked its cheek softly with her fingers. Her voice had changed to a low monotone. The fetus seemed basically healthy, without obvious defects.

Blütfink grunted, with the boredom of having heard this all before, and then looked away. "Karolena, we get a lot of our tissues for our experiments from fetuses, you know that. Why, it's an accepted procedure everywhere in the world. Fetuses are an important tissue source for us, just as they are for a hell of a lot of other labs, including those of our competitors. And you know that we use fetal tissue for scheduled transplants on patients over at The Winston, too." he nodded in her direction, adding a personal implication to his logic.

The use of human fetal tissue in medical experiments had become accepted years ago, and Karolena had no doubt that this very practice had allowed accelerated development of advances in areas as diverse as transplantation and neuro-pharmacology. She also realized almost from the start that some aspects of particular research protocols at FirsThought could be troubling. At first, she felt she could handle her feelings. As for Blütfink, though, it was obvious to her that there was no objection at all, because there simply were no feelings.

"Everyone uses donors just like that one you're holding now," he said, gesturing to the tiny fetus. "Look, you got a bad liver, right?" he said, pointing to her abdomen.

Karolena reluctantly nodded agreement, but made a point of looking away from his manipulative little eyes. She knew where he was going with his argument, having used it before, herself, and she didn't want to hear it again. It was simultaneously right to the point, and hopelessly irrelevant.

"Sure you do," he said, his face displaying an odd mixture of distant compassion for the fetus and paternal concern for her. "Well, someday, you might need a fetus just like this to stay alive, and believe me, if you ever do, I'm sure you'll take that opportunity. Did you ever consider that?" He crossed his arms in front of his chest, and slowly nodded his head at the logic of the point he had made.

"There are alternatives, aren't there?" Karolena replied, almost pleadingly. One could always use volunteer donors, as rare as they had become. The problem was, she realized, the wait was often intolerably long, and people who were forced to take the voluntary donor route often died before a suitable donor finally became available. Same problem for perhaps a hundred years, no solution in sight. Blütfink was, unfortunately, most likely correct about what course she might be forced to take in order to live. She felt like a coward, a moral coward and a hypocrite because she loved life to such a degree, or was so terribly afraid of death, that, like a vampire, she too might choose to live off an innocent baby's blood.

"Where did we get it from this time, anyway?" he said, gesturing with striking disinterest at the fetus.

Karolena looked oddly at Blütfink, but couldn't reply, wondering whether he could possibly be so unaware of how pitifully devoid of compassion he was appearing to her. How could he survive so successfully in medicine, how could he manage the intricacies of interacting in a tertiary medical center like WCMC, and yet not care what negative influence his acting so callously had on what little they still had left in their relationship?

"Well, what's the problem now?" he asked,

sounding totally perplexed and unaware?

"I just thought you knew. I mean, you often do, that's all. Our contract tissue procurer retrieved this baby, this fetus, as you call him, from the 'discard' holding area of the Neuse Family Planning Clinic only a few hours ago. It was kept alive on life-support just for our purposes, Rick, but it was unwanted," Karolena muttered, in a hushed voice, starring motionless at the floor. Her voice cracked even more and trembled as she almost choked on those words, wondering who else that applied to. "Can you believe it, Rick? This child was going to be destroyed. Even its own family didn't want it." Karolena clearly felt in danger of totally losing her composure at any moment, and struggled to regain control, not wanting to appear like a fool, a sniveling little weakling in front of Blütfink, especially in front of him.

"You know what?" Blütfink grunted. "It looks like a minority. Are you sure the mother was retro-negative?" He held his sleeve up to his mouth and belched, then smiled as if it were an accident.

"Wake up, Rick. These days, we are the minority," Karolena angrily said, ignoring his poor control of even his own bodily functions, and pointing between them. "Anyway, the mother and fetus were tested again this morning, and both were negative for HIV and all the other retroviruses and other organisms. Is that good enough for you?" Blütfink always seemed to her to be such an elitist, although she had to admit she could at least appreciate his point of view about retros, the singular failure of modern medical science. Retros were outcasts, undesirables, a burden to society, a danger to others. They were virtually a separate society onto themselves that she knew little of and had absolutely no interest in learning any more of.

"Yeah, sure," he replied, apparently satisfied the tests were good.

Taking care to avoid looking in "its" eyes or "its" face, Karolena gently placed the fetus on a separate operating table. When she tried to insert some intravenous lines into the umbilical vein for fluid and drug administration, she immediately encountered difficulty. Her hands suddenly seemed to lack any agility to move gently or act in coordination, and her fingers visibly shook, making her every act uncharacteristically clumsy. The blurry vision she had earlier was returning. To make matters worse, the fetus' veins seemed too delicate to stand up to a needle's puncture, and tended at their early stage of development to collapse around the needle. Her own anxiety, palpable and raw, only added to the problem.

"Look, Karolena, I think that those umbilical veins are too small and fragile, and maybe it's a little dehydrated, too," Blütfink observed as he watched Karolena's difficulties.

"It? What do you mean, 'it's a little dehydrated'?" she fumed. Couldn't Blütfink just for one minute acknowledge that he was working with another human being? This unborn innocence probably possessed higher ethical qualities then he did, or for that matter did she.

"Obviously, I was referring to the fetus. Touchy

today, aren't you?" he countered, making a clucking sound with his tongue. "Now, I think that the easiest solution is for us to perform a vascular cutdown. That way we can use the large femoral vein for fluid and drug administration." He pointed to the fetus' femoral area near where the leg and groin met, and outlined the femoral vein's tract with his finger.

Karolena nodded her agreement and turned around to reach for some additional catheters. She had to admit this approach would probably end up hurting the fetus the least. In a real O.R., a surgical ‘bot would hand her the appropriate caths, but here she did for herself. She remember her father telling her that when ‘bots first became an everyday part of society, people resented them. Workers were afraid of losing their jobs to the never tiring, never complaining ‘bots. That all changed when massive population shrinkage began just before she was born.

The numbers on the catheter package seemed small and blurry, but she knew the correct ones by the color codes.

Blütfink hurriedly injected some local anesthetic into the fetus' groin, stared at the area for a moment, apparently pondering something, and then made a wide inguinal incision using a scalpel blade. Staring at the open area for a moment, he suddenly gasped and said "Oh shit." under his breath.

Turning to him quickly, Karolena asked, "What happened? Is something wrong?" Her eyes darted back and forth between Blütfink and the fetus on the operating table. Nothing seemed to have changed, the fetus, the vital signs indicator on the monitors, nothing except for the worried look on his face.

"No, nothing, no problem," Blütfink blurted out. "Just that I hate working under such pressure for success, that's all." After placing a few quick sutures over the area he had been working in, he then went on to slip a large green plastic catheter into the exposed femoral vein. Blood from the fetus returned into the clear plastic line almost immediately, demonstrating to him good flow. Next, he inserted a breathing tube down the fetus' trachea and connected it to a respirator unit, and then injected some anesthetic and analgesic into the intravenous line.

After a few more minutes, Blütfink gave the fetus some additional muscle relaxant to cut down on reflex contractions from pain. "The tissues we transplant into this fetus should last for at least two more weeks with good care," he coolly observed. "By then we'll know how the amino acid substitutions that were made on the growth factor will affect the half-life." This said, more as a justification than an explanation, Blütfink quickly finished opening the fetus' flank area with another deep, wide, although this time slower, incision.

Karolena recognized that she was more bothered by today's surgery than usual. Maybe it was the early hour, maybe Blütfink's technique was too rapid for her, or maybe she was concerned that they would cause some additional pain for the fetus. She didn't know which demon she was wrestling with, she only knew that ever since her spontaneous miscarriage last year -- Karolena never did tell Blütfink -- she had become much more nervous about experimental human surgery. Before that, the area of research she had dedicated her life to and all those years of training had provided ample motivation and justification. She also felt a real drive, an intense motivation to study transplants after learning she might herself need one. But after her own loss, well . . . their research model gradually became too personal for her, too immediate.

"Look," Blütfink reassured Karolena, "I'll have the kidney out of thc fctus in a minute. Just hold on to the retractor." Blütfink dissected rapidly, and once he reached the fetus' kidney, he expertly clamped the right renal artery and vein. After the blood vessels distal to the clamps were cut, he removed the kidney, then tossed it in a bucket labeled 'HUMAN WASTE,' where it made a soft ‘plop' sound after hitting the bottom.

As Karolena watched Blütfink, she was unable to suppress a slight wave of trembling, more like a shiver, from running up her back. She could feel her own sense of revulsion churning in her stomach, making her dizzy. Could this have happened to her own baby? Worse yet, could it someday happen to her? The possibility of someday receiving a liver transplant, inevitable as it sometimes seemed, despite all her elaborate precautions, made her so anxious she almost couldn't breathe, and at that very moment, she wondered if she would faint. She considered the fine distinction between intellectual abhorrence and a gut-level revulsion.

Just then, the fetus's left leg unexpectedly jerked. "Shit." Blütfink cursed, and then glanced toward

Karolena.

Karolena felt her body stiffen in response, and she winced and looked away.

"It's probably just an involuntary reaction to pain," Blütfink said reassuringly to Karolena. "Anyway, I'm sure it was felt only on a subconscious level," he added, more for Karolena's benefit than his. He quickly gave the fetus a little more anesthetic and muscle relaxant, and soon, the jerking movements mercifully stopped.

Karolena didn't reply, lost in thought as she remembered how, once before, she had looked this closely at a fetus used for experimental surgery. The effect of the needless suffering she had witnessed lasted through months of self-analysis and self-doubt. Now, she liked to think that she was better, though perhaps still not fully recovered from that tortuous experience.

Karolena glanced at one of the AllSee units that seemed to her to be focusing on her facial expressions. She immediately dismissed it as paranoia on her part and switched her mind to the immediate task at hand.

Despite all that was happening around her right now, Karolena still thought she appreciated the importance of the research she and Blütfink did, research that might finally allow using animals as long-term organ donors for humans -- as 'xenografts'. *She must appreciate this*, she thought. After all, she had chosen this line of research herself, no one had made her. Of course, she also hoped that her own work would someday be of benefit to her too, should she, like so many other people she had known, ever need a liver transplant. This was always an uncomfortable thought and more than just a vague possibility, no matter how careful she was to avoid irritating her liver. Karolena continually hoped her career choice, blessed and supported by her father, was the correct one and that its inherent importance exceeded any feelings of guilt or doubt she might have about their 'experimental design.'

Trying to refocus her thoughts, Karolena turned away to the other operating table, and, after adding more nerve paralyzer to the anesthesia, went on to quickly dissect out the kitten's kidney. The forced concentration, thankfully, helped clear her mind. She rinsed off the outside of the donor kidney in a basin of sterile saline solution, by now tainted burgundy red, then attached the renal artery to a perfusion pump, circulating saline through the kidney to 'flush it out.' Finally, she placed the cat's donor kidney into the human fetus's tiny abdomen, where it sat as out of place as a retro in a public restaurant.

As Karolena slid over to make room for Blütfink to get into the operative field, her loose scrub blouse fell away from her chest, and she caught Blütfink's less than subtle glance down her front. Icily returning his stare, she scolded, "Rickhard, please, try to concentrate on our work here. Let's get our mind out of the gutter, shall we." Catching his insincere smile, his almost boyish, non-caring attitude, she firmly told him, "Look, Rickhard, I want to keep things between us on a strictly professional basis from now on, okay? What we had once is over, finished. We did agree to that, didn't we?"

"Yes, sure, yes," he said, struggling to appear serious.

"So, are you ready for reattachment?" She paused, looking over at Blütfink smiling back over at her, and then clarified, sternly," Are you ready to reattach the kidney?"

Blütfink seemed to give a little smirk back and then resumed working rapidly under the dissecting microscope. "I know what you meant, Karolena; I'm neither stupid nor heartless."

'Yeah, sure.' she thought. Still, at this point, Karolena had to admit her feelings toward Blütfink were at times terribly conflicting and confused. On the one hand, she couldn't help harboring a great deal of animosity over the callous way he still treated her, used her. At times, though, and only in his presence, a few thoughts of the old attraction still seemed to leak through. She was certain it was hormonal, sensual, and therefore controllable, rather than a true romantic interest, for that would have been for her both impossible to comprehend or to accept.

Blütfink used a laser pointer to identify to the optical scanner those arteries and veins which needed re-connection. Then he asked, "Karolena, can you hand me the glass vial with the yellow stopper? It's in the ice bucket." After she handed it to him, Blütfink used a clean alcohol wipe on the rubber stopper. He inserted a syringe needle, and then withdrew the vial's cloudy white suspension of recombinant Nerve Growth Factor.

The kitten's kidney now lay deep in the human

fetus's exposed abdomen. Blütfink consummated the experiment by injecting the experimental growth factors directly into the renal artery that supplied the implanted foreign kidney. A momentary, visible flush passed through the kitten's renal tissue as the nerve growth factor quickly entered and then exited the kidney and emptied into the fetus's renal vein.

Using the dissecting scope, Karolena could see the main renal sympathetic nerve trunk and the draining lymphatic system lying in the operative field. For a moment, she had to blink and refocus her eyes when the field of vision under the scope began to shift. Probably from all the stress, she thought, as she waited for her eyes to focus again.

Under a low magnification, the glistening gray white nerve ends were juxtaposed but not connected yet. Blütfink told Karolena that he would just leave them unattached since intact nerves weren't critical to the experiment's success, and cut nerves rarely functioned well even when surgically reconnected.

Blütfink gave the voice command "Re-attach," and the neural network directed the Auto-Suture 'BOT to finish the surgical connections. Millions of digital computer commands per second controlled the electric motors and solenoid actuators, which governed mechanical arms and 'grasping units' that functioned as amazingly agile little mechanical hands. The Auto-Suture 'BOT stopped when the myriad vascular connections were complete.

Once the transplant surgery itself was finished, Blütfink aimed the needle of the syringe into the operative field and cavalierly squirted the remaining experimental growth factor onto the kidney's surface and into the cutdown area by the groin. Smiling like a naughty little boy, he told Karolena, "Hey, it's for good measure."

Karolena really had not wanted to participate in this experiment to begin with, and Blütfink's joking only seemed to trivialize her own feelings. That was just like him, she thought.

With their experiment nearly complete, Karolena checked the leak sensor on her new pair of puncture-resistant gloves one more time, and was relieved when it showed green. Although there didn't appear to be any retro risk here, one could never really know, and she believed in playing it safe. She would never knowingly risk ruining her life by accidentally joining the ranks of the hated retro outcasts, let alone associate with one. Again she looked at the fetus, briefly wondering what it might have looked like if it had lived to full term. For reasons of sheer self-protection, she quickly forced that poverfully destructive thought clear out of her mind. Looking up, she noted that Blütfink already was preparing to leave, confirming that he really couldn't care less. Fetuses were a commodity, a research tool to him, and nothing more, and she pitied him for that.

Blütfink told Karolena he would call her shortly to check on the post-op recovery, left the cleanup to Karolena and the ‘bots and returned to his office to dictate the procedure into the lab's computer record. A draft of the dictation had already been prepared by one of the surgery ‘bots, and all he really had to do was proof it.

Once Blütfink was gone, Karolena carefully moved the fetus to the recovery area, and turned its care over to the recovery staff. The entire procedure had left her physically exhausted and mentally drained. With another thirty minutes before the next post-op check point, Karolena allowed herself enough time to leave Red One for just a few minutes breather, and hopefully to regain her composure. Perhaps she could walk over to the animal holding facility, to visit some animals recovering from surgery yesterday – anything, she thought, anything to get her mind off the shame she had just participated in.

Chapter 2

@The moment Karolena left the stifling confines of Red One, she took out another sim-cig unit, activated it to the “relax” mode, and inhaled deeply. Her hands had a perceptible tremor, which appeared amplified while she held the sim-cig. She moved off to the side of the expansive entryway, on to a concrete tarmac facing the upper part of the complex, where she could be alone. An AllSee with its hologram displaying was suspended nearby. Before her stood several acres of rolling hillside, dotted here and there by featureless buildings, a gas storage tank, a sewage processing unit, and ribbons of private roadways tying FirsThought all neatly together in one expansive corporate scientific package. When she had first joined the company, viewing its size had filled her with confidence in the future, and with pride in the importance of her work. Now, the terrain seemed empty, and she felt only estrangement from her research which had lately taken on such a macabre tone.

Once the sim-cig's medicated vapor began to settle her nerves, she collected her thoughts and started the short walk toward the Animal Holding Facility. Walking was one of her few forms of exercise, allowing her to get some "fresh" air, such as it were. Just getting away from the intensive atmosphere of Red One for even a few minutes made her feel much less stressed. After inhaling deeply a few more times, she began to feel a little calmer, less tense, and needed to inhale less often. There were times when the sim-cig vapors gave her such an intense sense of relief that she wondered how she had ever managed to live without them.

Her thoughts about the transplantation experiment she had assisted Blütfink on were interrupted by movement near the side of the stream, down near where the bridge crossed over. She thought it might be from a small animal, although wildlife didn't often show on the company property. Then, just as quickly, the movement stopped. Curious, she walked down the road and approached the edge of the stream, stepping carefully over rocks and tall grass to keep from dirtying the slacks under her white lab coat.

Once at the stream's edge, Karolena found herself looking at a collection of motionless feathers piled like so many discarded rags on the wet rocks. A light breeze ruffled a few of the feathers, imparting the illusion of animation and was apparently what had first attracted her attention. The faint odor of putrid flesh and acrid bile bit at her throat and made her certain that, whatever it was, it was now dead. Moving closer, she used the tip of her shoe to cautiously nudge what appeared to be a small, lifeless bird, but wasn't surprised in the least when she failed to elicit movement.

Karolena rolled the bird's carcass onto its side with her shoe, hoping for a better look. It was a rather large red Finch, and its belly and neck were bloated and discolored. The tiny eyes were open, jaundiced, and gazed out into nothingness. The decaying odor of lifeless flesh gagged Karolena, stinging her nose and throat, forcing her to quickly step back.

Coughing several times at the smell, Karolena felt dirty, and rubbed her shoes clean on some nearby grass before continuing on. The dead bird's general state, although nonspecific, had some of the disturbing markings of toxin ingestion. She took another deep drag from her sim-cig, and then slowly exhaled as she looked up and around her.

Remembering she had once heard from an older laboratory technician of a toxin spill at FirsThought, an 'unfortunate incident', as it was described, which occurred long before Karolena had started working there, she wondered if another spill into the stream had just occurred and poisoned the bird. FirsThought security would need to be notified, so they could at least clean up the carcass, and check for evidence of a spill.

Karolena had seen more than her share of toxins and pollution, both here and back in her troubled homeland and for her own very good reasons avoided them whenever possible. To the amazement of her fellow FirsThought workers, she actually considered the deteriorating environment in North Carolina to be of only a mild severity, at least when compared to the tragic eco-disasters of Central Europe. Feeling herself fortunate, in a way, just to be here in the US, she rarely voiced displeasure.

As she walked on toward the animal holding

facility, the background stench became more noticeable. Karolena looked around, then seeing that she was not being watched, spit several times to clear the bitter taste that had accumulated in her mouth. It didn't work, her nausea being of a more persistent nature than an aftertaste.

Better known to FirsThought employees as 'the cell', the animal holding facility was a nondescript single story concrete and steel building, one like so many of the others at FirsThought. After first turning off her sim-cig, and displaying her wrist ID unit to the AllSee by the door, Karolena entered once the computer system recognized her face. The outer office was no more than a small cubicle, and most of the available space was occupied by a metal desk and another smaller AllSee terminal standing in front of a featureless wall.

Inside the animal holding facility, she greeted one of the animal technicians, an acquaintance of hers. She told him about her seeing the dead bird, and expressed her concerns. He seemed sympathetic to Karolena's worries, but was unaware of another toxin spill, nor had he seen any other dead animals on the property.

Changing the subject, she asked, "So, how are my animals doing?" One animal in particular came to mind.

"Not bad. Go see for yourself," he smiled, gesturing into the facility.

Hearing good reports always made Karolena feel better, and helped assuage the guilt she often felt at using animals for experiments. Her extensive training in surgery oriented her toward healing rather than preparing test animals to be disposable parts in some vast research machine. She thanked him for being so conscientious, then put on a cover smock and face mask and entered the holding facility.

The inside of the building consisted of one long corridor from which branched dozens of nameless, identical housing chambers filled beyond reasonable capacity with animal cages. Some of the rooms, the rat rooms for example, housed hundreds of frightened little animals, all nervously scurrying about for a safe place to cower in the dark. The sharp smell of rat excreta was almost as nauseating as that of pigs, and Karolena avoided going into that room.

Toward the end of the echoing corridor was the 'dog' room, her destination. She entered, easily found the beagle she was looking for, and walked up to its cage. The dog instantly recognized Karolena, and sprang up and started wagging its tail and yelping. It was only three months old, and had various patches on its skin covering areas where test chemicals had recently been applied. Fortunately for the beagle, which Karolena had unofficially named Carlo, none of the test substances had elicited an adverse reaction. It saddened her to think that, with such minimal trauma, Carlo would now become available for another experiment, perhaps one less likely to let him off so 'easily'.

After making sure that the door to the room was closed, Karolena bent down and opened the cage, and Carlo sprang out and started licking her hand. Picking

Carlo up, Karolena laughed as he now eagerly licked her face and tried to climb up her arm. Stroking Carlo's head and back, Karolena wanted to come back for him and take him to a better home, although she full realized her own living situation regretfully wouldn't allow that. Leaving a dog home alone, unattended, all day long was cruel; dogs were pack animals who appreciated human company and the stimulation that play, companionship and talk provided. She often thought that, if her apartment rules would ever allow it, she would get her own animal, a real pet someday, perhaps even Carlo. For now, she made do at home with a holographic parrot named Renata. He could talk, didn't require food or water, and never made a mess. By changing the parameters of Renata's artificial intelligence – AI program, Renata could interact at various levels with Karolena, like showing a friendly interest in her, and responding to her moods. In her work area at FirsThought, she kept two small live fishes in a tank on her desk, and assorted real plants by the window sill. Since there was no natural light possible through her window, Karolena used a desktop light to supply healthy sunlight to the plants. Her computer screen displayed continual images of Animals of the World, and her collection of holographic pets, including a remarkably realistic Llama, seemed so authentic as to almost be alive. Noticing how much time had passed, she gently placed Carlo back in his cage, then left in the direction of Red One.

As she walked away, a little girl named Sarah

came to mind, one who could have a dog but whose mother couldn't afford to have one. The mother tended a small convenience store Karolena often stopped at on the way home from work, and Sarah frequently was there helping her mom. Once, when Sarah's mother asked Karolena, in light conversation, what kind of work she did, Karolena mentioned that she took care of animals, not being one to announce to the world at every opportunity that she was a physician. Sarah picked up on that right away, and wanted to know if Karolena had any extra dogs. Sarah would know how to care for Carlo.

Chapter 3

Nearly a half hour had passed before Blütfink, always the controlling perfectionist, called Karolena to check on the fetus' progress post-op.

"Everything seems to be as expected," Karolena reassured him, having just been on the AllSee in the recovery area herself. Although the fetus was doing well, she herself was not at all, still experiencing continued doubts over the nature of the work she had become involved in. Even her visit to Carlo had not completely cheered her up. After wondering self-consciously how awful her face must look after suffering through so upsetting a morning, Karolena tried to move out of the direct view range of the AllSee, hating even the thought of ever appearing like a sniveling weakling in front of Blütfink.

"Good." Blütfink paused a few seconds, staring quizzically at Karolena's image in the screen, and then asked, "Mind if I come by just to look?"

"No, no, not at all," she stammered, wondering how long she had to fix her appearance up a bit and still meet him over at the recovery area. Why was he asking her if she minded? Did he suspect a problem, and not want to make her upset?

"Good. It might be a few minutes, though. I really had a struggle with the elevators this morning."

Blütfink entered the recovery room in Red One

nearly twenty minutes later, and nodded to Karolena, who herself had arrived only a few minutes earlier. He began to discuss the post-op course when his sentence was cut short by the upset look on her face. Apparently sensing a problem, he walked directly over to the incubator.

A green "Retro-negative" sticker was plastered on the incubator's side near a viewing window, and various lines of tubes and telemetry monitor cables led into and out, making it difficult for Blütfink to observe what was happening within. The fetus's vital sign indicators for blood pressure, pulse, temperature and respiratory rate were all within normal range, which at least appeared to reassure Blütfink. Karolena busied herself checking the split function drains from each kidney, both of which were providing an adequate flow of urine.

"Well, I'm glad to see the kitten's kidney appears to be a ‘take'," Blütfink smiled. He glanced back toward the door, and then frowned. A black plastic "Animal Waste" label covered a black tie-string bag sitting on the floor. Blütfink started to look away when he noticed another label on the incubator, this one said, "*HG-227, Aug. 24, Human Fetus: Christopher*."

"Look, Karolena, I think you're making a big mistake here," Blütfink cautioned, shaking his head in disapproval. "Don't you see, it makes no sense to give the fetus a name? I mean, it's not like it ever was an actual person."

"If I want to give the fetus a name, it's my business. Okay? I'm not anyone's little girl, and I don't need a man's protection, particularly not yours, Rickhard." Karolena, visibly shaken, wanted to say nothing more, and leaned heavily against the wall. She felt the energy drain from her body, and with it, her will to resist Blütfink. In some ways, she knew she was relying on Blütfink for strength, for approval, just as she did with Wolfgang Kreisler, her father. Reliance was a trait fostered by her father, and one also reinforced by Blütfink, once he realized its presence and its usefulness. This was a pernicious trap, and one basic part of her personality she truly hated and knew she needed to change.

Rather than pursue the issue of naming the fetus, Blütfink instead asked, "So, how is your hand?"

With all else going on, Karolena had completely forgotten about the cat scratch. "Oh, that. It stopped bleeding right away," she said, looking at the raw red line on her palm. "I suppose I'll live."

"Good. I just hope you cleaned it well." Blütfink turned back toward the incubator, and then stiffened suddenly. "Look," he said, pointing to the fetus's right leg. "That's not supposed to be happening."

Karolena's gaze nervously followed his. "What are you talking about? The fetus looks okay to me."

"Well," he said, "actually, you couldn't have known. During the cutdown, I . . . ugh, well, I accidentally severed the fetus's right femoral nerve."

"You did what?" The large femoral nerve innervated the leg muscles, making the leg move; there had been no note of such an error in the experimental log.

"I severed the fetus's right femoral nerve," he repeated, more excited than nervous. "It was an accident, but that should have eliminated any movement of the right leg," he insisted as he moved closer to the fetus and examined its legs for additional signs of movement. "That's not what's important here, though. Look at this, it's incredible."

"I don't recall your saying anything about severing a nerve, Rickhard." She looked closely at the fetus's right leg, and it was indeed flinching, ever so slightly.

"I didn't mention cutting the nerve because it had no influence on the evaluation of the experiment," he countered.

"Still, you know you're supposed to note all observations," Karolena reminded, coolly. "It's essential to . . . "

"Listen here, Ms. Perfection, I definitely don't need lessons from you on experimental surgical procedures. I'm the chief surgeon here, remember? Besides, we may have something really big here. Can't you see that?"

"Don't you forget that I'm a surgeon too," Karolena countered angrily. She hated when Blütfink tried to push her around, like when he would lose his temper. She felt bad enough having participated in this surgery, and didn't need his criticism, his tantrums and his verbal abuse. "One thing I can see is what harm we may be doing. Maybe I shouldn't be doing these experiments on little kids, anyway."

"First, let's clear up one little thing: it's a discarded fetus, not a little kid," Blütfink mumbled. "I know how deeply you feel about this, and I sympathize with you, I really do, but let's at least agree about that from the start, okay? Anyway, we're probably only seeing involuntary muscle twitching." Opening a syringe pack, Blütfink jabbed the needle sharply into the fetus's right heel. The pink little foot withdrew quickly, leaving a small droplet of blood where the needle had pierced the skin.

"Rick, that wasn't necessary."

"Sure, sure, I'm sorry," Blütfink uttered as he rapidly connected nerve conduction probes to the leg over the nerve path. As he poked the needle into the fetus's foot, gently this time so as not to draw blood, electrical spikes flickered unevenly on the monitor, indicating nerve function. Quickly hooking up the test equipment to the other leg for comparison, Blütfink detected a similar but slightly stronger nerve stimulus.

"Well, how do you explain that?" Karolena asked.

"I don't know," Blütfink replied, staring at the oscilloscope, "I just don't know. I'm certain I cut the nerve." He paused a few seconds, and then said, "But I think we should open her up again. I have to find out what's happening here. It could be very important."

"This isn't a 'her'. It's a boy, Rick," she said, tearfully shaking her head.

"No. It's an experimental animal, Karolena, that's all. Grow up already, will you?"

You egotistical ignoramus, she screamed in her mind, then paused for a minute to collect her composure. Losing her cool would not strengthen her hand, she repeated to herself, pausing to regain her composure. "What do you mean, open *him* up again?" Incredulous, she thought she must have heard Blütfink incorrectly, for they had just completed the surgical transplant only a few hours ago.

"Look, Karolena, the femoral nerve has activity, electrical activity," Blütfink explained. "There's evidence of innervation and muscle contraction on both legs, despite the cut nerve on the right. If that's what's happening here, that would be truly remarkable. That's why I think we should at least have a look at the cut nerve and see how this could be happening. Perhaps we've found a new property for the nerve growth factor."

"That might not be necessary, don't you think? I mean, maybe the nerve isn't really completely cut."

"No, it's cut, all right. I know a nerve transection when I see one."

"You mean *'when you cause one',* don't you?" Karolena shot back. Giving Blütfink a tearful look, she warned him, "You screw up, you take the consequences. You may have blown the whole experiment, and in the process wasted a fetus, killed it for nothing. Don't you even care?" She had never felt more infuriated and betrayed, and wanted to run away from this frustrating hellhole she called work. At moments like this, she seriously considered returning home to her father in Germany. "And now you want to make Christopher suffer even more?"

"You make mistakes too," Blütfink retorted icily. "And don't call it Christopher. Now, first off, we need to open the surgical areas, right now. I want to look at the femoral nerve I thought I cut and maybe the nephric nerve net too. You didn't reconnect them while I wasn't looking, did you?"

"No, of course not," Karolena countered as she rapidly anesthetized the fetus again. Deftly, she reopened the surgical field and found the central kidney area -- the hilum. After moving the dissecting scope in, Karolena spotted the operative field, and then increased the magnification until she was looking directly at the nerve fibers. Her vision blurred momentarily, making her squint, and made her question whether she needed corrective contacts. Under the microscope, she could identify the tiny renal nerve ends, neatly juxtaposed, just as they had been before closure of the incision. No connecting micro-sutures were present, but there was a curious bump over the injured areas, and the cut ends looked unusually well-placed next to each other.

"It looks okay to me," Karolena reported to Blütfink. "As a matter of fact, it's hard to detect that there ever was a nerve transection here. I see nothing out of the ordinary, except a bump near where the renal nerves on the donated kidney were cut. Maybe it's a healing callus or a hematoma."

"No, no, no. It's way too early for that to be a healing callus," Blütfink scoffed. He attached neurophysiologic testing leads to the kidney and to the renal nerve, and then stimulated the nerve at the point where it entered the kidney. Sharp spike waves lit up the oscilloscope, suggesting that nerve function was intact. "That's just not possible," Blütfink said to himself, shaking his head as he stared in amazement at the tracing. "Those nerves were cut only an hour ago and we never even attempted to reattach them."

While Blütfink closed the surgical site over the kidney, Karolena carefully reopened the suture lines over the fetus' right femoral nerve. She gently teased back the overlying muscle layers and tissues, then retracted the sides back with surgical clamps. Unlike the renal hilum, the femoral nerve ends appeared traumatized, but it was not so clear that they had been severed, as Blütfink had reported. The nerve ends were now neatly close together, something she never would have expected to see.

Karolena stared under the microscope for a long time before saying, "I don't see any micro-sutures here either. One thing, though -- that same odd hump of what could be healing tissue is over the cut you *accidentally* made." Using a probe, she stimulated the femoral nerve by touching it proximal to the accidental incision. The muscle immediately contracted, again causing the fetus' right leg to jerk. Blütfink appeared less surprised and excited that when he had seen the renal nerve net healing. "I've never seen healing as rapid as this happen before," Karolena told him. Recalling the small vial of test solution, Karolena shook her head and asked, "Exactly what was in that stuff you injected, Rick?"

"It was just a test growth factor that should have cut down on the rejection of the kitten's kidney. It had nothing to do with nerve injury or repair, at least it wasn't supposed to. It was a renal tissue growth factor, period. I'll tell you one thing, though," a smile of satisfaction spreading over his face, "if the nerve really did repair itself this quickly because of something in that growth factor, why, that would truly be remarkable. The therapeutic possibilities, not to mention the economic potential here, is phenomenal. Maybe now they won't close our program," he smiled nervously.

A month ago, she probably would have felt as elated as Blütfink; instead, Karolena now could only listen, and look with trepidation and a deep sense of shame at what fundamental alteration of nature their experiment, and her actions, had wrought.

Chapter 4

The remainder of the day passed rapidly, and, her duties surrounding the experimental transplant complete, Karolena left her office and walked down the hallway toward the parking area. Trying to place all the uncomfortable events surrounding her work aside, at least for a few hours in order to finally have some peace of mind, she thought about the early dinner date she had arranged for after work. It was with her friend Susan Wilder, the wife of the WCMC Administrator, Bob Wilder. Although she hardly knew Bob Wilder, Karolena had developed a good relationship with Susan, having first met her at a local aerobics studio. They both liked the classes, and the trainer 'bots were very realistic, pleasant and didn't push them too much. Outside of the studio, they tried to meet at least once a week for lunch, and occasionally Susan invited Karolena out with Bob and to her parties. Susan, a short, thin, attractive red-head, was a refreshingly good-hearted person who tended to think in basic, simple terms. Bob, a handsome man, at least for an American, was of medium build, and seemed perpetually preoccupied and self-absorbed. He was pleasant to Karolena, and seemed to treat Susan well, but that didn't change her basic feeling that all the "natives" were basically lazy. If the environment were only less toxic, she would certainly move home in an instant, and find herself a real man.

Coincidentally, Karolena had also been asked out tonight by Larry Summers, the FirsThought corporate project manager. Larry, an athletic man a few years Karolena's junior, had actually been trying to ask Karolena out for a date on several occasions, and she had given him ample opportunities. Still, it seemed to take too long for everything to fall into place. She had, of course, done a pre-check using an AllSee. Just about everything about everyone was, by law, public knowledge. He was retro negative, unmarried, so the big blocks were not there. When he asked, Karolena had accepted. Karolena had previously gone out for dinner with Larry on a few, not so memorable occasions, and Mister Time-Based Competition almost blew his opportunity for any future date with her when, at work recently, he had the nerve to comment to someone else, while in her presence, about his cardinal rule never to date a fellow employee. *Lucky her.* She scoffed to herself, having already traveled that awkward route with the "charming" Blütfink.

Maybe Larry was intimidated by her position at FirsThought, or perhaps he was just shy, Karolena wondered, although she found it hard to believe that someone who acted as the corporate barracuda while at work could be in the least bit shy. Her feelings toward Larry were mixed, at best, and if it wasn't for his persistence, he wouldn't be any possibility. Yet, Karolena did find certain aspects of Larry's personality attractive, or at least interesting. He was very self-confident, not afraid to speak his mind, rather intelligent, although in a practical and not at all a deep way, and still not at all a turn-off -- in other words, a contradiction and a contrast to her. In more than one way, he actually reminded her of Blütfink. Perhaps that was the type of man she was attracted to, she wondered -- decisive, protective, controlling. She cautioned herself never again to fall into the same self-destructive relationship she had previously become embroiled in with Blütfink. Although unattached, she hardly considered herself desperate. Preferring time with Susan to a date with Larry, she made a rain check with him for tomorrow night.

Stopping to check her reflection in the window as she left the complex, she had to admit she felt better about her appearance lately, despite her difficult day at work. Her tight black body suit was topped with a new short cream-colored skirt, which seemed to accentuate the best parts of her figure, and made her glad she had finally managed to put on a few more pounds. Along with complementing the outline of her figure, the body suit allowed her the freedom of not having to show her legs, something she was rather self-conscious about. For a moment, the edges of the mirror seemed to blur, and Karolena found herself blinking and staring at her fuzzy image. Looking back up into the mirror again a few seconds later, she was relieved to find that whatever distortion she thought she had seen was gone, although she had no problem recognizing the beginnings of another headache. She made a mental note to have her vision checked soon.

Karolena continued down the hall and entered the cavernous underground garage. Practicing a phrase Karolena had been taught once during a visit to Texas, she said, "Howdy, partner" as she passed through the metal detector and in front of the AllSee, and then smiled to herself. Apparently, neither her choice of colloquial nor her discernible German accent caused a problem for the software.

Karolena took the elevator down to the third level, walked quickly to her car and keyed her ID code into the door handle. Standing back, the door of her new yellow NWO model Electric Coupé gracefully raised open, assisted by the dry hiss of pneumatic actuators. She climbed inside, and then punched in her personal ID code, activating the motor. She waited for the charging cable to drop before pulling out toward the exit. The protective steel door to the garage slowly ground open, allowing Karolena to drive out, and she eased her coupé down the service road and pulled in to the back of the animal holding facility.

Only an AllSee was at the front desk, it being after closing time. She used her wrist ID to let herself in to the main area. Walking quickly down the corridor, she entered the dog room, opened Carlo's cage, scooped him up and covered him with a blanket, and exited quickly through the back door. Placing Carlo on the floor in the back, she started her car, drove up the hill and keyed the back gate to open.

Once out of FirsThought, Karolena turned onto the main street toward downtown Neuse. A slight twinge of pain occurred in Karolena's right palm when she grasped the steering wheel tight. She simply attributed the pain to the cat scratch she had acquired earlier, and dismissed it. Carlo lay quietly on the floor, uncertain of why he was there, but not complaining in the least. She reached over, petted him, and said, "Don't worry, Carlo, I've got someone for you to meet." He licked her hand and lay his head back down.

Driving along the two-lane road, Karolena looked around her car's interior with satisfaction. She kept it clean and neat, exactly the way she liked it, and completely the opposite of Blütfink's rather messy car. Her personal environment was one of the few things in her life that was without clutter or odor, one of the few things she had any control over, and the order soothed her.

Addressing the driver's console, Karolena announced, "Destination: Winston County Pet Supply," and watched as a local map of Winston County and a blowup of the city of Neuse displayed in green. The personal navigation unit considered any late information on driving conditions; police activity and traffic, then automatically outlined in blue the best drive route to the store.

Neuse, where Karolena and many other FirsThought employees lived, was a small, older city located on the Neuse River less than an hour away. Shortly after the turn of the new century, Neuse had been a center of light industry. It gradually changed to communications and housing. It still retained a Southern flair, although she had to admit she had no idea what exactly that was. Neuse provided a reasonable opportunity for social activities, and Karolena had over the last year grown to like living there.

The long drive through featureless country passed in a typical blur, then changed gradually from rolling farmland and woods into a medium-sized suburban area of small collections of shops intermixed with multiunit housing. The traffic seemed unusually slow, and as Karolena moved to the passing lane, she noticed a long line of large tank trucks passing her, apparently also heading toward Neuse. A small paramilitary escort drove at the front and end of the convoy, providing protection. Her car's radio gave no clue to their purpose, although paramilitary convoys were not uncommon when the truck convoy carried precious cargo.

Once she entered Neuse, Karolena pulled into the parking lot of the pet store. She went in, quickly chose some essentials, and had an attendant 'Bot load the supplies into her car. She then drove over to the convenience store where Sarah's mom worked.

Karolena greeted the mom, and then Karolena and she spoke quietly as Sarah ran to see the dog in the car. Having gained the mother's permission, Karolena and she walked over to the car. “Do you like Carlo?” Karolena asked.

“Oh yes, he's so cute. I wish I had a dog. Please, mommy, can I have one?”

"Carlo hasn't had an easy life, and he needs a lot of love. Can you give that to him, Sarah?" Karolena asked.

As Sarah promised to care for Carlo, Karolena opened her car and handed Carlo to her. The mother smiled, put her hand on her daughter's shoulder, and petted Carlo. Carlo looked at Karolena, then barked a few times, and snuggled into Sarah's grasp and licked her arm.

Finally feeling good about herself today, Karolena gave the pet supplies to Sarah's mom, promised to visit Carlo as often as she could, then left, confident that Carlo would be taken care of. She then continued on to the restaurant where she was to meet Susan Wilder for an early dinner. Within another few minutes, Karolena pulled into the parking lot of The Natural Disaster, and went inside.

The dinner with Susan Wilder was uneventful, pleasant but too short, due to last minute plans that had developed with her husband Bob. And they had so much to catch up on. After arranging to go shopping together the next weekend, Karolena bid Susan goodbye and drove back to her apartment. She passed WCMC, a large collection of mostly below-ground concrete and metal buildings scattered over a square kilometer of land, along the way, and then continued another mile before turning into her apartment complex. The unit in which she lived was a cramped collection of plain-appearing towers, one of the few newer buildings in Neuse. Finding a flat in an area of Neuse that was still relatively safe had taken a great deal of searching and bargaining and required a stroke of luck. Karolena supposed she should feel fortunate to even have the apartment, but, after living alone for over a year, it only reinforced the social isolation she sometimes felt. At first, Karolena rationalized that her homesickness was due to having left most of her friends and her family in Greater Germany. Greater, she scoffed, Greater as in Greater Pollution, Greater Social Discord, Greater in so many negative things. Then, for a while, her loneliness diminished, and her desire to stay was reinforced by a growing confidence in her career choice at FirsThought. Now, with that confidence changing, particularly after suffering through a day like today, she again contemplated giving it all up and returning home.

As she approached the front entrance to her building, Karolena wove her car carefully through a set of concrete roadblocks, each pitifully concealed with artificial potted plants and graffiti. Off to the right she could see a "*Stiff*" crew loading several corpses of vagrants who had died on the streets overnight. The workers indifferently tossed the bodies, destined for the county incineration facility, into a pile already on the flat bed of a pickup truck. Watching the sanitation workers lift one of the bodies, she quickly realized how the "*Stiff*" crew got its name. Karolena wondered why deaths of street people were happening so frequently of late, especially here, so close to where she lived. That fact made her feel less secure than she already did in Neuse, with its ever-present crackle of evening gunfire -- a din she sometimes could only drown out by playing the stereo system at an irritating level all night long.

Karolena displayed her wrist ID to the AllSee, who requested Karolena to remain in her car while her security clearance and *retro* status were verified. This AllSee's holo image was possessed of a thin, transparent clarity, which, although appearing fairly real as he smiled, could be seen at an angle to merely represent a holographic projection. Holographic simulations, commonplace over the last ten years, were generally thought to be as good as the current state of neural network programming could allow, and relieved humans from the dangers inherent in certain high-risk jobs.

After a short delay, the AllSee cleared Karolena's ID and she was given the okay to pass. The heavy reinforced door of her apartment building's parking garage slowly opened with a rumble, allowing Karolena to dart forward and down into the underground area, where she parked in her assigned spot. Several overhead light panels which had been nonfunctional for weeks were still out, giving the area a dark and isolated appearance. Parking garage rape and robbery were all too frequent, even in 'secure' apartment complexes like hers, and even in this 'good' area of town. Without all the overhead lights on, Karolena feared, it would be difficult for her to be absolutely certain she was alone. Yet, she reassured herself, the area did appear completely quiet, and she had to admit she had never experienced a personal attack against herself. Karolena made certain that her car's charging cable was coupled, cautiously looked around again to be sure the garage was unoccupied, then, with her personal stun probe in her right hand, quickly got out of the car and dashed toward the safety of the elevator.

The door to the small elevator opened as soon as it sensed her approach. The cramped inside was only large enough for three to four people, the floor was littered with trash and the walls were defaced with innumerable and indecipherable messages and symbols angrily scarred in the paint. The air was wet with mildew, and imparted a choking sensation. It reminded Karolena of elevators in Red One at FirsThought, but still a relative improvement over those in her own homeland. As Karolena slowly descended to her 15th floor apartment, she left another message on the elevator AllSee, diplomatically reminding the apartment manager to fix the parking garage light panels, and to do something about the awful smell in the elevator. She couldn't imagine the cause of the smell, and didn't want to know. Realistically, Karolena never was too hopeful that her messages were read, let alone acted upon, as managers of *Retro*-negative apartments held all the winning cards these days.

The elevator stopped at floor 15, moved sideways to her area, and opened so Karolena could exit. As she neared her apartment door, the silence of the corridor was interrupted by the loud, intimidating barking and snarls of a vicious-sounding dog, emanating from the direction of her apartment. After looking up and down the corridor to check that she was alone, she used her wrist ID to gain entry to her apartment, the door sliding open just long enough for her to enter before closing behind her.

Immediately upon closing the door, the computer-generated barking, which had been activated by the detection of movement in the hall outside her door, stopped. The voice synthesizer for the apartment's AllSee announced, "Greetings, Karolena. The status of your apartment is: SECURE. I detect one person: Karolena Kreisler." Such reports were the custom whenever she first entered her apartment, and the added touch of the AllSee's voice often made her feel as if she wasn't alone. Even after living here all these months, the AllSee sounded so real that Karolena often found herself looking around to see if someone was actually there. The AllSee had a holograph option, but she found it a little creepy and had recently turned it off. In the background, Renata, her holographic parrot, happily chirped at her return. Karolena had never considered Renata to be anything but living, and marveled at all the tricks it could learn.

Karolena lived in a small one bedroom unit, with a dinette area attached to a small kitchen, and a living room. Being fifteen floors below ground level, there were no windows, but several walls had projection simulators which could give the appearance of almost any exterior, from alpines to Carolina summer to undersea. With all its flaws, she still found her apartment a warm, charming place to live, especially after she had fixed it up exactly as she wanted it. By late afternoon at work, she looked forward to leaving and returning there, and in the evenings, she hated leaving her little island of sanity.

She quickly straightened up around her apartment a little, more as a means to relax into being at home again than to restore order. The house-'BOTs kept that well-enough. Afterwards, Karolena sat in her favorite floral pattern cloth chair near her matching sofa, wondering what to do with the rest of her evening. Had Neuse not been so dangerous, she might have been tempted to go for a walk on her own. In reality, to do so would be most unwise. Besides, she felt tired from her day at work and her long drive home.

Even with a well-stocked library of e-books and films available on her AllSee, she felt not at all interested. Although a few of her books and films were interactive, they provided only an illusion of company, a vicarious and cheap imitation of moments shared with a true companion. For a moment, Karolena even considered calling Rickhard, ostensibly to discuss a technical issue related to today's experiment. Perhaps he even might call her, inquiring after her difficult morning in the lab. But that was not Rickhard's way, and she could not lower herself to give even the appearance of pursuing him again. He would have taken too much satisfaction in that.

After taking a few moments to stretch, Karolena instructed the AutoBev unit to brew her some cappuccino. She really wasn't that thirsty, or hungry for that matter, after having earlier dined with Susan. She asked more out of her habit to drink a cappuccino or café-au-lait in the early evening -- she found them most relaxing. To her left, a diverse set of optical diskettes she had brought home from the office sat on her table, but she had no desire to look at this work, even as a distraction; some new exercise opticals also sat unused.

When the AutoBev announced in its pre-selected French accent that her drink was ready, she laced it with simulated whipped cream and at least an inch of crème de cacao liqueur, her favorite way to perk up the cappuccino. This she 'hid' in a bottle inside a panel by her optical book case -- out of sight, out of mind, she reasoned. As she sipped from the steaming cup of cappuccino, Karolena was reminded how, on each of her visits, her primary care doctor dutifully reminded her of the seriousness of her chronic liver injury. The illness, usually nothing more than an annoyance, had been with her since a chance exposure to a hydrocarbon toxin spill while in her teens.

Occasionally she suffered from bouts of fatigue, but those episodes of illness usually resolved on their own, with rest. Still, she knew that relapses of the hepatitis were to be avoided, for they might increase the underlying damage. To forestall an exacerbation, especially as bad as one she had suffered through last year, she was cautioned to avoid a long list of items known to irritate the liver. Alcohol was among the 'potentially hepatotoxic' items, yet, for Karolena, as it had been for her mother, alcohol had always been a little difficult to abstain from completely. Well, she thought, I guess my liver can probably stand one more little insult. After all, she sulked, she had made nearly a career out of protecting her liver from danger, and had made a studied art form of toxin avoidance. She paid as much attention to her lousy liver as Susan Wilder did to her diet, as Blütfink did to making money, as Bob Wilder did to impressing people, and as Larry Summers did to looking good even at the expense of making others look bad. She took out a sim-cig, set it to High Relax, activated it defiantly, and inhaled deeply, holding the warm, stinging vapor in her lungs for a long time, before slowly exhaling through pursed lips, anticipating the drug's soothing effects.

Tonight's cappuccino wasn't made particularly well at all, being possessed of a subtle, tart aftertaste which surprised and disappointed her. The taste actually left her slightly nauseous, and she put the unfinished cup down on the table, momentarily eyeing it suspiciously. With pollution the way it was, anything tasting out of the ordinary was cause for concern. She speculated at first on an error in the AutoBev ground coffee program, then wondered exactly what her "privileged commodities" supplier was using this week to cut the outrageously expensive brown ground material purported to be coffee. Opening the top of the AutoBev unit, she sniffed the coffee reservoir and had to admit whatever was in there really did smell like coffee, although she remained skeptical -- chemistry being capable of making anything smell like coffee. These days, good coffee was harder to acquire than real tobacco cigarettes or quality alcohol, and she was in no position to complain about the quality of any coffee she could find. Karolena ignored the cappuccino's bitterness as best she could and instead, concentrated on savoring the warmth from the added liqueur as she finished the cup and felt the contents slowly travel down her body.

It was then that Karolena considered another uncomfortable possibility: the coffee's bitterness could instead be from contamination in the city water again. A vision of the dead bird lying by the stream at FirsThought appeared in her mind, and Karolena felt disgusted and angry with the way her environment was deteriorating all around her; she had no influence, no control anymore. Was she in no better position to control even the quality of the very water she drank than were the animals in their little cages at FirsThought, she had to ask herself? She paused and looked around her as she said that. Was she as helpless and at the whim and will of others as they were? Was she someone else' little experimental animal?

Karolena instructed the AllSee to turn down the intensity of the light panels, and to report on the published toxin levels in the water supply this week. A slight touch of nausea returned, and with it a feeling of fatigue and a mild frontal headache, making Karolena resolve to make an effort to get more rest this weekend. Then, surprisingly, when she tried to push herself up from the couch, she fell back, slightly dizzy, her vision a little out of focus. "Maybe I'll add only one finger full of liqueur next time," she chastised herself, staring into the now-empty cup of cappuccino. The AllSee overheard her, perhaps that was her intention, and it relayed that feedback to the AutoBev unit, which flashed once in acknowledgment. Fortunately, after a few moments, the dizziness and nausea seemed to pass, although the faintest touch of a headache persisted. She went to the medicine cabinet in her bathroom to locate some pain reliever.

The medicine cabinet was mounted in a recessed area of her bathroom wall, behind an old-style mirror. The door slid open on touch, but as she reached inside, Karolena noted another transient blurriness of vision, this time accompanied by a shifting and doubling of images. She stared forward at the cabinet, forcing her eyes to focus, which they seemed to be able to do, and after another minute her vision returned to normal. That uncomfortable episode convinced her that, if nothing else, she really needed to take it easy tonight, and try and get an early rest. In her subconscious, just below a conscious awareness, images of the fetus she had named Christopher floated, images she now was forcing herself to suppress and deny.

Having decided not to go out on her own this evening, Karolena looked around the room for something to keep her mind occupied and off of Larry and Rickhard and all the other men who called her up and used her without really wanting her, and off of all the terrible moral issues she faced in her work at FirsThought. At times like this, she wondered if there were any eligible men of the high moral character and kindness of her father, and she realized that she missed him very much.

She ordered another hot drink from the AutoBev, this time hot chocolate, and again heavily laced it with crème de cacao, with the justification that it would settle her nerves and allow her to sleep. The AutoBev flashed a short message cautioning about use with liver disease, which she had programmed it to do, and promptly ignored it. The AutoBev flashed once to indicate that it had tried. Taking the cup in her hands, she put her feet up on the couch, lay back, and began to read from an e-book. She preferred historical romance, and often fantasized what it was like to have lived in the last century.

Soon, Karolena found herself simply starring at the e-book unit, still displaying the same page she had brought up over an hour ago. The words seemed intermittently blurry, which she attributed to fatigue, yet, her usual concentration wasn't there, nor the will, nor still the energy, and instead of reading, she found herself preferring to play absentmindedly with some dried flowers in a vase. Placing her half-empty cup on the table top, she asked the AllSee for the time.

"Eleven ten p.m.," the unit replied, although she paid the unit little attention. The AllSee noted from a distance her heart rate, pupil size and reactivity to light, and general sense of awareness.

Thereafter, the hours passed even more quickly and at the same time also more slowly, almost without her noticing. Karolena was not used to staying up this late and was beginning to feel its effect. Even after the liqueur, she found it difficult to sleep, nagged as she was by a mild headache. Unfortunately, the pain medication she had taken earlier in the evening for her headache wasn't helping at all. She nervously brushed her hair back with her fingers, stretched her legs, and stared critically at her reflection in the tabletop.

Trying again to concentrate on the time indicator

readout flashing below the table's surface, squinting to see better, she watched the numbers pulse: "12:31 a.m., 12:31 a.m.," the numbers now nearly blurred to past the point of recognition.

Karolena looked across the room at an antique style chest of drawers near the wall leading to the kitchen, the edges of its form shifting in and out of crispness. The chest had been a going-away gift from her father, Wolf Kreisler, and was one of her prize posscssions, and she wondered again how he was doing, and where he was. He traveled frequently on business, and lately they didn't touch bases often enough, and she planned to reach out to him tomorrow.

"AllSee: Hot chocolate milk, please," she addressed the unit, which relayed her desires to the AutoBev. After the customary whirl of syrup leaving a package, the trickle of water flowing into a cup, and the low hum of the microwave kicking in, viola.

"AllSee: News, sound low." Karolena settled down in the corner, propped up against the far wall facing the AllSee holograph image. The house 'bot brought her the hot drink, asked in a perfunctory way how she was doing, and then returned to its charging station.

"The NWO Network News is reporting that another Eco Disaster, this one of possibly major proportions, has just occurred in Winston County, North Carolina." Oh no, not another toxin spill, she thought. The News continued, "Night workers at the sprawling Industrial Petrochemicals Corporation discovered a large leak in the number two funnel pipe, a large conduit between what are called synthesis reactors."

Karolena stared suspiciously into her glass cup, and then put the remainder of her drink down on the table top. Pictures of the damaged pipe, and of the toxic spill, covered the AllSee screen.

"A toxic chemical called trichloroethylene, or TCE, has apparently been leaking into the Neuse River, and into the water supplies of the cities of both Neuse and Raleigh. Medical and environmental experts told NWO News that TCE is widely used in the manufacture of plastics and pharmaceuticals, and is very toxic to all life. Toxicity in humans often takes the form of liver and bone marrow injury."

The news report rang with uncomfortable familiarity to Karolena. How much like life in Greater Germany had her existence here become? What had she gained by emigrating, compared to what she had given up? Her headache was increasing now, and took on an uncomfortable, throbbing character.

"The duration of the spill isn't known. Plant officials, who spoke on condition of anonymity, speculated it may have increased slowly for more than ten days. Automatic leak detection equipment apparently was functioning, but wasn't designed to detect a small leak which gradually increased. No information was available on how today's leak was found."

A picture of a polluted waterway flashed up, and reminded Karolena of the stream at FirsThought.

"An environmentalist with the Earth Legal Network expressed outrage at the spill and indicated plans to sue IPC. National Shoreline workers have already found quantities of dead fish and small animals which presumably drank contaminated water from the Neuse River and its tributaries. Some environmentalists have claimed seeing many dead birds along the river banks, but only a few were present when officials went to investigate. The carcasses have been sent to the University of Raleigh Veterinary School for autopsy and toxicological testing."

Karolena barely listened to the newscast in the background, and instead, stared deeply into the cup of hot chocolate the AutoBev had prepared for her using city water.

"So far, we are told that there have been no human deaths. However, medical experts at the State Department of Health caution residents not to drink water originating from the Neuse River. A fleet of tanker trucks is bringing in safe water for distribution at local emergency stations."

Not very reassuring, Karolena thought. She remembered seeing what probably was that very convoy on her way home from work yesterday.

"This represents the fourth Eco Disaster this year in North Carolina, and perhaps the most serious yet, and state representatives have called for a full . . . "

Karolena now recalled noticing the "**Toxin Sensor Inoperative**" warning light flashing on and off above the sink. At the time, she had ignored it, an action she now regretted. The unit often didn't work well, she had rationalized, and frequently gave false-positive warnings. What am I supposed to do, she angrily wondered at the annoying message? Should I stop drinking water every time the stupid warning light goes on? The AllSee was supposed to let maintenance know of the malfunction. She depended on the AllSee taking care of all the annoying basics for her life, and assumed it had been doing so.

Her headache had now increased in intensity, and was really starting to bother her. Karolena walked into the kitchen and poured some water from the outlet into a glass, in order to take some more pain reliever. The water looked clear enough to her; the mere hint of a slick she had noticed yesterday, with its rainbow effect on the surface, was no longer present. Karolena had then attributed the residue to traces of dish soap, but now she wasn't at all certain, and to be sure, she lifted the heavy, cut glass to her nose and sniffed. Translucent, the water possessed no telltale odor. Yet, when she brought the glass up to her lips, she found the water definitely not tasteless, although this in itself was neither unusual nor definitive.

Karolena smiled with an uncomfortable resignation, swallowed her pain medication, then poured the rest of the water into the sink and walked toward her bedroom. Along the way, she noticed feeling slightly nauseated and dizzy and found herself holding onto the wall for support.

The warning "**Do Not Drink City Water**" continuously flashed across the bottom of her AllSee screen, but it was now too blurry for her to read, and its meaning didn't register. Returning to the kitchen, she filled her glass, this time with bottled water, which she again poured into the sink, slowly and without drinking. Doing so reminded Karolena of a recent incident at work, when some "friends" mocked her preference for bottled water. To push the point, they had designed a "*taste test,*" unexpectedly presenting her with three glasses of water. Two were from the city water supply, ostensibly from the water fountain in the hall outside her office. The third glass was from her own bottled spring water dispenser: Low Sodium. The others took great pleasure contending that Karolena had been unable to correctly identify the Spring Water, and claimed she therefore couldn't taste the difference from tap water. Yet, Karolena immediately recognized the water tasting exercise for what it really was: a petty attack on her private preferences and her own cautious standards.

Now, she wondered who had been right. Perhaps if those involved had seen and actually lived through as much toxic pollution as she had in central Europe, they would have felt a little different. Karolena had been insulted by the implications that her preferences were all in her mind and resentful that others dared test her personal beliefs. She also hated being the object of public ridicule and humiliation, no matter how much in jest it supposedly was. She still believed that she had chosen the correct glass, and they had just been trying to harass her again, although, for some reason, this time a few of those involved wouldn't let her forget it. However, even if she had chosen the wrong glass under those circumstances, it didn't change her convictions, confident as she was of the logic they were based upon.

Karolena turned to another stack of optical documents in front of her, work she had brought home to finish. The disk labels were clear plastic with a light red tint, allowing the FirsThought corporate logo to show through. At first, when she looked at the logo, she almost didn't recognize it, although its image was clear, and it was only after looking away and back again that its identity was discernible

Each set of optical documents, if printed, would have been at least an inch thick. God, there could be over ten sets here, she thought. Under the best of conditions, each set could take hours to read and digest. All sets were supposed to have been finished sometime in the recent past. She was not sure just when that was, only that with her vision becoming more blurry, it was unlikely she would be able to read much of anything in the remainder of the night.

Sighing, Karolena changed into a fresh set of pastel colored disposable, paper evening clothes, as was the local fashion, then pulled a thick sim-woolen robe tightly around her body and secured it with the cloth belt. The robe was old-fashioned but functional, a gift from her father. He had purchased it for her on her last birthday, remembering how she disdained the artificial feel of the newer, self-heating disposable clothes.

Still unable to sleep because of her persistent headache, Karolena attempted to read again, but found her vision now so blurry she had difficulty even making out individual words.

Renata moved back and forth on a perch in its

cage, chirping nervously. "Parrot holographic sim off," she told the AllSee, having no patience for nonessential distractions for the moment, and especially while suffering from a stubborn headache.

"Play some music. Anything will do. Softly." The AllSee chose a Liszt piano concerto, filling the background with bright, pleasant music. Karolena always had felt alone in the apartment, vulnerable despite its high-tech security, and the occasional gunfire she heard every night in the distance only reinforced her uneasiness. Security flows from strength, not from someone else promises, she remembered her father reminding her on more than one occasion.

At difficult times, times she felt totally alone, times like now, Karolena wondered why she had leap at the opportunity to work in the U.S. anyway. Certainly, in terms of her career, the offer had come at an opportune time. Yet, despite her having visited here several times before and feeling that she understood the U.S., Karolena had to admit at least to herself she still didn't feel safe or welcome in this violent and dangerous part of the world. Fortunately, she had developed a few good friendships here, and had made some quality social contacts, like Susan Wilder, although none substituted for having her father nearby. Nevertheless, Karolena clearly knew why she emigrated here - and it centered on survival, her survival.

Much of the world was a toxic dump, with North America the least contaminated. With her liver already damaged as much as it was from toxins back home, any step she could take to avoid further toxic injury could only help her avoid the failure of her own liver and postpone the dreadful necessity of a transplant. Even the remotest possibility of her liver failing was more than enough motivation for her to move just about anywhere and to do almost anything.

Karolena reached for a memory stick from the slide pocket of the top folder labeled: "Critical Points, FirsThought Scientific," pushed it into a slot under the top of the coffee table she was using as a desk, and told the unit to use the video mode. The introduction was from Larry Summers, who occasionally asked her opinion on evaluating new technologies for their scientific potential.

"Karolena, this brochure contains background information on FirsThought Scientific's Growth Hormone Projects," the document began.

Researchers had been looking for truly effective and clinically-relevant growth factors for as long and as unsuccessfully as for a cure for AIDS. With so abysmal a track record and as little likelihood of success, it was no wonder to Karolena that attracting venture capital for these projects was so difficult, and why their latest experiment with growth factors, and especially with their unexpected positive finding, may have turned out to be so important to science, and to FirsThought.

"As I'm sure you're aware, we're involved in a second round of expansion funding. This should allow final preclinical development of our new nerve and liver growth factors. These growth factors are produced with recombinant technology, fill an area obviously in great demand, and supposedly have minimal competitors."

It was common knowledge in the biotech area that few companies could afford to pursue their probably unattainable goals any longer. Blütfink had already told her that was happening at FirsThought. Perhaps the nerve growth factor results would turn out as promising as they initially looked, and assist in attracting to FirsThought needed funding.

"NWO Bank has been asked to provide funds and has committed a response within five days, although this request has also gone out to other lenders," Larry droned on. "What's your assessment of the earliest time to more widespread human trials? A rapid response could be crucial to our success. Karolena, I value your judgment and await your conclusions and recommendations."

After trying unsuccessfully to concentrate on the video report, and finding her vision deteriorating to the point where she almost couldn't see straight, Karolena became more concerned that something more than simple fatigue was bothering her sight. She called out "finished," and the top of her table became transparent again. Lifting one of the first optical disks, she felt its feather weight in her hands, rotated it, stared at it almost as if it were something unrecognized and seen for the very first time, then gently put it back down in its place. Although she continued to gaze at the blurred image of the stack for a few more minutes, she didn't pick another disc up again. *I know that I'm exhausted, but could that be why I can't see?* Karolena thought. She wondered about the toxin spill she heard about on the news, the warning sign on the water tap, and the health of her liver. The connection was too obvious and too horrible to consider. But, what could she do now, she wondered, feeling like another trapped animal?

Nearby, dried flowers filled several cut-glass vases on various cabinets, tables and shelves. Disposable ceramic dishes, caked with dried food, sat in her sink, waiting to be loaded into the recycling unit. Coffee, also dried long ago, caked her cups in the sink, on the tables, and in her room.

Karolena instructed her AllSee to change the picture window display on the wall from a curtain pattern to a daytime local mode, revealing the changing fall weather that had in the past always interested her. The image was transmitted from a camera mounted way above ground, giving the impression her apartment was anywhere but buried like a coffin hundreds of feet in the other direction. Leaves fell in a dance to death, spiraling their way to earth to join the ever-growing pile of compost, and watching this made Karolena feel melancholy. The far-off trees were brush-stroke combinations of pure orange, flaming red, deep olive greens, and browns. Oh, how she wished she could paint, and how she wished specifically to paint those trees, and to paint in oils, not water colors or pastels. Yes, oils had the substance and depth to capture her feelings best, and oils wouldn't fade with time. She was aware of her thoughts wandering, but was not alarmed. She was glad the AllSee was not so aware.

Only a few leaves remained on most garishly naked branches, stuck on at unnatural angles with some natural glue. Karolena knew more nude branches would soon emerge, skeletons of what had once been full maples. Snow would come next, and then the barren land would languish for months. Winter in Neuse always stayed too long for her liking and depressed her. Watching the birds that still remained, sitting idly on the building edges and the bare branches, she wondered what they did to survive unharmed. Did they really need to simply do nothing, and could such a basic strategy ever work for her?

Karolena got up, stretched her arms and legs, and nervously paced around the room. She felt at that moment like a caged animal, confused by strange, blurry surroundings her captors constructed, rendering her incapable of understanding the means to escape. She pulled off her rings, her earrings, her bracelets, all except her wrist ID - for that wasn't permissible. But at least taking off the jewelry had somehow made her feel lighter, more mobile.

Sitting back down on the couch, she turned toward a large impressionist lithograph, hung artfully on her living room wall, centered over some antique Oriental-style cabinets covered with a set of vases she had purchased years ago, and nearby a set of Hopi-style cloth patterns. At first she couldn't recognize the painting, but forced herself to remember, although not by using the graphics itself, but rather, the painting's position in her apartment. Karolena had always believed the litho's soft texture blended well with the decor of her apartment, and lent expression to some of her choices in life. Now, it seemed so irrelevant, so meaningless. She no longer made an effort to focus her thoughts.

Turning toward the wall, Karolena said "TV" to voice-activate and animate the art that reflected life. Karolena had always loved the way the newer paper thin flat-screen displays came with a wide set of programs that, in standby mode, looked like works of art. Karolena tried to watch a replay of her last visit with her parents, a tape quite dated at this point as they were shown together and with her mother still alive, but her vision was too blurry to see them well, and before long she gratefully fell asleep.

She thought she remembered awakening with an anxious start a few hours later. Opening her eyes in that vague haze between sleep and wakefulness, Karolena was surprised to see a woman in her apartment, standing near her bedside, perfectly still in the darkness, Karolena at first thought the woman was a nurse checking on her patients. Then, on closer inspection, Karolena saw that the woman, whom she couldn't recognize, seemed rather young for a nurse, and was wearing a summer dress instead of a uniform. When Karolena tried to speak to her, the woman turned, her bruised and bloody face a contorted mixture of pain and sorrow, held tense fingers to her lips, and whispered only the plea, "Remember me." Those two words lingered for a moment like ethereal sign posts at her bedside before slowly dissipating into the night air, mixing with the background music of electronic hospital sounds and the ghost-like moans of nearby patients on death's door. Moments later, the image herself vaporized much like an AllSee, like a holographic person's, leaving Karolena with the impression she was still dreaming.

Later the next morning, Karolena awoke from a fitful sleep, marked by a number of unpleasant dreams, to find that her vision had become even worse. She remembered vaguely her disturbing dream, but soon its memory faded. Trying to look around her apartment, it seemed as if she were instead inside a thick fog. Objects which only yesterday had been familiar now were surrounded by fuzzy borders, and she was now able to recognize most only by their position and their feel. Moving around her apartment was difficult, and it was only with effort that she was able to touch enough objects to literally feel her way slowly back into the kitchen, holding against the wall as she groped for stability

The growing sensation of disorientation was unnerving, and Karolena fought to control the feeling of panic. Quickly taking stock, she was certain she was not dizzy, and although her heart rate was faster than normal, she believed this due to all her anxiety. Her sensation and her ability to move her arms and legs seemed normal, that much she was thankful, for at least her visual problems couldn't be due to a stroke. Having never experienced any problem like this before, Karolena was certain it would just pass if she left it, and she returned to the living room to sit down and remain calm.

As she walked, feeling her way along, her concern, her anxiety over her condition increased, yet she had a hard time staying awake. Finding a comfortable spot on the water couch, she verbally set the heater to forty degrees centigrade, stared deeply into some holograms showing a picture of her home in Germany, and promptly fell asleep again.

Nearly ten hours later, the AllSee called out "Karolena" to notify her of the arrival of some urgent video mail. Getting no response on the third try, it increased its level of volume threefold and tried again. Again without a reply from Karolena, the AllSee amplified its own microphone unit until it located the room Karolena was in, and then monitored first her respiration, and then her heart beat. Satisfied that both were within accepted limits, its logic sequence decided to let her sleep another hour before attempting again to wake her.

Karolena awoke with difficulty later in the day, feeling more nauseous and disorientated than before. Her vision, although it had not gotten worse, was definitely not any better, but the problem had drastically changed in nature. Although the blurriness seemed to have improved, Karolena now found herself having a distinct difficulty recognizing objects that she felt she should know. Despite having slept for several hours, she still felt very tired, and the headache, now directly behind her right eye, persisted, untouched by the medication. This, together with the nausea that dogged her, made Karolena more certain than ever that her problem was more than simple fatigue. A sense of foreboding, deep and undeniable, flooded her presence, as she faced the true extent of her problem. At the same time, her illness weakened her, made her confused and indecisive and paradoxically left her lacking a good grasp of what immediately needed to be done to save her.

Karolena now was certain she had to get to a doctor, but given her basic distrust of American physicians, decided to wait it out just a few hours more. She was sure that her difficulties, even though visual in nature, somehow centered around her underlying liver disease, and just as so often in the past, whatever problem her liver was having should be temporary, and should pass.

Ignoring occasional questions from the AllSee's programmed neural network's logic, Karolena cautiously got up and felt her way along the wall to near the AllSee, and asked it to contact her father. After a few moments, the AllSee reported that, unfortunately, Wolf couldn't be located and instead a message was left for him. That was just like her father, she thought, going away unexpectedly and incognito for days at a time.

Under different circumstances, the programmed neural network responses of her AllSee trying to talk to her would have been an annoyance, and she would have turned down the threshold or changed the program for another logical response. Today, however, she was glad that artificial intelligence terminals were an option provided -- although at considerable expense -- by the phone company. The AllSee's presence seemed to comfort her, in that it allowed her the illusion of thinking she was not alone. It was probably more trustworthy than any human companion she had recently been with, Karolena reflected.

As a few more hours passed, Karolena's fatigue overtook her, and, assisted by additional doses of pain killers for her persistent headache, she again fell asleep. After a few minutes, the AllSee could only detect shallow breathing, which at least indicated to its rudimentary level of understanding that Karolena was both present and alive. The circuit automatically amplified the microphone input signal to detect heart sounds, and patiently waited.

Toward nine in the evening, Karolena was awoken by a throbbing headache. She was also nauseous, and this was accompanied by an uncomfortable, bloated feeling. After first unsuccessfully searching for relief by lying down, then by sitting up, then by walking a short distance, Karolena continued restlessly shifting positions. After a while, Karolena began wandering her apartment aimlessly, looking with an odd, disheartening sense of unfamiliarity at many of the objects she came in contact with, before finally flopping exhausted back down on her bed.

Rolling onto her back, Karolena looked over at the

wall, and realized with horror that she now wasn't able to recognize even her own image in a mirror. The suddenness with which this happened, coupled with the shock of not being able to say for certain the face she saw was her own, snapped Karolena briefly out of her confusion, and for the shortest moment she was back in control, knew what to do and did it without hesitation.

Turning toward the AllSee hologram floating near her bed, she cried out, "Medical Emergency. Help." The AllSee's loyal logic set in motion the necessary actions she had carefully programmed in long ago.

Karolena was now mercifully oblivious to her loss of vision, her surrounding, her confusion, and collapsed into a deep sleep.

Chapter 5

Winston County Medical Center
Emergency Room

Karolena arrived at the ER semiconscious and too weak to move, much as the ambulance crew had found her sprawled on her apartment floor. The gurney's legs popped open and swung down spider-like with a loud metallic click, allowing the paramedics to rush Karolena's cart down the loading ramp, and up toward the ER's outer doors. Just to the entrance's side, four heavily armed guards in flak jackets and helmets -- members of a local paramilitary group -- stood watch behind bulletproof shields. In the open parking area beyond the ambulance bay, a restless sea of the sick and dying milled about like an encamped army laying siege, huddled around burning trash receptacles and cardboard huts while trying to keep warm.

Projected down from the ER entrance overhang, a large flat panel display flashed in an ever-changing stream of languages:

VERIFIED *RETRO-NEGATIVES* TO THE RIGHT, ALL ELSE TO THE LEFT

The lead emergency medical technician steered the head of the gurney carefully watched the blinking sign with one eye and the paramilitary with his other. He knew all-too-well that '*To the left*' meant transfer to a *Retro* Positive facility elsewhere. Medical care there would be of a lower quality and the wait very long. The Winston, in contrast, was a Level 3 hospital; it handled complicated traumas and specialized surgeries, and possessed the most advanced laboratory and diagnostic equipment in the state. More to the point, access to this particular Level III facility was restricted to '*Retro-negatives*.'

The paramilitary had been expecting Karolena and waived her gurney to the right, around a team of barking police dog-‘bots on chains that helped enforce the directions displayed on the flashing sign. The ER charge nurse on duty, an experienced 'float' from the surgery wards, directed Karolena's gurney into a holding room halfway down the dingy hall. An ER record had already been prepared before Karolena's arrival, based on data supplied through telemetry by her wrist ID, including her medical and surgical history, medication list, allergies, and date of last verified *Retro* test.

Switching the infrared telemetry link on Karolena's monitoring cuff over to the ER system, the cuff's pressure sensor now operated under its own power. It remained on Karolena's upper arm to provide intermittent measurements and also served as a temporary monitoring lead. These numbers were automatically noted on the ER record, and were also displayed on a continual digital readout:

"**Nature of Admission**: AllSee-Initiated Medical Emergency
Retro: Negative
Identity of person requesting help: Kreisler, Karolena
UN identity: uncus212-22-36543x
Citizen: Greater German Republic
Biotype: F A658B333C983475D243, 32 y/o
Address: 2232a St. Joseph's Terrace
Neuse NC USA 074123g-3141
Justice: none outstanding, no known criminal record

Blood Pressure::	70/40
Heart Rate:	141
Heart Rhythm:	Regular
Body Temperature:	97.4
Blood hemoglobin:	12.0
Oxygen saturation:	94%

The telemetry unit digested the information through an artificial intelligence trauma algorithm, and displayed a notation that the values detected were clearly abnormal.

After carefully looking down at the new patient, the ER doctor checked the name before exclaiming,

"Oh, oh. This is Karolena Kreisler."

The nurse stared at them, indicated she didn't understand the significance.

"I heard Dr. Kreisler speak at a recent hospital symposium on growth hormones, along with Dr. Blütfink. They both work at FirsThought. Could you notify Dr. Blütfink that she's here?"

Karolena could hear the doctor speaking, and when she thought he said something about asking Blütfink to handle her case, she tried to raise her head and object. In her nearly delirious state, unfortunately, her words only came out garbled, and echoed inside her head.

Digitized diagnostic information emanated from the Doppler stethoscope almost immediately after the doc ran the unit along Karolena's chest and abdomen, "Lungs clear, heart tachycardic but regular and without murmur," he reported. "Abdomen: enlarged liver, perhaps 20 centimeters in the midline. Awfully damn big. Skin dry and without lesions." A voice transcription unit kept track of his observations, and prepared an EMR-electronic medical record as he spoke.

Next, the ER doc requested a set of blood samples for the usual labs, including an assay of Karolena's coagulation system and ammonia level, after noting her enlarged liver. From the medical information recorded on her wrist ID, they knew that it was a chronic condition.

"I'm way ahead of you," the nurse reported. "Blood specimens for the labs were drawn five minutes ago, and the results should be available soon."

"Good. I wonder if that new toxin spill over at IPC set her liver off? The low blood pressure and tachycardia are certainly consistent with dehydration, vomiting and possibly some internal bleeding."

The laboratory results, which came back within minutes, all were unchanged from recent blood tests whose results were encoded in Karolena's wrist ID. After noting that Karolena continued to be medically stable, the ER doc left to examine his next patient while waiting for Blütfink to come in and assume care of his new patient.

Semi-awake, and feeling disoriented, Karolena pleaded to the ER nurse, "The pain, my headache, nausea, too much. Can you give me some medication, please?"

The nurse quickly checked Karolena's medication chart, then went to the nursing station, and returned with a foil package of anti-nausea skin patches and an analgesic patch. "These medication patches should help with your nausea and headache, Karolena. And here's an extra one for you to use in about four hours if you still feel like throwing up," the nurse offered, knowing that as the ER became more hectic, Karolena's access to the nurses, as long as she remained medically stable, would be spotty.

Karolena reached out, but completely missed the foil package. Instead of trying again, Karolena let her hand drop helplessly onto the bed, a shocked look sweeping across her face.

Not having a great deal of time to spend on any

one patient, the nurse took the medication package and placed it firmly in Karolena's hand. "Here, you better get a good grip on the patches this time before I let them go, Karolena."

"I'm afraid holding onto it isn't the problem," Karolena admitted.

"Then I don't understand. What IS the problem?"

"I know this is going to sound strange, but I, I can't seem to recognize what it is you're handing me," Karolena stuttered out, her face a mass of confusion as she stared blankly at the patches.

"That's the nausea medication you wanted," the nurse told her. "Why, what do you think it is?"

"I'm just not sure. These last few days, my vision has really deteriorated, and I don't recognize things too well."

"You mean your vision is getting blurry?"

"No, not blurry, not that, at least not completely. Actually, much of the time I see okay, everything seems in focus. I've never experienced this problem before, and it frightens me, and it's difficult to explain to others."

"Then I don't understand." The ER doc had just returned to the room, and also listened intently to Karolena's symptoms.

"It's just that I don't seem to know what things are anymore. I feel confused, real confused, and it's making me very scared."

"Dr. Kreisler, can you see me?" the ER doc asked. When Karolena nodded unconvincingly that she could, he attempted to perform a cursory visual exam, concentrating on areas that might be helpful in evaluating her visual symptoms. With Karolena only semi-conscious and unable to follow commands completely, it was difficult to determine whether she was able to move her eyes or to focus. Still, her pupils and retina seemed normal to the ER doc, as was the movement of her eye muscles. Despite her grossly normal exam, Karolena's complaints were most credible, and the ER doc considered it prudent to order ophthalmology consult before he again left to care for some new arrivals. Fortunately for Karolena, the medication patches had a rapid effect, allowing Karolena to again fall asleep.

Several hours passed before Blütfink was able to see Karolena. After all, she fumed, why should he make any special effort to see her instead of any other of his lucky patients? After all, they had only worked together for over a year, had in the past slept together, dined together, argued and laughed like normal people who one very might expect cared about each other.

By now, Karolena was formally admitted to the hospital, although she still was 'lodged' in the ER and without an actual room and bed assignment. "Karolena, what happened to you?" Blütfink asked as he approached her bed side.

Hearing Blütfink's voice, Karolena turned her head slightly, reached out and held his hand. Still feeling somewhat disoriented, Karolena looked askance in the direction of Blütfink's voice, but only saw the unrecognizable shadow of a large man. His voice, though, was clearly Blütfink's, and even though he took longer than she expected to arrive, he was at least finally here with her.

Although she thought she would probably have preferred another doctor, someone whom she didn't know as well, or as intimately as she did Blütfink, he was at least a known quantity. His competence as a surgeon was unquestionable, although just how capable he would be in evaluating her visual problems was doubtful.

"I started to feel dizzy at home several days ago," she explained, “and everything began to appear blurry. I had trouble recognizing anything." I got very tired, and the next think I knew, when I awoke, I was here," she gestured around the ER with her hand. Closing her eyes, she told him, "That's all I remember. I guess I must have passed out in my apartment." She realized she was lucky to be alive, and wondered if she would ever walk out of the hospital. Feeling suddenly very choked up, Karolena asked, "Could you hand me a glass of water, please?”

Blütfink had ears to get what he needed to know from the nurses, and eyes to watch his patient, and had already been informed of Karolena's visual difficulties, although he had absolutely no idea what they could be due to. He did immediately notice that, as he tried to hand Karolena a simple glass of water, she acted confused when he presented it to her. *No, not confused*, Blütfink thought, as he carefully observed her unusual reactions. The difficulty Karolena displayed was quite different from simple confusion. It was as though she simply didn't recognize the glass of water. He turned to ask Karolena more about her symptoms, but she seemed on the verge of falling asleep, and he knew better than to awaken her to perform a physical exam, especially when the ER staff had apparently already thoroughly evaluated her so recently. Instead, Blütfink held the voice translation unit up in his hand and began his dictation from the records he had.

Patient: Karolena Kreisler:
Conclusions:
1) Syncope, possibly due to dehydration,
2) Headache, nausea, possibly due to viral infection,
3) Acute visual loss, bilateral, cause undetermined,
4) Chronic liver disease

Plan:
1) Ophthalmology consult, rule out visual agnosia problem,
2) Maintain adequate tissue perfusion and blood pressure via fluid intake.

The computer unit digested Blütfink's words, entered them into the electronic medical record-EMR and regurgitated a timed and dated thermal printout to document his observations and plan of care, although his thoughts were another matter. Slowly, Blütfink folded the laser-generated document, repeatedly ran his fingers over the crease, and then fit the paper snugly into the pocket of his long white lab coat, in-between a package of oversized oatmeal and raisin cookies and his personal AllSee, underneath where a monogram "*Dr. R.* Blütfink" was neatly sewn into the pocket with red thread.

An infrared link from the voice unit automatically forwarded copies of Blütfink's dictation into Karolena's EMR and on to Blütfink's office, where he could proof the report later. The ward computer scanned the words "Ophthalmology consult" and automatically scheduled a 'routine' visit, which would not take place for two weeks. "Acute visual loss" was copied from Blütfink's conclusions into the "Reason for Consult" line of the request form.

Blütfink shook his head, slowly looked up and examined the ceiling, seemingly for answers. He was unable to believe how ill Karolena had become just in the short time since he had last seen her. It seemed only yesterday they were in the lab over at FirsThought, working and arguing together, and now all this. Just then, his wrist ID notified him of an incoming call, from W. Kreisler.

After a rush of new admissions to the ER, Karolena's cot was wheeled to an open spot in the outer hallway, until a bed opened up on the wards. Heavily medicated for her headache and nausea, she slept there for long periods, depending nearly completely on intravenous fluids for her intake. Around her, a sea of patients and hospital staff moved in a continual flow, indifferent to her presence, awakening her at odd hours by occasionally bumping into her bed or arguing nearby. Soon after her bed was moved, Karolena awoke to the voices of people arguing by her bedside, then the sound of someone calling her name.

"Karolena, Karolena Kreisler?" The voice was unfamiliar, heavily accented, and seemed to come from the shadows, from afar.

"Yes?" Karolena almost croaked a response through her mind's fog. The pain inside her head was both sharp and dull and loved inward from all sides, alternatively pressing and squeezing. Karolena turned her head with some difficulty, even the slightest movement bringing a jarring ache. Her brain pounded, her eyes refused to focus, her mouth was dry and tasted like an old sponge, and she felt like she had fallen off a building. Groggily starring at the shadowy figure by her bed, Karolena made out an older woman, short and squat, dressed in a long, dark robe of crimson color. A red dot accentuated the center of her forehead, and when the woman smiled, Karolena could see several large gold teeth. Karolena also noticed a mild body odor, which was partly responsible for waking her up. Water was short for everyone, and these days many took fewer baths and resorted to more deodorant with fragrance.

"Karolena, I am Dr. Nabula Fromposi from County Ophthalmology Associates," the woman said. Strangely, her face seemed to Karolena rather expressionless.

Oh, no, Karolena thought, after having already just

been examined by both the ER doc and by Blütfink. Not another doctor. Not so soon.

"Dr. Blütfink asked me to examine your vision," Dr. Fromposi continued, echoing Karolena's thoughts. "Apparently you are having some problems seeing." Fromposi nearly threw an old style heavy black leather exam bag, full of instruments, onto Karolena's bed, almost knocking over the glass of juice on the bedside tray. "OOPS, sorry about that."

"No harm yct," Karolena said, but had trouble hiding her annoyance as the shaking jolted straight through to the center of her headache.

"What is the hurry here, anyway?" Fromposi asked. "The hospital administrator himself called me in from home. This is most unusual."

Karolena suspected that Susan Wilder must also have heard of her admission and exerted some pressure in speeding up her care. Blütfink most likely had some input here too; there were times with the current medical system that such personal intervention was absolutely essential, and could make the difference between life and death. Her position as a physician on staff at a large local company, one with plenty of influence with the hospital, must also have been helpful.

"Facilities are limited for a bedside exam," explained Fromposi, "however, Dr. Blütfink believes it would be too difficult to move you to the Ophthalmology Services area given your present condition. So, I will just have to complete my workup right here," she sighed in an exaggerated manner.

Firmly grasping hold of her ophthalmoscope like an ax handle, Fromposi sighed again, then pointed to a spot on the wall. "Now look straight ahead, please."

"Dr. Fromposi, I'm having problems recognizing things, not seeing things."

"Oh, I see," Fromposi acknowledged. She paused a long time before saying, "Okay, but I still do need to complete a baseline visual exam regardless. This is very very important. Now, look straight ahead, please." Fromposi used her ophthalmoscope to complete a detailed examination of Karolena's retina and optic disk, which appeared normal. Moving her face to within inches of Karolena's, Fromposi next attempted a good look at her retinal arteries and veins.

Karolena sensed that Fromposi was, for some strange reason, losing her concentration and not acting quite normally. She watched, puzzled, as Fromposi carefully considered the sight of Karolena's face reflected in the shadows. Then, suddenly, Fromposi blinked, shook her head briefly and seemed to regain her composure and clear her mind of whatever mysterious subject she had been considering in private.

"Look straight ahead, and fix on a point," Fromposi instructed, briskly and coolly. "Do not move your eyes, please." After a few minutes, she said, "I can see some yellowing of the retinal background. It is probably due to escape of bile from blood vessels. It is not too unusual in chronic advanced liver disease. I am surprised they do not just give you a liver transplant. It is so easy to do, no?"

"I probably could use one someday, but so far, my

own liver is still holding out just fine, thank you." Just having to admit out loud that she had chronic liver disease depressed Karolena further. It was almost a failure on her part as a person, ridiculous as it may have seemed.

"Oh, that is very good, really it is, no?" Fromposi asked, taking hold of Karolena's hand and patting it.

"Right now, I don't think my liver is bothering me at all. The problem is that all of a sudden I can't see correctly." Karolena felt uncomfortable, and she withdrew her hand from Fromposi's grasp. She had had other women take hold of her hand, without making her feel uncomfortable, but somehow this was different.

"Well, your retinal arteries and veins themselves appeared normal. The optic disk appeared normal, as well, without enlargement or degeneration. So far, Ms. Kreisler, I can see no reason for a problem with your vision. Maybe the problem is neurologic."

Karolena acknowledged Fromposi's remarks with an emotionless nod. She clearly felt, though, that there was something quite strange about Fromposi that made her want to limit their conversation.

"Follow my finger, please," Fromposi instructed. After moving her finger left, right, up, down, and in and out, she noted that all Karolena's eye movements were intact. This implied that the brainstem, extra-ocular muscles and the third, fourth and sixth cranial nerves were functioning normally and were not the cause of any visual deficit, leading Fromposi to suspect a problem elsewhere.

Fromposi held up a small plastic card with rows of numbers in decreasing size, about one meter from Karolena's nose. "Okay, Karolena, I want you to read the smallest numbers on the chart that you can."

"Actually, I can't," Karolena hesitated to reply, wondering how she was ever going to explain the problem to Fromposi without sounding like an illiterate.

"What do you mean, you cannot? I thought you just told me you did not have trouble seeing clearly."

"That's correct, in a way. I mean, I see writing but I can't read it."

"But you do see the numbers, no?" Fromposi demanded, impatiently. She clicked her teeth again, and then tapped her shoe against Karolena's bed.

"Well, I think so. I see 'things', but I can't always say exactly what they are." Karolena gave a nervous laugh, then said, "It's very hard to describe, so you don't need to get angry. I'm not intentionally acting evasive, you know."

"Of course you are not. I know that. Karolena, there are simply numbers on this card. Do they not look like numbers? Are they very blurry or indistinct?" Fromposi impatiently asked, pointing repeatedly to the figures on the card. "I am afraid that I have several other patients to see, and this is already taking too much time," she muttered out loud.

"I can see them clearly, but I can't tell you what they are." The experience was very frustrating for her, too.

Rather than persisting, Fromposi tried a different

approach, this time using symbols representing big letter E's, opening up, down, left or right, printed on test cards usually reserved for the illiterate. "Can you tell me which way the open sides are?"

This worked better for Karolena, who now seemed to display good visual acuity. She could recognize changes in the orientation of figures, even if she was having problems interpreting symbols. Then, acting on a hunch about something she had heard a few colleagues discussing lately, Fromposi showed Karolena an old style key she had been given once. "Do you see this object?"

"Yes, I can see it all right." I must really sound stupid, Karolena thought.

"Okay, then, what is it you see?" Fromposi prodded.

"I don't know." Karolena shook her head, a confused and worried look covering her face.

Fromposi angrily flicked her ophthalmoscope off. "Okay, okay, let us try this. Close your eyes." Fromposi placed the same key into the palm of Karolena's hand, closed Karolena's fingers around them, and asked Karolena, "Do you know what you're holding? No?"

Karolena felt the key with her fingers, examined its shape and knew instantly. "It's just an old-fashioned key, isn't it?" she offered, glad to finally show that she was not a complete invalid.

"That is right, Karolena. It is most definitely a key. So you could recognize it by touching it." Fromposi took the key from Karolena and showed it to her. "See?

This is the very same key I was just showing you. Do you not recognize it now? No?"

"Yes. No. I don't know." At this point, Karolena didn't know if she was more confused, frustrated, angry or embarrassed.

"Then how come you knew what it was when I placed it in your hand? Please tell me this." Fromposi looked at Karolena as if she was crazy.

Karolena looked puzzled, but didn't reply. Her embarrassment and confusion was changing to fear as she began to consider what her life might be like without the ability to visually recognize things. She contemplated whether her vision in general would deteriorate, too.

Fromposi arranged for a radiology technician to wheel in a portable Magnetic Resonance Imaging Unit and move it over to the bedside. The large silver sphere had projecting cables and antennae and a cylindrical opening to adapt to whatever body part was to be examined, in this case the head. The technician lifted Karolena's head, placed it entirely inside the halo, and plugged a long black cable from the imaging unit into the wall receptacle labeled 'MRI Remote'. Fromposi keyed some numbers into the panel on the halo which activated the unit, and then moved a scanning wand over Karolena's wrist to link the scan to her UN ID. "There, that should do it," Fromposi said. After a few minutes, interrupted only by an occasional low pitched hum, the scan was over and the halo was moved away from the bed.

A three-dimensional color coded holographic

image of Karolena's brain hovered over the imaging unit's control console, rotating slowly in space. Shortly after that, a printout of the scan of Karolena's brain appeared, followed by a typed interpretation:

> Magnetic Resonance Imaging scan normal in all areas, except some early lucency in the right occipital area corresponding to Visual Association Area 19.
>
> Clinical Correlation advised.
>
> Thank you for choosing Winston County Radiology Associates."

Her suspicions confirmed, Fromposi told Karolena that she would need time to prepare a report, and would be in contact with Dr. Blütfink, then got up and prepared to leave.

"But what did your scans and your exam tell you? Don't you have even a preliminary diagnosis, something, anything you can tell me?" Karolena pleaded. How could Fromposi just leave, after spending so much time examining her, without saying anything?

"It is best not to speculate. Please, be patient and wait for my full report," Fromposi said as she slowly backed out the door, leaving Karolena behind.

As Fromposi vanished, Karolena stared helplessly at the MRI Remote Unit, wondering just what was happening to her, and whether she would ever recover.

Chapter 6

Having just completed her assessment, Fromposi asked the ward clerk to put in a call for Blütfink. Fortunately, Blütfink wasn't in surgery just then and responded immediately.

"Dr. Blütfink, this is Dr. Nabula Fromposi, from County Ophthalmology Associates."

Blütfink recognized the name Fromposi, and immediately tensed up as he wondered what conclusions Fromposi had come to.

"I am calling about the consult you requested for the chronic liver patient in the ER, the one with a visual problem."

"That would be Karolena Kreisler. What have you found?" Blütfink asked.

"Karolena's vision is 20/20 uncorrected. She can recognize objects by touching them, but not visually. Further, her brain scan showed a lesion in the cerebral cortex, specifically in Area 19 of the occipital lobe. This is the Visual Association Area, which we commonly call the VAA. Are you familiar with this?"

"I know of it, but not a great deal, I'm afraid." Blütfink admitted, trying to recall what little he could. Neuroanatomy was not his strong point, and, in fact, he had specialized in transplantation to such an extent, that he was for all practical purposes no longer competent in most other areas of surgery, let alone medicine.

"Now, damage to the VAA leads to visual agnosia, and I think that your patient Karolena Kreisler is exhibiting a symptom complex consistent with visual agnosia. I cannot be certain without examining actual brain tissue from a biopsy, which, I think you will agree, is not appropriate at this time."

"Of course," Blütfink readily replied. He recalled his recent call from Karolena's father, alternatively pleading and pressuring for action to be taken. Blütfink had never met the man, but certainly knew the type.

"However, I believe a preliminary diagnosis of damage to the VAA can be made even without the biopsy. Given the limited treatment options, being more aggressive in trying to make the diagnosis makes little sense in terms of risk vs. benefit."

"That's very interesting, and I certainly agree. But, how did Karolena develop a problem in her VAA?"

"We do not know for sure. Lesions in the VAA are very rare. But, she has liver disease, no?"

"Yes, but what does that have to do with her visual problem?" Blütfink asked Fromposi.

"This is very very interesting. Liver disease seems to predispose patients to an infection with the Oculocortical Virus, known as OCV. The OCV has a propensity to infect and damage the VAA. Lately, several cases have been reported in association with acute or chronic liver failure."

"That description seems to fit Karolena, all right. Do you think that Karolena has an infection with this

OCV?"

"Quite possibly," Fromposi agreed. "That virus lives in animals, they can transmit it. Did she get scratched or bitten lately?"

He remembered the cat scratch back in the lab. How ironic, he scoffed. He shrugged a response to Fromposi's questions, and then asked, "But what kind of precautions do I need to take? I'm around her all the time." The thought of needing to protect himself against one more kind of virus irritated him, worried him.

Taken aback at Blütfink's sudden interest more in his own welfare rather than that of his patient, Fromposi added, "On this you can feel somewhat safe. OCV appears similar to spongiform encephalopathy virus of sheep. It isn't highly infectious to the other patients."

"To hell with other patients. I want to know if this OCV is infectious to me or not? Could I get it from contact with her?"

"Dr. Blütfink, OCV is definitely not, I should emphasize, not very very infectious, except perhaps for animal scratches, or intimate personal contact with a victim."

"Oh, great." he exclaimed.

"Besides, OCV isn't even in the Retrovirus family. But if you want to know more about precautions you need to take, I suggest you consult the Infectious Disease Service."

"I definitely will do that." Every day, Blütfink thought, there seemed to be another infectious agent his patients might have that he needed to protect himself from. The laying on of hands was definitely old century, back when practicing medicine must have been so much simpler, and safer to the practitioner.

"Please remember that this is only a preliminary diagnosis, based on the results of the visual exams, the bedside Magnetic Resonance Imaging scan, and her medical history, including exposure to trichloroethylene. So, has Karolena had any recent animal bites?"

"I don't know for sure."

Fromposi paused, considered her words carefully, and continued. "There have been some cases of OCV infection linked to animal bites."

Blütfink looked at his hand and remembered how a cat scratching Karolena back at the lab. "How about a cat scratch?" He thought about how close he too had come to being scratched.

"Well, yes, I guess. Why?"

"Oh, it was just a guess," Blütfink added.

"There seems something very very unusual about this patient, though. Your patient did not have contact with people infected with unusual viruses, did she?"

Blütfink shrugged his shoulders. "I don't know who she has had contact with lately, really," he admitted, the thought bothering him somewhat.

"I see. We are also running the appropriate blood tests now to confirm. But I doubt given the similarity to cases we have seen lately that the diagnosis will be different."

"Let's say she turns out to have this OCV. Can you

treat this?" Blütfink asked. He was well aware that neural tissue didn't regenerate well, and was sure occipital cortex of the brain wouldn't. For a brief moment he wondered if the nerve growth factor that his laboratory at FirsThought was developing could help Karolena. He considered mentioning that to Bob Wilder, who somehow also knew of Karolena's admission.

"I am afraid there's a uniformly poor prognosis for restoration of visual recognition in this illness," Fromposi replied. "Anti-viral drugs have very very good efficacy in eliminating the virus and arresting disease progress, but not in restoring visual comprehension and recognition. Once it is lost, vision never returns. However, as the OCV only attacks the VAA, once treated, the virus does not progress further. At least it will not kill her."

To that last, telling remark, there was only silence from Blütfink. The possibility of Karolena dying left him with an unusually empty feeling, and a certain uncharacteristic sadness enveloped him for the rest of his day.

Chapter 7

Blütfink hurried down the corridor to the emergency department early the next morning to begin rounds on his patients, his open white coat with the monogrammed letters "BR" flapping at his sides like floppy wings. He busily argued with the hospital radiologist via his AllSee, while simultaneously munching on a half eaten red chili horse meat burrito, both hands and his mouth constantly busy as he went. A small paper bag stuffed halfway from his side pocket. It was late the previous evening when Blütfink had last examined Karolena Kreisler, his research assistant, his former lover and now his patient. Fromposi's shocking diagnosis and prognosis for Karolena had upset him more than he was willing to admit. He had spent a miserable night worrying, had not slept well, and wanted to see Karolena as soon as possible.

Blütfink took a few moments to first quickly look in on his other patients in their regular hospital rooms. Although the surgical residents were responsible for the day-to-day care of the patients, he usually stopped by first thing to head off any problems and to offer advice on therapeutic strategies. For the most part, he seemed totally unaware of the world's ability to function without his micromanagement. Fortunately, today everything was quiet, and with that responsibility completed, he went down to the ER to see Karolena.

Karolena had spent the remainder of the previous night again lying on a gurney jammed against the wall near the nursing station, still waiting for a room to open up. Her bed was partially hidden by a portable x-ray unit which abutted Karolena's feet and a linen cart pressed near her head. With a gray hospital blanket loosely covering her body, and her head uncomfortably propped up on an undersized pillow, she was nearly unrecognizable from a distance.

When shc awoke by Blütfink's gently prodding at her side, Karolena felt weak and disoriented, sapped by her illness and the less than therapeutically healing accommodations. It took her a few moments to remember where she was, and why she was there. Looking around her, the ER seemed to be in a typical state of disarray, full of patients on wheelchairs and gurney beds moving in steady streams out the doors and back into the doors of the large unit. Armed guards in fatigues leading guard dog-bots on chains circulated in the corridors. Because they were actually bots, very real-appearing bots, Karolena knew that the use of chains was unnecessary, but definitely added a sense of aggressive potential danger. Her vision seemed more clear now than it had last night, but many objects with which she had the feeling of vague familiarity were at the same time still unrecognizable, like the sea of faces at a crowded mall.

Karolena looked up through glazed eyes at a man in a white coat standing at her bedside and attempted a smile. Although he looked vaguely familiar, she could not place him, and she pulled her blanket up around her chest.

"Karolena, how are you feeling?" Blütfink asked in a subdued voice. Although looking directly at her at first, he soon started up at the ceiling, avoiding her eyes.

"Rickhard, is that you?" Karolena asked when she recognized his gravelly voice with its characteristic German accent. She was surprised at the extent her visual recognition had further deteriorated. Having Blütfink here also made her feel self-conscious -- Karolena knew she looked horrible -- the illness had left her fatigued, her hair must have been disheveled and her face drained of energy. Although Blütfink had seen her several times before in bed, it was of course never in such an open and vulnerable context, and she felt totally out of place. In other circumstances, she might have felt merely embarrassed, but this obviously was different. Even though she and Blütfink were no longer emotionally involved or intimate and hadn't been in a while, looking into his eyes, Karolena couldn't help wonder if he felt even the least bit concerned about her as a person. How could he not have?

"Yes, I'm here, Karolena. Are you feeling any better?" he asked, anxiously.

"No, not too good, Rickhard."

Blütfink stood several feet away from Karolena's gurney and nodded with concern as she spoke. Although usually speaking in Karolena's general direction, Blütfink was frequently interrupted by conversations with other staff and patients or calls on his personal AllSee, and the lack of his complete attention, especially when she was so sick and really in need of him, irked her. Seeing her annoyance and understanding it in a way only one previously intimate could, he reached into his pocket and took out the bag. Removing a cold cup from it, and taking off the lid, he handed the steaming cup to her. "Here," he smiled cheerily, "I got something for you."

Karolena thanked him, and took a sip, then broke out in a smilc. "Thanks for the cappuccino. How nice of you to remember."

"No problem. Look, Karolena, I just want you to know how bad I feel about your getting sick like this. I know we've had our differences, but I still like to think of all the good times too."

Karolena reached out and took hold of his hand and gave it a squeeze. "Thanks for saying that, Rickhard." She set down the cup with her other hand, took a corner of the bed sheet and wiped a tear that had formed in the corner of her eye.

"Karolena, Dr. Fromposi told me what she saw on her exam of your eyes," he said, shaking his head gravely. "It wasn't too good, I must admit, but we're going to do everything in our power to help you."

"Dr. Fromposi didn't tell me too much when she was here. Exactly what did she say was wrong with me?" Karolena asked.

After her initial visit, Fromposi had not returned to give Karolena her diagnosis and recommendations, preferring instead to work through Blütfink. Unfortunately, whenever Karolena tried to discuss her own interpretation of the situation and her fears and desires with the nurse who apparently had charge over her case, she didn't appear too interested, and within minutes, was gone again. Karolena, of course, realized at a gut level all too well just how desperate her situation was, but she had no intention of giving up hope; her will to survive was very strong.

"Apparently, you have damage to the area of your brain which associates vision with recognition, your VAA, and this is possibly the result of a virus."

"A virus?" Karolena asked. She wondered where she could have contracted the infection, and if it could spread to other parts of her brain and body, causing even more damage. "And what am I to do?" Karolena asked, horrified at the implications of going functionally blind. "Can't you treat the infection, reverse it?" The hopeless prospect of enduring a progressive viral infection of her brain sickened her and filled her with dread.

"I certainly hope we can treat it. For a start, we have many new antiviral medications that might help you. It's not like the old days, you know," Blütfink said positively, trying his best to reassure Karolena, although not too convincingly. It seemed too soon to discuss in more detail without knowing whether medication alone would work.

Karolena looked in Blütfink's direction, trying to gauge his thoughts, sensing he was withholding certain aspects of the complete picture. Her voice cracking with emotion, she told him, "You don't think that will help me at all, do you?"

"Same old Karolena, aren't you? How about trusting your care to your doctors?"

Noticing that he deftly avoided answering her, and suspecting that she knew why, she could only say, "Only to a point, Rickhard, only to a point. I appreciate all you're doing for me, but as long as I'm able to think clearly, I want to participate in making decisions that affect my life." She hoped he would understand, having always found Blütfink to be the controlling type, and wanted him to at least partially let go, if just this once, for her.

There wasn't much more for either of them to say, right now, and with his AllSee constantly going off with messages, and a string of other patients to examine before returning to his office at FirsThought, Blütfink nodded, then left Karolena's bedside and slowly walked away.

Chapter 8

After several days lying on an open gurney tucked against the wall in the ER corridor, a bed finally opened up for Karolena. The small barren cubicle was designed for only two patients, now stuffed with four beds, each separated by a holographic curtain. Karolena felt it not much improvement over her former spot in the hall. The make-shift arrangement left little room to walk about, and provided even less of a sense of privacy. No pictures decorated the walls, which were painted a blue-gray, with white primer showing through in spots. A single oblong light panel ran across the ceiling, and individual light panels lit up each bedside. Connected to the head of each bed, but often inoperative, a video panel controlled the video monitor and communication with the nurses, Arm cuff telemetry units attached to each patient continuously relayed vital signs to the central nursing computer where the data were supposedly analyzed via the hospital's neural network artificial intelligence computer programs to detect problems as they occurred.

The Infectious Disease consultants called in by Blütfink made certain that Karolena was given the latest 'smart' antiviral chemotherapy to inhibit the virus that had attacked her vision. The medications were linked to antibodies to make them more specific and less toxic, like "designer drugs." Their effect was predictably rapid and complete, and although Karolena experienced no further deterioration in her vision, the injury to the Visual Association Area of her brain's cerebral cortex was significant and seemed irreversible.

The days of treatment with antiviral medications slowly passed, and, with her ability to visually recognize objects not returning, Karolena found her life as she had known it totally destroyed, and her hope for the future empty. People she knew from work, even her friend Susan Wilder, appeared like total strangers to her, save for their characteristic voices. It was a surreal contrast, for, even though she could tell to whom she was speaking, without recognizing their face, it was as if they were impostors.

Like a stranger in a strange land once again, Karolena became devastated, and gradually gave up hope that the antiviral medications she had been given would work. To look, but never to see again -- this seemed to be the depressing end of her career, and she would effectively be blind for the rest of her life. It was at that lowest point in Karolena's life that Dr. Fromposi, recognizing the failure of standard therapy, contacted Blütfink on his AllSee.

After reporting on the lack of progress, Fromposi told him, "I realize that this sounds very hopeless, but I would like to mention an experimental procedure for VAA injury. It is an operation which has been performed lately with some success on non-human primates in a few Indian centers."

"Oh yes, what's that? I'm not familiar with any such experimental surgery," Blütfink told her.

"The procedure is intended for physical injury to the VAA, like blunt trauma and penetrating damage. This surgery has never been used to treat damage from viral infection, and has also not been attempted in a human," Fromposi cautiously explained.

"What does this surgery consist of?" he asked, all his attention now focused on her unexpected and hopeful remarks.

"Cerebral tissue from cortical area nineteen is transplanted from one animal and placed on top of the similar but damaged area in the recipient." Not hearing Blütfink acknowledge what she was saying, she asked, "Hello, Dr. Blütfink, are you there?"

"Yeah, I'm here. I was just thinking that this treatment sounded like something tried for Alzheimer's disease before the turn of the century. As I remember it, that didn't work very very well and the procedure was dropped," Blütfink replied, smirking as he attempted to mock Fromposi's odd vocal inflections.

"Maybe so, but that was well over half a century ago. Medicine and surgery were so primitive back then, you know. Now we are experimenting with cerebral grafts like this. When the transplant is followed by massive doses of recombinant Nerve Growth Factor administered every fourth day, regeneration of the engrafted nerve tissue is stimulated in animals, with the donor nerve fibers integrating with those of the recipient. I've also heard that the Clinical Research Laboratory at The Winston is participating in a protocol to study the efficacy of nerve growth factors in spinal cord injury, and I think it's possible we could see some effect here, too."

Blütfink listened as Fromposi spoke, taking occasional notes. "I'm familiar with nerve growth factors. My research laboratory at FirsThought is the one that has been studying nerve growth factors, you know," he proudly told her.

"Yes, I think I heard mention of that at a hospital conference recently," she noted, eyeing Blütfink seemingly with more respect.

"Actually, Karolena assisted me in some of the testing on animals. However, I guess the real question is: can we perform surgery on the VAA here? And I have to know whether it would be safe for her. After all, I'm sure she would rather live blind then die on a gamble." Fromposi could only offer a shrug, with no real answers to these hard questions. "Any reaction to the graft would kill her, and I supposed that the graft would have to be very well-matched, too."

"Perhaps we could add this surgery onto the spinal injury protocol?" Blütfink suggested.

"Yes, with so few alternatives, it is worth looking into, do you not agree?" Fromposi asked.

That was the central point. Although he knew he had no right to gamble with Karolena, nor treat her like an experimental animal, he felt that he had to try something. At that moment, he recognized that he still cared about her, and just the thought that she might get worse or die made him feel terribly sad. Karolena's father also called again, pressuring him again to do something, and a transplant certainly would qualify as doing something. "Okay, let's say for the sake of argument that we could try this experimental surgery and perform the graft. I could get some nerve growth factor for you to use on a protocol; it's produced by Genetic Generics, which is a subsidiary of FirsThought Scientific, about an hour away from here. In fact, now that I think about it, the nerve growth factor is already available on a compassionate use basis until it's licensed."

"Good. Then why don't you ask about its availability in a circumstance like this? If you can get it, I'll consider trying the transplant on Karolena. But remember, no one is certain this procedure will work in humans, or to what extent, or how it might function in humans. Besides, do you really think Karolena might consent to undergoing a procedure as experimental as this one is?" Fromposi asked.

"At this point, what's Karolena got to lose?" he asked. He didn't know for certain, but would guess that Karolena was depressed enough by her illness to consider something as risky as the transplant Fromposi was proposing. If there was any doubt, he would try to persuade her.

"Yes, I certainly see your point. But even if she would consent, and the hospital would allow us to proceed, there are additional problems I must tell you about before you choose to bring this up with your patient. As opposed to the situation in liver transplantation, the donor of brain tissue must be greater than 95% bio-compatible with the recipient, no matter what regimen of immune suppression is used. That means no adult unrelated donors, although fetal tissue might be possible, and of course, no animals."

Blütfink indicated that he understood. "And, as you can imagine, unlike donation from living donors, only a nonliving donor can donate brain tissue from the cerebral cortex."

Thinking carefully about what she seemed to be telling him, Blütfink told her, "I see what you're saying. But that certainly makes finding a donor much more difficult." Insurmountable would be more like it, he thought.

"Definitely," Fromposi nodded. "But, in case luck should come your patient's way, I will ask Dr. Malawassi from the Neurosurgery Service to perform an additional consultation, so we could be prepared. I do not know if he will approve of our proposal," she shrugged, "but if anyone is technically capable of successfully performing such a transplant, he is the one."

Blütfink nodded his approval. He would mention this to Wilder, to get the hospital behind this. There were actually several potential advantages here for Wilder, and few downsides, so Blütfink was sure Wilder would support the plan.

"Perhaps your patient would consider having the VAA graft performed in India," she suggested. "Neurosurgery is very very advanced there."

"Perhaps, but I don't think so, Doctor Fromposi," Blütfink said, knowing Karolena's poor opinion of medicine even in the US, as opposed to central Europe.

For her, the world seemed to revolve around Germany, and he could relate to that. He was certain that, for Americans, the world seemed to revolve around North America, as, in the past century, it seemed to have, before the great die-offs.

"Do you have any additional questions?" Fromposi asked, seemingly eager to end the conversation.

"Not really, you've said it all. I'll explain it to my patient, and let her make the choice. Thank you, though, for your very detailed and careful consultation, and your interesting suggestion." Blütfink reflected on how much more difficult everything was becoming. He felt sorry for Karolena, with at least the extent he felt sorry for any of his patients and their families, and given their relationship, of course more so for her. He wondered who, if things just didn't work out, would take care of her. Probably her wealthy father Wolf Kreisler, he surmised. The guy called him just about every day, pressuring him to "just do something" as if that was all it took. Wolf seemed to think that money and influence would buy him and thru him Karolena anything she needed. Of course, it was a lot more complicated, a lot more complicated. But he didn't make the problem, he could not fix it, and he just was not sure that Fromposi and Malawassi could either. Maybe he could direct Wolf on to them for a while, instead of always calling him.

"You are welcome, Dr. Blütfink. A typed report is being prepared and will be placed in her EMR. As ever, thank you for this interesting consult," Fromposi concluded as she hurried off to her next patient.

Blütfink turned off the AllSee, and docked it in the case on his belt. His mind was immersed in thought about how he was going to tell Karolena about the "exciting" options he had just learned, and when Fromposi would do it. Rather than go up to her room just yet, he decided it would be better to think over all he knew about her situation first. Undoubtedly, Karolena would be asking him for his recommendation, and at this point he wasn't certain what that would be. One thing he knew, no matter how much he wanted to try the operation and test the efficacy of the nerve growth hormone on humans, he had to make Karolena understand it was her best interests that he had in mind. And he did, he told himself, for she had little other choice, except the possibility of this tiny bit of light at the end of the tunnel.

Chapter 9

The next day on morning rounds, Blütfink spent an unusually long time examining Karolena's flat screen patient chart, looking for any sign that her disease was abating. Unfortunately, there was none. Her visual recognition remained spotty, and her headaches persisted. At times like this, he felt totally helpless, and was unsure what his advice to her would be. What alternatives, after all, did he or any of the other doctors have to offer her? His powerlessness reinforced his preference of the surgical specialty over that of medicine: surgeons could always cut, assuming they were presented with an operable lesion. The Internal Medicine docs cowered behind their potions in the face of the incurable.

He had hoped that Karolena would be the first to bring up her condition, but this morning she seemed unusually glum and silent. Under the circumstances, Blütfink certainly could understand. Finally, still not looking up from his chart, Blütfink took the initiative and asked, "How do you feel today?"

"Not any different than when I saw you. I mean, when you were here last."

Blütfink could see the pain on her face as she had to correct her sentence. It struck him as odd how little figures of speech could sound so clumsy and embarrassing in the wrong context. Sensing that Karolena preferred not to be talkative, he added, "Look, Karolena, it's obvious to me you're becoming less responsive to the antiviral treatments." Producing a graphic display of her visual tests over the last several days, in the form of a holograph suspended in front of her, he added, "The headaches you're still having may indicate brain swelling; it's even possibly that your infection may be spreading to other parts of your brain."

Karolena closed her eyes, swallowed, and then said, "We don't know that for certain, Rickhard."

"Look, I'm sure you're aware, although your visual acuity continues to be stable, your visual recognition is severely damaged and hasn't shown any sign of improvement or recovery."

"Yes, I know, and I'm very worried about that. I

have to wonder what good living in that condition would be, functionally equivalent to being blind, but twice as confusing."

"I know several people who're blind, Karolena, and they seem to live quite well." Karolena responded with a scoffing sound, and turned her head away. Realizing how much something hopeful would mean to her, Blütfink decided that now was as good a time as any to mention what might turn out to be her only chance for a cure, and a way to get back her normal vision. "Dr. Fromposi seems to think that there's a small chance your VAA's damage may be helped by transplantation."

Karolena looked surprised, and turned her head back toward him, although the idea was not totally unexpected.

"There have been a few experiments on grafting the VAA between non-human primates with some success, and, because of the seriousness and urgency of your situation, this procedure might be tried here." Seeing her interest, rather than outright rejection at this risky suggestion, he attempted displaying a confident expression on his face, and continued, "In these experimental surgeries, part of a normal visual cortex was grafted on top of damaged nerves in the Visual Association Area. There's reason to think that the administration of a recombinant Nerve Growth Factor, perhaps the very one you and I were studying in our lab at FirsThought, could result in a repair and intermingling of the donor's and your visual nerve fibers, giving an edge to a successful surgical outcome." The whole idea seemed to Blütfink more a long shot than one likely to result in a therapeutic success, but he knew Karolena had very little hope otherwise.

"Donor, what donor, Rickhard?"

"Well, we'd have to find one, of course. And it would have to be a very good match." Realizing just how impossible in today's transplant market this was beginning to sound, even to him, he put his hand on her shoulder, and gently told her, "I'm truly sorry about all this. I know how depressed you must feel, and how outlandish all this must sound, but if you'd consider trying this, I just hope we can find an appropriate donor in time." Karolena uttered a low moan, and turned her head away. "Please, Karolena, I can understand how . . ."

"Like hell you can," Karolena shot back, pushed to exasperated tears. "How could anyone truly understand these pressures unless they were facing it themselves?"

"Well, if you really want to know, Karolena," Blütfink warned her, shaking his head, "I think you've got little choice here, although I certainly can understand your reticence. We've got exceptional surgical facilities here, and this experimental surgery has apparently led to some restoration of normal visual recognition in a few animals."

"In a few animals." Karolena groaned. "Am I an animal?"

"No, of course not. And I emphasize the word 'experimental,' for this procedure is highly speculative, and you must realize that."

After taking a moment to cool down, Karolena's attitude became slightly more open to the suggestion, open but skeptical and not yet accepting. "I do realize all that, Rickhard, and of course I'm appreciative for anything you can do for me."

Blütfink wondered for a moment why, in general, transplants didn't seem to work out as well as they used to back at the turn of the century. Surgical technique was much better now, immune suppressants were far advanced, but for somc strange reason the outcome results lagged. He hoped that would not be the case here. "I probably don't need to tell you that trying this surgery entails a great deal of risk."

Karolena nodded, her face belying the apprehension and doubt she truly felt for this desperate proposal. "It certainly doesn't appear that there's not much of an alternative, though, is there?"

"No, I guess not, as far as the visual problem is concerned, short of leaving you saddled for the rest of your life with the terrible disability you now have. But, I can understand why you would not consider that a good option."

Karolena shook his head that she too understood what he was proposing.

"If you have any questions about anything I've told you, please don't hesitate to ask." Blütfink offered, then added, "Ironic, isn't it?"

"How's that, Rickhard?"

"I was just thinking how the very research that you had objected to so strenuously might be responsible for restoring your own sight, and your life as you knew it.

Maybe this will finally convince you that it's important to use fetuses for experimentation."

"I doubt that, Rickhard, I really do doubt it. Immediate practicality and overall principles are two different ethical issues, and ethics is not relative nor situational."

"I see your point," he admitted, not wanting to debate medical ethics in this forum.

"By the way, who will be willing and able to perform this neurosurgery, assuming we go that route?"

"I understand from Dr. Fromposi that the surgery may be performed by Dr. Malawassi from the Ophthalmologic Surgery Service."

"Dr. Malawassi? Have they done anything like this before?" she asked, but Blütfink's face said it all.

"Oh," was her only reply. The discussion left Karolena shaken, as she had fully expected the antiviral medications to have worked at least a little by now. She had anticipated by now to be well on the road to a full recovery, rather than being presented with desperate last-ditch surgical options. After a long moment of silence, she asked, "When, I mean, how long, before this will happen?"

"Within one to two weeks, maybe sooner, maybe a little longer. There's a lot here we still don't know."

The conversation was making Karolena more agitated by the minute, but she was glad, in a way, to at least get these essential issues of her future out in the open. Looking disapprovingly at a burrito wrapper protruding from Blütfink's coat pocket, partially recognizing it from its characteristic smell, Karolena chided, "Mexican food never agreed with you, Rickhard, did it? Anyway, you really ought not to eat while rounding on your patients. It's unprofessional, and it's unbecoming of you." She wondered again how she had ever been romantically interested in such an uncouth slob.

"Maybe so, but what I eat is my business, thank you. You're not my mother, Karolena."

"And I wouldn't want to be either, Rickhard." The concept of being his mother was not humorous, and the possibility he thought of her in that way bothered her. She had detected a hint toward that in their old relationship, and, liking strength and independence in men, she found it a real turn-off.

"Look, Karolena. You know Dr. Fromposi and I wouldn't recommend so radical a course of treatment unless it seemed to be absolutely necessary. We both agree that medication won't work here, at least totally. Sure, they may slow down or stop the infection, but I think we're all in agreement that we can't expect a damaged area of your brain, especially one so crucial, so vital, so advanced like the VAA, to repair itself. Perhaps you ought to give the go-ahead for the surgery right now, and not continue to monkey around with the fleas."

Karolena had heard Blütfink on several occasions in the past refer derogatorily toward Internal Medicine and Infectious Disease specialists, and for that matter anyone with non-surgical remedies, as fleas. When she had asked him what being a "flea" meant, Blütfink shrugged and told her no one seemed to know any longer where the term originated, but that it was definitely 'last century'. He was sure that it was some arcane American or English slang, or inside joke, and ignored it.

Karolena was silent for a long time, thinking what course was in her best interests, before finally saying, although feeling less than confident, "No, I'm not ready to consent to getting a VAA transplant, at least not yet. I want to wait."

"Wait? Wait for what, Karolena?" Blütfink asked, disbelievingly.

"I think there's still some time before I need to decide. For one thing, I'm not convinced that we really have given the antiviral medications enough time to work. Besides, I want my father here if I'm going to undergo major surgery." She stared at a thick drop of hot sauce on Blütfink's coat and again realized just how little he had changed.

"Maybe so, but in your case, I think your options are limited, to say the least. You know that too." He wanted to tell her that her father had been pressuring him to do something radical for a while, but decided against mentioning it, for now. Wolf had asked him to keep his concerns and offers quiet and unknown to Karolena. "Try to make a goddamn decision on your own for once, will you, and save your own life." Noticing that she was staring at his coat, he tried to wipe up the hot sauce with his finger. "Sorry about that. I was in a hurry."

"You're always in a hurry." *Even with their relationship*, *even in bed*, she thought, always i*n a* *hurry, never having enough time to relax*. Yet, his concern for her welfare now seemed to be genuine, and she found that at least consoling and touching.

"I'm not always in a hurry," he replied, defensively, and looked down at the floor. "Just when I need to be. I don't like seeing you incapacitated like this, and I want you to get better, but you hold the key here to your future, Karolena."

"Rickhard, if I didn't know better, I'd say you still care about mc. Look, don't take this wrong, but do you think you should have primary responsibility for my medical care? I mean, considering our past, our recent past, . . . "

"Yes, I DO think that I can be objective. Besides, the hospital assigned me to your case. Of course, I want to be sure you get the best of care, too. And you know how hard it is to find a *Retro-negative* surgeon these days, okay?"

Karolena meekly nodded agreement; Rickhard spoke the truth this time.

"Once you give the go-ahead, Karolena, we sometimes can find a fetal donor with matching biotype in a matter of hours, and . . ."

"No," Karolena interrupted. "I don't want fetal tissue used in me, Rickhard, under any circumstances. Is that clear? Adult donors only." She tried to sit up in bed, anxious about being understood and for her wishes in this regard to be strictly obeyed, only to fall back, exhausted. What Blütfink proposed was out of the question. After a moment she regained her composure, and some strength. "By the way, how is Christopher?"

"Christopher? Christopher who?" Blütfink asked, before remembering. "Oh yes, the experiment we did recently. It was successful, so we, uh, we terminated it." He quickly looked away after seeing the devastated look on Karolena's face. "But Karolena, remember, that fetus may be responsible for saving your life. The properties of the growth hormone, the ones which we accidentally discovered that day, seem to have some very interesting nerve healing abilities. Perhaps they have just the properties that will make this experimental graft work for you, impossible as it seems, and maybe, hopefully allow your sight to return."

Not wanting to so glibly change the subject from growth hormones, she asked, "You terminated it? What did you do that for?" She could hardly believe what he was telling her, or that when he referred to ending an infant's life, it seemed to be worth so little feeling on his part. How, she wondered, could Rickhard be so cold and detached and callous?

"It was too young, it wouldn't have survived anyway, you know that. And besides, it was already discarded for dead when you saw it in the first place. Believe me, I took your personal desires to heart and I want you to know it didn't feel a thing or suffer at all. But, we both knew that was the intended end, as it always is in experiments like that. I'm sorry."

That was the first time Karolena had ever remembered Blütfink saying he was sorry, and he did sound genuine, so she believed him and was actually touched. Maybe he had changed, and she felt glad. But she was becoming very tired again from all this talk, and her demeanor changed and she no longer wanted to discuss treatment options, or upsetting experiments at FirsThought, or anything at all for now. She was confused and weak and simply needed to rest. Blütfink must have sensed that too, and decided to let it go, to not pressure her further concerning a commitment to undergoing a transplant.

"You'll be interested to know that, since that chance discovery of ours back in the lab, we're already progressed very far," he confidently told her. "I don't know how much of an exaggeration I'd be making if I told you that cut nerve ends, as long as they are just about in the same body, will connect up if you use this new nerve growth factor. Can you just imagine the potential."

Karolena knew he was referring to commercial potential, not the potential for benefiting mankind, although she was fairly certain that, in his mind, both outcomes were the same. She could only nod her head, for neither her mind not her heart was on the commercialization of the nerve growth factor.

"I'll see what I can do," Blütfink reassured Karolena, as gently as he could under the circumstances. After holding her hand and trying to smile encouragingly, he left to see other patients. Once out of the room, he immediately called the Infectious Disease and Hepatology consultants back in on her case. Maybe they could provide him with some further suggestions or helpful alternatives, short of a transplant. Then he painstakingly dictated a full memo into Karolena's chart, documenting what he had informed her. His own appraisal of the situation, born from years of experience with legions of patients in somewhat similar conditions, was depressingly dismal, and, knowing Karolena the way he did certainly didn't help him keep his emotions detached or his priorities straight.

Chapter 10

\
Over the next few days, Karolena in essence continued the same frustrating waiting game that she had been playing against herself for years. She managed to check in place her vision, as she had for her liver, and so far she had carefully avoided checkmate, leaving her to wonder wearily if the end game may finally have arrived. The stakes, though, this time were way too high for her to be a gracious looser.

Karolena had learned of the IPC chemical spill through Susan Wilder, shortly after her admission. Perhaps a few hundred unfortunate persons who lived in the communities whose water supplies originated from the Neuse River went on to develop an unexplained toxic hepatic failure. It occurred to her that toxin exposure may have also compounded the problems of her already weak liver, and made her susceptible to infection with the OCV. When thought about in this way, it only made Karolena more angry and resentful. She had, after all, left central Europe to avoid exactly these types of problems. She hated to have her past weaknesses, like her liver problem, following her around, stalking her, continually waiting for a moment of weakness to strike out at her.

Perhaps, she thought, a liver transplant, in addition to a VAA transplant, would finally free her of this legacy of illness. But, she would never use human fetal tissue; she could never mentally allow that morally objectionable choice for her present problem. Better to be blind. If she were to give the go-ahead for the suggested VAA transplant operation, risky as it sounded, she would allow the use of only an adult human donor, perhaps that of an accident victim. It was all too obvious to all, but never spoken out loud, that the donor could not be living, as no one could live without their VAA. Although she knew the retro risk to be small, still, it would not be zero. There were false negatives, especially if tested too early after exposure. Obvious to her, organ donations from family members or friends, although much safer, were unlikely in her case, given the need for a near-prefect match and for the donor to have died.

Karolena realized all too well that, if she survived and went back to FirsThought, and that was a big IF, she could never again have anything more to do with using human fetuses for research. The haunting memory of the discarded fetus she had named Christopher still roamed her most private thoughts daily, looking back at her from whatever distant place he had finally arrived.

Blütfink visited Karolena again early the next morning on his way to the operating room. Although outwardly he expressed to Karolena no interest other than of a medical professional and of a colleague at work, he could little disguise his increasing dismay at Karolena's deteriorating vision and her persistent headaches. "Karolena," he warned her, "when the pressure inside your skull rises above a certain point, there's very little supportive treatment that medical science can offer."

"I know that, Rickhard, and I have for the most part decided to go ahead with the transplant, but I still want to wait until my father arrives. Please try to understand that I don't want to be left alone, particularly if something should happen."

"I'll be here for you, Karolena," Blütfink added, sincerely.

Looking at Blütfink, Karolena thanked him, then laughed almost bitterly as she said, "You know, this is the most that I've seen of you or talked to you in months. Funny, isn't it?" It was a bitter-sweet theme of her life, a life that, seemingly, could very well end soon. Perhaps she had misjudged Blütfink, or judged him too harshly. She was capable of error, certainly, and of change.

"I don't think there's anything 'funny' about your condition at all, Karolena."

"What I mean is, it's really very sad that I had to get so sick to finally have a good conversation with you. And when I finally do get to talk to you, it's about my medical care." This was one more sad characteristic of their failed relationship, and she thought if perhaps one day Blütfink would even bring her flowers, even one flower, it would make a difference. But that was too much to expect of him, and she well realized it, but the knowledge only left her melancholy. Yet, she clearly saw his changing attitude toward her, and she wanted to believe.

"Yeah, funny," he said, looking uncomfortable,

then asked, "Do you have any idea when you'll hear from your father?" He had called Blütfink twice now, first to inquire about his daughter and to offer resources, and then again to less subtly pressure Blütfink to take action and get the transplant done. Kreisler had asked Blütfink not to tell Karolena that he was intervening in her behalf, least she take it as an attempt to treat her like a child, or to imply that she was not capable of actions. Next time Kreisler called, though, Blütfink would ask his permission to tell Karolena

"Very soon, I hope," Karolena replied distantly, having no idea why this time it was proving more difficult than usual to reach her father, but believing he would contact her in time. Although she sometimes resented her father for being too protective, she did appreciate his help. Karolena realized that she would need a transplant very soon -- she had faced the reality of her situation and had grown willing to accept the inevitability of undergoing a transplant, but she feared going to surgery, and perhaps dying, alone. Being in the health profession left her too close, too aware of the unpredictable nature of surgery's outcomes and risks.

Ultimately, that was why she still preferred to wait for her father: not to discuss treatment options, just not to be left alone while she underwent surgery. Her father was the only true family she had, and the only person she was close to, although she had no interest in admitting that to Blütfink. In her heart of hearts, Karolena was certain that Blütfink's concern for her, like that of Larry Summers, was superficial at best.

Her mother's face briefly flashed in her memory. She had died from chemical poisoning when Karolena was only a child, and Karolena had hardly known her. Karolena felt suddenly choked up, and stared silently into her empty hands.

"Again, it's my opinion that your only hope would be a transplant, and it needs to happen soon," Blütfink repeated, as he turned to walk out the door. He stopped, turned back to her and added, "The more you delay, the less likely it is that I can help you. You need a certain amount of strength just to survive the surgery, you know."

"Yes, I know," Karolena sighed. But physical strength was not all -- basic will power was as important as surgical technique, a fact she had seen demonstrated in people and animals alike time and time again.

Blütfink nodded, as if he understood not to pursue the question any further, and then left.

Chapter 11

Tucked in her bed in a corner of her room, Karolena watched the continual stream of indistinguishable hospital personnel move in and out. For the most part, their activities didn't involve her, mostly dealing with pre-surgical care and consultation of other patients, and transporting patients to and fro. She could see the same hectic confusion out in the hallway, and was glad she was at least inside her room.

Reading e-books and newspapers was becoming increasingly difficult, and she was forced to switch almost entirely to audio books. Now, her days consisted of watching movies which she could barely understand save for the dialog on the video screen, and short visits and conversation with the nurses, and rarely, with Blütfink, whom she often could only identify by his characteristic German accent. Her fatigue and headache had once again stabilized, but everyone assumed she was playing a waiting game. Although Karolena had never actually consented, it seemed the plan for a transplant was simply a *fait accompli,* and that was an assumption she never challenged.

Another few days passed without Karolena hearing from her father, leaving her to wonder more seriously, if he ever would arrive, and if it would be too late? Sensing that the time for decision was finally here, she accepted the inevitable and gave the go-ahead for the transplant surgery to Blütfink, and felt much relief at having just made a decision. Then, Karolena lay back and tried to mentally prepare herself for surgery, expecting to be transferred to the preoperative area almost immediately. Interestingly, nothing happened.

Several more days passed, uneventfully waiting for the transplant surgery, before Karolena was forced to ask Blütfink, while on his morning rounds, "I'm surprised that you haven't done the transplant by now. You seemed to be in such a hurry just a few days ago." She had expected the surgery to happen imminently, and now that it wasn't, she sensed something could have changed, that perhaps some aspect of her medical condition that she was not aware of, or not been made aware of, had changed for the worse. In her slightly confused and nauseous state, a strong sense of panic ensued, heightened by her very condition.

"We're having a little trouble finding a suitable donor," Blütfink admitted.

"But you were so hot to start the transplant surgery a few days ago. Was it any easier then?" Thinking clearly above a recurrence of her headache -- was it from her viral infection or simply tension? -- even finding the strength to speak took increasing efforts.

"No, of course not. But, look Karolena, a VAA transplant just isn't routine at all; you know that as well as I do. And I'm sure you're well aware that organ donation is severely down, especially one like this. Only after you said 'go' could we even begin to look."

Karolena had known that, on a basic level, but had

not really considered the more practical aspects. Now, she worried whether she had waited until, as Blütfink had so recently warned her, it was too late.

"Only after you consented to the operation could the transplant coordinator tie a donor down, and dedicate an organ match just for you. Look," Blütfink said, nervously glancing repeatedly at his watch, "I have to go now."

"Thanks for talking," Karolena muttered under her breath to Blütfink's back as he left the room. Their brief conversation left her wondering if Blütfink had been having a discussion with her or just working things through in his head out loud.

At a meeting in her room later that day, the transplant coordinator reminded Karolena of the number of other patients in the hospital waiting for donors, a figure that Karolena found truly astounding. Both the coordinator and Karolena realized that she needed a donor, and she needed one fast. Fortunately, in her case, she wasn't competing with others for a limited pool of specific common transplant organs like livers or kidneys, as her surgical procedure was unique. Still, there were many other desperate people in the greater Eastern US waiting along with her for a suitable donor to become available. The difficulty was the same as it has been since transplantation surgery began some 80 years ago, although it seemed to be getting worse lately. It was a case of supply-demand at its simplest: an increasing demand for *Retro-negative* organs, and decreasing *Retro-negative* donors on the supply side.

Leaning forward, Karolena's shadowed face showed the fatigue of carrying too heavy an emotional burden, and doing so alone, and she felt so very tired and so very old.

"You know," the coordinator reminded Karolena, "there are only about 130 million or so people living in the United States, and only around three quarters are *Retro-negative*, and that leaves less than 100 million potential donors. From this group, and other similar pools around the world, one has to find an appropriate match. And in your case, it really has to be a nearly exact match. Sometimes it's easy and sometimes very hard," she sighed, spreading her hands with the palms up. "This time, I'm afraid it's going to be a problem, but I've also learned to be patient. Hopefully, something will become available soon."

Desperate for a solution, Karolena reluctantly offered, "I've heard about contract organs." Occasionally, people who had healthy organs of interest, and who knew they were going to die soon for reasons unrelated to the health of an organ, would bid on an exchange for the rights to parts of their body. It was not Karolena's first choice, but one option she might need to take. "Does that still go on?"

"Sort of. There are very few matches on demand from organ contracts, but you don't want to get involved with that, do you?" Not getting a response, the coordinator continued, "Organ brokering is still illegal in North America, Europe, and the like, but I've heard that it's a thriving business elsewhere. Occasionally organs can 'suddenly and miraculously' become available along the US/Mexico strip or the US/Canada strip. But, you know how that goes," she frowned at Karolena.

Looking out the window at the rest of the world functioning quite well without her, Karolena added, "I've heard that hundreds of 'illegals' are shot each day. That's not what really happens, is it?" she asked, hoping for reassurance otherwise.

"Unfortunately yes, but they rarely survive long enough to make it to transplant centers, and those that do usually aren't *Retro-negative,* so that doesn't help your problems."

"No, I guess it doesn't." Talking about potentially being on the receiving end of a transplant only depressed her further, and, for the first time, she considered if she would be better off dead. Especially considering it was her dead or someone else dead. It was then she admitted to herself that this was not the first time thoughts of self-destruction had wormed their ugly way up from her subconscious and fouled her life. In the past, she had ignored the thoughts, or suppressed them, or tried to laugh them off, but now, this seemed different. She had never felt so depressed and hopeless before, so desperate. What would she do? Who could she depend on? She looked in Blütfink's direction, and the answer was clearly not him.

"Look, Karolena, because Dr. Blütfink is a friend of yours, I'll see what I can do." The coordinator smiled, put her arm around Karolena's shoulder, gave her a hug, and left.

Surprised at the offer of preferential treatment,

Karolena was nevertheless not in the least offended. Although she had known Deborrah for only a short time, she liked the woman, and felt she had true, deep convictions and sensitivities. In her desperate situation, Karolena realized that she was in no position to refuse offers of help in any form.

Still, it was clear, from what the coordinator had said, that the IPC spill had only made the matter of donor availability worse by increasing demand for donors. Now, many potential, hopeful transplant recipients, productive and good people like Karolena, would die waiting before a suitable match would become available.

An additional complication was that transplantation surgery was again not being funded this year, due to another recent national medical budget reorganization. As a result, for all practical purposes, only those who could personally afford the expensive procedure would end up getting one. So much for universal health care, she mused.

The estimated cost at WCMC, according to the transplant coordinator, was roughly the dollar equivalent of 700,000 Euro, the international standard of currency for as long as she could remember, and came to almost fifteen years average US single income. Karolena had to accept that, and she did. *She could endure the cost*, she thought, *much more easily than others could.* Besides the generous medical coverage she had from her employment at FirsThought, her family position also made this a non-issue. One half of the fees had to be paid up-front, in Euro, but the rest was due before the transplant went in. Perhaps this was because, given the experimental and risky nature of the neurosurgery, Karolena might not live to pay the rest, and, knowing her father, she considered, he wouldn't pay for a poor outcome. “A poor outcome” -- that was truly a most depressing and sobering thought. Unlike repairs on a car, there would be no warranty of success for this transplant.

Chapter 12

On rounds the next morning, on his way in to visit a woman he truly cared about but whom he had a difficult time expressing his affection, a woman who could see him but not recognize him, a saddened Blütfink shook his head. After each exam of Karolena, he was unable to believe the disastrous way the entire case was turning out. *It seemed only yesterday* they were in the lab over at FirsThought, working and arguing together. Now all this. The unexpected infection, the rapid failure of her visual cortex, the desperate rush to an experimental transplant that might just as well fail or even kill her, it all had happened much too fast for either of them.

Although Blütfink felt, on the surface, upset with Karolena, for her complicated medical problems only added to the heavy pressures he was already under, his deeper feelings for her, once forced out into the open and fully examined, really examined, were another matter entirely. Having their brief romance unexpectedly fall apart after only a few months together, Blütfink thought Karolena was finally out of his system forever. Yet, whenever he got near her, touched her, listened to her talk, looked at her as she could no longer do with him, at those now precious times his feelings for her as a good friend, an attractive woman, a sensuous and caring and exciting lover, those primal feelings were aroused once again. He had felt that strong attraction back in the FirsThought O.R. when they had worked on that last fetus together, the one she had foolishly insisted on referring to as Christopher. Although he had discouraged her from taking so serious a personal interest in the welfare of ‘experimental subjects', he at the same time actually silently had admired Karolena for her strong moral convictions, her sensitivity, her caring, although he never could say that to her. Karolena's was a personality totally opposite his, and she attracted him, not simply because he enjoyed the contrast that opposites shared, not only because she seemed to fill a deep void or some other sentimental nonsense, but because it made him feel proud to actually know someone like her, to be friends with a person, a woman of that high a caliber. Although he knew a lot of people -- professionals, the famous, the powerful, none to him were quite like Karolena, and now, she was sick, very sick, and she perhaps might die, and there seemed so little he could do for her, partly because those very convictions of hers he admired so much were frustrating the very efforts he needed to take to help her.

"There's not a lot new that I can tell you," he glumly admitted to Karolena, the disappointment in his voice evident. “For now, we'll continue giving you massive doses of antiviral drugs to slow and possibly reverse the infection," Blütfink added, "although, so far, the anti-viral medications you’ve been receiving have had a poor effect, at best. That's a bad sign, and, if it continues, soon the virus' effect on your overall brain function may become intolerable."

Karolena nodded, gravely, at the hopelessly depressing news Blütfink gave her, after finishing her exam. Although she had not noticed any further deterioration in her overall condition, she had not detected any improvement either, and Blütfink's exam merely confirmed this. Looking up at Blütfink for a moment, Karolena frowned, and then turned away. She choked up and was totally at a loss for words.

"Now, things don't look too good, Karolena, and unless you get your transplant very soon . . ."

Karolena winced and looked even more worried.

"Oh, I can really emphasize with you, Karolena, but, unfortunately, it's simply a supply and demand problem. I do have some good news, though, and I'm sure you'll want to be the first to know. Because of the urgency of your condition, we've placed you on the highest organ recipient category. When, that is to say, as soon as a donor becomes available, we want to be ready to proceed with the transplantation surgery immediately."

"Thanks, Rickhard. I want you to know that I really appreciate your efforts for me, and, and no matter how this all turns out, . . ." Karolena tried to finish, but became choked up again and lost her composure and had to stop speaking.

Blütfink came over to the bedside and sat down. Holding her hand in his, he felt truly sorry, both for her as a patient, one he would like to help but could not, and sorry for her as a person, a friend he cared about. For a moment, he wondered if, should she recover, they might give their relationship another try, a thought he had had before, but never was able to share with her. "Karolena, The Winston and the Transplantation service are facing an unusually complex and rigid matching requirement for your experimental transplant. Using a visual cortex has severely narrowed the list of available donors down to nearly an identical twin, virtually a genetic twin. Locating such a match has been very difficult so far."

“”A genetic twin,” Karolena exclaimed."Yes, I'm sure it has been difficult." Karolena's forehead furrowed, then after a few moments thinking, she added, "But, a donor must become available if I’m to survive. Strange, isn’t it Rickhard?"

"How’s that, Karolena?"

"Just that someone must die in order for me to live. How tragic. It makes me seem like a parasite, no, worse, like a vampire," Karolena sighed, a certain pained weariness in her voice, obviously upset by the unexpected morbid turn in direction the conversation was taking.

As the level of anxiety Blütfink felt for Karolena's survival rose, he desperately searched his mind for options, answers, alternatives, anything he had missed or discarded up to now that could save her. Unfortunately, few viable options seemed left for her. It was odd that, after not being very involved in her life for months, she and Blütfink were in a way together again. Yet, Karolena would die, and soon, if matters seemingly were left to take their own slow, natural, random course. Without his personal intervention, it was obvious to Blütfink that Karolena would never get an adequate organ donor.

"There's always a way, Rickhard, and I know a donor will be available in time. Please," she pleaded, holding on to his hand, "if you love me, or even if you ever loved me, please, Rickhard, help me find that donor."

"Karolena," Blütfink said, holding her hand tightly, "I assure you, The Winston is doing all that can be done. We can only react to the offer of a donor when one - if one - becomes available. Why, there are only fifteen or so people with matching biotypes in the entire western world who could even donate in this particular instance, and they're all healthy."

Karolena stopped in her tracks and starred directly at Blütfink, as if she had just determined the secret to everlasting life. When she thought she had understood his meanings, she asked, "When you say available, you mean when someone dies, don't you. It's terrible to admit, Rickhard, but someone must die then, either me, or some unnamed donor on your list."

"What do you mean? What list?" Blütfink asked, unsuccessfully trying to sound ignorant.

"You just said that there were only fifteen potential donors, didn't you?"

"Well, yes, but . . ."

"Okay, that means you apparently checked into the numbers, and so you must have a list," Karolena insisted. "Show it to me."

"I'm afraid I can't do that, Karolena," Blütfink said, nervously letting go of Karolena's hand like she had leprosy, and glancing at his watch again. "It's not that simple. Now, I must really go on to see my other patients. I'm really pressed for time today."

"No matter. You have time, plenty of time, but unfortunately I don't. Good-bye, Rickhard."

Their conversation, unnerving as it was for them both, only further strengthened Blütfink's resolve to help Karolena live on. Clearly, that meant getting her transplant accomplished, and it now appeared obvious to him that he would need to intercede personally in some way to facilitate the seemingly stalled process of locating a suitable donor. But how, that was the question? Certainly every desperate person in Karolena's precarious position, and their frantic families and friends, were seeking the same answers, and as their diseased organs slid further along that irreversible path toward hopeless failure, their degrees of desperation only heightened. He recalled the quote, "Desperate diseases by desperate means were cured, or not at all," but could not remember by whom. No matter, for now his former lover was the desperate person with a desperate disease, and she obviously needed an inside advantage to help herself compete successfully against the thousands of patients, the wealthy, the powerful, the connected, in the same hopeless predicament as her.

Although Blütfink had no clear idea how to exert an advantage in locating the precious graft, it didn't take him long to decide that perhaps he did know someone who seemed to understand those things very well. It was clear to him that he would need to see that person as soon as possible, if Karolena was to have any hope of a future.

Chapter 13

Karolena had been enjoying a dream of visiting her childhood home in Germany when a loud crashing sound awoke her from a deep sleep. Looking around, the room was deathly quiet and empty, save for the peaceful sleeping sounds of the other patients and the unintelligibly distant resonances from the nurse's station. Still, certain she had been awakened by an unusual noise, Karolena managed in her disturbed state to pull a robe on and get out of bed. It didn't take her long to notice, even with her vision so disrupted, the shattered spiral of glass in the window pane.

Walking over to the fractured but still intact glass pane, Karolena first thought the break was from a rock, or worse yet, a random bullet fired from Neuse. Then, looking down on the outside window sill, she noticed a small red bird, lying motionless on its side. Apparently it had accidentally flown into the window, killing itself in the process, its head slightly mis-aligned, wings twisted at odd angles, and fresh red blood soaking its tiny feathers.

Never a believer in omens, Karolena was nonetheless deeply disturbed, for she seemed to feel at some deeper, subconscious level there was another significance here than simply an accident, although she as of yet couldn't fathom what that was. She looked down at the bird's lifeless body and said to herself, '*Blütfink.*', which meant Blood Finch in her native tongue."

Later that evening, Dr. Rickhard Blütfink received an unexpected call on his wrist AllSee from Bob Wilder, the hospital administrator. "Rickhard," he said, excitedly, "You won't believe this, but UNITED ORGAN NETWORK just called. They have a match for Karolena, a nearly exact match, and they'll be arriving in two hours from Brighton, England. Can you get things ready?"

"Wonderful," Blütfink exclaimed, wondering whether his impassioned request last evening for Bob's direct intervention had anything to do with the organ's sudden availability. Ultimately, that question was irrelevant to him, and to Karolena. "Yes, of course I can, we can," Blütfink volunteered, as he looked at Bob's enthusiastic holographic image on the AllSee.

"Great, Rickhard. I really hope this new operation works. It sounds pretty risky, and a lot is riding on it, you know."

"Yes, it is very important to Karolena's health."

"Her health, right. And more, Rickhard, much more actually. This could be our answer to improving unrelated graft donors. Success of those growth factors of yours could bring a lot of funding in to FirsThought and pay for a lot of your research projects. And the fame, Rickhard, think of the fame."

Blütfink nodded at Bob's holograph image, although his mind clearly was on the risky surgery his patient, his former lover was about to undergo. Of course, he hoped for success, they all did. But what if it didn't work? Karolena was strong, and should be able to recover and adapt, with time. But this was, after all, neurosurgery. What if she didn't recover well? What if she died? How would he feel being a party to so strongly recommending what could very well become her death instrument?

After disconnecting from Bob, a greatly relieved Blütfink immediately placed a call to Drs. Fromposi, who agreed to contact Dr. Malawassi and the Scheduling Desk in the O.R. to arrange for a room. Next, Blütfink rushed up to the nurses' station, puffing and out of breath. "Where's the charge nurse?" he exclaimed. "We just got a donor. You need to get Karolena Kreisler ready, now."

"Calm down, Dr. Blütfink," the ward clerk said. "You're going to have a heart attack."

"Thank you very much for the free medical advice," Blütfink glared. "Now get a move on it. We have to get Karolena ready for surgery, now." For a moment, some thoughts of a particularly good conversation he had had with Karolena months ago flashed in his mind. Although he had his doubts about the advisability of this surgery, it was Karolena's only hope for even a semi-normal life, maybe a life he should be taking more of an interest in.

The head nurse, and the nurse responsible for all four patients in Karolena's room, bounced over to the nursing station. Looking as though she belonged more at home than at work in her pink electro-heater sneakers, pink jump suit, red sweater, and bauble earrings, she hardly inspired order or professionalism among the people she was supposed to supervise. "What's all the excitement here?" she sang out in a heavy Philippine accent. "Dr. Blütfink, are you the one making all the commotion?"

Blütfink had become accustomed to the high-pitched squeak-squash of her sneakers whenever she shuffled around the ward. Looking away from the monitors, TV screens and telemetry units, Blütfink excitedly told her about the sudden availability of a donor for Karolena.

"Oh, that's good," she replied. Will the donor be coming here?" She asked, suspecting that the conversation was leading up to more work for her. "I hope she's *Retro-negative*, Dr. Blütfink," She added.

Looking at her strangely, Blütfink exclaimed, "What's the matter with you? Get with the program. Of course the donor is *Retro-negative*. Otherwise, her organs wouldn't be coming here, now would they? The *Retros* aren't acceptable donors; you know that, especially here." As the charge nurse nodded that she understood, Blütfink added, "Most importantly, though, the data indicates the donor is biologically compatible with Karolena. Now, can you get Karolena ready for the O.R., prepare an electronic packet, and have her there in thirty minutes?"

"Thirty minutes. You've got to be kidding, doc. I've got over fifty patients, and it's only me, one other nurse, a few inexperienced aides, a few BOTs and a clerk," She exclaimed, looking disapprovingly in the ward clerk's direction. Shaking her head and gesturing at the nurse's station, She asked, "Besides, are you sure you actually want Karolena Kreisler?"

"Of course I'm sure. Don't I look like I know who I want to operate on?"

She had seen several big mistakes on patient identification before, including at least one of Blütfink's. Given his typically rushed attitude, she looked askance at Blütfink and left toward Karolena's room, but resolved to check with the transplant coordinator first, just in case.

Impatient not to miss a perhaps once-only opportunity, Blütfink personally called the O.R. scheduling desk to make sure the neurosurgeon was already busy making all the proper arrangements. Then, reassured, he walked over to Karolena's room. There, he found her awake and somewhat alert -- probably enough to consent to the procedure, he thought. Shortly after arriving, Blütfink was joined by Dr. Malawassi, whom he introduced to Karolena, in case she didn't remember or recognize her.

"Karolena, your prayers have been answered. I just learned that a donor has been located. Are you ready for this?"

"Yes, of course, I guess," she stumbled, but at the same time added, "Frankly, I'm very nervous."

"I can understand that, Karolena, but I'll be right there with you, and I'll do everything I can to assure your safety. If any problem comes up that looks like we should stop, I'll try to act in your best interests."

"Thank you, Rickhard, she said, squeezing his

hand.

“”Karolena, do you remember everything we talked about last week concerning the transplant?” Blütfink asked, “specifically, why you need it, what it entails, and the kind of problems that can occur during and after the procedure?"

Karolena moved the bed controller so that she was sitting up, adjusted her electric blanket down over her legs, pulled her robe closed over her nightgown, then told him, "Of course I understand. I'm a medical doctor, remember.” A bad headache, probably from all the stress, made her less than receptive to the rush in Blütfink’s mannerisms at that moment, understandable as they might be.

"I know that you're a lot more informed than the average person, Karolena, but also I'm sure you understand why I have to tell you all these things. It's the rules, and your consent to the surgery must be considered informed."

Karolena nodded acquiescence. Her headache was now even worse -- Karolena attributed it to all the increased tension. She was also feeling more nauseous than usual, and at this point she only wanted to get all this over with as soon as possible. She was sick of worrying about the dangerous surgery she so desperately needed, and was wearily ready to accept the consequences, whatever the outcome would be. She could not go on as she was.

"The procedure we are going to try involves the transplantation of a small segment of optical cortex," Malawassi explained, one more time. "It's just a section, not all of it, but it should be more than enough."

Karolena nodded, apprehensively.

"With the help of the nerve growth factor, we can expect growth of the donor segment to occur soon after transplantation," Blütfink added, his voice struggling to express encouragement and hope.

Malawassi nodded agreement, and then said, "Because of the small size of the section we'll be engrafting, we may not even need to remove any section of your own brain to make room. There should be enough room to leave your diseased optical area in place and still transplant in the donor segment, by overlaying it on top. I also anticipate only a minimal need for vascular connections, if at all, and the entire surgery should go reasonably quickly."

As Karolena nodded, Malawassi asked, "Do you have any questions?"

"Will it hurt much?" She had always had a low tolerance of pain, and most medications she knew of for pain also were toxic to her damaged liver.

"Not really. I doubt you'll feel or remember a thing," Blütfink volunteered.

Sort of like what I feel after a night alone with you, Karolena reminded herself. She was surprised at the magnitude of the resentment and anger she still harbored against Blütfink. Her conflicted feelings were mixed in with all her other conflicting emotions, carefully suppressed and tightly packaged up as they typically were. Momentarily she felt guilty and ashamed for feeling so negatively toward him. After all, Blütfink seemed to be expending a great deal of effort in her behalf. Just then, she remembered to ask, "What kind of donor is it?"

"The donor is an accident victim. This isn't fetal tissue, if that's what you're getting at."

"Yes, that's what I wanted to know," Karolena admitted. She had plenty of time to think about this as she lay in The Winston, possibly approaching her death, and had long ago decided not to continue to live if it was at the expense of another, particularly after witnessing the suffering of the innocent fetus she had named Christopher. Her feelings, though, didn't exclude accident victims, for there would have been no possible causality in their availability.

As she had anxiously waited for a donor to become available all these past weeks, her vision inexorably deteriorating, Karolena, in her desperation, had at one low point begun to rationalize, as had Blütfink, that a fetus probably was not exactly a "person." It hadn't, after all, actually been born, walked with parents, played with other children, thought about who it was, or tasted any of the pleasures of life. Even the particular fetus she had named Christopher was the result of an abortion, and a fetus could only be officially sanctioned for use in transplants if it was aborted. This ruling supposedly prevented intentional abortions on demand as a source for transplants, which had occurred for a number of years. That practice was now banned, at least it was officially banned. The availability of fetal tissue to serve as a donor was therefore not related to the need for a donor -- at least that was the official line. Still, Karolena never believed the official assurances, having worked inside that very system, and she harbored her own doubts. Even though it was ridiculous to even think such a causal relationship could exist, Karolena had almost convinced herself to accept a fetal donor for her transplant when Blütfink tried to offer her one early on. Still, she eventually changed her mind, deciding to hold fast to her original convictions. Karolena accepted that she would rather live essentially blind, or even die before accepting a fetal donor tissue. Now, she was glad that holding to her standards of right and ethically wrong was finally going to pay off for her.

"Here's the consent form for you to sign," Malawassi said, interrupting her thoughts as he moved a silicon consent plate toward Karolena for her hand imprint. It was the equivalent of a signature, but much more specific, and he waited for Karolena to finish signing before continuing. "Since, in your condition, you probably won't be able to read this, I'll switch it to audio. This consent form outlines the risks, including bleeding, infection, failure or rejection of the graft segment, and other even less likely complications. By the way, the nurse anesthetist will also be by soon to get your informed consent for the anesthesia." Malawassi paused to let the audio consent play. When it was finished, Karolena asked, "How long after the surgery before I can expect to begin feeling better?"

"Hopefully not too long," Malawassi paused, then added, "But you never can predict these things, particularly in relatively experimental circumstances like this. "Malawassi saw Karolena look expectantly at him, and asked, "Do you have any other questions?"

"No, no more questions. It's just that, now that the moment is finally here, I feel a little nervous, and now I'm not so sure I want to go ahead with this, that's all."

"That's quite understandable, Karolena," Blütfink reassured her, "and not at all unusual, but there's no need for further delay now. Besides, you know how it goes around here -- first come, first serve. If you don't take the donor tissue while it's still available and fresh and warm, then I'm afraid someone else will."

Realizing the practicality of Blütfink's advice, Karolena reluctantly placed her hand imprint on the digitized surgery consent plate. Malawassi placed his hand imprint in the witness area, and minutes later Karolena was loaded onto a gurney and whisked off to the preoperative suite.

The nurse anesthetist, a short, dark woman in her forties, met Karolena as soon as she arrived inside the preoperative area. "Karolena, I'll be administering the anesthesiology medications to you during surgery. I understand that the surgeons have already met with you and described the surgical procedure to you."

Karolena weakly nodded yes. She felt something odd about the anesthetist, similar, in some vague way, to the uncomfortable way she felt around Fromposi, but didn't have the energy to pursue it.

"You are having a transplant of your visual cortex?" The anesthetist was certain this was the procedure she was scheduled for, but checked

Karolena's wrist ID tag one more time anyway.

"That's right. Dr. Blütfink and Dr. Malawassi told me that, although the operation is experimental, it should go reasonably well, and they said I probably won't remember anything." Although she had tried to stay calm, a rigid terror gripped her body and she wanted very much to get out of bed and run away, to be somewhere else, anywhere but here. Working as a surgeon had exposed Karolena too much to all the potential errors of surgery and their unfortunate results, and had given life to her worst fears. Now, Karolena imagined she was going to die and felt a full panic seize control of her, making her dizzy with hyperventilation. Her lips became numb and her finger tips tingled as she anxiously stared at her unfamiliar surroundings, and wondered what, if anything, she would see next.

"The visual cortex, how interesting. And yes, you’re correct, you probably won’t remember anything about the surgery. Few people ever do remember their surgery, the anesthetist added, as she checked the intravenous line to Karolena’s arm for patency, then reassuringly told her, “Now, just relax while I give you some more oxygen." The anesthetist placed a translucent flexible mask lightly over Karolena's mouth and nose, and gently instructed her, "Now breathe deeply, just rclax, okay, and don't worry about a thing."**Chapter 14**

Blütfink quickly drove over to FirsThought to take care of some rushed details on other matters, and then headed right back to The Winston. He parked in the underground bunker area, and then briskly walked toward the staff entrance of WCMC. Armed irregular militia guards lined strategic positions behind protective bunkers outside the hospital entrance. The guards recognized Blütfink and the outline of his ID pass, and they let him pass through the fortified entrance way, and then under the weapon scanner. The **UN identity** scanner picked up Blütfink’s wrist ID and let him pass into the hospital. He stopped in the lobby to look at the Location Plaque on the front lobby wall:

O.R. FLOOR 2

Taking a deep breath, Blütfink quickly climbed the stairs and strode past the main entrance to the operating suites. The insides of hospitals were no strange ground for him, and he located the staff's entrance and went inside. Blütfink paused by his locker, and then began undressing. He donned his typical medium scrub uniform top and bottom from a stack he found in a corner open shelf, and then put on a paper surgical mask, cap, and paper booties to cover his set of ER sneakers, which he always left in his locker.

Hearing the door to the changing room open, Blütfink quickly pulled up his pants. Another surgeon entered and looked in his direction.

"Wow that was One Long Case. Which one are you on?"

"The transplant," Blütfink replied, forcing him to take several long, deep breaths.

"Yeah? Which room is it in?"

"Three, I think, isn't it?" "Yeah, three," Blütfink repeated, as he rushed to complete his changing.

"Well, good luck," the O.R. nurse sighed. "I heard the electricity might go out again later today." The nurse quickly changed and left the room.

Taped to the wall, Blütfink found the O.R. schedule for the day and located Karolena's name. He confirmed that it was scheduled for Room 3 in thirty minutes, and then went out into the corridor.

Outside the O.R. door, a flat panel displayed Malawassi's name and the words "Optical cortex Donor for TRANSPLANT."

Inside, O.R. #3 was deserted, save for some

equipment carts. It was a small O.R., with typical tile walls lined with metal cabinets, a central operating table, several large overhead light arrays, and wall receptacles for various gases and suction. On a side table, he found a printed sheet of paper inserted inside a clear plastic cover, with the letters **UNITED ORGAN NETWORK** in double height bold red. Under this, Karolena's name appeared with a listing of various internal organs and their destinations:

Organ	**Destination**
Cornea	unassigned
Lung	Ontario, Canada
Heart	Ontario, Canada
Liver	unassigned
Optical cortex	Winston County, NC.USA
Kidney, right	New Orleans, LA.USA
Kidney, left	Vienna, Gr Germany

In the pre-op area, it took only seconds for the anesthesia to take hold, and Karolena lapsed into complete, unfeeling unconsciousness. Moments later, her limp body was moved into the busy specialty operative room #3 reserved for neurosurgical cases, where she would finally receive her transplant. Her mind, though, freed of all corporeal constraints, drifted off in another direction. The technicians wheeled Karolena's gurney parallel to the O.R. table and set the parking brakes. Positioning themselves on both ends of the gurney, they prepared to transfer her. An O.R. nurse took the lead, saying, "Now, all heave together on my count of three. Be careful, we don't want to drop another person on the same morning. That would be even harder to explain than the first one," she quipped, causing them all to chuckle nervously.

"Ready? One, two, THREEEEE . . . " Blütfink joined in to help, and they not too gracefully transferred Karolena from the gurney over to the O.R. table. Her motionless body landed with a dull heavy-sounding thud like one gigantic side of beef on the O.R. table. Blütfink did his best to cushion Karolena's fall, and was surprised how light and limp the small body felt, and also how cold. Karolena's blank face was emotionless and ivory white, as if it had been flushed clean of blood.

IV lines had already been started in Karolena's arm by the preoperative nursing team, and her IV bags were transferred from the gurney onto special poles attached to a corner of the O.R. bed. A telemetry unit clung to her wrist, and the output was redirected to the small crowded anesthesiology cart computer unit sitting nearby.

The O.R. technicians took turns draping and preparing Karolena's head for the organ donation surgery. Karolena now lay totally exposed, arms outstretched, waiting to receive the nails in sacrificial manner on what soon could become her cross. The analogy was not lost on Blütfink, who now was more determined than ever to give Karolena a good outcome.

Blütfink looked down at Karolena's scantily clad body and smiled inwardly at a momentary remembrance, before his face again went blank. After inspecting the IV lines and the setup of the O.R., he glanced around at the various O.R. staff. The head O.R. nurse caught Blütfink glance, then quickly turned away. Blütfink, sensing something out of the ordinary, began slowly moving toward the head nurse, but got distracted as the anesthetist approached him to discuss the case.

By now, surgical nurses and residents had flooded the O.R. Some of them busily swabbed Karolena's shaved forehead with iodine-based cleaning solutions, which left the skin with an unusual green-brown discoloration.

In a corner of the O.R., a small section of human donor brain floated in a cryopreservation unit, unconscious in a light red pool of oxygen and nutrient-rich medium, waiting to finally be joined with Karolena.

. . . The essence of the donor, in complete detachment, looked down from a spot near the top of the operating room, and, for the first time since her death, she felt unusually light and in no pain at all. Although not totally sure what had happened or what would soon occur, she wasn't frightened in the least. On the contrary, she now felt very much at peace, and instinctively understood that her immediate purpose was to help others.

Moving away from her own body with wings of angels, her essence stopped and reached down to touch Karolena's cheek, thousands of miles away, and tried to understand the desperate situation of another young woman, herself near death's door. She kissed Karolena's and silently whispered into Karolena's ear, "*Now you will be me. Now we will be one. Now you MUST remember . . .* "

An unusual series of jagged lines appeared on Karolena's electroencephalogram tracing, then just as rapidly disappeared, attracting only the vaguest of attention by the anesthetist.

Blütfink nervously looked over his left shoulder, then his right. Just then, several remote cameras units came on-line and began movements to scan the faces and objects in the O.R. The Neurosurgical Team, led by Dr. Malawassi and assisted by Dr. Fromposi, arrived at that time, and, acting as assistant surgeon, Blütfink moved to the side of the operating table where he could best observe the surgical procedure.

Malawassi began preparation for placement of the donor **VAA** by dissecting back a minute section of scalp, exposing Karolena's cranium. Using an electric saw with a circular blade, the lead surgeon cut open Karolena's skull, and removed a small section of the parietal bone, pealing it back like the peel off a grapefruit. This exposed the thin but very strong triple layer of neural membranes, and after they were incised, the off-gray, semi-firm brain lay open. The whole procedure, which resembled scalping as much as surgery, took less than five minutes.

Deep in the exposed skull, Karolena's living but unconscious brain -- the consistency of warm tapioca pudding -- pulsated slightly and quivered whenever someone jarred the O.R. table. Beneath lay the sought-after brain Area 19 - - the visual association area VAA. Recognizing where she was from the anatomic landmarks, Fromposi sprayed a mist of surgical glue over the approximate area of Karolena's own, damaged VAA, followed by a layer of recombinant nerve growth factor to prepare the surface for the donor graft tissue.

The smell of smoke from cauterized brain and blood started to make Blütfink hungry, and his stomach, in independent response to his more primal thoughts, elicited a loud, grumbling sound. Embarrassed, Blütfink looked around in feigned amazement, as if to deny that the disgusting sound had originated from him.

The anesthetist looked up from her cart, surrounded by gauges and dials and monitor lights, and after several minutes searching for something in particular, anxiously asked, "Has anyone seen my pancuronium bromide syringe? It was just here. It's the one with the red and yellow bands . . . " After looking for the missing syringe of nerve paralyzer for a few more minutes, she had to return to the anesthesiology cart when one of her instruments emitted a loud, continuous beep. She looked at the cardiovascular monitoring unit, then warned, "The patient's blood pressure is starting to climb," as she quickly prepared another syringe of arterial relaxant for use.

Looking over at the instruments anxiously, Blütfink knew that, with all the arteries and veins lying open and partially connected, this was the worst time for hypertension. Any of the vessels might spring a leak into Karolena's brain, and the results could be disastrous.

"Her heart rate is tachycardic, too," reported the surgical resident, thankful for something to finally do.

"I got it," the anesthetist said as she began to play with her anesthesia gauges to fine-tune Karolena's blood pressure. "It's probably just a physiologic response to pain," she commented.

Taking the donor VAA from the transport unit, they carefully bathed it in saline to remove extra perfluorocarbon oxygen-carrying chemical which had been added to aid movement of oxygen into the tissue, then they gently placed the donor brain over Karolena's own VAA. Fromposi had already applied the growth factor to the brain's surface, and blood vessels on the surface of Karolena's brain around the donor site blanched slightly, as if complaining about the presence of 'foreign' tissue.

Some red and yellow lines flashed across the electroencephalograph-EEG, and a warning message was generated by the cardiopulmonary computer. "We've got some spontaneous EEG activity," the anesthesia nurse called out. "And Ms. Kreisler's blood pressure is dropping also."

The neurosurgeons nervously stared at the monitors. The EEG activity consisted of some sharp waves and a few spikes, then quickly died down, with Karolena never displaying any spontaneous seizure activity. "I think the electrical activity was just due to irritation from placement of the graft," Fromposi called out, reassuringly," and the hypotension should pass, too."

A few minutes later, the relieved anesthesia nurse reported, "The blood pressure is okay now. It must have been just a transient shift from disturbing the patient's brain surface with the donor graft tissue."

"That does happen," an obviously strained Fromposi confirmed, nodded her head. She took the syringe containing the remaining nerve growth factor and liberally squirted the surface of the engrafted tissue one more timc, 'for good luck,' she said to herself. Turning to Malawassi, she said, "I sure hope this nerve growth factor Blütfink's been working on is effective." Malawassi nodded back, but his face displayed the deep concern for the surgery's success he was feeling. They both looked to Blütfink for confirmation, and he returned with a confident but constrained smile.

Because of the near amorphous, loose texture of living brain tissue, the VAA transplant didn't require suturing or vascular connection, and the entire VAA transplant procedure was completed in only a few minutes. Looking down at Karolena's head, Blütfink jokingly thought to himself that it resembled a little coconut, but immediately felt guilty for the unkind thought and was glad that, for once, he hadn't said it out loud.

Once the neurosurgeons closed her skull and sutured the cut scalp edges together, Karolena's ground-breaking transplant surgery was complete. The surgeons left soon after, and the O.R. nurses prepared Karolena for transport. After covering her with a blanket, pulling the electrocautery pad off her buttock, attaching her IV lines to a pole, and heaving her unconscious body onto an adjacent gurney, Karolena's next stop was the Surgical ICU for further close monitoring. If all seemed well, she could be moved to the surgical floor later that day.

Chapter 15

Several hours later, while still in the Recovery Room, Karolena slowly regained consciousness. A prolonged period of postoperative unconsciousness was not unusual for neurosurgery patients, and, as in her case, it was often longer. As she again struggled to open her eyes, Karolena felt deathly tired, and her general feeling of disorientation was further clouded by a gnawing headache. "Where am I?" she groaned, thinking she was still in a dream, or a nightmare. At first, the room around her was a fog, and what little she could manage to see appeared to be only an amorphous gray mist.

As she opened her eyes further and looking around, Karolena struggling against a monstrous headache and an almost overpowering nausea. Her mouth tasted dry and crusty and her eyes could barely focus, and it was with difficulty that, out of the fog slowly crystallized a hospital room, one full of strange instruments she could not recognize. The same dull walls and peeling paint were close to her bed side, and a dirty picture window looked out over a parking lot and backup power generator. Oxygen and suction outlets hung from the walls, and gurgling tubes ran back and forth to her bed. Several objects did have a familiar appearance, but not enough to recognize, leading her to the depressing possibility that her surgery, and all the risk and pain and anxiety, had failed and been for naught. One thing she did recognize, though, was the chemically sharp, pervasive hospital odor. Her nausea rapidly increased in severity until Karolena had to gag. An acidic retching caused a sharp, crimpy pain in her abdomen, almost as if a hot knife was being plunged in there.

Beyond a monstrous headache and the nausea, Karolena felt a stinging, burning sensation in her right nostril. Then she remembered about a tube that, just before surgery, was inserted in her nose and ran down the back of her throat into her stomach. The nasogastric tube -- NG in hospital jargon -- caused a sick, ticklish feeling and made her gag. Just the thought of it going in, the very idea that a foreign object was in her nose and violating the back of her throat made her sick to her stomach. Karolena heard the tube making a sucking noise as it ran out her nose to a pump by her bedside, and she looked over and saw the suction receptacle bottle filled with a slimy green-brown semisolid material pumped from the pit of her stomach; the site only made the nausea more severe.

Several clear plastic lines for administration of intravenous fluids ran into her arm, limiting her movement. Karolena tried to shift her weight in bed, but a searing pain in her head instantly limited her. Oh yes, she thought - *the surgery*. She remembered going to the preoperative area, the black rubber mask placed over her face to give her "more oxygen," and then . . . nothing.

"This is Surgical Intensive Care, the recovery area," the nurse said. "Your surgery is over, and your surgeons tell me it went pretty well."

Karolena tried unsuccessfully to focus her vision, and didn't reply.

"How do you feel?" the nurse asked, as she took Karolena's hand, felt her wrist pulse and checked her blood pressure.

"Tired, very tired. And my head is throbbing."

"I'm not surprised, after all the surgery you've been through. Do you have any pain along with the throbbing?" Although the recovery room nurse felt obliged to ask that question, she doubted Karolena would be experiencing a great deal of pain. It was too soon for all the strong analgesics given during surgery to have worn off. In addition, the surgical orders had included the placement of a continuous nerve stimulation unit over Karolena's left temple to control any discomfort.

"Yes, I have quite a headache, and some throbbing, too." She hesitated for a moment, not wanting to sound like a complainer, before saying, "Can I ask you something?" She knew how stupid she would sound, but had to know what was real and what was imagined.

"Sure, but try not to exert yourself too much," the nurse said, as she busily noted the instrument readings.

Karolena struggled to speak, to concentrate despite her head pounding every few seconds. "Are you supposed to dream when you're under anesthesia?"

"The textbooks say no, and I've never had anybody tell me otherwise. Why, do you think you had a dream during your surgery?" the nurse asked. She bent closer to Karolena and carefully examined the surgical dressing wrapped around Karolena's head. A small amount of blood stained the bandage, without evidence of continued oozing or frank bleeding.

"I'm not really sure if something I think happened back in the operating room was imagined or real. Were you there for my surgery?" Karolena asked.

"Yes, I was in there pretty much for the whole procedure."

"Did anyone kiss me on my forehead?"

"I don't understand. Like who?" the nurse asked, taken aback.

"I'm not certain. Perhaps it was after I was unconscious." She knew her question sounded ridiculous and immediately regretted asking it. Although Karolena tried again to look at the nurse, pain kept her from moving her neck, and she now was able to distinguish only areas of light and gray, but no definite objects.

The nurse shook her head, smiled faintly, and told Karolena, "I can assure you that none of the surgical staff kissed you. That's just not professional conduct. It must have been a dream," she smiled reassuringly, although a slight annoyance laced her voice.

"Maybe so. But it seemed very real," Karolena insisted.

"I've read that, under the influence of certain medications, dreams can take on a sense of power, and an almost terrifying reality," the nurse said, reassuringly.

"Maybe so," Karolena repeated, very tired from the surgery. She smacked her lips and moved her tongue around her dry mouth, yawned, then tried to shift her position around a bit to get more comfortable, but was immediately restrained by a sharp pain in her head. "I certainly seem to have had my share of strange dreams lately," Karolena added, grimacing.

"Oh? Like what?" the nurse asked her.

"Well, in one I dreamt I could run forward and leap into the air and fly. I've dreamt variations of that same dream at least a couple of times already. What do you make of that?" Karolena asked.

"Well, I certainly don't claim any pretense at interpreting dreams," the nurse laughed. "But I read once that dreaming about falling can be associated with anxiety. With all your medical problems, I would be anxious and have bad dreams too."

"But I was flying, not falling, and the dream was quite peaceful," Karolena said, as she remembered the pleasant sensations she had during the dream.

"Maybe it had something to do with your viral infection. When did you first have such a dream?" the nurse asked, interested.

"I think it first occurred around the time I was lying unconscious in my apartment and was brought to the ER, although I did have some bad dreams before that." She knew there was a sharp difference: her prior bad dreams could easily be attributed to aggravation with work, with Blütfink and with men in general, and with her life in the states. These new dreams were quite different, though; they had to in some way be related to her illness, and they were getting worse.

"Perhaps that particular dream was a near-death experience. Who knows?" the nurse asked, shrugging her shoulders. Looking at a slight rise in Karolena's blood pressure noted on the monitors, she pulled the sheets up to cover Karolena better, and gently told her, "Let's have less talk about frightening dreams and more rest for now, shall we?"

"Sure. Anyway, it's not important right now. The operation is finally over, and I survived." Karolena tried to smile. Whether the operation was successful was another matter. She doubted that any change would be evident so soon, and wasn't disappointed at this early time, although she had hoped there would have been at least an indication.

"Right. Just concentrate on resting for now. We're going to take you back upstairs to the regular ward soon," she started to say, before noticing that Karolena had already fallen asleep.

Chapter 16

After the transplant surgery, Karolena experienced a very rocky recovery, with little change in her ability to recognize even common objects, and a nagging persistence of headaches. The slowness of her progress was disappointing to everyone, the continuous headaches seemed to take forever to abate, and there were days when the amount of pain meds Karolena needed to control the pain left her completely in a fog, unable to think clearly, almost beyond caring.

She also struggled with more bad dreams, disturbing dreams. They were not of the intensity of nightmares, and not all easy to remember details of. Not sleeping well contributed to her general fatigue, and she often grabbed a nap whenever she could, which frequently was during the day, and made it hard for her to establish a good sleep cycle.

It was only the strength she was able to take from the daily visits from Susan Wilder and Blütfink that seemed to make her painful existence at least tolerable. Susan provided the daily encouragement, the company, the friendly voice; she helped Karolena to eat when she was too weak or disoriented, answered her AllSee, and kept her up with events in the outside world. Blütfink gave her continuity with her professional life, and also with a reassuring sense of value of herself as a woman.

Gradually, Karolena was able to struggle out of bed, then walk, with assistance, to the bathroom. Her appetite slowly returned, and with it her strength, and Karolena could notice a difference as her interest in living, in being alive again, slowly return.

Several entirely indistinguishable, nameless weeks slowly ground by before Karolena began to realize that a subtle change finally was coming over her vision. First, the ubiquitous fog abated and objects could again be seen, although with sometimes ill-defined edges. Then, slowly, she began to recognize objects, albeit still assisted by touch, sound and smell, objects whose identity had up until recently been foreign to her; she could reach for things and know, recognize, actually understand their use, and these final incremental triumphs lifted her spirit and in a basic way buoyed, and accelerated her physical recovery.

Blütfink continued to come by every morning for a few minutes to perform his daily exam and direct her post-operative care. Malawassi came by separately, but less and less frequently as her surgical wounds healed; some nurses Karolena had become friendly with also stopped by more often, and this in itself signaled her new attitude, as she also began to entertain occasional visitors from her lab at FirsThought. For those welcome moments, some happy, some strictly business, each short but as a total quite fulfilling, she was thankful.

A few days later, Karolena lay awake in her bed in the evening, having awoken for the third time that night. Each time, she had the same terrifying nightmare. She had been walking in an open field, a flock of birds followed her, and then attacked her. She could still feel the pain of her flesh being ripped down to her bones, and the helplessness, and the lack of anywhere to run. Now, too upset to sleep or to even try, she found herself able only to stare at the ceiling and ponder the meaning of her existence, and she remained that way for hours before finally falling asleep once again.

On ward rounds the next morning, Blütfink was stopped by Karolena's nurse as he walked by the nurse's station; she expressed her concern about a small but persistent elevation of liver enzymes. Blütfink, distracted into studying his schedule of appointments for later in the day, replied to her, "First off, the readings of liver enzymes taken by sensors taped onto Karolena's skin are not as accurate as those obtained by the usual blood tests. But, sure, I'm concerned about that, although my experience is that the enzymes are nonspecific and typically will normalize over the next few days even if, or perhaps because, we do nothing at all. Has Karolena reported any changes in her headaches?"

"No change," the nurse told him. "Just that she still gets them often, and asks for a lot of pain medications. But her neurologic checks are improving, and for the last few days I've noticed the first real improvement since her surgery in her ability to recognize objects. Maybe she needs medicine to help her stay asleep."

Spurred by the nurse's observations, Blütfink

headed for Karolena's room. As the nurse followed, he told her that Karolena had complained of headaches as far back as he could remember, and long before needing any surgery. "According to the neurosurgeons, so far, the optic graft appears to be healing well, and Karolena's visual recognition has been improving daily, albeit not at the rate we would have expected." He, in fact, was surprised that the optical graft, experimental as it was, had been working even this well. As a concept it seemed to make sense, but also appeared to be way too technically demanding for mid-twenty first century surgical technology. And what about all the billions of connections within every section of the brain? Flopping one set of foreign brain tissue on top of a fully integrated section of brain was one thing, but expecting all those nerve cells to connect up exactly right on their own seemed almost too much to ask. Yet, he remembered the last experiment that he and Karolena performed, how all the nerve nets almost instantly connected, and wondered, could they have finally found the magic formula? Would someone in his professional circle finally remember his name?

Walking up to Karolena's bedside, they found her awake, and staring peacefully out of the window. "Rickhard, is that you?" Karolena reached out.

Blütfink sat on Karolena's bedside. "Karolena, it's Dr. Blütfink and your nurse."

"Hello, Rickhard," she said flatly. Sometimes he seemed so formal, even though he probably wanted the D work because the nurse was there and he didn't want to appear too familiar with her. But the nurses knew of their relationship, she was sure, or they could surmise.

Ignoring her lack of enthusiasm, he asked, "How are you feeling today?" in his standard matter-of-fact clinical voice. Picking up her bedside flat panel chart, he began flipping through the various medical and nursing screen displays.

"Rickhard, I'm over here, in the bed, not on the flat panel," Karolena reminded him. Drumming her fingers on the bedside rail, she chided, "You're not having trouble with visual recognition, are you?"

The nurse laughed nervously, glanced at Blütfink's annoyed face, then excused herself from the room.

"Yes, sure, right. Real funny, Karolena. I see you're getting your lovely old sense of sarcasm back, too." Blütfink looked toward her, saw that she was annoyed, but didn't put the flat screen medical record down. "I was just trying to check your numbers. And, look, since we're not back in the lab at FirsThought, I really think it would be better if, at least around other patients and staff, you addressed me as Doctor, okay?"

"That's just fine with me, Dr. Blütfink, if you think that our relationship has deteriorated to that point. But in return, I prefer that you address me as Dr. Kreisler, as I'm a medical doctor too, and I also request the courtesy of your looking in my direction when speaking with me. I think that's only reasonable. But you don't have to address me as Doctor. Everyone here knows that I am."

Blütfink noticed with some irritation Karolena's assertiveness and self-confidence returning, which ordinarily would have been a good sign in another patient. "Let's not have any more of that old subtle Karolena hostility, now, okay?"

"Oh, do you find me hostile, Rickhard? Karolena asked. When she got no immediate denial from Blütfink, she seemed disappointed. "There is something that I need to talk to you about, Rickhard."

He looked at her questioningly, but relieved they weren't going to have another fight, especially in public again. "Sure. What's that?"

"I want to talk about the problems I'm still having with headaches."

"Yes, your nurse mentioned the headaches, and also some difficulty sleeping." Blütfink glanced at the medication screen, and noticed that Karolena had indeed been requesting analgesics rather frequently. "What are your headaches like?"

"They hurt a lot and last for hours at a time. Medicine does help them, though." Karolena held her hand to her forehead and said, "The pain's here, right here."

"I'm sorry to hear that," Blütfink said, looking at the area Karolena was pointing to, over her forehead, but far away from her surgical site. "Are you having any nausea, dizziness, stiff or painful neck? Any weakness or difficulty moving your arms or legs? Any deterioration in your vision?"

"No, I'm not having any of those things, fortunately, just a headache. It's a continuous, low level headache, and sometimes it gets really bad." She thought a little more, then added, "well, maybe I get a little nausea with it too."

"I hope that the headaches don't represent some intracranial swelling," Blütfink explained, "possibly from your optical transplant. That was pretty serious neurosurgery you had there, Karolena."

"I know that much, Rickhard. Give me a little credit, will you?"

"It's probably to be expected," he sighed, "but I'll discuss it with the neurosurgeons. Have they been by to check you yet today?"

"Yes, they come by every afternoon. I've already asked them about the headaches, and they said the same thing they always do: headaches after any form of craniotomy are to be expected and should pass with time."

Blütfink made some notes on the flat panel patient log, including a request for the Neurosurgeons to reexamine Karolena and for them to report their findings to him personally.

"You know, Rickhard, in some ways I feel deep down that all the bad luck I've been having with my vision, the deterioration and then the transplant surgery, is because of the horrible thing I did to Christopher." It was a disturbing worry she knew floated just below her consciousness, but something she often considered. "Of course, I know that there can't really be a causal connection, but it worries me a bit."

"Christopher?" Blütfink asked.

"That's the name I gave the fetus we last worked on together. I know that's the problem here. Sometimes," Karolena paused and looked out the window, "I feel so bad for what we were doing, or the way we were doing it." She felt suddenly on the verge of tears and of totally losing control, and perhaps losing her mind as well.

"Oh, Karolena, don't say that." Taking hold of her hand, he sternly told her, "I hope all the stress from you're illness isn't making you suicidal. Just look at how full your life is." Never one to be able to counsel patients in ways to effectively deal with their illnesses, he instead suggested to her, "Have you talked about your feelings of depression with a counselor?"

"No thanks, getting that on your record can ruin your career in a hurry. No, I think it's just better to keep some things to yourself. But I did want to mention it to you, because you have known me for a longer time than just about anyone."

"Look, Karolena," Blütfink said, frustrated with revisiting this issue, "you weren't responsible for the birth of that fetus, and you didn't recommend or perform the abortion, did you?"

"No, I guess not, but ..."

"Did you design the transplant experiment we worked on, or request it?"

"No, but . . . "

"There, you see. The fetus would have been aborted and discarded anyway. It would have died whatever experiment you and I were planning for it that day, so you definitely aren't responsible. We're as guiltless and clean as the new fallen snow."

Karolena looked away, and muttered only, "I doubt that," seemingly unconvinced by his tepid attempt at situational ethics.

"But, I'll tell you this much. If participating in research with fetuses bothers you so much, you really shouldn't do them once you recover and get back to work. I think you need to do something you find much less morally objectionable, don't you?"

"Perhaps you're right. I've been thinking the same thing for a long time," Karolena admitted. Finally, a breakthrough in understanding with Blütfink, she sighed to herself. "Thanks for talking to me, I feel a little better now," she said, patting his hand and attempting a smile. At times like this, she felt she could really relate to Blütfink as a person, although to varying degrees, depending on where their personal relationship was at the moment. In her less melancholy moods, Karolena hoped that, if she were to recover, perhaps they might even resume seeing each other socially.

"Any time, you can talk to me any time, and do get better, please, Blütfink smiled at Karolena, squeezing her hand. "I really hate to see you like this," he added with a convincing sense of sincerity, before turning to leave.

"Thanks, Rickhard, and you know where to find me," Karolena quipped, and they both laughed. After he left, Karolena stared at the window, motionless, for almost an hour, enjoying the beauty of once-familiar objects just now returning to recognition. For a moment, she wondered if rejection by a transplant recipient of a living tissue and rejection of one person by another living person were equivalent, and she found herself unavoidably and unknowingly slipping into another depressing despondency, and fought against falling down that downward spiral. Still, she had to wonder sometimes why she went on living, and what was her life's purpose. But these were questions for another day, and the silence was kind, and she soon fell into a peaceful sleep.

After leaving Karolena's room, Blütfink stopped at the Nursing Station and instructed the nurse to keep him informed of Karolena's progress, particularly about her nausea and headaches. In addition, he ordered a nuclear medicine liver scan and a daily set of liver enzymes and coagulation factor levels to monitor the status of Karolena's liver more closely, before hurrying off to see his other patients.

With a great deal more disappointment and apprehension than acceptance with her experimental surgery's outcome, Karolena showed little further improvement during the next week. Although her chronic headaches had abated quite a bit, albeit with the steady assistance of analgesics, there was still no clear resolution or further perceptible improvement of her vision. Had her progress plateaued out, she worried? Was this inadequate level of recognition of faces and of objects all she could expect to achieve, especially after all the pain and suffering and risk she had put herself through, she fretted? Karolena also was left with little energy to walk around her room, let alone the ward, perhaps a side-effect of prolonged bed rest and all the pain meds she was forced to consume, or had become dependent on, and even eating often took too much effort. As a result, Karolena found herself forced to spend almost all of her time in bed, thinking and dreaming, and occasionally speaking with visitors, and also with her father, who was for the moment back in touch via the AllSee. She forced herself to take daily strolls with one of the more human-appearing exercise-bots, who could be rather entertaining and conversant in the way it was programmed, and it did speak several languages, which piqued her interest more. Yet, like with the AllSee, she was always careful of what she said, as it was all recorded, all noted. And you never know.

Blütfink, noting Karolena's disappointing lack of real progress, suspecting a mild form of graft rejection, but continued to hope for a recovery. Occasionally, a mild rejection occurred shortly after a transplant, he well-knew from experience. Such minor rejection incidents often resolved on their own or with only a "touch" of anti-rejection medication. But he would leave that to the specialty consultants to manage. Eventually Karolena's lack of progress prompted Blütfink to consult with Malawassi on how best to confirm this unfortunate possibility, and what they might actually do about it.

A closed needle biopsy was really the only way to know for certain what was happening to her graft, and after Malawassi's concurrence, and Karolena's reluctant acquiescence, the risky procedure was performed. Fortunately, there were no complications to the procedure, and they all waited anxiously for information from the hospital pathologist.

"Just as I suspected," Malawassi commented to Blütfink, as he looked over the pathology report on the biopsy specimen. "It seems our patient is experiencing sub-acute rejection of her graft."

"I'm surprised and I'm really disappointed, given the high degree of tissue compatibility we were able to achieve here," Blütfink replied, all hope seemingly draining from his face. "She got nearly a perfect match."

“”Sometimes it happens,” Malawassi shrugged, “although in this case, she hasn't even responded to the most aggressive anti-rejection monoclonal therapies we've got. It just makes no sense to me whatever," Malawassi admitted, shaking his head. "I agree, though, that the tissue match was pretty good, at least as far as compatibility markers go. The transplant operation technically went really well. And, for just those reasons, I never would have expected this particular graft, of all the transplants I've performed lately, to react this way. It's almost like the graft, for some reason known only to it, just doesn't want to stay there.”

“That sounds a bit too unscientific, don't you think," Blütfink replied. "But, as you say, maybe the graft just doesn't want to take hold in Karolena's body," Blütfink nervously chuckled.

"Maybe, but that can't really be our working hypothesis now, can it?" Malawassi asked, skeptically.

"No, of course not," Blütfink replied, looking into his open hands. He had meant the comment almost as a joke, but now he reconsidered. "Obviously, we're going to have to try something else to suppress the rejection, before the swelling affects other areas of her brain."

"I don't follow you -- try again with what? There are no additional treatments we can try at this point," he insisted. Truth be told, Malawassi had tried last week to make Blütfink aware of the unwelcome possibility that graft rejection was occurring, so that early action could be taken, but Blütfink back then wouldn't listen, wouldn't act any sooner. "Additional medication may not work, I'm afraid," Malawassi said, with a great deal of hesitation in his voice, before offering, “I think perhaps it would be advisable if you would schedule Ms. Kreisler for another transplant; you know, just tentatively, just in case this one gets rejected. After all, it did seem to work a little, at first. And it was a very new and experimental procedure. Maybe a second one would take better?"

Blütfink couldn't believe he was hearing those words. "Another transplant?" Blütfink almost screamed at Malawassi. "That's most unusual, isn't it?" A look that blended surprise and disbelief colored his face, and he began to cough out a string of objections, although he had to admit to himself that he, too, had also entertained that awful possibility.

"Unfortunately, you heard me correctly; I think that we need to schedule Karolena for another transplant. How else can she get back on a donor list, in case we are seeing an uncontrollable graft rejection here? Look, I can understand why you're concerned, but sometimes these things just have to be done." Not getting further objections from Blütfink, Malawassi straightened his white coat, then continued, "Frankly, though, I must warn you, I doubt that the next transplant will be accepted either. Once you reject, subsequent rejection episodes tend to occur more frequently." That had been the unfortunate experience of transplant surgeons for perhaps fifty years, and was unchanged. Summarized a little differently, it went: 'Shit happens.'

Despite Karolena's rather dismal overall prognosis, Blütfink tried, at least when in Karolena's presence, to display confidence of a satisfactory outcome. Sometimes you just needed another graft, and that was the luck of the draw, he thought, all the while recognizing that was only the flimsiest of rationalizations. Considering the difficulty of getting any donor, let alone a high match of a living section of the brain, it seemed entirely too unlikely to even seriously entertain.

Later that day, while speaking with the ward nurse, she asked Karolena, "What has Dr. Blütfink told you lately about your progress?"

"I speak with Dr. Blütfink almost each morning, usually on his rounds," Karolena replied. "He's been pretty good about that, I must admit. Apparently, these last few days I have been having a slowing of my healing process, and that's a little disconcerting to us both."

She nodded her head in agreement as she watched Karolena closely.

"I know that I've had recurring headaches, which isn't unexpected, I guess, given the type of surgery I've just had. And I understand that the neurosurgeons aren't too worried about the headaches at this point, although, frankly, I certainly am. My biopsy did show some rejection of the graft, but they're treating it with all the medications at their disposal, and I'm still hoping for a good response."

"Yes, we all are hoping for that, Karolena," she replied, a worried look on her face.

"Why? What else then has Blütfink been saying?" Karolena asked suspiciously.

"If I tell you more, will you swear that you didn't hear anything from me?" she insisted, taking hold of Karolena's hand.

"Yes, of course," Karolena promised her, knowing she had to keep any promise she made to keep future lines of information flowing. If there was some vital fact on her condition, or some change in her treatment being contemplated, she of all people needed to know about it right away.

"Let me just ask you this, Karolena. Has Dr. Blütfink mentioned a need for another transplant?" she whispered. She appeared to have heard some sounds from behind her, but, after turning, all she could see was a security patrol with a dog-bot, and a utility bot delivering nursing supplies.

"Another transplant?" Karolena tried to laugh at

that absurd suggestion, but instead almost ended up choking. Incredulously, she managed to ask, "Surely you must be kidding." Not hearing the nurse deny this, she nervously asked, "Do you mean they think I might need a liver transplant?" She hadn't heard of any change in the condition of her liver, and wasn't aware of feeling increased nausea or fatigue.

"It's not a liver they're considering, I'm afraid," she replied, sadly shaking her head.

"No. No no no. Not another visual graft." Karolena nearly chocked. "But ... don't you think they should give the anti-rejection medications more time to work? I mean, it's not like I'm in acute graft failure right this minute," she cried at the very thought of undergoing another surgical procedure.

"You got that right," the nurse nodded. "You know, I think that Blütfink and Malawassi may be brilliant at what they do, but really, perhaps they're both a little out of their minds this time."

Karolena motioned in silent agreement, wondering just how she could locate Blütfink and discuss this with him before he started doing something she didn't really need, something she wouldn't agree to anyway and something they both would regret.

Once the possibility of looking for another transplant donor was raised by Dr. Malawassi, the transplant coordinator, acting on Malawassi's request, began the painstaking and laborious search for a suitable donor, just in case one would be needed. An appropriate donor of neurologic tissues, however, was not immediately available, to the relief both of the surgical team and also the ward nurses. Except for Malawassi, they all felt certain that Karolena probably wouldn't tolerate another graft just now; she simply lacked the physical fortitude so soon after her last surgery, and they all hoped that she probably just needed more time to recover. Everyone hoped that this would happen, forcing Blütfink and Malawassi to come to their senses.

The next morning, Blütfink's secretary informed him he had a call on his AllSee from a parent of one of his patients. Before Blütfink had a chance to say anything, he was greeted with, "Rickhard, this is Karolena . . . "

"Good morning, Karolena, What do you want, I mean, what can I do for you?" Blütfink was a little annoyed at having Karolena call him at the office, instead of waiting to speak with him while he was over at the hospital, and made a note to have his receptionist screen out future calls from her.

"There's really no need to get derogatory, Rickhard."

"Not at all, Karolena. You can interpret my tone of voice any way you choose, but derogatory it is certainly not. As I've already said, if you're touchy about what you do, or rather don't do, then it's your problem," Blütfink quipped. His disdain for certain patients was well known; they were all troublemakers and instigators in his eyes. Unfortunately, Bob Wilder, the hospital administrator, always the PR man, didn't share that opinion.

"I hear that you're planning another graft for me," Karolena started out. "I naturally found it hard to believe that you would seriously contemplate taking so serious an action at what's so obviously premature a time, especially without even discussing this with me first. I certainly hope, for your sake, that what I was hearing wasn't true."

"How did you find out about my surgical plans?" Blütfink nearly exploded. He hated to have his surgical plans discussed behind his back, his decisions questioned; it was one thing that made him particularly angry.

When Blütfink tellingly didn't directly deny what she had related, Karolena pressed on. "So, is it true?"

"Look, Karolena, apparently you're suffering from sub-acute rejection of your transplant," he explained, "and I'm doing exactly what's considered appropriate."

"Appropriate?" she angrily shot back. "My graft has not rejected. It's got some sub-acute reaction, but it's not going anywhere."

"Yes, my having a backup plan is very appropriate. Besides, considering a second graft was Dr. Malawassi's idea. Why don't you question him if you're so against it?"

"I certainly will. You can depend on that."

"Karolena, Karolena, be reasonable, please. These are unusual times. What would you have me do? Nothing?" Blütfink stared at Karolena's hologram on the AllSee; it was the look of someone who still was going to challenge him, cause trouble, and made

Blütfink come to dislike Karolena. He knew that particular look very well.

"Don't you think that you should be a little more aggressive in trying to first reverse the graft's rejection, if that's what it really is? And wouldn't a consult from a transplant immunologist be helpful?" Karolena asked, fighting to remain calm and appear helpful, despite the sense of desperation in her voice.

"Okay, Karolena, I'm willing to get an outside opinion, if it will make you feel any better, but I doubt they will report anything different. We already have many people in addition to Malawassi working on your case. We all care for you and your outcome." In fact, he considered, that was generally true, and perhaps more so for two people besides her basic team. Her father continued to meddle from the sidelines, or so he heard from Bob Wilder. He had money and he certainly seemed to have the right connections. And of course, Bob Wilder was concerned and pressed for a good outcome, although not so much because of concern for the patient, or pressure from her father, but because, Blütfink speculated, of the upside economic potential. That would make a big difference for them all.

After quickly arranging for a transplant immunologist to give an opinion on the management of Karolena's case, he left for the relative peace of his office.

Chapter 17

It was not long after Blütfink returned to his office, that he was contacted by the hospital's transplant immunologist, who had just completed performing a consultation on Karolena. Not unexpectedly, there was agreement on both the diagnosis of sub-acute graft rejection, and on the treatment. As a result, Karolena was given more frequent Nerve Growth Factor for her visual graft, now every four hours, and, in addition, some newer, but still investigational, immune modulators.

The change in therapy Blütfink had instituted at the recommendation of the consultants fortunately resulted in a rapid acceleration of Karolena's recovery. Within a few days, she began to respond to the changed medical regimen, feeling more at ease, less nauseous, had a better appetite, and even ventured out of bed again. After a few more days on the modified therapy, Karolena's headaches nearly completely abated, and her sight recognition began to improve considerably.

As she lay in bed, Karolena finally felt with confidence that she was on the road to recovery. Curiously, she found she could anticipate almost like clockwork when her growth factors were wearing off, and when it was time for her next dose. Colors, for example, appeared stronger when she had just had a dose of medication, and less intense and gray when she was due for another dose. Although she interpreted this as dependence on the medication, a dependence which potentially could last her lifetime, this she could accept, for the alternatives were to her totally unacceptable.

It wasn't long after that any talk of Karolena needing another graft finally ended, and with her ability to recognize objects continuing to improve and without the burden of crippling headaches, that long-anticipated day finally came when Karolena was able to be discharged home. Early discharge had become the almost universal pattern for the last half century, and Karolena soon found that the psychological benefits of recuperating at her apartment also helped her recovery a great deal.

Technicians at The Winston had modified Karolena's AllSee to monitor her vital signs and perform certain laboratory tests and relay the results to Blütfink's office. In this way, she actually had better and closer follow-up than as an inpatient at The Winston. The AllSee gave her personal training and assistance with object recognition.

Like a prisoner recently released from some Kafkaesque sentence, Karolena found her return home overpowering in intensity. Now, having survived the ravages of pollution, which left her liver damaged but not yet crippled, and having overcome the odds and benefited from an experimental transplant which restored her vision, it seemed to her that she could finally look toward her future with a renewed confidence. It was a time of moral renewal, a reaffirmation of the values she held most dear, and, although she would continue her work at FirsThought as an experimental surgeon once she was more fully recovered, she would work for the health of animals, and no longer use them as unfeeling tools of research.

The first thing Karolena did, once home and alone, was have a sim-cig and a grand size cappuccino. Once she was finished, she was almost moved to tears as she recognized just how much she had lost and missed of life's little pleasures. She found the intensity of relief and of pure joy she experienced at being home again almost too much to bear.

Her first days back at her apartment were both uneventful and just a little frustrating. The memory of her last days and hours there before being taken by ambulance to WCMC still lingered like an invisible veil, reminding her of just how close she had come to death. Making an effort to place negative thoughts out of her mind, Karolena forced herself to concentrate on the positive turn her health has again taken, and how fortunate she was to have benefited from the surgery, highly speculative and experimental as it was. She now realized how much she benefited from Blütfink and Malawassi being aggressive and open to trying new things.

With her visual recognition still incomplete and inconsistent, she found herself dependent on continued use of nerve growth factors. She quickly realized just how much her life, particularly when living alone, had changed. While a patient at WCMC, she had unconsciously become dependent on the nurses to prepare and bring her food, help her out of bed, and provide her with new sets of disposable clothes. Her hospital room had become familiar, by all her frequent movements around, so that she seemed to navigate by measure and by touch, much as did the blind. Now, having been away from her apartment for so long, she could find her way around only with difficulty, needing to learn the numbers of steps and appropriate directions like the blind. Although the times when she could recognize a familiar chair, a cabinet or a door gradually increased, she had not yet advanced to the point where she could trust to her site alone to get around. Her AllSee was a great advantage, providing her with spoken responses on her location, and directions, much like the Seeing Eye dogs of years ago. And her hologram Parrot Renata helped her too, once she adjusted the AI settings to increase spoken interactions.

To make her life at home more facile, Karolena soon went about rearranging her apartment for her convenience of movement. Her house 'bot cleared areas of likely travel such as the halls and kitchen. No heavy objects were left out over which she might trip. Each room now had its own functional AllSee, and Susan helped make arrangements to deliver prepared food and pay her bills automatically.

Within hours of her arrival at home, the intercom rang unexpectedly, notifying Karolena of a visitor. As she was expecting no one, she was surprised, and carefully instructed her AllSee to determine who was there.

"Karolena, it's Rickhard. Can I come up?"

”Rickhard, what a surprise,” she exclaimed, as she realized what a mess her apartment, and she, must look like. “I just got home only a few hours ago, and I haven't had a chance to clean up yet, but you're welcome to come up." She indicted to her AllSee to allow Blütfink entry, then sat down on the couch and waited. She also instructed her house ‘bot to quickly clean up any messes. Renata, her holographic parrot, chirped in the background, seemingly happy at the prospect of having a visitor.

A few moments later, the barking program was activated as Blütfink approached the apartment door. In other circumstance, she would have checked to see who was outside her door by using the video camera, but in her current state that would have been of little assistance. Instead, she had the AllSee certify via the wrist ID who it was that stood outside her door. Once she was certain it was Blütfink, the barking program stopped and the door opened.

Blütfink struggled inside, carrying a large package. As he passed her, he leaned down and quickly kissed her on her forehead. "Welcome home, Karolena. How are you?"

Unsure just how to respond to the unexpectedly pleasant Blütfink, unexpectedly and uncharacteristically pleasant Blütfink, she said, "Fine, Rickhard. Thanks for stopping by.” She motioned for him to have a seat in the living room, and he set his package down on a table top nearby. "To what do I owe the visit?"

“I brought you a little welcome home surprise,” he

told her, gesturing to the box. Renata chirped, "What's in the box, what's in the box," as Rickhard got up, walked over to the table and opened the box.

Despite her limitations, Karolena had no difficulty recognizing a bird cage. Inside, a real, live red and yellow parrot chirped real, live bird sounds, and the sound was a symphony a thousand times more rich and varied than even the authentic recordings Renata was programmed to produce. "Oh Rickhard, how thoughtful," she exclaimed in both astonishment and delight at her marvelous gift. Getting up, she walked over to the cage, and watched the bird move back and forth on its perch, cocking his head this way and that.

"I know you've always wanted a real pet," he smiled. "Isn't it beautiful?"

"Yes, but how, I mean where ...." Parrots as a species had proven unusually sensitive to environmental pollution and had nearly disappeared from existence years ago.

"Let's just say that a former patient owed me a favor. I'm glad that you like it. Here," he said, opening a smaller package, "I also brought along a box of assorted seeds for food. I know it's kind of soon, but perhaps you will give it name."

It I was in a vengeful or comical mood I'd probably name him Larry, she thought, and then answered, "Yes, I think I'll name her 'Corina.'" Renata chirped approvingly at the naming. "Thanks again, Rickhard, I'm truly touched." She walked over and gave him a big hug, and they stood holding each other for a long time, savoring the pleasant feeling of renewed closeness, before Karolena asked, "Aren't I the rude hostess. Can I offer you something to drink, or to eat?" Susan had arranged for her AutoEats unit to be replenished before her arrival home.

"What do you have?"

"Coffee, various teas and soft drinks, juice, cappuccino," she listed, knowing that he would stop her at cappuccino, which he did. She also quietly spoke to her wrist AllSee, telling it to program the house ‘bot and Renata to take care of her new bird.

Karolena ordered two cappuccinos from her AutoBev, via her AllSee, then carefully guided herself to a seat on the couch. Rickhard seemed uneasy as he watched her move, then sat down on the soft end chair nearby. "Anything to eat?" she asked.

"No thanks," he said, glancing at his watch. "I'm not all that hungry, and I have a case to get back to in about an hour. But, now that you're back home by yourself, how will you manage to cook, with all the problems you still have?"

""Cooking isn't than much of a problem. I'm mostly a vegetarian, I’ve got plenty of frozen vegetables, and the AutoEats does a fairly good job of preparing the recipes I’ve programmed in. Susan, Bob Winder's wife has food deliveries set up. Also, I can get deliveries from The Natural Disaster,” referring to a favorite local restaurant of hers.

The AllSee announced that the drinks were ready, and Rickhard got up to retrieve them. Before either of them knew it, almost an hour had passed, and Rickhard left to the hospital, promising to return soon. “I’m very glad that you survived the surgery, Karolena. I really worried about you," he smiled sincerely, then bent down for a quick kiss on her cheek before leaving.

As she closed the door behind him, Karolena thought that this was the first really pleasant encounter with Blütfink she had had in a very long time, and the possibility for more such visits made her feel warm inside.

It was in this way, cheered on by her new pet, and occasional visits by friends, including Blütfink, that Karolena managed to convalesce for several weeks after her discharge from WCMC. Her AllSee read to her often, and Susan Wilder came by occasionally to take her out to lunch and shopping. Although a few friends from FirsThought called, Karolena had not yet decided when, and under what conditions, she would return to work. For now, with her recovery incomplete, the entire issue of career seemed rather premature.

There was also a dark side to Karolena's return home, for she had not at all left her disturbing dreams back at the hospital. Whatever was bothering her -- her liver, her graft, the medications she depended upon, doubts over her future -- her evenings were often an uncomfortable time, filled with apprehension over whether she would again be torn from sleep, her heart racing, her body sweating. Her sleepless nights wore on, each in the same disturbed way, struggling to stay awake and avoiding returning to that uncomfortable surreal land of fear and uncertainty for as long as possible, until, through sheer exhaustion, she could resist no longer, and involuntarily drifted off.

The disturbing dreams seemed to be increasing in both frequency and in intensity. In one of those occasions of a battle lost, soon after falling asleep, her disoriented body lay remote while she experienced yet another dream of fantasy, but this time it was a dream unlike those she had ever had before, a dream of unreal power and a dream of distant travel . . .

. . . Karolena sprinted a few feet forward, fretfully wrenching the necessary impetus with her leg muscles, and, when the moment was right, catapulted herself forward against the earth that held her back and sprang up into the air. Her lithe body strained against the wind as much as her strength would allow as she flung forward and upward, upward toward freedom. The lack of resistance gave her the momentum she required, and she lifted off, gracefully but with power, almost as if the gods themselves had willed the action and had their divine hands underneath Karolena and were protectively holding her aloft. Now the gods served as the wind beneath her wings.

With her hands outstretched, soaring above the trees, Karolena aimlessly circled her house for hours, lazily watching from afar the inconsequential lives of all the microscopic rats that scurried below her. Karolena continued circling leisurely, moving effortlessly among the trees much like an eagle might have, watching, endlessly searching.

Like a goddess, Karolena felt supremely powerful, and she was no longer afraid of heights as she had been in the past. Now, she didn't fear falling, and she didn't even entertain the thought. She now believed herself omnipotent, definitely stronger than those mortals whose trivial lives haphazardly passed far beneath her.

Slowly Karolena moved her arms down toward the earth, and diving from her cumulus springboard, descended into her ethereal swimming pool. Flying low, she headed through the village. In an instant, she landed softly and began walking, and it occurred so naturally that she was left without even a thought that only seconds earlier she had been airborne. A warm breeze blew against her cheeks, the sun felt delicious against her face, and the scent of flowers bathed her senses. Karolena felt happy and uncharacteristically at peace.

A young lady, whom Karolena felt she may have met before, waited for her. She wore a pastel-colored dress and a wide-brimmed spring hat. Karolena asked the young woman for her name, and could see her mouth move in reply, but strangely heard no sound. After a few moments, they began walking together along a row of shops and restaurants with the familiarity of having walked there many times before. Soon, they entered a small country store with a definite old English atmosphere. A bakery filled the front, its glass-covered shelves crammed with cookies, pastries and breads. Other shelves held an assortment of jams and teas.

They went through the shop to the back area, which served as a modest tea room. The room was crowded with small tables but otherwise empty of clientele. They sat at a circular table covered with a blue cloth, and all certainly seemed as neat as her own apartment might be. Tea and freshly baked scones were served without her asking.

A waitress dressed in surgical garb suddenly appeared at their table and asked them if they wanted to try their special today - an English liver pastie. Karolena, never having been one to eat liver, was revolted by the idea and shook her head. The young lady in the pastel dress similarly replied, "No thanks, not yet."

The young lady in pastel mentioned to Karolena an upcoming trip to the US. This would be her first, she told Karolena, a gift from her mother after finishing another year of school. Apparently she didn't really want to go, but had not been asked, and this was upsetting her.

After a while, the conversation abruptly ended. Karolena left the restaurant, ran a few steps, took off into the air and flew again. She could fly anywhere, and was no longer afraid. She could soar up, swoop down, see all, know much . . . Now, she was truly free . . .

Her previous evening's dream had left Karolena exhausted when she awoke. Its inherent meaning escaped her, as if the entire dream sequence had occurred on another world, and in a different language. Still, for some unknown reason, the dream also seemed to make perfect sense, possessing a hidden but vital and inherent meaning, a meaning that must have had a special significance to her and her alone.

Her disturbing nightly dreams were only a mild bother, particularly when compared to her numerous other physical difficulties. Karolena tended to attribute their cause to an unusual side-effect of her surgery. Soon, though, the pattern changed, the dreams became more threatening and violent, and she was awakened in terror several times a night.

When she became convinced that these disturbing dreams would not go away on their own, Karolena spoke with Blütfink about them. Having no background in psychiatry, and having never before dealt with a problem of this nature, Blütfink had little to offer Karolena other than doubting that they were a side-effect of her medications. Neither did Doctors Malawassi and Fromposi, with whom Blütfink discussed the problem, have any helpful suggestions, although they seemed fairly certain the nightmares were not the result of the transplant. Karolena thanked Blütfink for his frequent inquiries and his sincere concern, but declined the offer of referral to a psychiatrist. That was just not her way. Instead, she elected to wait the dreams out, and fully expected them to resolve on their own.

Chapter 18

“So, how's your patient, Karolena Kreisler?" Bob Wilder asked as he passed Blütfink in the lobby of WCMC on the way to a meeting.

"Not much change; headaches, mostly resolved, and just slow progress. She had a mild episode of rejection to the transplant, which we were able to control with a change in medication."

"Yes, I heard about that, and I'm glad you have it under control."

"Anything in particular you want to know?" Blütfink asked. It was unusual for Bob to ask him about the progress of any of his patients, and left him wondering the motive.

Wilder, who had been made aware of Karolena's progress and problem's through conversation with his wife Susan, said, "I heard that she wasn't doing as well at home as you'd like, and I'm a little concerned. After all, we gave special permission for this very unorthodox surgery, and there could be repercussions if there were problems."

"Repercussions? Perhaps, if you got your medical information from the doctors who work so hard at The Winston you'd have a different perspective," he pointedly told Bob, and then, toning down his reply, proceeded to update Bob on Karolena's progress at home since discharge.

When Blütfink was done explaining, a relieved

Bob told him, "I'm glad to hear that Karolena is at least stable. Her success is very important to me."

"I'm sure you want all patients to do well, just as I do, Bob."

"Yes, of course, but even more so in this case."

"I'm afraid I don't understand."

"There are many things scientists like you can't understand, Rickhard. There's an entirely different side to what you do, called paying for it." As Blütfink listened intently, Bob pointedly continued. "Do you remember how the nerve growth factor project was basically a dud for so long that we almost closed it down?"

Blütfink nodded apprehensively, then added, "but when we discovered this new nerve growth factor, you came through with the funding."

"Yes, but only really for one last experiment."

"Karolena?" Blütfink asked cautiously, seeing where Bob was going. Karolena was simply Bob's guinea pig.

"Of course, Karolena. I needed a showcase, and she provided it. Once she conclusively demonstrates a healing property to the nerve growth factor in a human, we'll be able to attract even more research money to fund more of your projects. And if she doesn't, then . . ."

"We're doing everything we can, Bob, believe me," Blütfink reassured him.

"Good. Say, Rickhard, I've told a few interested local business persons about this nerve growth factor from FirsThought that you tested, and it seems they're willing to put in a little seed money to set up a small scale manufacturing plant."

"A manufacturing plant?" Blütfink exclaimed. "But why?"

"You yourself have told me you could only manufacture a limited number of doses over at FirsThought."

"Yes, that's true, Bob. Where is this manufacturing facility to be located?"

"Not too far from here. I've named it Genetic Generics, and I have plans to take it public, if things work out. GG would market nerve growth factor as their first and lead product, a product pioneered by you, Rickhard, and first tested in Karolena. If we're successful, we're going to need you even more."

"In what way?" Blütfink asked cautiously.

“We, for starters, we want you to have a share in the company's profits, a position on the board, and the directorship of research."

Taken aback at the generous and flattering offer, Blütfink soon regrouped his composure, and indicated his willingness to participate.

“Of course, there's really one problem in all these plans to fame and fortune," Bob explained coyly, "and that problem is Karolena. You see, she must do well for us to do well."

"But I think the graft rejection is resolving with steps we have taken, Bob," Blütfink tried to reassure. "She's already been discharged, and is recuperating at home.

“I understand that. Maybe so, probably it will. But

I understand that now she is having problems with disturbing dreams, recurring, frightening dreams. If these are due to some unusual side effect of nerve growth factor, then registration and the license to sell might be delayed, perhaps even denied."

Blütfink knew of Karolena's friendship with Susan Wilder. She must have been Bob's inside source, relaying every problem Karolena experienced directly to Bob. Blütfink reassured Bob of his intent to mobilize the medical and psychiatric resources of WCMC, to help resolve Karolena's problem. He also promised to keep Bob abreast of any change in Karolena's condition.

Blütfink contacted Karolena immediately, and was upset to learn that she still experienced nightmares, almost every night. Yet, despite extensive tests, no real organic cause for the terrifying dreams could be determined. Although Karolena continued refusing seeing a psychiatrist, she did finally consent to allowing Blütfink to start her on a course of mood-altering drugs. Over the short-term, they had no discernible effect on her disturbing dreams, but did manage to make her very sleepy. Their long-term efficacy in eliminating her disturbing dreams was still to be determined.

Chapter 19

During the ensuing days, Karolena was at peace, free from the fantasy life which continued to torment her every night, taunting her with its hidden meanings, taunting her despite the sleep medication and the counseling and the rest, and even despite the significant improvements which continued in her vision. Each evening, Karolena, while waiting apprehensively for her bazaar nightly images to return, pondered their haunting meaning, with the hope that, through understanding could come relief. It was in one of those moments of deepest reflection that an insight finally occurred.

Karolena sat at her bedside, looking out through the window toward the town of Neuse, below. She was used to being able to select whether her window was transparent, or displayed an image of her choice, and tried to make her selection, when she became very sleepy. She lay down and noticed that the scene before her gradually shifted from trees and buildings to something else, a place unrecognized where she saw . . .

. . . A young business student had just finished her last class of the day, and was finally preparing to drive home. After piling her optical texts and notes into her backpack, she paused at the mirror near the classroom door to do a once-over before leaving. About five foot

six, one hundred twenty pounds, the young woman had a healthy, youthful appearance. Straightening her businesslike gray coat over her cream-colored pastel print dress, she quickly brushed her sandy blond hair and put on her favorite wide-brimmed hat, and, liking the image of efficiency and no-nonsense she saw, she strode confidently through the weapon scanner, past a set of paramilitary guards, and out of the building.

Passing the administration building, the young woman stopped to ask a guidance counselor who she was friendly with if she could use her AllSee before beginning her drive.

"Sure, help yourself," the counselor said, handing the small flip unit to the young woman.

Entering the UN ID number for her mother, which would allow the system to ring at her last known location, the "bounce-back" message showed the local newspaper, where the mother worked. Her mother had been working there six months now, six successful months, her first stable position in the year since her discharge from the psychiatric hospital. There, she had been a patient after undergoing psycho surgery, which the state had required after her last bout of acute schizophrenia brought her to such a heightened sense of paranoia she almost killed someone. The young woman knew her mother's threats were harmless and unintentional and that her mother couldn't have helped herself any more than a diabetic could do without insulin. Still, she was glad that her mother's violent, frightening outbursts and disturbing dreams were now controlled. Those terrible dreams, perhaps induced by prior psycho surgery, had disrupted both their lives long enough, and even scared her on several occasional.

Wanting very much to meet her mother for dinner again tonight, the young woman hoped to reach her mother at her office before she left. As her mother's only social contact, she knew that frequent meetings were important for her continued recovery and successful functioning in society.

The young woman also was concerned because her maternal grandmother, an author and psychic who died before she was born, had also experienced hallucinations. Could this problem be inherited, she worried? She found it depressing that she, after having worked so long and hard for her degree, one day might also have to struggle with psychosis, and perhaps be forced by the state to undergo the barbaric surgery, just like her mother had endured.

Strangely, there was no final connection of her call through, and, after clicking the receiver button several times, she no longer even got an "ON" signal. Pressed for time, she decided to try calling from her car and left for the parking area.

The young woman enjoyed the walk to the parking lot along the garden-like path, which paralleled the 250-year-old stone buildings now used by the Science Department. Loose red gravel, unique to this area of England, covered the path, flowers lined the sides, and the trees were alive with squirrels and birds. Today had been a particularly sunny day, and life seemed to spring from everywhere, but now the afternoon sun was beginning its descent, and she felt a bit chilly in the slight breeze.

Trying to be cheerful, she nodded to the campus police and the paramilitary patrols as they rode by. Today, for some reason, her greeting seemed to her forced, an effort rather than a pleasantry. Odder still, the police patrol didn't return her greeting, and instead only stared at her without speaking; their response made her nervous. She also noticed, as she walked, a stranger seated on a bench, a stocky man with pale brown hair the color of birch bark, gray eyes with the coldness of steel, who momentarily looked her way as she passed near. When she looked back at him, the stranger indifferently turned his head and returned to reading from his e-reader. Their unspoken exchange, although superficial and brief, left her palpably cold.

Stopping by the side of the walkway to look at some small red finches which were perched on the railing by the bicycle rack, one bird in particular caught the young woman's eye; it was slightly larger than the others, with splotches of red coloring painted onto its leading wing edges and on its forehead. It's big yellow eyes angled down, and a pointed beak protruded forward. The bird appeared restless as it rocked back and forth on its feet, and as she approached, the bird cocked its head and turned to watch her.

The woman believed since childhood there was a certain intelligence present in animals that humans could never appreciate, a concept not reinforced in biology classes in college. Although her mother agreed with her, her friends and teachers often dismissed these thoughts as unfounded superstition.

As the young woman slowly moved closer to the bird, making some cooing sounds as she cautiously advanced, the bird seemed puzzled but not at all afraid. It continued to look at the woman, tilting his head first to one side, then the other, then responded with a deep, lingering, almost haunting cry. Slowly, it lifted off its perch and circled overhead, as if it were beckoning the young woman to join him, and as it did so, she felt a distinct chill run down her arms.

Off to her right, she noticed that the man who had been seated reading from a tablet had gotten up and now was walking rapidly toward her. He was foreign-looking by the style of his clothes, appeared perhaps ten years older than she, was rough shaven, and muscular. As she had moved to the side of the walkway to let him pass, he seemed to have stared at her face, nodded politely and coolly without saying anything to her, then walked on toward the parking lot. . .

Karolena bolted up in her bed, terrified and cried out for help. Her AllSee popped up and asked her what was wrong. She gripped the bedside with sweaty palms and felt her heart racing. She felt paralyzed, and knew that if she didn't get up and run this moment she would surely die. Then she remembered the horrible dream. Someone was after her. She had tried to fly away and just couldn't lift off. It was SO REAL, as if she could just see it happen. It was a dream, of course, but why then did it seem SO REAL?

Karolena reassured the AllSee, who had responded to her screams, that she was all right, but told it nothing more. Resting her hands on the window sill as she leaned forward, Karolena wondered about the real significance was of this dream and all the other terrifying and strange dreams that she had had experienced since her operation. One thought kept recurring to her, a distinct feeling of realness to the dreams, as if they had actually happened. Further, she couldn't seem to shake the belief, ridiculous as it seemed, that the dreams, and particularly the dream of last evening, a dream different in depth and character and seeming realism from the others, that dream especially had happened, not to someone else, not to her dream-self, but had actually happened to her. Perhaps not to her as Karolena Kreisler, but to her as - - as some other woman. But who?

Karolena stayed by her bedside for several minutes until she had managed to calm down, now recalling a scene with a dead bird by her hospital window. Now that seemed to have been ages ago, and the advancing seasons had changed the landscape quite a bit since then. Most of the leaves had fallen off the trees, and they now stood barren and unshielded against the coming frost. The tree's stick figures interrupted a garish wasteland that had once been covered with life, and Karolena, almost fixated on her terrifying dreams, became more depressed than she had been in a long time.

Chapter 20

It wasn't long before the pattern of the terrifying dreams started to change once again, and Karolena now had to endure several terrifying dreams during the day time. Even more disturbing, some of the more vividly realistic visions were of someone trying to kill her. The memory of each and every dream was now terrifyingly permanent, staying with Karolena long after she awakened.

It was then that, in one moment of unusual clarity at home alone in the evening, Karolena began to lose her vision. It happened suddenly, and it occurred with surprising completeness. Yet, rather than fearing for a return to living in the fog of unrecognized objects, she felt oddly at peace and not at all afraid.

Staring frantically around her room for objects to

recognize, Karolena hoping to reach her medicine cabinet where she stored her nerve growth factor, thinking that another dose would restore her ability to see. As she turned toward where she remembered needing to go, she was startled to see the vague shape of a person standing at a distance. Not expccting to recognize whoever it was, she was startled to clearly see the very woman who was in her dreams.

"AllSee," Karolena cried out, "intruder emergency. Call the police," she screamed.

"Negative. You are alone," the AllSee replied.

The reassurances and contradictions of a machine did little to allay her fear, and she asked, "AllSee, number of persons?"

"One, two, one, ... error," it responded. "Repair has been notified."

The apparition stayed floating stationary in the mist, several feet in front of Karolena, her substance alternating between a solid, corporeal form and the virtual image of a hologram. Fighting to remain calm, Karolena called out, "AllSee, I need to know now if there is an intruder here or not."

For the first time she had known, her AllSee was silent. The apparition slowly floated toward her, reaching out toward her, speaking in whispers to her. "Karolena, Karolena, you know me, yes, you know me. Don't be afraid, Karolena."

"Who are you?" she stuttered, too afraid to move.

"*I am you, and you are me*," the vision laughed, a long, deep, haunting laugh, a sad laugh, a laugh empty of happiness but still full of peace. As the vision began to break up, she smiled, reached out toward Karolena, and said, "*Karolena, please, remember me, so I can live.*"

And it was with those last words that Karolena finally recognized the woman who had appeared at least once before to her, at night while she was hospitalized and awaiting surgery, when she was hoping desperately beyond hope for a donor to become available. And it was at that very moment that Karolena realized exactly who the woman was.

Surprisingly, for what she had been through earlier, Karolena finally was able to sleep that night, for the first time in months, a profoundly peaceful sleep, a sleep without terrifying visions and nightmares.

Later, in the morning, Karolena received a call from Susan Wilder. Susan had been one of Karolena's more frequent callers, although their conversations often were one-sided, and concerned her unstable marriage, or one of her several extra-marital affairs with a string of the world's worst losers. Still, Karolena found Susan amusing to talk to and a loyal friend, and looked forward to her calls.

After some small talk about the progress of Karolena's recovery, Susan asked Karolena if she was interested in meeting for lunch. At first, Karolena objected, not feeling so strong, just weeks after her surgery. Susan, though, insisted, explaining that she thought it would do them both some good. Without much further discussion, Karolena had to agree. She needed to get out of the apartment, if for no other reason beyond her strange experience last evening, the fact that her AllSee would occasionally come back on-line, and cycle in a confused manner between detecting one and two persons in the apartment before automatically requesting repairs and going off-line again.

Karolena suggested lunching at *The Natural Disaster*, because it was familiar, had reasonably good food, a pleasant atmosphere, and was located near her apartment. Susan picked her up shortly, and they found a good spot in the local parking structure, one of the few benefits of the dramatic population decrease due to toxins and the retro infections.

They stood together for a few minutes outside the parking garage, engaged in small talk. All the time, Karolena desperately wanted to talk to Susan about what she had just come to know of the meaning of her dreams, but decided to hold back, at least for now. Getting together right now seemed too soon. Perhaps a more opportune time would develop over lunch. Anything more immediate, Karolena feared, might be perceived as a turn-off by Susan.

They walked the short distance to the restaurant and lined up in the screening cue behind a well-dressed and petite young woman. The popular and trendy restaurant was located in a posh section of Neuse, only a few blocks from the shopping mall. Outside, tastefully done-up accouterments of toxic waste - drums, cans, discolored slicks - ‘decorated' the front and the parking area. A retro negative-only symbol displayed prominently on the door, near a set of credit card symbols. They smiled at each other while waiting in the queue to pass through the security scanner positioned in the restaurant entrance, but, as was the custom, kept their conversation to a minimum so as to not confuse the security-bot. After the woman in front of them wristed to enter, a red light came on over the scanner tunnel, followed by a loud buzzing sound. The maitre d' immediately approached the young woman and said, in as polite a voice as he seemed capable of forcing, "I'm sorry, miss. According to your wrist ID, you're *retro* positive. I'm afraid I must ask you to leave, as this is a retro negative establishment."

The restaurant guard, a dirty looking young man in black overalls and an old army uniform, picked up his Stun Gun and moved toward them. Short and too lean, he was possessed of small, wide set eyes with a vacant stare, with a scar over his lower lip. Saliva dripped from the jowls of his guard dog, tipping Karolena off that it was not a 'bot, and therefore was unpredictable.

"You must be kidding," the *retro* woman protested, visibly agitated but trying to remain civil. "Why, I'm no danger to you or your customers, none at all. I don't see why you have to make an issue of this."

"I'm afraid that this is NO joke. And you're the one trying to make an issue of being able to enter our restaurant, not me. Our customers choose to come to our restaurant because all of our clients and staff are *retro* negative. That's who they want to associate with, eat with, and be served by." The maitre d' nervously pointed to the '**Retro Negative Only**' sign, a bright green notice prominently displayed on the windows, the door, the reservation desk and on the front of each menu. "We're certainly within the law to insist on that." The maitre D's face had a facial twitch which grew more obvious by the minute.

"Why, you creep? Isn't my money good enough?" the *retro* screamed, then began to cry in frustration. "Are you afraid of me? What's the problem?" The *retro* inched forward as she spoke, and then quickly jumped back as the guard dog's loud bark scared her.

"Look lady, this is a *retro*-negative establishment," the maitre d' persisted, again pointing to the green sticker on the door and backing away from her. "What part of NO don't you understand?" he firmly asked, nodding in the direction of Karolena and Susan.

"Where do you expect me to eat? On the street? I'm a citizen too."

"I really don't want to stand here and debate with you where you choose to eat, nor is it my concern. I hope you don't force me to make a scene and have you removed," he told her threateningly, while nodding at the security guard and his dog.

Deciding that to dispute would be futile, the *retro* turned to leave, and said, "Every dog has his day, asshole. See you later." She stuck out her tongue at the maitre d', gave him a foul gesture with her hands, and quickly disappeared down the street.

The maitre d', his face flush and his hands trembling slightly, turned back to Karolena and Susan. He seemed visibly relieved when they had successfully stepped through the security scanner and wristed.

"Sorry for the disturbance, ladies. Welcome to *the Natural Disaster*. Two?"

"Yes, please, for lunch," Karolena replied, then paused and said, "Could I ask you something?"

"Of course," the maitre d' warily said, stretching the space around his neck by running his finger under his collar, then patting his forehead dry with a handkerchief.

"If that *retro* woman had been a guest of mine, couldn't she have eaten with us?"

"Now, ladies, rules are rules. Of course not," he nervously told them.

"Well, I wouldn't have had a problem having her join us," Karolena replied to the maitre d's authoritarian directives, but when she looked to Susan for confirmation and support, she was disappointed.

"I can understand your feelings, and I respect you for them, although I don't share such radical views," he unconvincingly reassured Karolena, then asked accusingly, "You're a foreigner, aren't you?"

"That's not the issue." Karolena protested, making an effort to Americanize her German accent. In a way, the subtle anti-foreigner bias she often witnessed made her appreciate just how worthless and unwanted the retro must have felt.

"Perhaps. Nevertheless, you wouldn't have been able to eat here with that . . . that *retro* as your guest," the maitre d' countered. "I can see you find that disagreeable, but, well, THOSE are our rules, and in THIS country, it's perfectly acceptable. I'm sorry if you find it unacceptable." He started to put the flat screen menus back in their holder.

Placing her hand reassuringly on Karolena's shoulder, Susan pleaded, "Karolena, let's stick to having a pleasant lunch. Don't cause an argument, okay?"

The maitre d' nodded appreciatively to Susan, reached for the menus again, and cheerily asked, "Ladies, do you prefer to sit at any particular disaster *motif* today?"

Karolena looked around at several theme rooms, and then asked, "Do you have any preferences, Susan?"

Susan shook her head 'no,' having no yet gotten over the nasty confrontation any more than had Karolena.

"Do you have a special this week?" Karolena asked. "Something particularly contemporary, perhaps?"

"Why yes, we do. In honor of the IPC spill, today we are featuring the '*Neuse noose*.' Right this way," he said with a pride and flair that made Karolena give Susan a quizzical look.

The maitre d' led them to a special section near the back of the restaurant, where a hologram of a small stream flowed through, complete with a walkway labeled "Neuse River." A yellow jelly slick lay along the bottom of the water, and several very realistic toy animals lay on their backs on the river bank, simulating poisoning. In concert with the true sterile nature of the restaurant and its typically vapid clientele, a peppermint scent emanated from the stream, rather than a toxic stench. Realism, too, had its acceptable limits.

After being seated, Karolena turned to Susan and commented on the surrealistic nature of the art. "Very a . . . interesting."

"Yeah, I guess so," Susan said glumly, as she arranged her napkin, and opened the menu. Although it was printed, in the old-fashioned style, each item had a touch sensor for ease of electronic ordering.

Karolena sensed that now was a good time to change the subject from retros and pollution to something more personal.

The waiter brought bottled water, labeled toxin-free, to their table. Susan ordered an imitation spinach salad with light natural French dressing -- on the side -- and a glass of orange-flavored juice. Karolena ordered the *Disaster of the Day* special, and some cappuccino, which for her was more a coffee-substitute than an after dinner drink.

Susan glumly looked at Karolena, but didn't speak for a long time, apparently still disturbed by the unpleasantness associated with entering the restaurant. Finally, she had seemed to calm down sufficiently to say, "I'm glad that you're getting better, Karolena. For a while there, I was really worried about you ever recovering."

"Yes, I think I am finally on the road to recovery, thanks to the transplant, and to Rickhard." The recovery of her ability to recognize objects had been both unexpectedly rapid and astonishingly complete, especially considering how severe the symptoms were, and had exceeded her and Blütfink's wildest expectations. Although she had wondered whether her recovery was really due simply to a resolution of the viral infection, or to the transplant, she realized there was no way to ever know for certain, nor did it seem important to know. She cared about the results, not the cause and effect of another human experiment. Pausing a moment to consider whether to even bother trying to discuss her continuing problem with Susan, she finally decided to say, "Susan, I really want to know more about my organ donor."

Susan sadly began to shake her head 'no,' and told Karolena, "I don't think that the hospital can release any information to you."

"I know that's probably the official policy, but maybe they can make an exception for me," Karolena insisted.

"Why, Karolena, why? You got your transplant, you got your health again, and soon you can go back to your interesting little job at FirsThought and do interesting things and live in a nice apartment. What else do you want?" Bob had warned her against discussing donor information, although she really knew very few details anyway. Nobody knew anything, as far as Susan could say.

"I don't know what you mean by that," Karolena replied coolly, ignoring Susan's little implied digs, and her condescending attacks on Karolena's personality. Karolena had come to accept that as one unintended but unpleasant aspect of Susan's personality. "But Susan, I really want to know who my donor was. I need to know, believe me."

“There are a lot of things that I would like to know too, Karolena. But I am interested in results, not details. Why, Karolena, what is so important here, anyway? Just explain to me why this is so important to you? Maybe I'm missing something.”

"Okay, I'll tell you why. You know those dreams I get every night? Well, I had another last night, only this time, it was different. I saw her, Susan."

"You saw who, Karolena?"

Karolena related in the greatest of detail that she could remember her most recent dream, then, confident in the meaning of her vision, she told Susan, "I know who that person was, Susan. I saw the person who donated the brain tissue for my transplant."

Susan coughed loudly, and nearly chocked, before taking a long time to catch her breath. "Look, Karolena, you had a dream, a disturbing dream, but a dream never-the-less. We all have dreams, and you've had more than your share of medical problems. Now you're on medication for those dreams. Don't you think it's possible that the medications caused you to have some sort of hallucination?"

"Hallucinations don't occur in dreams, Susan. But I do know that what I saw was real, as real as you are here talking to me, and I know who she was. She was trying to tell me something important when she went away, but she wanted desperately for me to remember her. How can I forget, now, after all this? But I don't think it's enough to remember a person whom I don't even know. I have to know her name. Please, help me, Susan."

"Karolena," Susan said, shaking her head, "I just don't know about you. You're so persistent, especially with something as foolish as this."

Karolena knew, though, in answer to Susan's question, exactly what it was she wanted. Karolena used to think that what she wanted most was a meaningful career, then, after she was graduated from medical school, it was a meaningful relationship, whatever that was. Then, when her sight began to fail and she needed a transplant, she wanted to be well again more than anything else. But now those wants and priorities had all changed and Karolena knew that above all else she had to have the answer to a question she was asking herself every day ever since having her first terrifying nightmare. The possibility even existed - now that she let her reasoning lead her on - that the donor of her transplant wouldn't be dead if Karolena hadn't needed the organ in the first place. That bothered Karolena terribly, damaging her self-confidence further. Now, Karolena needed to find out if, incredible as it sounded, that was true. She felt the same sense of guilt and shame and the same confusion she had felt back at work whenever the issue of fetal research came up. It was the same causality trap that surrounded baby Christopher, and she felt just as bad and just as guilty. Only now, she was the experiment, she was the block of tissue in question.

The waiter returned and set the salads and juice glasses on the table, returning Karolena's attention to the immediate present. Susan was the hungrier of the two, and was the first to peel off the safety cover from her salad bowl and open the tamper cover on her juice. Lying right on top of the lettuce was a *Retro* strip, which remained green, and a Tox strip, also green. Reassured, Susan took a bite. "Hey, this stuff tastes almost like spinach, you know?" Susan smiled.

"No, I can't say that I've ever had the pleasure of eating real spinach. But, I'm glad you like it," Karolena said. Her lunch special was a pasta dish with pesto sauce, and tasted as good as it smelled. She had no idea what it was supposed to taste like, just that she liked it.

"Well, not changing the subject, but WCMC has an agreement with the transplant organ donor pool, and it's a strict policy not to disclose these details to patients or to their families. But," she winked, "under the circumstances, I think it might be possible, as long as you keep my strictest confidence." Susan smiled uncomfortably and shifted around in her chair, then glanced nervously around the restaurant. "I just don't want to make Bob angry, you know."

"Why? Are you afraid of him?"

"No, of course not," Susan quickly replied, then told Karolena, "I think you'll be disappointed, though. My knowledge of transplant donor details is very limited. I probably wouldn't know anything useful to you anyway."

"Maybe so. But, I'll take my chances," she said, fairly certain the contrary would be true. For someone totally unaware of the health sciences, Susan could occasionally be party to some amazing facts.

"Actually," Susan smiled mischievously, "if truth be known, I've already sort of looked up some information on your organ donor." Karolena's attention perked up immediately. "All I can remember showing up on the donor information list from UNOS was that the donor was a person named P. Forest from Brighton, England."

"P. Forest, from Brighton, England, huh. Nothing more? Not even a complete first name?" Karolena asked, disappointed, but now understanding what she would have to do. If this woman, P. Forest, possibly the woman who visited her in a dream state, if this P. Forest died only coincidentally with Karolena's grave need for an organ donor, Karolena could accept that, could live with that. Yet, if this woman died in order for Karolena to live, if her death were not coincidental, then Karolena would have to know that too, and she would have to discern the how, the why, and of course the who, for there would have to have been a person who had arranged everything. She had never asked for such a horrible thing to be done in her behalf, never even implied it. Who could have arranged for something evil like this without her permission and knowledge was a complete mystery. Certainly not her or a member of her own family.

"Sorry. UNOS gives the donating and receiving hospitals very little personal information of the people on both ends, other than what is medically necessary. Of course, the donor was bio-compatible and *Retro* negative."

"Of course," Karolena added, glumly, “and dead.". She certainly hoped that the donor was Retro negative. As she half-listened to Susan, ideas churned in her head about who the woman was who donated part of her brain to Karolena. What did she look like, who were her friends, how old was she, where did she live? The more she thought, the more questions she had, and gradually Karolena began to fixate on the means to learn more about this woman -- including how she died.

"Yes, I guess the donor certainly must have been dead, at least in this case." Susan stared at what appeared to be perfectly shaped simulated lettuce which lay stiffly in her salad bowl, then accidentally knocked her glass over, spilling her drink on the table cloth and onto the floor. "Sorry," she apologized, her hands visibly shaking.

Karolena threw a napkin on the spill, then waited while the wait-bot cleaned up the mess. Karolena could see that Susan was quite disturbed by their conversation, and she had a fairly good suspicion why. Deciding that she had reached the end of useful information for now, Karolena changed the subject again. They continued their lunch, now discussing some gossip around The Winston, how Karolena was getting along in her apartment, and the possibility of Karolena's part-time return to work at FirsThought.

With Susan no longer talkative, Karolena paid via her wrist ID, and Susan and she got up to leave. Having learned as much from what was said as what was not said, Karolena and Susan walked back to the parking structure. Along the way, Karolena offered Susan a sim-cig, and she accepted. She set both to Calming, and they both inhaled as they walked along. A few minutes later, they arrived at Karolena's car on the first level, and after promising to meet for lunch again soon, Karolena got in her car and instructed it to drive back to her apartment. As she watched Susan get into her car and drive away, Karolena had already begun planning the many phone calls and arrangements necessary to make before tomorrow.

Karolena arrived home a ball of ideas, her imagination in a frantic flight, her mind in turmoil, incapable of resisting the thousand urges to test the horrid hypotheses she had formulated during her disturbingly revealing lunch with Susan. What had happened several months ago, back in the hospital, when she was so desperate for a transplant? When an organ donor suddenly became available, she had felt so fortunate, but was she really? And at whose expense? The potential answers filled her with apprehension, but what could she do now with the knowledge? And if she could really do nothing, then why should she even try to find out, if knowing the ugly truth would only lead to needless and useless self-recrimination?

Collecting her composure, Karolena made her decision. Using her home AllSee to access her computer at FirsThought, she ran a web search. Concentrating on news from England, Karolena without much difficulty was able to locate an article describing the death of P. Forest. The P stood for Penny, who was indeed murdered and in an unusual way and for no apparent reason. The article contained little about Penny herself, and certainly nothing that

Karolena could use to know better the person whose death probably resulted in her being able to see once again. Yet, she felt a strange familiarity to this woman, Penny Forest, and it was that compelling but unexplained closeness that initially drew Karolena away.

After an hour searching on the AllSee, and with all her necessary arrangements complete, Karolena felt better. The actions she had taken provided a needed sense of release of her anxieties. Perhaps soon she would know more, she hoped.

Sighing heavily, Karolena walked into the kitchen and took her evening dose of nerve growth factor. The pills were tasteless and easy to swallow, and within a few hours after she took them she typically felt her vision improve. Whether that really was happening, or just perceived to be, she really didn't know, and had no interest in risking finding out. She was no guinea pig.

Karolena considered having something to eat, but didn't feel very hungry, and decided to forgo food for now. Her AutoEats had prepared a steaming cup of cappuccino, which it brought to the living room, and placed it next to where Karolena sat down on the couch. Her bird real Corina was nearby, as was Renata the hologram. There were many evenings, especially the quiet ones when she was alone, and not out shopping, or meeting with Susan or her other friends, when she preferred simply to drink a cup of cappuccino, and perhaps eat a croissant, preferring to have heavier meals more around mid day. Tonight, the cappuccino was excellent, giving her a satisfied smile.

Corina chirped happily, and Karolena cooed, "Pretty bird" in response. The bird moved back and forth on her perch, and played with her toys, a small copper bell and a tassel of seeds on a string. Karolena actually referred to Corina as a her, but she had absolutely no real way of knowing. Karolena watched the bird move around for a little while, finishing off her cappuccino, then lay back on her couch and had the AllSee read to her from a novel she had started long ago, but never finished. It wasn't long before, exhausted, she fell fast asleep.

Chapter 21

Early that next evening, Susan and Bob Wilder stood together in the kitchen food preparation area near their AutoEats unit. After first keying in their solid food choices, they selected beverages and walked over to the dinner table to wait. "I understand you've been seeing a lot of your friend Karolena lately," Bob said, a certain tension in his voice.

Susan looked up, but away, and replied, "Well, of course. We went for lunch again just yesterday. Why?"

"She received a new growth factor during her operation, one of great importance to FirsThought, and

I was curious how she was doing. What did she have to say?" Bob asked.

"Not much, she just wanted to say hello to me, that's all," Susan answered in a subdued voice, staring into her empty plate on the table.

"Your entire conversation during lunch consisted of her saying hello?"

"No, of course not," Susan laughed nervously. "It was small talk, that's all."

"Small talk? So, how *is* Karolena doing?"

"She said she was doing much better; in fact, she might be going on a vacation; she said it was a sudden inspiration."

"Vacation, huh. I could use that. I hope Karolena enjoys herself, wherever she goes," Bob commented drolly.

The AutoEats chime went off, and Susan, glad for the interruption, went to retrieve their dinners. "Here you are," she smiled as she put their plates on the table and peeled off the security tops. Most of the time, Susan preferred to serve the food herself, instead of letting the 'bot do it. Cleanup was always left for one of their bots. "These prepared dinners taste so good, I wonder why people used to make fun of them? Didn't they call them TV dinners or something like that?"

"TV dinners: now that's really an old century term. They probably weren't as good as these are." Bob looked over at Susan, who avoided his glance. He stuffed a large portion of food into his mouth, then tried to get back on the subject. "Yeah," he replied, a few food particles spraying out of his mouth and onto the table top. "We all could use a vacation. It's really very nice to be so independent that you can just take off like that. Where did she say she was going?"

Susan looked askance at Bob, and then stared down at her plate. "She really didn't say, exactly." Susan knew it was a lame answer and didn't look up, afraid to see the disbelief on Bob's face.

The next day, a highly suspicious Bob Wilder called Karolena's apartment. She wasn't in, and her AllSee answered. "This is Mr. Robert Wilder. I'm the hospital administrator at The Winston. Can I speak with Ms. Kreisler please?"

"I'm sorry, Mr. Wilder." The AllSee knew exactly who he was, but didn't have any specific directions for his calls. "Ms. Kreisler isn't in. Can I take a message?"

"Well, I don't think so. You see, I'm calling about some time-sensitive information she asked me to get about a biotech company. I'm afraid that if she doesn't get the information soon, it will be useless, and it could hurt a major client of FirsThought. Perhaps I could send it as an attachment to Ms. Kreisler."

"That might be possible," the AllSee said, aware of the working relationship between Karolena at FirsThought and The Winston. "Let me get the AllSee number of the hotel she'll be staying at for you."

"Thank you," Bob said after the number was transferred, then hung up. He swiped the number into his AllSee unit and was surprised to see the bounce-back location: "Plaza Hotel, Brighton, England."

Bob shook the desk with his fist. "That meddling

bitch." Although he knew he wasn't personally responsible for the donor's death, there was a connection to The Winston. He could see it all now: he could be incriminated, his career ruined, his startup to make the NGF implicated, all he worked for at The Winston destroyed.

Bob's mind reeled and his stomach sickened as he considered what could become an easily misinterpreted trail of circumstantial evidence. Picking up the AllSee, he hit a pre-coded sequence and simply said, "Guess who's going to Brighton?"

Chapter 22

Higher atmospheric turbulence shook the Ilyushin Concordski 211 as it cut through the night sky at Mach 4.2, hurtling Karolena toward England. In those disconcerting moments when the sudden jolts were more marked, particularly up and down, stress on her still-healing surgical adhesions caused headaches. The pain was typically brief but very sharp, and she knew it all too well. The surgeon's scalpel had sliced through her flesh months ago, yet its mark was still there, a constant reminder of just how vulnerable her life was.

Karolena reached for her facing seat back AllSee to check for messages, although she knew that if there had been any the unit would have notified her. As she looked in the AllSee screen, she noticed the reflection of a man sitting across from her seat. He appeared to her to be the "stud" type, and even resembled her friend Larry Summers, he had looked at her one time too many for her liking. Although she didn't think that she would find him interesting, she thought he bore watching.

Opening her briefcase, Karolena pulled out an interesting but bizarre article that had shown up on her monthly biomedical literature search. It appeared in the *Eastern Journal of Comparative and Developmental Zoology*, and involved experimental reattachment of tadpole heads severed and engrafted onto other tadpoles. The researchers used only minimal surgical technique, no micro-vascular connections, no nerve-to-nerve approximations, but instead employed various epidermal and bone growth factors, mixed with some new kind of surgical super glue. Bizarre, she thought, as she considered the analogies to the surgical procedure she had recently undergone.

Karolena planned on jokingly sending a copy of the article to Blütfink, who had once mentioned to her that he wanted to transplant his head onto a young body so he could live forever. Perpetual Blütfink, yuck. Perhaps he would look more appealing in a new body, a new designer body. Now that was something she herself could use, Karolena jokingly thought. She considered asking Blütfink his opinion on the scientific validity of this article when at her next follow-up visit or back at FirsThought, but then decided that it was so ridiculous and impossible that she would only be making a fool of herself giving it any credence. Her self-esteem was low enough, and particularly more so in his presence, and Karolena didn't see any need to help him ridicule her.

Karolena returned the back of her seat to its upright position after unsuccessfully attempting a nap. There was too little time for relaxation on these SSTs, she thought. The transatlantic trip seemed more like a rocket trajectory to her: thirty minutes up, a one-hour cruise with drinks and snacks, then thirty minutes down. She had really not rested adequately before making the voyage this time, but she promised herself that after landing she would go straight to the hotel and lie down; she would need to rest before visiting Brighton hospital tomorrow. She hoped to arrange a meeting with a doctor at Brighton Hospital who had taken care of Penny Forest around the time of her death. Unfortunately, she wasn't certain how exactly to learn who that was.

Less than an hour later, the Ilyushin slipped into Brighton International Airport on a runway which had been specially lengthened to allow for this craft. The plane's elongated composite body approached the airport with a rather severe appearing down tilt angle to cut down engine noise to the cities below. Its leading wing edges still glowed red in the evening light from the heat they had developed from friction on reentry into the stratosphere. Karolena felt a sharp jerk when the drag chute popped open, and waited for the short taxi to the terminal, staring at the nearby city through the tiny windows.

Once safely inside the Airport parking ramp, the IL-221 taxied to its special docking area, where chocks automatically rose from the ground to secure the wheels. A refueling 'BOT immediately connected itself to the lower wing and began feeding the hungry baby a formula of liquid oxygen and nitrozene fuel. Moments later, a JetWay 'BOT positioned itself to allow for the discharging of passengers. Looking out her window, Karolena saw a European Defense Forces tank pull up to the plane to guard against terrorist actions. She noted with some pride that the tank's side lettering indicated it had previously been attached to the Greater Germany Air Base 30 minutes out of London. German armed forces were the major part of the UN peace-keeping forces assigned to maintain order in England after its disintegration into smaller states.

Karolena quickly exited with the other r*etro-negative*s, who deplaned out of the forward door to enter the terminal proper. *Retro*-positives, by generally accepted convention, exited via the aft aircraft cabin door, from whence they were bused to a separate Customs hangar.

Karolena thought about the double sense attached to wristing as she flashed her wrist **UN ID** at the airline door to exit. In one light movement you both increased your level of security, and lowered your level of privacy. Karolena knew that there was no winner in this sort of act, still, she longed for the days she had read about before the new century, long before she was born, when no one knew who you were when you traveled. Now you could know quite a bit about someone if you wanted to: too much, perhaps.

The voice synthesizer connected to the ID scanner at the cabin door asked her, "Karolena Kreisler, is this correct?"

"Yes, it is," she replied, looking down the ramp and into the crowded terminal.

The holographic scanner picked up her image and assured itself that Karolena was the registered passenger she claimed to be. The computer verified her citizenship, that she wasn't wanted for crimes anywhere in the UN sphere of influence, and that she wasn't listed as carrying a retrovirus. Karolena started to leave the scanner when it suddenly began to pick up a variation in the image being recorded. "Wait in place please for internal verification," it blared out at her.

"Is there a problem?" Karolena asked. She noticed that other persons standing around her began to look suspiciously at her and moved away from her vicinity.

"There is no problem, Frau Kreisler," the cabin supervisor reassured her. "The scanner image was malfunctioning - it was fluctuating between detecting one and two persons where there is obviously just one, but it seems fine now. You may go," she gestured forward.

"You may pass," the scanner said, speaking in her language of preference: German.

Flashing her **UN ID** again, Karolena now easily passed through every stage of security and at the baggage carousel she picked up her one case. Then, she stopped at the terminal bar and took a seat at a tiny table near the window looking out onto the runway.

The barkeeper 'BOT approached her table and set down a napkin and menu in front of her. "Drink, Miss?" It was a standard service-sector model, round, four feet tall and painted a cheery red with pin stripes. When she was much younger, the trend was for bots to look move human or humanoid, and to sound more human. People, real people, resented that overwhelmingly, and now bots were in general round-ish and not at all human-like. A few bots could be astoundingly human-like, especially certain personal service bots, but in general they were not welcome around people.

Karolena nodded toward the unit, which began to list the special of the afternoon. The terminal bar offered the usual rums, tonics, fine wines, and nonalcoholic drinks; assorted sandwiches, salads, and light things to munch were also available. Along the bottom of the menu was an array of convenience items: toothbrush and paste, condoms, retro test gum, and generic anti-retroviral drugs. Karolena looked at the last few items and lost her appetite.

"Drink or something to eat, miss?" the unit repeated.

"Do you have nonalcoholic Mai Tai?" Karolena asked.

"But of course. Right away."

After relaying the codes into the AutoBev, the barkeeper 'BOT returned with her virgin Mai Tai. "Here you are, Miss. Do you want to pay by wrist?"

"How else," Karolena answered, wondering if there really was any other choice. No one she knew ever used money, or even had seen some in years. "Yes, please," she said, and waved her wrist ID over a credit scanner. She disliked doing business this way because of all the dangers inherent in exposing one's identity, but generally found it necessary. She had to admit that there were no secrets anymore.

"Are you alone?"

"Yes, I'm afraid so," she sighed, then stared at the BOT, wondering why it was asking so many personal questions. She soon decided it must have been programmed for polite conversation. Her identify, her itinerary and just about everything else about her was known to this ‘bot, or to one like it.

"Are you waiting for a plane?" the barkeeper 'BOT asked, stationing itself next to her table.

"No, I'm just awaiting my limo driver. Thanks," she said, as she activated another sim-cig, this one set for stimulation, perhaps her tenth today. She knew she smoked too much, even though they were listed as non-toxic; she found the smoke relaxing, and kept her mind occupied. The BOT was asking far too many questions, making her suspicious and she wanting to terminate any further conversation. She waved it away.

Shortly, a hologram popped up from her AllSee, notifying her of the arrival of her limo, and a few minutes later, the driver came over to the bar area. She had expected a limo 'BOT and was pleasantly surprised when she got a real person to drive her; it was a nice touch.

The driver helped Karolena with her bag on the long walk through the terminal. They weaved their way past several layers of security, then down to the parking area several hundred feet away from the reinforced concrete roadblocks in front of the terminal. Karolena saw that the anti-terrorist measures here were a degree stronger than at Neuse or at Morristown International Airports, and guessed that they probably saw more action here.

The converted NWO Electrocar that was her limo was in a state of deterioration from overuse and poor upkeep; Looking around, Karolena was disgusted to see dirty mats on the floor, scattered old papers, and even a real cigarette butt, which she had not seen in years. A ragged old flier offered cash for a variety of items: cars, jewelry, mortgages, organ donors, surrogate mothers, sperm donors. After lifting the flier up and examining its not-too-appealing holographic images, she disdainfully dropped it back into its home arrangement on the floor.

"Looks like it's going to be a long ride to the hotel tonight," Karolena said, trying to make conversation.

She got no reply and wondered if the driver didn't hear her, before seeing what was occupying his attention: a string of ambulances rushing onto the runway toward a group of large hangars. "What do you think that's about?" Karolena asked.

The driver held his fingers up to his lips to signal Karolena to be silent, then switched his car radio to the police band. A call for airport security concerned a report of blood seen dripping from the trunk of a maintenance vehicle parked near the long-term parking lot. A body had just been found inside.

"The victim's wallet and wrist ID are missing," a voice on police band said. "It appears the victim was shot after parking his car. We're trying to determine his identity now. We recommend full security alert."

The limo driver shook his head sadly. "I sure hope the guy who did this gets caught. It's just terrible the way so many people are getting killed these days and how all the retros are left to just die like dogs on the streets. You know, things were different back before the turn of the century, . . . "

Karolena looked at him more carefully and decided that he could indeed be that old, then tuned out his dialogue. The reminiscences of old men never interested her. Their ride past decaying landscape was both uninteresting and sad, given the rich history of England before the collapse of the European Union. But that was then, this was now. Although she had never been to this area of England before, she noticed a strange sense of slight familiarity with the landscape.

Arriving at the Plaza Hotel, she paid for the limo in exchange credits via her wrist **ID** and stepped out onto the entrance walk. A few local militia guarded the hotel entrance, and seemed disinterested in her arrival. The driver removed her single piece of luggage from the trunk, and a porter 'BOT helped Karolena take it through the luggage scanner for transfer to her room. Karolena wristed to enter the lobby, then walked through the security scanner, which alerted the desk attendant to her arrival. Karolena was made to go back through the scanner twice, and the second time she thought she heard the security guard say something about the unit momentarily indicating two persons, but she was finally allowed to pass. Nothing works right these days, she sighed to herself.

A recent terrorist poisoning of the Brussels water supply already had the Plaza hotel filled; the resultant population shift moved tens of thousands of Eco-refugees into the city. She was glad that she had made her reservation several days in advance.

Inside, in contrast to the militia outside the hotel, security was very tight, more so than she had ever seen it in any other hotel. Heavily armed private guards with dog-bots patrolled the lobby. Several were seated in the restaurants.

She slowly approached the mahogany front desk, avoiding a team of snarling guard dog-bots. "Good evening. I have a reservation under the name of Karolena Kreisler."

"Certainly, Ms. Kreisler. It's definitely fortunate you have reservations. We're completely occupied," the clerk noted, gesturing to the hoards sleeping in bags on the lobby floor. "You're staying for two nights?"

Karolena thought about this again, and decided that two days might not be enough. "No, I think I'm going to be staying for three. Will that be possible?"

The clerk examined his computers, then her wrist ID information. "You are a German citizen?"

Karolena nodded yes. In the states, admitting to that didn't help, but here, . . .

"Hum, let me check my reservations computer. Ah ha, I think I may have found a way to change things around a bit. I'll text your AllSee when I can confirm this." Giving Karolena a relieved but harried smile, he added, "Enjoy your stay in Brighton, Frau Kreisler. Your wrist ID opens the door to your room." He handed Karolena welcoming information to Brighton and a token for a free drink at the lobby bar, and repeated his wish for her to have a good stay. "And Ms. Kreisler, . . . "

"Yes?"

"Please, only attempt outside walks during daylight hours. And, Ms. Kreisler," the clerk added after looking at her neck, "it's not advised to wear jewelry at any time. No necklaces, no earrings, no rings, no watches, and no handbags, please. It's for your own safety," he warned. "You'd do well to leave your valuable jewelry here in the hotel safe during your stay."

Karolena nodded "yes" and immediately took off her watch and earrings and handed them to the reception clerk. She then went to the lift area, and waited for an elevator up, cautiously looking inside first before entering.

"Good evening, Frau Kreisler. Are you going to your room?" the elevator computer asked.

Somehow the scanner had known who she was, probably by detecting her wrist ID, and spoke to her in German. Karolena was surprised at how far the technology had advanced, even in England. For a moment, she had thought there was someone in the elevator talking to her, and it had frightened her. The voice sounded so real. "Yes, yes, I'm going to my room," she replied, the fatigue in her voice obvious to her.

The elevator knew her room number, ascended to floor seven automatically, then moved laterally to 768. A gray metal door which linked the elevator to her room slid open at her instructions, and the elevator car waited for her to exit. The elevator unit replied, "Voice recognition definite. Your room is confirmed empty; security status is adequate. Good night, Frau Kreisler." Running lights on the floor, resembling a runway, rippled a path through her room. She said, "Good night" and went inside.

Karolena found her room decor comfortable but simple and designed to be clean and efficient. There was a main room with a double bed with floral spread, a desk stand and adjacent desk with lamp, a window overlooking Brighton, and several AllSee units. Off to the side were a private bathroom and a closet. There were no messages or printouts by her AllSee, and her bag had already been unpacked and searched by someone from hotel security.

Karolena showered, then put on a fresh paper jump suit in a style she had chosen from a catalog while still on the plane. Looking in the mirror, she carefully checked the state of her two-week Permaface Makeup, making some minor adjustments. Once she was satisfied, she went down to the lobby lounge for a before-dinner drink and music.

The lounge was a large open area on cut green glass tiles and packed with small glass tables too closely arranged. Karolena ordered a bowl of soup and a salad, pulled out her AllSee, linked to a book she had started to read several times, and read for an hour before going up to her room and bed. Her vision within the last week, and particularly after a good rest, had improved a considerably, and boosted her confidence in her future life and career.

The next morning, feeling refreshed after a good night's sleep, and particularly one free of disturbing dreams, Karolena put on a new set of fresh paper clothes from the hotel shopping mall, and got ready for her visit to Brighton Hospital. Today she had many important questions to ask about Penny Forest's death, and hardly knew where she would begin. She first stopped at the city hall, Division of Vital Statistics. There she found a public secretary, and asked, "I'm trying to learn where I can find information on someone, whom I believe died in or near Brighton approximately three months ago."

"Are you from the police or are you a private investigator?"

"No, I'm neither. Ms. Forest may have had some medical information that is of personal interest to me. You see, in a way we're related. I hope to speak with her treating physician to learn more."

"Oh, I'm sorry," the secretary laughed, as if to dismiss the request offhand. "That kind of information is just not available to the public, especially without," she paused and smiled, "prior approval."

Finding the secretary devoid of subtlety, but understanding her all too well, Karolena took out a 1000 credit note, placed it under the open leaf of a book on the subject of information access, and slid it forward. England was notorious for graft with public employees. "Do you have additional books of this type on public access to records?"

"Yes, I think that we do have just the book you're looking for, Miss . . . ?"

Karolena didn't reply with a name; she only smiled and waited for an indication that all was acceptable.

She almost uttered her usual curse of "Typical English," then felt inclined to hold back, for obvious reasons. Why, she wondered, was it that truisms and characterizations were so amusingly valid?

"Just a moment, and let me see what I can find. Ah, here it is. It's no trouble at all, really. Yes, Penny Forest died almost exactly at the time you specified; apparently she was shot during a robbery. I see that she was treated at Brighton General, where she died. Would you like a copy of her death certificate?"

When Karolena nodded yes, the clerk pressed some touch sensitive buttons. Karolena's personal AllSee unit beeped twice, indicating it had received the document. "Dr. Brian Humphrie signed the certificate at Brighton General Hospital."

"Thank you so much for the document." On the way out, Karolena phoned ahead to Brighton Hospital using her AllSee to clear her path, and, as a fellow physician, was able to secure an appointment to speak with Dr. Humphrie without too much difficulty.

Brighton Hospital was an aging, gray, 27-story inner city facility that stood on a hill just above Brighton University. It had been built years ago, near the turn of the century, for advanced cancer research and treatment after the great plutonium waste spills that caused thousands of cases of leukemia. With the rise of NeoAIDS and the decline of Brighton as a commercial center, it was converted to a retrovirus and trauma treatment center, a fate common to so many inner city hospitals.

Karolena located the tiny reception desk in the cramped lobby. The receptionist ‘bot directed Karolena to Dr. Humphrie's office near the ER, and she started on her way to find him. The haphazard manner in which the corridors were arranged soon caused Karolena to lose her way. Before long, she had to stop in the Medical Records department for directions, where she was helped by a pleasant young lady named Daisy, who was cheerful despite being quite advanced in her pregnancy and appearing uncomfortable. Her faded and wrinkled clothes clearly spoke of low wages and a hard life. With the help of a map and directions provided by Daisy, Karolena set off again to find Dr. Humphrie.

Karolena eventually found the aging outer ER office, and marveled at the difference in health care that still existed between England, WCMC and her German homeland. The strong odors of hospitals, long familiar to her from her own recent long stay, permeated even the cloth of the room, and were mixed with mildew and smog from the city. The equipment was antiquated and the room was crowded and not very clean.

A wide assortment of patients and their families were packed into a waiting room in overflow capacity with too few chairs. There were no tables, no magazines, no flat screen with informative programs or entertainment, and Karolena found the barrenness of it all depressing. She announced her presence as Dr. Kreisler to an actual human receptionist, and stood against the wall, waiting. Karolena had become accustomed to the holographic receptionists at the Winston with their rapid neural network artificial intelligence responses, and she found it hard to accept how much slower and inefficient an actual person could be.

Dr. Humphrie, a very distinguished man probably of Scottish accent, sporting a small red mustache, came out shortly and introduced himself. He wore the traditional white clinical coat, with an old style stethoscope crammed into one pocket; notes and pencils were stuffed to overflowing in the other pockets.

Karolena stood up, extended her hand and said, "Dr. Humphrie, let me thank you for taking your time to meet with me on such short notice. As we discussed on the phone, the circumstances are somewhat unusual, and your candor would be greatly appreciated."

Humphrie took Karolena to his office and freely and openly told her what he knew about the Penny Forest case. He related to Karolena how Penny had been found by the police and taken to the ER essentially dead, and then placed on the donor list, which he assured her was the accepted default practice. Everyone on the planet was default donor, and this had been accepted practice for over 50 years.

Just then, one of the older patients who had been forced to stand for a long time due to lack of chairs finally fell over in a faint. The back of his head hit the metal back of a chair while falling, resulting in a cut his forehead. Blood splattered on the floor, on his face and on the clothes of those who rose to help him, and the scene in its unnecessary total disorganization disgusted Karolena.

"I'd like to review Penny's records," Karolena said, looking back at Dr. Humphrie. Off to her side, the fallen patient was being loaded onto a stretcher.

Agitated at the turmoil and at her request, Humphrie shook his head. "I really can't understand why. And due to confidentiality rules, I can't allow your request to look at any medical records of the deceased, unless her mother authorizes it. And I doubt that she will."

"Because?" Karolena wondered, as she considered how hard Penny's parents must have taken her loss.

"Well, because Barbara Forest is a very strange person. I knew her somewhat well. She used to work here as a nurse, but quit a few years back. She left I think because she had a nervous breakdown. She never came back to nursing, and took up medical reporting for the local e-paper."

Karolena wondered where this was going, and noted that Humphrie had difficulty concentrating, with all the other things going on. "Do you know how she reacted to her daughter's death?"

"Quite understandably, Barbara became extremely depressed after her daughter's shooting, and never really seemed okay after that. Still, she was here only a few weeks ago, I think to look at her daughter's records. Maybe she can tell you something."

"I'll try that. Where can I get in touch with her?"

"She works at the Brighton News."

"Thanks for the information."

"I hope I was of some help."

"Yes you were, although I'm disappointed at not being able to examine Penny's medical records, but I understand." Pausing, she asked Humphrie, "You mentioned a donor list?"

"Yes, as is the custom in your country too, all dying patients are placed on the presumed organ donor list, unless there's a medical contraindication, such as infectious diseases or cancer, of it they're a retro, and then they go onto another list."

"And what organs were donated?" Obviously in this case, part of the brain, at a minimum, Karolena thought.

"I didn't say that any were, just that we followed standard procedures and entered Penny's biotype on the UNITED ORGAN NETWORK available list. Information on actual donation is confidential." Humphrie glanced over to the packed ER waiting room and began to tap his foot against the chair.

She could see Humphrie was both nervous, pressed for time, and apprehensive about something. "Was there anything unusual that you noticed when treating Penny that you think might help me, other than what you would have expected for such a victim?"

"I really can't say that there was." He looked away at the receptionist, then over to the full waiting room, then at his watch, then back at Karolena again. An intake-bot circulated among the patients, reading their writs IDs and collecting triage information.

Karolena could detect some evasion and hesitancy in his voice, but wanted to try one more question, one that had been circulating in her subconscious for weeks. "Can you at least tell me what Penny looked like, and what clothes she was wearing when she was brought in?"

"Yes, I think I can tell you that, but then I really have to be going," Humphrie said, nervously nodding in the direction of the waiting room. "She was pretty, a thin girl, really, with blond hair, and as I recall, she had on one of those summer dresses."

The vision of the woman Karolena had seen in the hospital when wakened from sleep after her surgery immediately came to mind, lending support to her frightening suspicion. Feeling that she was at the end of useful conversation, Karolena thanked Dr. Humphrie for his time, and left. She then headed straight for the medical records department.

Karolena found Daisy right where she had last seen her, and started a conversation. Penny's medical records would reside here, and Daisy would have access, Karolena knew. If she only were given the opportunity to explain her particular situation, Daisy would understand and perhaps help her. Looking for an opportunity, Karolena, played the lonely tourist and suggested meeting Daisy after work for some tea. Daisy accepted.

Karolena called *Brighton News* next, looking for Barbara Forest. She wanting very much to talk to Barbara about her daughter Penny, but simultaneously feared meeting Barbara, and imagined how easily and how quickly that a conversation between them could become strained. But there were still things she had to know.

The operator at the Brighton News told Karolena, "I don't think Barbara Forest works here anymore. Let me connect you with the City Desk."

The City Desk editor picked up the phone, and Karolena again asked for Barbara Forest.

After a short silence on the phone, the voice curtly replied, "She no longer works here. Sorry."

"Wait, please. Do you know how I might get in touch with her? Her number is unlisted." Something was wrong, Karolena could sense it.

"I think she moved. I really don't know. Sorry." The line went dead.

After five p.m., Karolena met Daisy at the employee's parking lot. As they drove to a small restaurant Daisy had chosen, Karolena took the risk that Daisy could be trusted, and explained just what she was looking for. When Daisy seemed taken aback, and perhaps a little frightened, Karolena calmly showed Daisy one month's equivalent of salary, and waited for the return smile.

Karolena, inexperienced in these matters, and occasionally a poor judge of character, at least in men, soon found out that she had made a mistake here. After a short and uneasy serving of tea and scones, punctuated by long periods of silence, Daisy spoke. "I'm sorry, but I still feel uncomfortable about letting you look at the records of a deceased person, and one not related to you at that. If Dr. Humphrie can't help you, there must be a reason. Don't worry, though, I promise not to tell anyone at the hospital that you asked me to do this."

Karolena surmised that Daisy would maintain her word about keeping her confidence, and smiled politely. "Thanks for your help, anyway. You can still get in touch with me in the usual way, in case you reconsider," she said, and they exchanged info by touching their wrist IDs together.

Although discouraged and disappointed at not being able to examine Penny's hospital records, Karolena at least had tried to find out more. Seeing no point in staying in Brighton any longer, Karolena returned later that day for North Carolina and FirsThought.

All along the return trip to Neuse, Karolena thought about poor Penny Forest and how terrible her mother must have felt after learning of her death, however it may have occurred.

The short flight on the SST from Brighton to North Carolina was uneventful, and after the customary long wait at customs, Karolena took a cab to her apartment. She immediately went in her room, changed into paper night clothes, and lay down, and sleep came instantaneously to her tired body.

Chapter 23

The sudden and impulsive trip to Brighton, short by time but long by distance, left Karolena with more unanswered questions than answers. She regretted not knowing much more about her graft donor than she knew before leaving, and wondered if she had better planned beforehand whether she could have learned more about the strange woman whose body part she apparently now carried within her.

Neither did the unsuccessful attempt to discover who Penny was relieve Karolena from her haunting dreams. Karolena soon discovered that, not only did her painful dreams continue, but they now changed character in a disturbing way. The dreams displayed more and more detail, as if scripted by a psychotic artist who had patterned her nightmares from a surreal painting, their oils mixed with the blood of terrifying realism and an ominous feeling unlike any dreams she had experienced in the past or had ever heard of.

At times, Karolena felt as if another personality were actually at work inside of her -- not in possession of her will, but more like making subconscious suggestions. Now constantly reflecting on the inner meaning of what she was experiencing, and fearful as each night approached, she became frightened by the possibility that she was carrying, not just the memory, but the actual part of another person's consciousness around with her. Was this due to an adverse effect of the nerve growth factor - a distinct possibility in itself, or to the actual presence of the graft. As she considered these questions, her mind shifted in and out of awareness, until she could see herself back with the woman who apparently was Penny Forest, walking toward some as of yet unknown parking lot.

. . . In some ill-defined way, Penny was bothered by the encounters with the birds along the walkway, and with the strange man who passed her by. She hurriedly got in her red NWO Coupé and immediately started the electric motor with her wrist ID. The car's artificial intelligence unit quickly recognized her identification, and gave her access. "Greetings, Penny. Notice: there is only one hour of driving time left before needing a recharge."

"How could that be? The car's been charging all day?"

"Checking." The unit paused, then replied, "Charge cord failure. What is your destination, please?"

Thinking for a moment, she decided to ask a friend of hers at the apartment building where she lived to look at the cord. She lived less than a half hour away, and apparently had more than enough battery to get there. "Home," she commanded the unit, then looked out her windows and around the parking lot. Fortunately, there was no sight of the strange man who had been watching her. A local road map, with a blowup of her particular location flashing, displayed on the dash screen.

Releasing the defective charge cord, Penny backed up with a sharp jerk, steered the car into the street and turned south toward her apartment, unconsciously driving a little faster than usual. After waiting a minute, a small tan ElectroVan followed her out of the parking lot and into the street from a distance; she barely noticed it in the rear-view mirror.

In another ten minutes Penny was out of the city and nearing her apartment building. Turning onto a small street near a strip of farm land, her mind concentrating on a lengthy class assignment, she glanced into the rear-view mirror. That's strange, she thought, isn't that the same tan-colored van I saw parked back at the University?

Slowing only briefly to make a tight turn, she accelerated at the first opportunity, triggering her car's logic unit. "Careful, Penny, that turn was approaching the safety limit and could result in an accident and injury. Also, you now have only ten minutes of battery time left. You need to consider stopping for a recharge before proceeding. My calculations indicate that you do not have enough range to reach home."

Nervous and preoccupied, she wasn't paying complete attention. "Acknowledge, please," the logic network said.

A sickening feeling, the gut-wrenching fear of panic, overcame Penny. Somehow she knew who was in that van -- it was that strange man, and she knew that she had to get away, quickly. Her eyes began desperately scanning the road for a police car, for traffic, for a crowd of people to safely surround herself with, and terror gripped her as she realized she was absolutely alone. She pressed her red alarm button, but it did not respond. She asked her car to call the police, but it did not respond.

Penny watched the ElectroVan following her from a block back, and after making another rough turn, the ElectroVan accelerated right toward her, rounding a corner, outside of her rear view mirror's site. She again tried using her car's AllSee to contact the police, but it wasn't functioning correctly. About a half kilometer away down the street and to the right, she spotted a food market, and accelerated in that direction.

Trying desperately to turn her car into the market parking lot, Penny just about made the turn when a school bus full of children suddenly crossed her path to her right. The bus forced her away from the entrance to the parking lot, and she barely avoided an accident. Her eyes flashed up to the front and then back to her rear view mirror in a staccato of terror, anxiety gripping her stomach, her head swimming, a powerful sense of nausea making her want to vomit. Then suddenly, there was no tan van. Maybe, she hoped with a sigh of relief, just maybe she had managed to lose him. .

.

Fear pulled Karolena back to reality, and she found herself back in her own home in Neuse, sweating and feeling terror stricken herself. She wondered what Penny feared, and what danger Penny had been in. Was this dream her final flee from death's grip, or a problem earlier in her life?

For several nights in a row, Karolena tried to wall the disturbing dreams off. The visions and dreams proved stronger than she, and they remained as insistent as ever. Although the dreams were frightening and often terrifying, there was no direct communication, no demand, no direction from Penny, and unfortunately no clue to ending the dreams. Finally, assuming that the dreams were related to the presence of the graft, Penny's graft, Karolena decided to attempt to try placating Penny. Although she had no idea what Penny would want, other than obviously not wanting to have died, Karolena felt it was an approach that she should try. Certainly, up to this point, nothing else had worked.

Chapter 24

While seated at her desk at home the next day, Karolena heard the beep of her pocket AllSee. Flipping open its top, the unit announced that she had a message waiting. Karolena touched the "display message" area, and was surprised when she read:

To: Kreisler, Karolena uncus212-22-36543x
From: Bob Wilder, Administrator, WCMC
Subject: Annual Dinner Dance
Message: Please plan to attend this annual event honoring the staff and volunteers of The Winston. We'll also be keynoting select patients such as yourself to represent to the media the dedication and medical skills shown by our employees. Please contact my office for details.

Karolena was of course interested, although she thought it rather odd she had been invited. Assuming that Susan Wilder was involved, she contacted Bob Wilder's office to find out more details.

"Yes, hello, Dr. Kreisler, this is Paulette Whitness, executive secretary to Mr. Wilder. We would like to officially honor you as representing the success of the transplant program."

It sounded to Karolena as if Paulette was reading

from a script, but she listened anyway, waiting for her to stop on her own.

"In addition, after the various awards honoring our hospital employees, we will be asking you to take part in an interview with a member of the international press service. This would be a way to highlight the organ donor shortage problem and build better international cooperation," Paulette continued." Would you be able to attend, Dr. Kreisler?"

"Possibly," Karolena answered cautiously. "When would the event be?"

"Next Friday."

"Let me check my schedule . . . " Karolena consulted the calendar section of her AllSee, then replied, "Yes, Ms. Whittles, I think I'll be able to attend. You can plan on it."

"That's Whitness, not Whittles. But, there's no need to apologize. I'm sorry to say it happens all the time. Anyway, I'm glad you'll be coming to the awards banquet. See you then."

Perhaps too coincidentally, that afternoon, Larry Summers called to say that he heard that she was being honored at the banquet and asked if they could go together. She accepted, as she did enjoy his company and wanted to see him again.

On the evening of the awards banquet, Karolena dressed in a new black crepe paper party dress, with a matching set of dark red earrings, necklace and shoes. It seemed perhaps a little too serious for the occasion, but, not having attended an awards banquet at WCMC before, she wasn't sure and felt more comfortable playing it safe. Besides, she knew she always looked good in black, and the little hints of red helped pick up her color.

Larry picked her up a few hours before the dinner. He seemed to Karolena to be more outgoing and complementary than usual, which certainly pleased Karolena. After parking in The Winston's secure underground garage, they walked together to the service elevator and went inside. The elevator greeted them both, closed its doors, and started up. Karolena immediately became aware of the irritating odor of oil and rust and mildew inside the garage elevator. It seemed such a telling contrast to the flashy image The Winston wanted to portray, that they could let slip so minor and so easily remedied a detail. The elevator's paint was peeling, imparting to Karolena an uncomfortable, closed-in feeling. The control panel of pressure-sensitive buttons was visibly damaged by vandalism in several places and scarred with indecipherable graffiti. The AllSee in the elevator automatically directed them to The Penthouse, the location of the banquet. Their voyage upward began with an uncomfortable jerk that jarred her abdomen. The ride made Karolena feel even more claustrophobic and she found herself fighting against the urge to stop the elevator and get out.

As she listened to *inconsequential* music droning on in the background, Karolena couldn't help but feel mildly annoyed and uncomfortable in some ill-defined way, although she attributed her feelings to stress from her continued difficulty sleeping well. Halfway up the building, the elevator unexpectedly stopped and the doors opened. Two workmen waited outside next to a roller cart, piled high with seven foot-long body bags, each obviously full. It wasn't long before Karolena recognized the bags as being similar to those stacked at the nightly pickup point near her apartment for the city's homeless. The top, sides and end of these bags, though, were marked with the internationally recognized *Retro-negative* symbol, suggesting probable safety in handling. Karolena moved a little back into the elevator and to the side, and Larry, appearing very uncomfortable, nearly hid behind her.

"Sorry, lady," one of the men gruffly apologized, after looking at the upset expression on her face. "We was waiting for an empty one to go down to the incinerator." The workers looked at each other, then laughed coarsely and waved her on.

Larry nervously pressed the "Door Close" button and then the "P" button several times, and as the doors slowly closed, Karolena moved more to the side to avoid the stares of the workmen. A momentary shiver passed through her body.

The elevator continued up for what seemed like an eternity before opening onto the penthouse deck. Karolena felt relieved as the door opened, exhaled deeply and they gladly stepped out of the elevator as quickly as possible. The doorway area itself was crowded with people who nearly prevented Karolena from exiting, and she almost had to push her way into the Penthouse foyer. Once in there, a receptionist checked Karolena's and Larry's names off a long list, compared their holographic images and ran their wrist IDs through a scanner.

"Thank you for coming, Dr. Kreisler and Mr. Summers," the receptionist-bot smiled, politely. "Mr. Wilder is expecting you." Please step through the metal detector, and hospital security will take your coats on the other side. The party is off to your right."

Inside the spacious penthouse, the awards banquet was already taking off into the "Hyper" business mode. Pushing her way through the crowd at last, Karolena met Susan Wilder, dressed in a low-cut evening gown of black chiffon, with a matching set of pearl necklace, pearl bracelet, flat-black metallic wrist ID and matching earrings completing her outfit. They both seemed momentarily aware of the vague similarity of their outfits, but there were enough differences so that they didn't appear like twins, nor want to run home and change.

Susan introduced Karolena to several of her friends, none of whom Karolena knew, and quickly forgot their names. Larry was typically shy and silent, and seemed content just following her around.

"Susan, where is Bob?" Karolena asked as she looked around.

"The last time I saw him, he had wandered off to talk to the administration gang," she shrugged. "I think they went over to the sushi table. Why, what do you need him for?" As soon as Larry heard sushi, and Bob, he excused himself and took off too.

"Oh, I just wanted to say hello, that's all. And of course to find out what he wants me to do tonight," Karolena said. She noted Susan's possessiveness, but let it pass. She, unlike many at The Winston, was definitely not a threat to Susan. The likes of Bob Wilder would be the last person she would be interested in having an affair with. She had hoped to meet up with Bob early on, hoping he would give her the courtesy of a briefing before asking her to speak. Karolena had already asked Paulette for more information on what The Winston was interested in her saying and not saying to the foreign reporter, but had not gotten a reply.

Toward the elevator entrance, off to the side near one of the security surveillance cameras, something subtly odd brought Karolena's attention to an older woman. Her style of clothes was slightly out of date -- a casual blue dress with a gaudy scarf draped over her right shoulder, and flat white working pumps -- and not at all in the fashion trend of the US. The woman appeared to Karolena to be rather thin and ill-looking, and slightly agitated, and although Karolena couldn't place this woman, she felt a vague familiarity upon seeing her. She also experienced an unexplained uncomfortableness, imprecise and free-floating. It almost seemed to be a warning sign, and it's compelling nature was such that Karolena was reluctant to simply dismiss it.

Although Karolena asked several people about the woman in the blue dress, no one seemed to know who she was. Karolena followed the woman with her eyes as she retreated into the background, and Karolena was drawn to look her way from time to time.

After not being able to locate Bob Wilder, Karolena found a quiet area near the wall. Soon, Susan joined her. "Why are you hiding here near the back, Karolena? You're the star of the show, don't you know?"

"No, I didn't know. Actually, there seem to be several '*stars*' here." She preferred to be reclusive at parties, having always found socializing to be a rather difficult chore. She avoided notoriety and preferred to just be by herself.

"Well that's true." Susan seemed about to say something, but her thoughts interrupted her before even starting. "There's Bob now," Susan said, pointing over to some men huddled in the corner.

"Yes," Karolena agreed, "of course," as she instead found herself again staring in the direction of the older woman in the blue dress. At first Karolena couldn't see her, then spotted her standing alone by the elevators, holding a drink in one hand and a plate of food in the other. Something deep within Karolena felt it important to watch this person. "Who are all those people with Bob?" Karolena asked.

"Bob is with the top management of the hospital, the department chiefs, and some representatives from the National Medical Insurance fund," Susan waved her hands for emphasis.

"Tell me, Susan. Who is that older woman in the blue dress standing alone by the elevators? I've asked around, but no one seems to know." Karolena didn't want to admit that she got a bad feeling from that person, although she had been watching her carefully.

"Oh, her. That's Barbara Farmington, the foreign correspondent Paulette told you about. She's visiting from England to get material for a story about international organ exchange. She called me several weeks ago asking if The Winston had any experience with human organs originating from England. I looked up the information in our UNITED ORGAN NETWORK log book, and I found that you had been our most recent recipient. The reporter asked to meet you, I had Paulette ask your permission, and the rest is history."

"But no one from the hospital has given me a press briefing." Karolena protested, nervously sipping from a glass of champagne she had taken from a serving tray, and puffing on a sim-cig. "In fact, I'd rather . . . "

"We will, just give us some time," Susan reassured Karolena.

Always acutely aware of her liver problems, Karolena usually didn't consume alcohol. Tonight, Karolena, perhaps as a reaction to her nervousness, had already had two glasses of champagne. Even half a glass would have been more than enough to have a dizzying effect, although today the alcohol was having a paradoxical effect, a dangerous, destabilizing influence.

While attempting to politely listen to Susan discuss this evening's agenda, Karolena had the opportunity to say hello to Deborrah, the transplant coordinator at The Winston. Conversation at the party suggested her to be Blütfink's current live-in. Karolena saw at once that there were definitely qualities that would attract the likes of Dr. Rickhard Blütfink to Deborrah -- former surgical nurse extraordinaire. She remembered how Blütfink had jokingly told Karolena, while they were still dating, how an outstanding location of adipose tissue and a willingness to please had earned Deborrah the title, 'Beaver of the Year.'

"Oh, Ms. Farmington . . . " the voice rang out from across the room.

Barbara turned quickly to find Susan Wilder bearing down on her with someone else close in tow. "Ms. Farmington, here's the person you simply must meet. I know you came all the way from England to interview her. Well, this is the lady, Ms. Karolena Kreisler."

Farmington had already started to take Karolena Kreisler's hand when the color suddenly drained from her face. A champagne glass she was holding fell loosely from her hand and shattered on the floor, staining the bottom of her dress with a light red color. It took more than a few moments for her to recover her posture, and she apologized profusely, then took a napkin and nervously wiped some drops that spilled onto Karolena's clothes.

Finally taking Karolena's hand, Barbara said in a rather flat voice, "Pleased to meet you, Ms. Kreisler. Susan has said so much about you."

Karolena smiled politely but felt extremely uneasy with this woman, who obviously was having extreme difficulty retaining her own composure upon meeting

Karolena. For some reason, she got that sense again that there was something familiar about her. At the same time, something was just not right about her. Karolena was quite certain they had never met. She almost never had such strange feelings about strangers she met, and was a little surprised.

"I'm so glad that I've got the opportunity to meet you and talk to you. My newspaper sent me here to get a story about the importance of international sharing of organs for transplants," Farmington said.

"Yes, Susan told me," Karolena replied coolly, trying to better size this woman up. "Organs certainly are a scarce resource."

"I thought it might be a particularly effective story if I spoke with the recipient of an English organ." Ms. Farmington slowly eyed Karolena from top to bottom, her face bearing the traces of an ugly sneer.

"So I've been told, Ms. Farmington." Karolena felt increasingly uncomfortable about the situation, but couldn't say why. Her instincts were crying out that something was wrong, and she had to fight to repress an almost uncontrollable urge to run. But, as a representative of The Winston, she needed to cooperate and remain civil. "Well, I'm available to discuss this if you like. When would you want to conduct the interview?" Karolena felt almost smothered and had to fan the front of her face. She quickly reached for a glass of sparkling water as a server passed by, hoping it would settle her a bit.

"Right now would be fine. Perhaps we could sit and talk. I have a Voice Transcription Unit right here with me." Barbara reached into her purse and pulled out a sleek, blue plastic unit with an interesting color pattern. Most people Karolena knew simply used their own AllSee units.

Farmington's face was completely serious and devoid of emotion, and looking at her made Karolena feel just a little threatened, in some non-specific way.

"As you know, the exchange of organs between our two countries is growing. Susan has already told me a great deal about the workings of the UNITED ORGAN NETWORK, and how this hospital participates. Her husband, Bob Wilder, whom I understand you know," Farmington smiled at Karolena, "has already told me all about your problems with financial reimbursements in the States. And Dr. Blütfink has briefly taken the time from his very busy schedule to tell me a little about how transplant surgery is performed. Apparently he had primary responsibility for your surgery."

"He participated, but I think Dr. Malawassi had primary responsibility," Karolena corrected.

"I see," Farmington said, noting Karolena's less than enthusiastic response. "Well then, perhaps I can interview Dr. Malawassi another time. That still leaves the aspect from the individual patient, and that's where you come in."

"What would you like to know?" Karolena asked, looking at the time on her AllSee and at the door several times.

"Can you tell me what's it like to be carrying another person's organs, parts of someone else's body, inside you?"

Although the nature of her question was tactless, Karolena kept her composure, and replied, "I'm certainly grateful to have had the transplant."

"I'm sure you are," Farmington said, coolly.

"I had a viral infection of my brain, I lost my sight as a result, and this operation saved my life."

"I've already been told that, Ms. Kreisler, but I guess what I mean is this. If it weren't for the donor's death you wouldn't be able to see, now isn't that true?"

"I can't say, really." She could in fact say, but truly resented this woman's unsavory insinuations. She really had few choices – get the transplant and see, or be blind.

"Oh? Why?" the reported asked Karolena.

"Because I don't think about it much in that light. I'm grateful, of course, for having received the gift; after all, it's made me whole again." Her undefined feelings of both strange familiarity and discomfort with this woman continued to grow, reminding Karolena over and over that something was just not right. If she could only place it . . .

"I really don't understand how you can tell me you 'CAN'T SAY,' when you know that to be true," Farmington persisted, irritation growing in her voice. "Well, perhaps you could answer this for me. Do you think the converse might also be true, I mean in an existential sense, of course?"

"Converse? I don't understand you," Karolena said, warily, not sure where this discussion was going.

"Well, the converse is that the donor wouldn't be

dead if you hadn't needed the organ."

"Of course not, that's utterly ridiculous," Karolena nervously laughed. "As a matter of fact, Mrs. Farmington, I think you have a hell of a lot of nerve even suggesting that. I mean, are you implying a causal relationship? If you are, I think that you're sadly mistaken." Karolena angrily said. Several people standing around them stopped their conversations and stared at Karolena.

"Look, I'm a reporter, and I'm only looking for interesting angles. That's all," Farmington shot back. "You say *GIFT*," she pressed on, her voice rising as she glared at Karolena. "Well then, does that mean that the organ was donated, not sold or taken?"

"Of course it was donated. What's the matter with you, anyway? I don't really know much about the donor. We're not told, and we don't ask. It fits, it works, it's *retro-negative*. What else is there to know?" Karolena drained her champagne glass, hoping that the interview would be over soon.

"Well that really does depend on what interests my readers."

Unexpectedly, Karolena felt a strong grip on her upper arm. Looking around, she saw Susan holding her. At first she was annoyed, and then felt relieved as she realized she had found an excuse to get away from the reporter, if even for a moment. She needed a breather to think.

"Come on," Susan said, propelling Karolena across the room. "Bob wants to show our Board of Directors how well you've recovered from . . ." Susan waived her hands in the air "from whatever kind of brain transplant it was you had."

Something suddenly awakened deep inside her, a fear, a painful but subconscious remembrance, caused Karolena to react to Susan's grasp by firmly digging her fingernails into Susan's wrist. "Hands off." she yelled at her.

Susan yelled out and grabbed her wrist. "Ouch, that hurts. Hey, I was only taking you over to Bob. You said just a few minutes ago that you were looking for him. I didn't mean to startle you or anything. Really."

Realizing that she had overreacted, Karolena said, "I'm sorry, but I don't like it when people grab me like that." The feelings she had just experienced were clearly not appropriate for the circumstances, yet her over-reaction had happened automatically. Although she couldn't understand what she was feeling, she wanted to find out. She did know in the past that when people had held her and tried to move her around at parties, she had never had a problem. Now, it seems her personality had definitely changed.

Susan nervously tried to downplay the incident, and quickly apologized, explaining that Karolena's interview seemed to be taking a confrontative turn. She had thought it would benefit from an interruption.

"Susan," Karolena admonished, "I was speaking with that woman reporter from England, and your grabbing me by the wrist startled me. Your interruption, though, really was welcome, believe me."

"That reporter from England gives me a strange feeling, too. I'm glad I don't look weird like that,"

Susan attempted to laugh.

"Now, actually, I want to go home. I'm still not feeling very strong yet." She had an almost irresistible urge to run, and wanted in the worst way to get away from the banquet and far away from The Winston.

"If you don't feel well enough to drivc, I could take you home. I am sure Larry could drive you too. But, if you can, please wait just a few minutes more, until after Bob introduces you as an honored guest. I'll have him put you on first so you can leave right after. Think about it, Okay?" she smiled reassuringly.

Karolena smiled weakly and told Susan, "Okay." She definitely didn't want to cause a scene, or raise concerns about her health when her purpose here was to illustrate how well her transplant had made her.

Standing near the podium, someone from hospital security whispered something into Bob's ear, and Karolena overheard him reply, "Yes, I guess so. She is kind of eccentric, now that you mention it. Leave your security people with me. When the booze flows, some of our more infamous guests might need a little 'assistance' leaving early." Bob smiled lightly, and then returned to his guests.

In a few minutes, Paulette Whitness announced over the public address system: "May I have your attention, please. Mr. Robert Wilder, our hospital administrator, would like to say a few words about tonight's activities." Looking toward Bob for approval, she said, "Mr. Wilder."

"First, I want to welcome you all to the Second Annual Medical Center Appreciation Dinner," Bob oozed from the podium, the excitement in his voice contagious but forced. "This is our yearly way of saying thanks for all the efforts you have made to further health care in Winston County." He smiled at the polite applause and waited patiently for it to die down. "I would like to acknowledge our fine medical and nursing staff for their outstanding efforts. We live in a particularly trying time for health care. Those who work in any facility, *Retro* positive or *Retro-negative*, certainly deserve our support and gratitude," he praised, then turned and clapped at the senior nurses congregated near the front.

As Bob read off the list of those being honored, Karolena looked around for Farmington, but couldn't find her. Susan moved to Karolena's side and whispered, "It's kind of boring, isn't it. Don't worry, this shouldn't take too long."

"And finally we would like to honor our patients, to whom we owe our very existence," Bob continued. "Exemplary among them is our own Dr. Karolena Kreisler, a surgeon with FirsThought Scientific, who is here tonight." Bob reached out his open hand toward Karolena and smiled.

Karolena returned the smile and nodded her head at the polite applause. She wondered whether, if she hadn't also worked for Blütfink or FirsThought, she would have been so honored.

"Karolena signifies the new spirit of international cooperation in the organ donor area," Bob continued. "This international cooperation is increasingly important, given the organ shortage that exists everywhere. We're pleased to have Dr. Kreisler a patient, and to have her continue to receive her outpatient follow-up care at The Winston also, under the expert direction at Winston Transplant Associates."

Upon hearing his group's name, Blütfink enthusiastically joined the applause, and gestured proudly to Karolena and Bob.

After several more minutes of awards and honors, Bob said, "And finally, I've saved the best news for last. I have an important announcement to make." Extending his hand toward Karolena, he said, "Let me just say something about Karolena before I start the main part of my presentation."

Karolena was surprised and edged toward the side wall. She could only hope and pray that whatever he would say wouldn't be too embarrassing.

"Karolena came to The Winston one night suddenly blind, stricken with a vicious viral infection that crippled her ability to recognize what had been even the most familiar of objects. Up to now, despite all the miraculous information that medical science had learned, we would have had nothing to offer her, and her life, her career would have been tragically changed forever. Fortunately, we were able to help her."

Everyone had turned toward Karolena, and she blushed self-consciously.

"A significant part of Karolena's amazing recovery that I just mentioned was directly attributed to a new front-line, state-of-the-art nerve growth factor. I'm proud to say that the pioneering research effort on that very factor took place in the lab of Dr. Blütfink at

FirsThought." Everyone's attention was directed over to Blütfink, momentarily sparing Karolena from all the stares.

"There are several areas of research here at The Winston that we're developing in cooperation with FirsThought Scientific. Perhaps it would be better if I asked Dr. Blütfink to comment." Bob motioned for Blütfink to take the podium.

After pausing for some polite applause, Blütfink said, "Research at FirsThought is concentrating on developing nerve growth factors. As you may know, nerves are notorious for their poor regenerative ability." All attention was fixated on Blütfink, as if he were about to transmit the very words of God.

"Nerve growth factors may be useful for nerve injuries such as traumatic nerve cuts, spinal cord injury, and maybe even multiple sclerosis and other degenerative syndromes," Blütfink enthusiastically continued. "I am currently conducting animal experiments in this area and we are just beginning some limited human trials on this. We are certainly all pleased that Dr. Karolena Kreisler is a living example of their effectiveness and safety."

Blütfink had to pause again for some applause. "Hopefully, when she returns from medical leave, she will continue to work with me in this exciting area."

Hearing Blütfink's comments, Karolena noted that it was the first time she had admitted to herself or to anyone she would more than consider returning to her old job. Karolena flashed a grateful and positive smile at Blütfink as he continued, "Thank you all for your attention." He smiled at those listening to him, and then started down from the podium as the more than polite applause continued.

Bob stood up from behind the speaker's rostrum and said, "Thank you, Dr. Blütfink." Turning to the audience, Bob continued, "As you can see, there are many activities at The Winston that will lead to better health care now and in the future. I thank you for your patience, your support, and wish you all a good evening."

All the activity, aided by the champagne, had left Karolena feeling drained, and, sensing an opportune moment to leave, she headed toward the elevator. Her movements caught Blütfink's eye, surrounded as he was by a large group of hospital staff, and she motioned for him to join her off to the side. After excusing himself, Blütfink walked over to Karolena, and asked, "Going so soon?"

"Yes," she said, more than a little guilty for skipping out so early, then added, "I still haven't gotten all my strength back after the surgery, and the fatigue still decreases my vision. Susan has arranged for a ride back to my place. Please let Larry know, as he drove me here and," glancing at Larry having fun in the distance, she added" I think it's best if I just bow out without ruining his evening too."

"I understand," Blütfink told her in an understanding and concerned voice, comfortingly placing his hand on her shoulder. "If you're really too tired to stay, then perhaps you should go. I am glad that Susan fixed things for you. How about lunch or dinner tomorrow or some other time this week?" he smiled.

Karolena wasn't sure how she felt about the offer, made in so seemingly innocent a manner, but full of unseen implications. Certainly she wasn't interested in or ready to restart a relationship with him, although when she reflected on it, and considered her current options, it didn't seem too impossible either, even compared to Larry. "We'll see," she smiled. "I'll call you tomorrow. And thanks for the offer to drive me." They shook hands, and Rickhard unexpectedly leaned down and kissed her lightly on the cheek, and it felt remarkably good, and she momentarily reconsidered his offer. Then, just as the elevator door started to slide open and Karolena began to step in, she heard Susan yelling her name. "Oh no." Karolena cursed under her breath.

"Karolena, I hope you're not leaving just yet. Why, you're one of the most important guests. What about the newspaper reporter who has come all the way from England to interview you?"

Karolena glanced to Blütfink for support, but he only shrugged and smiled. "I know, Susan. I've already spoken with her."

"But, she wants to see you again, one more time." Susan's voice had a slightly annoying, whining quality to it.

"Karolena is feeling very fatigued after the surgery, Susan, and I think she just wants to go home and rest," Blütfink added.

"She can rest any day, Dr. Blütfink, but this is an important function for The Winston. Karolena, please?" she pleaded. "I did arrange for your ride, but it's really for after you speak, not just now."

Karolena shrugged helplessly, then firmly added, "Oh, okay, but just for a little while. I really must be going, Susan."

Susan smiled, then clutched Karolena's arm and led her over to the sushi table, where Barbara Farmington had been waiting for her. Blütfink moved back to the executive group, near the bar. "That's strange, the reporter was just here," Susan said.

Not at all disappointed, Karolena told her, "That's all right, Susan. Just now I need to go home. I'm not feeling well at all."

Susan started to reply to Karolena, but her words seemed to drift off as something strange caught Karolena's attention. A small ruby red pinpoint of light flashed slowly across Susan's forehead. The light trace seemed to come from nowhere, and trembled slightly in an up and down motion. Before Karolena could react, she watched the red pinpoint zigzag wildly, then rapidly move across Susan's face, down her neck and then onto her own center chest where it rested for several seconds. She felt a burning on her skin right there and quickly stepped back. Karolena watched the red dot as it came to rest again, this time on the forehead of another of the guests, a local reporter, standing nearby.

For an instant, she wondered if it were some sort of weapon, or a way to target one. Then, just as quickly, the light disappeared. Karolena looked around for a source, but could see none. By this time, many of the attendees had either left or started to leave. Feeling tired, she also made a few perfunctory greetings, then found Larry and got a ride back with him to her apartment. On the way, she kept hearing that question from the reporter. Was it the chicken or the egg? Was she the lucky recipient or the cause for the donor's demise?

Chapter 25

Karolena went up to her apartment on her own without Larry, who had to finish some administrative tasks at The Winston. Once inside, she collapsed exhausted onto the bed. Despite all she had been through, somehow she just couldn't fall asleep. She got up, turned on all the lights, and went to the living room, and asked, "AllSee. Security Status."

"Hi Karolena. Welcome home. There is one person in the apartment: Karolena Kreisler. All security systems are functioning." The AllSee paused for an unusually long time, and then said, "There may be a detection problem. I am running internal diagnostics now. Otherwise, there are no faults, and no messages."

"Specify nature of this detection problem," Karolena asked as she nervously looked around her, then got up and checked behind some of the furniture. Corina must have sensed her agitation, and moved nervously back and forth on her perch.

"There is an unspecified internal conflict. One **UN ID** is present: Karolena Kreisler. The number of persons registering as present in your apartment fluctuates between one and two."

"Notify apartment security now," Karolena said as she nearly ran out the door and into the hallway, turning to look back over her shoulder as she went. Three people from security, two with dog-bots and one tractor type of bot met Karolena in the hallway almost immediately. They had been briefed by the AllSee on their way up, and went straight into her apartment.

Several long minutes later, the apartment security guards came back out. Karolena had seen one member of the security team before - a large, older woman, who spoke for the team. "Your apartment is clean, Ms. Kreisler. The AllSee security sensor seems to be malfunctioning. You should definitely have it checked. There's no one in there but you." Security wiped her brow with her sleeve, scratched her side, turned to leave, then looked back and told Karolena, "Look, I'll get someone up here from maintenance as soon as I can, but you know how that goes," she shrugged. "Until then, don't worry. This building is locked up tight. Call me if you need me, okay?" She bumped her wrist ID next to Karolena's, transferring her contact info.

Karolena was more convinced than ever that, just as she had needed the transplant to stay alive, she now needed to find more out about her organ donor in order to continue to live with sanity. She thought it ironic that the very act of surviving could have lead to another's death, unintentional or not.

As the morning approached, her AllSee reminded her of her routine transplant follow-up appointment. Noticing that only a few hours remained before the early morning appointment, Karolena checked the security status of her apartment once again, and then walked into the bathroom to get ready. She took off all her clothes, and placed them in the appropriately labeled recycling unit. Standing across from the full length dressing mirror on the inner door, she stared at herself for several minutes, turning around slowly. Quickly turning away from the image which she felt to be imperfect and in general a disappointment, she turned on the ultrasound shower and stepped in.

Chapter 26

As soon as the holographic receptionist at Winston Nuclear Medicine Associates detected Karolena Kreisler's body standing in front of its scanner, its programmed logic asked, "Can I help you?" The scanner had already picked up her **UN ID** off her wrist, and correlated it with the reason for her visit - her appointment.

"Yes, my name is Karolena Kreisler, and I received a reminder on my AllSee to come in for a brain scan." Karolena had been scheduled for a brain scan at The Winston as part of her routine follow-up care.

Karolena nodded a brief greeting to another transplant patient, a liver transplant patient named Robilyn Carter, whom she had become acquainted with casually during her own hospitalization. Other than for Robilyn, the Nuclear Medicine clinic was empty.

"Please have a seat, we'll be with you soon," the hologram said. It was always amazing to Karolena how lifelike the receptionist-bot looked and sounded, and she wondered if she had ever mistaken one for a human.

After a short wait, and some light conversation with Robilyn, Karolena followed a mini lab robot, resembling a motorized and talking toaster - Karolena had seen a real toaster in a museum once - into a laboratory area. The laboratory technician on duty that afternoon directed Karolena to be seated in a special phlebotomy chair, a setup which hadn't changed in perhaps a century. The brown simulated-leather recliner had a wooden armrest that swung out to accommodate Karolena's arm as it lay flat for the needle. The tech applied the tourniquet with the expertise of one intimately familiar with intravenous injections, then looked quizzically at Karolena. "I think I've seen you before, Ms.?"

"My name is Karolena Kreisler," she replied curtly, her mind occupied with the upcoming needle stick. Although having no compunction with sticking animals or other humans, she had a revulsion, almost a terror to needles going into her own body. "I don't remember your name, I'm sorry to say," she replied politely.

"Oh yes, now I recall," the tech said. "I drew blood on you when you came into the emergency room a while ago. I'm not surprised that you don't remember me, though; you were unconscious. But, I never forget an arm," she smiled, patting Karolena's arm lightly.

"Thanks a lot," Karolena replied sarcastically.

"I didn't mean that as an insult; you do have some outstanding veins. Now this won't hurt a bit. Don't move . . . there it is." The needle's user-safe point cleanly slid into Karolena's arm vein without any discomfort, exactly as the tech had promised.

The tech, pleased that the phlebotomy was indeed painless, bragged to Karolena, "They say that veins just miraculously appear in my presence; sometimes they're veins even experienced surgeons swear don't exist.

They simply swim under the skin over to my needle, just so they can tell other veins that they had been pricked with my point. What an honor." Both of them laughed at the analogy.

"Now this won't hurt, either," the tech promised. She attached the needle of another syringe, this one filled with Karolena's dose of radioisotope, into the rubber cover at the base of the needle.

The clear radioisotope solution imparted a short stinging sensation as it flowed into Karolena's arm, and she worried once again about the cumulative dose of radioactivity she received. The technicians typically reassured Karolena the radioactive isotope used to image her brain had a short half-life. Yet, no matter how many times they said that, getting the injection always gave her cause to be concerned, and, when the opportunity arose again, she intended to ask about this, just as she had on every previous visit.

"It kind of stings, doesn't it?" a man's voice said. Surprised, Karolena turned around, and found Blütfink standing in back of her chair.

"Oh, hi. I haven't seen you in a while," Karolena said sarcastically, as she smiled up. Looking at the needle protruding from a vein in her arm, Karolena said ruefully, "I'm afraid this is a bit awkward."

"You're right," Blütfink said. "Now that you're feeling so much better, I have an idea. Perhaps you could meet me at the Physician's Section of the hospital cafeteria in, say thirty minutes, for some coffee?"

"I'd love to," Karolena smiled back. She was pleased and grateful with the successful way the transplant surgery had finally turned out, and in many ways she felt Blütfink to be responsible for saving her sight and even her life. He still called her occasionally during her convalescence at home, to inquire on her progress and to ask, quite uncharacteristically, if there was anything she needed. She also remembered that they had promised at the banquet to meet soon. Since then many events had happened, including another terrorist attack at The Winston. Yet, in just a week's passage of time, most people stopped mentioning that terrorist attack. The killer escaped, and other terror incidents replaced that one in time and in magnitude. Such was the state of the world they had all become accustomed to, and to which she had resigned herself to.

"Good. Then I'll see you in a little bit," he said, then left, for her to finish her imaging session.

The executive dining section was an exclusive part of the cafeteria reserved strictly for the upper level of hospital administration. It was connected to the main area by a locked unmarked door which Blütfink opened using his wrist ID. Inside was a small, carpeted dining room with wood tables, table cloths, comfortable chairs, and quiet, tasteful music.

Physicians ate in their own area, also separate from the general cafeteria. The general cafeteria was used by patients, visitors and hospital employees.

Blütfink offered Karolena a seat next to him at a small round table with a red checkered table spread. After a moment, he got up and returned with some coffee in brown self-heating ceramic cups with gold "***The Winston***" embossing. "When you're finished you can keep me," the cup told them both, in a happy recorded message.

Karolena smiled back, thanking him.

After some small talk, Blütfink remarked that he was hungry. Karolena admitted she was a little hungry too and they put in their orders via a modified AllSee on the table top. Blütfink and Karolena knew that here they didn't need to go through a serving line like the patients, visitors and students.

A small motorized server unit brought their food, two dog meat burritos and some ice tea, from an AutoEats unit after a few minutes. Karolena had come to expect that AutoEats units could make almost anything taste palatable. Blütfink sipped from the iced tea, made a bad face, then returned to his coffee. Once they had started eating, their conversation gradually turned to transplants, a topic in which they certainly shared a common interest.

Blütfink emptied a pack of salsa onto the burrito, and asked, matter-of-factly, "Do you mind if I smoke while I eat? I find it relaxing." He offered a sim-cig to Karolena, who smiled and took one also. He set his to "Concentrating Inward" and she did too. Inhaling deeply, he held his breath for several long seconds before slowly exhaling the medicated vapor and his face became flush. He took another drag on his sim-cig, then sipped from the cup of coffee.

"How are your headaches, Karolena?" he asked, real concern for her welfare clearly showing in his voice. She was touched by the degree of sensitivity Blütfink was able to show, and wondered how much he had changed.

Inhaling deeply, she leaned back in her chair, thought about her response for a moment, then said, "Fortunately, they're getting less severe, and less frequent."

"And the nightmares, the hallucinations?" he asked, his voice now more medical exam than simply personal concern, but not totally.

"I still get them," she sighed, resignedly. The last time she had tried to discuss the terrifying dreams with him, shortly after her discharge from the hospital, he had tried to refer her to a psychiatrist. Wondering if now he would understand better what she would tell him, or whether she would still sound a little crazy, she said, "You know, Rickhard, sometimes I think the dreams are talking to me."

"Easy, Karolena. You're sounding a little psychotic."

There, her fears were confirmed, she thought, chastising herself for opening herself up so much to him. He really had changed so little. "What I mean is that it almost seems as if there's a message in the dreams," she continued, trying to better explain herself. She needed for him, for anyone to understand her fears, and not simply dismiss her like a hallucinating freak.

"Of that I know nothing," Blütfink joked. "But tell me, just what might that message be?"

"I think my graft donor was murdered, actually I know that she was murdered. To me, at least, that raises the possibility that the connection between the donor's death and my needing a graft may not have been strictly coincidental."

She noticed as she said that, a clearly uncomfortable look clouded Blütfink's face. Looking away, Blütfink seemed to redirect his attention to some food he was playing with on his plate. He remembered, uncomfortably, Karolena's father calling him several times and pressuring him to get a graft donor. The guy obviously didn't know how the organ procurement worked, Blütfink reflected. Or maybe he did, in his own way. The organ donation matching system was supposed to eliminate the possibility for preferences and pressures. Even though in some other countries you could sometimes "arrange" for an organ like a kidney, North Carolina was a completely different place. He had passed on her father's concerns to Bob, but was sure that would be of no avail. Still, he felt compelled to ask Karolena, "You really think someone murdered your donor intentionally?"

"I'm not sure, but I have to tell you that my dreams are very realistic and intense" Karolena had to laugh as she watched Blütfink, who seemed to lose his attention in what she was saying, and instead concentrated on cutting a burrito cleanly in half and then tried to push the ends back together. "Rickhard, just what are you doing?" she asked, annoyed at his apparent loss of interest in what she so strongly needed to tell him.

"Oh, just trying to use this hot sauce to connect up the ends of the burrito together. Hey," he smiled with a boyish grin, "maybe it will work. What do you think?"

"I don't know about that," Karolena told him, shaking her head playfully.

Blütfink's face took on a serious hue, and he looked right at Karolena and told her, "You know, Karolena, if you cut off the arm of a starfish, or the tail of a salamander, it will regenerate. And wouldn't it bc remarkable to be able to do that for people too?"

"Rickhard, salamander tails don't just *come together*. The injured areas regrow - nerves, bone, muscle and all," Karolena corrected Blütfink. "It's actually very complicated, and unfortunately the phenomenon is unique to only a very few species."

"Thanks for the biology lesson, Karolena. I mean, after all, what could I possibly know about something like transplant surgery?" he added sarcastically. "But follow me on where I'm going with this, will you. We know that certain organs can regenerate to some extent, repair themselves like the liver does, even nerves, like with the growth factor, although when they reach a certain point they must be replaced too. Transplants have extended the life of those with diseased organs -- like you, for example. But it really hasn't solved one of the foremost problems of mankind: longevity of the healthy producers," Blütfink insisted, fingering his own chest as he spoke. "THAT'S where I think medical science should look, Karolena. I think there's a real need here, and a big untapped commercial demand too."

"Meaning what?" she asked, wondering whether he was freely associating or really pulling her leg.

"Meaning that for normal, healthy, employed,

educated retro negative people, real ordinary people like us, Karolena, after investing a lifetime learning, experiencing, improving, what happens? Poof, it ends. That's what. And no amount of transplanting, medicine, anything can prevent that."

"But, that's what life is all about, Rickhard," Karolena said, gently touching his shoulder. "All life, including us have a natural and inescapable end. There's no need to fight it, it comes for us all. I accept that, especially after all that I've been through lately." In her short life, she had come so close to death, had actually welcomed it at one point, she had lost most, not all, but most fear. Hers was certainly not at all a religious revelation, not a resignation, but more an intellectual acceptance, a way of coming to terms with the inevitable.

"Well, let me tell you something that may interest you, then, Karolena Kreisler. It's NOT acceptable to me. I want to keep going," Blütfink insisted.

Karolena smiled patiently, waiting for him to continue.

"Who knows? Maybe we'll just find a way to just take my head off when my body gets old and put it on a young body so I can keep going."

After a split second of silence, they both laughed out loud at the patent absurdity of his suggestion.

"I'm afraid that's not too likely, Rickhard," Karolena said, shaking her head. She was slightly surprised when Blütfink reached over and held her hand as they laughed, then he gently let it go. She was pleasantly surprised at how natural and yet how uncomfortably inappropriate his touch felt. It was part of the contradictory character that their complicated up and down relationship had always had. "Besides, don't you see enough dead and dying people in your job to make it seem acceptable, natural?"

"Sure, sure I do see the dead and the dying, but I never could get used to it," Blütfink admitted. "Did you know that a group at FirsThought is doing some really exciting pioneering research on regenerating regions of the brain's thought center?"

"I think you're referring to central nervous system consciousness reconstruction. Yes, in fact, that was one of the things I heard you were collaborating on." She knew very little of the project in detail, but what she did know sounded more fantasy than reality. She could see perhaps a role for the nerve growth factor here. Maybe there was a wider meaning to her successful transplant.

"That's it," Blütfink said, "*thought reconstruction.* Even the name has appeal. We could be able to attract some big venture money here," he nodded, with enthusiasm.

"Sure," Karolena smiled politely at him, realizing though that it would probably would never happen, at least in their life time.

"And of course we're continuing our research in the repair of nerve damage. Why, some of the other researchers tell me they may be onto a way to repairing cut spinal cords using one of our nerve growth factors we're working on. Now that's closing in on immortality, if you ask me. And nerve repair of any kind has got one hell of an economic potential."

Thinking about the meaning behind his enthusiastic, almost impassioned line of conversation, she asked, "Tell me, Rickhard, are you afraid of death?"

"No, of course not. That would be ridiculous." Blütfink sat up straighter in his chair and tried to smile at Karolena.

"I'm not so sure of that," replied Karolena, shaking her head. She sensed that he was not being candid with her. "You know, when I had surgery, I thought a lot about dying. It was a real possibility for me."

Blütfink nodded agreement. "And what did you do to deal with that reality? It must have been real scary."

"There was nothing to do, Rickhard. I had to have the surgery or I would've died, or at least remained blind. And while I was under anesthesia and unconscious, control over my life was out of my hands."

Blütfink shook his head. "Yeah, I've thought about that a lot in my position. I just don't know how I'd react, losing so much control." He shivered, then closed his eyes for a moment, then looked over to Karolena and tried to smile.

Karolena smiled back, then said, "I think ultimately, real control over our own lives is an illusion, Rickhard; it's entirely out of all our hands, totally." She raised her hands up in a poof motion.

"Does that mean you're a fatalist?" Blütfink asked, shifting uncomfortably in his chair.

"Fatalist? Perhaps. Realist? Yes. Anyway, I tend to

internalize things and not talk about my fears. But tell me, Rickhard, why do you want to live forever? It's just not natural."

"I want to go on living because I don't want to die. I've gone through so much to get to this point in my life, why should I give it all up? I'm at the peak of my capabilities. Is that so strange or unreasonable?"

"No, I guess not. I think, at least as far as I can understand it, people seem to fear death, or more so the dying process because it's full of such total unknown." Karolena watched Blütfink intensely watching her, and perhaps for the first time she felt he was actually listening to her. It was a strange feeling, one that she hadn't often had with a man, even with Larry, or perhaps especially with Larry. "Maybe it's because you're so much the controlling type, Rickhard, no offense, and death is the one thing you'll never have any control over."

"You'd think by now, with all medical science learned, there would be a better understanding of longevity, at least. But, no," he shook his head slowly back and forth.

"Well, we still haven't been able to conquer cancer or the common cold, and scientists have been working on those problems for hundreds of years and more. We've unraveled the entire human genetic code, although we can't understand it. We've mapped the brain, got localization of areas of compassion, insight, comprehension, but never found the soul."

Blütfink shook his head sadly. "All that effort, and I can't live any longer now than I could a hundred years ago. Probably less, for that matter," he said, as he inhaled anxiously from his sim-cig, then sipped on his coffee, his eyes staring far off elsewhere.

"But if you have such a strong desire to live, is there anything you would be willing to die for?"

Blütfink smiled wryly. "Hey, I know what you're expecting me to say. You think someone as cold and heartless as you perceive me to be would say that there's nothing I'd be willing to die for."

"Well, yes, frankly," Karolena said.

"Then you're very wrong, Karolena Kreisler. There certainly is something I would die for."

"And what would that be?"

"I would die if I could live again."

Blütfink's face became too serious, too intense for Karolena, almost frightening her, and she decided to change the conversation. With her recent brushes with death, and her familiarity with the limits disease imparts on longevity, she had more than her share of thoughts on death, and actually found their conversation a little depressing. Shortly after this, a page message emitted a series of short almost imperceptible subcutaneous shocks to Blütfink's AllSee. The pattern meant his office, and he got up to leave the cafeteria.

"This was nice, Karolena. Sort of old times," he smiled comfortably as he moved away.

Karolena nodded, and when Blütfink suggested, "Let's meet next time for dinner, like we had planned to at the banquet," she was only too happy to agree, and they made tentative plans for the next evening.

Karolena offered to send him the details of where and when.

Karolena remained behind, and ordered a cup of cappuccino. Then she 'smoked' another sim-cig, and, after the cappuccino arrived, savored the rich aroma and chocolaty taste from the cocoa powder which floated like fine brown dust on the surface. While watching the news on the flat screen display at her table, she was startled when she suddenly caught sight of a red laser light out of the corner of her eye. A warning shiver ripped through her as she remembered the scene at The Winston reception. She dropped her cup and in a reflexive move dove for the safety of the floor.

After several seconds, a very concerned server-bot came to her table. "Can I help you, Miss?" it asked. "Are you all right? Did you drop something?"

Looking around her anxiously, Karolena was relieved to notice that there had been no attack on the restaurant, and she suddenly felt very foolish. "No, everything is fine. I just got scared, but I'm okay. Thanks so much." Blushing, she smiled and returned to her seat.

Turning her head in the direction of the light, she saw that the source was a red "Ready Light" indicator over the fire detector. That's all, Karolena repeated to herself, trying to breathe deeply, just a stupid 'ready' light. Her heart was racing at maximum speed, and she became self-conscious about how stupid she must have appeared. Embarrassed, she threw a napkin on the spill and got up to leave. The whole incident made her angry, angry at herself for being so jumpy and angry at being put under such stress in the first place.

Chapter 27

That evening, Karolena used her AllSee to send Blütfink directions to a favorite restaurant of hers: "*The Natural Disaster.*" She noted to Blütfink that seven the next evening would work out fine, and asked him to be sure and call her if there were problems. Everyone was linked up thru their AllSee units, which managed to do a great job knowing where everyone was and what they were scheduled to do. Her AllSee would make the reservations, and order her any paper clothes or accessories that she would need in advance. Once she had made the arrangements, as she had told Blütfink that she would, she felt both relieved and at the same time maybe a little more apprehensive. What if, she asked herself, he had really not changed at all, and was the same insufferable, self-centered, egotistical creep she had come to know and to finally after too long reject almost a year ago? Why, she wondered, was she always making problems for herself? Was she not better off occasionally dating, and keeping herself open, like with Larry. Still, although Larry was pleasant, their relationship certainly did not seem to be going anywhere. Better safe but bland Larry than getting mixed up with people she had already figured out, and especially those she worked with and might again?

The night was uncharacteristically peaceful - she

slept very well, with no disturbing dreams - and the next day passed quickly. Toward seven in the evening, Karolena drove to The Natural Disaster restaurant, sarcastically named after the last great series of toxin spills into the Neuse River, which was not too far from The Winston. Blütfink met Karolena there after work, which was more convenient for him, as The Winston was only a short distance away. She occasionally met Susan Winder there also and felt comfortable.

Once together, they spent a long time talking peacefully in the lounge, a small and dimly lighted area centered around a holographic fire atop old tires, smoking and drinking and sharing small talk. The decor to the uninitiated would sound not at all conducive to a nice restaurant and lounge, but it was fixed up in an imaginative and almost humorous way, although in reality what had happened to the world's environment for the last 40+ years was certainly not funny at all. Neither of them had in the past been exceptionally good at small talk, but tonight's conversation seemed noticeably effortless, an observation which pleased Karolena. After a while, they moved from the lounge to the restaurant, and had a seat at a circular slab mounted on a mock toxin drum, next to the stream. The table was close to where she and Susan had recently sat, prompting Karolena to wonder how Susan was doing. It had been a while since they had spoken, and Karolena planned to give her a call in the morning. In some ways, she found Susan superficial and a little lazy, like most of the native Anglos seemed to be. She realized that was a bigoted generalization, but in her experiences it usually was true. At the same time, Susan was peaceful, friendly, without an identifiable ulterior motive, and usually available. She answered calls, and was one of the very few people Karolena could ask for a favor and be depended upon. Karolena knew that shc ccrtainly needed more people like Susan in her life.

A waiter-bot came by with menus, printed on simulated garbage wrappers, with matching stains in the carpet and table cloth to simulate chemical pollution. The bot mentioned the dinner specials, waited for a moment for questions, and then left to take care of other clients. The restaurant's particular theme idea, although potentially revolting, was so cleverly and tastefully done that the restaurant was the rave of the south. Karolena and Rickhard both paused to examine and discuss the menu. When the waiter returned, they both ordered the pasta special, and a bottle of red wine. That done, they returned to their discussion, which centered around the restaurant's unusual decor.

The restaurant's ambiance was particularly enjoyable tonight, and for Karolena quite romantic. For once, she actually enjoyed Blütfink's company, the gentle way he treated her, and the intensity with which he seemed to listen to everything she said. It was almost as if he were an entirely different person, that they had met for the very first time, and in many ways she was reminded of how gentle and interesting and fun she had found him to be when they first met in Europe.

Blütfink had the presence of mind to mention that, as their relationship had taken a significant change of direction again, perhaps full-circle, his professional relationship to her probably should change also.

She nodded thoughtfully at the reasonableness of his remarks. "Odd, isn't it?" she said, almost to herself, still not sure how she felt about becoming possibly more involved with this man again.

"What's odd about what I just said, Karolena?"

"It's odd that we're even here, together, and that is even a potential problem. That's what I meant, Rickhard," she reassured him, least he misunderstand her comment. Was it physical attraction? She doubted that, as Rickhard Blütfink was no model of attractive manhood, although he wasn't exactly repulsive either. Was it sexual attraction? She doubted that too, for sex was not a high priority for her, and never had been, and she didn't find Blütfink particularly sexy either. Besides, with all her physical ailments, she had rarely found sex to be all that enjoyable. Instead, she wondered if she was experiencing feelings of transference. Was she transferring her feelings of gratitude and dependency in her patient - doctor relationship back to him? Although this was also a possibility, she thought herself mature enough to avoid that trap.

The waiter-bot came by to refill their wine glasses from the bottle, announced that their order would be right out, and then left.

"What I'm trying to get at is that, since I currently am your doctor, in addition to our having a working and professional relationship back at FirsThought, I think I better distance myself in those senses from you, in the interests of propriety," he quickly added.

Karolena understood very well what Blütfink was concerned about, and admired him for being so ethically correct, although she still wondered why he had then taken the initiative to reopen their failed relationship. "What do you have in mind?"

"Oh, just to transfer your primary patient care responsibilities to someone else." Karolena nodded agreeably. “There are several fine surgeons that I think you could benefit from. There's Malawassi for one. You said that you like him.”

"Yes, I do like him as a doctor. I can understand what you're saying, Rickhard, and I certainly will give it some thought. For now, let's concentrate on having a pleasant dinner, okay?" she smiled as the dinner trays arrived.

After dinner, Blütfink held Karolena's hand as they drank wine and smoked a few sim-cigs and stared into the simulated fire back in the lounge area. Blütfink turned to her and started talking to her by addressing his napkin. "I know that this isn't very romantic, but these days . . . "

Karolena knew what was coming, and didn't object. It had been too long, and after their lovely evening together, she was ready.

Blütfink reached into his pocket and offered Karolena a stick of RetroGum that he had "conveniently" stashed in there. He was relieved when

Karolena accepted. "You know what they say, 'Chew before you . . . "

"I'm aware of that particularly crude slogan, Dr. Blütfink," Karolena replied in a stern voice, blushing. She understood all too well and just wanted to get this uncomfortable bit of necessity over with. "How convenient for you to keep RetroGum in your pocket like that," she commented sternly, nervously tapping her shoe against the table leg.

Blütfink smiled lamely, then shrugged his shoulders. "Hey, I'm a careful guy."

"I'll bet you are," she replied dryly, and drolly smiled in his direction. Such was the state of relationships, she reflected with resignation.

They both chewed the chemical-impregnated gum for a few minutes, savoring the sweet spearmint flavor before shyly showing each other the shiny fluorescent green color of freedom, of purity, of safety, suggesting they were dangerous only to each other's emotions. Red means Stop, but Green means Go, she said to herself, smiling.

Hours later, Karolena rolled over and pulled the pillow gently between her legs, curled up, and uttered a silent moan. "Damn," she softly cursed into her side of the bed. The discomfort of intercourse that she had experienced with Blütfink the last time they were together persisted, but was perhaps a little more tolerable now than she remembered it to be. Karolena was reminded again why she had sex so infrequently, and actually avoided it. Sex was supposed to be something she did for pleasure, particularly since she didn't consider herself a 'breeder,' yet she derived so little pleasure from it. What, she wondered, was wrong with her?

"What's the matter, Karolena?" Blütfink asked, seeing how distracted she looked, rather than appearing to be floating in ecstasy with him.

"My belly hurts a little. I'm sorry," she told him, feeling embarrassed and hurt, her conflicting emotions only further confusing her and muddling her already mixed experience with him again. "Maybe the dinner last night didn't agree with me."

"Maybe, but I ate the same food and my stomach is just fine. Could it be disuse atrophy?" Blütfink quipped, then adjusted the blanket over them both a little better. He glanced at the time on the bedside AllSee, then made some rather lame apologies and got up to shower and dress.

Karolena didn't argue with this explanation of her discomfort, crude and thoughtless as it was on Blütfink's part. But neither did she appreciate her '*duty to please him*', as she sometimes thought his attitude toward her was. After living together a while, she had found Blütfink's crude jokes were not very amusing at all, and the memory of her past failures now returned to soil her present.

In the past, when the discomfort – she didn't think that it rose to the level of pain, just discomfort - of intercourse became localized in her abdomen rather than her vagina, Karolena sought help, at Blütfink's insistence. After several gynecological visits and two tries with sex counselors and the latest mechanical "surrogates," her "*dyspareunia*" was explained as being due most likely to surgical adhesions from her past abdominal surgery. The tissue linings of her internal organs had become inflamed and stuck together, causing the painful pullings she experienced whenever her abdomen or pelvis were jostled. Apparently not much could be done about it, short of surgical exploration, and that was out of the question as far as Karolena was concerned, weighing the significant risks versus the limited supposed benefits.

Even though Blütfink had insisted that he didn't particularly like to make her suffer while he derived his own pleasure, Karolena suspected that her suffering actually held a certain bizarre, vicarious interest for him. In fact, sometimes she actually thought that her discomfort appeared to excite him sexually. In her eyes, Karolena thought that she probably tried ten times harder than any other woman would to please Blütfink, and wanted Blütfink to at least credit her for that and give the same loving gentle and caring effort made in her behalf.

Karolena also persisted in her habit of wearing clothes when she went to bed with Blütfink. She was self-conscious of her rather large and unflattering surgical scars, which she vainly avoided openly displaying to Blütfink. Somehow she deluded herself into violating one of her very basic precepts: "Never assume someone can't see what you're hiding."

Before he left her apartment, they discussed briefly the advisability of resuming their old relationship.

They both still seemed to like the professionalism and dedication each offered the other very much, although Blütfink made it abundantly clear that he was really interested in nothing more permanent. "I've been dipped in honey and strapped onto the ant hill of marriage before, babe," Blütfink emphatically told Karolena. "I hate commitments and just want to enjoy life while I can, while we can. Right?"

That comment seemed most telling and prophetic to Karolena, after their first time in bed together in months, for it didn't take long for their new rendezvous to again become less and less frequent. Soon she came to realize just how wrong Blütfink probably was for her, and how resuming her dependent relationship would only perpetuate a life-long pattern of dependence upon men. Soon, Karolena too lost interest and backed away from a more involved relationship. Better nothing than something, in this case, she truly believed. Instead, she prepared for her return to FirsThought, scheduled to occur in only a few more days. Although still suffering from fatigue, and occasional headaches, she believed that the work would provide a form of occupational therapy, and be healing to both her body and for her mind.

Chapter 28

Several uneventful days passed after Karolena's return to FirsThought, days without further information concerning her donor. There were times when she even forgot that she was ever interested in knowing more about her donor. The nightmares had provided such an impetus, but with their waning, so had her interest in interpreting them.

It was late in the afternoon, and although she had done little all day besides read some company documents from a holobook and set up a few experiments for Blütfink, Karolena still felt mentally and physically exhausted. She thought it might help if she left work early, and planned to stop for dinner at *The Natural Disaster* on her way home. The thought of eating home alone tonight held no appeal to her at all. Wanting a change from her usual fare, Karolena remembered that she had coincidentally received a holographic advertisement from that very same restaurant, and it took only a brief reminder of its interesting interior to entice her back. Susan once told Karolena that she found it odd that Karolena tended to eat at the same place all the time. For Karolena, she found peace in the consistency. She never craved new things all the time. Besides, The Natural Disaster was clean, and the food tasted good and appeared to be fresh and healthy, although who realistically could know about that these days. The local militia favored the place too, which added a touch more sense of safety, too.

After giving her order to the waiter ‘bot, Karolena became aware of someone watching her, a feeling which for her was almost never welcome or comfortable. Turning, she caught the eye of a good-looking man at a table nearby. Once their glances met, the man got up, smiled, and walked over to her. "Hello," he smiled down at her, a spark of familiarity in his voice.

Karolena pulled back into her chair, looking surprised and somewhat taken aback. Men hardly ever went out of their way to speak to her, particularly at restaurants. This person did look somewhat familiar, although she really couldn't remember where she might have known him from.

"I know this sounds phony," he smiled harmlessly, “but do I know you?"

"Why yes, I believe I've seen you around The Winston. Do you work there?" Not waiting for an answer, she blurted out, "Hi. My name is Karolena Kreisler," and she extended her hand to him.

"My name is Dieter Müeller," he replied. “Ah, yes, Karolena Kreisler. I think I've heard your name mentioned. Weren't you a patient there recently?"

Karolena replied that she had been.

"I do some contract work there occasionally."

After Dieter asked if she were alone, she said, "Yes, I am."

"Me too," he laughed. "Would you like to join

me?" he asked, sweeping his hand toward his table.

Dieter's invitation seemed to Karolena the natural and polite thing to do under the circumstances, and harmless enough. Dieter gave Karolena a very broad and open smile, and without too much difficulty, her defenses were lowered. Before finally getting up from her table, she briefly considered asking him if he were married. She held back, though, despite her need to protect her precarious psyche from further disappointments. It just seemed to her that to do so would appear rather presumptuous on her part, especially so immediately after just having first met.

After an enjoyable dinner and some light conversation, Karolena and Dieter enjoyed some drinks together - hers were nonalcoholic, in deference to her liver -- then agreed to meet after work the next day for dinner at a restaurant chosen by Karolena. She particularly liked the fact that Dieter was such a good listener. Karolena, by nature an introvert, nevertheless felt almost compelled to do all the talking. Social engagements came far between for Karolena, too far in between, and in the ensuing hours she looked forward to the next night. Ever since her last brief affair with Rickhard Blütfink had slowly wound down, she had few invitations out from men, and if she leveled with herself, the number actually was zero. Even Larry had seemed to drop off the face of the earth, as far as reaching out to her was concerned. She briefly wondered if Susan had tipped Larry off to the fact that she had started seeing Blütfink again. There would have been no reason for Susan to have done that, but with Susan, she seemed to have her own internal motivations which were mysterious to Karolena. At any rate, Karolena did not consider herself desperate, or really ever in need of a man, more for companionship, and she was generally satisfied being peacefully alone by herself most of the time.

The restaurant Karolena chose for the next evening, Sans Bolero, was trendy, authentic Italian, at least as far as she could tell, never crowded, and located in a small shopping complex attached to her apartment building. Dieter met Karolena at the restaurant's lounge and they had a few glasses of non-alcoholic wine before dinner. Karolena explained that she had run to the restaurant straight from work. She hadn't had enough time to stop in her apartment to take care of some important things, and excused herself for a few minutes, saying she would be right back.

Dieter followed Karolena with his eyes as she left the table, and saw her stop at a small store just outside the restaurant. He noticed that she left the store after only a few minutes, carrying a small bag. After giving Karolena time to walk to the elevator to go to her apartment, Dieter got up and walked over to the small shop.

"Good evening," Dieter addressed the clerk. "My wife was just in here buying some articles, and she sent me back to get some more . . ." he waived his hand vaguely in the air, and displayed a slightly embarrassed look.

"Certainly, sir," the clerk replied understandably, "Here's another box of RetroGum."

Karolena returned shortly, and she and Dieter dined together, laughed together, danced together. They sat by the artificial fire in the lounge, drinking wine punch and puffing on romance-scented sim-cigs, telling each other stories of their lives until late into the evening. Karolena began to tell Dieter about her liver disease, her transplant surgery, and the violence that she remembered growing up. As she listened to the words run from her mouth, she realized that she must be sounding terribly boring and a little paranoid. Bubbling over with enthusiasm and buoyed by spirited liquids and vapors and hope, Karolena found it difficult to stop talking, particularly when Dieter seemed so interested and willing to listen.

Finally, Karolena told Dieter about her dreams, and how she thought they might relate to her having received transplant tissue. Instead of turning away or changing the subject like the others, she was surprised when Dieter held her hand, then looked understandingly into her eyes and nodded that he believed her. She found his show of concern both unique and touching.

As the hours wore on, they happily drank too much, and then, later in the evening, laughed all the way to Karolena's apartment building. Dieter walked and Karolena nearly danced through the security weapons scanner at the building's foyer, and past the dog-bots and the glares and jealous smiles of the security staff. Then they held hands as they took the elevator up to her floor. Karolena felt dizzy and almost out of control and loved every minute, energized by the possibility that she had finally found a man who understood her, and who accepted her for whom she was. When she swayed as the elevator moved laterally, Dieter held her in his strong arms, but made no move which might have frightened her away. Pleasantly pleased and appreciative of her rare accidental find, she relished perhaps the first feeling of joy she had experienced in months.

The "Dog" program began barking as they neared the door to her apartment, causing Dieter to back off somewhat and seem ill-at-ease. "You don't like my dogs?" she asked, her voice the essence of understanding and concern.

When Dieter smiled uncomfortably, Karolena passed her wrist ID by the scanner and told the "dogs" to be quiet, and Dieter understood. Standing at the door to Karolena's apartment, Dieter started to say a very sad, "Good night, Karolena," when she put her finger to his lips and invited him in. Dieter feigned an appropriate reluctance, but not too much.

"Good evening, Karolena," the AllSee greeter her. "There is a second person with you, Karolena. He is Mr. Dieter Müeller. Is his entry expected, Karolena?"

"No, not at all. But he certainly is welcome," she replied, amazed sometimes at just how well her AllSee watched over her and protected her. She was relieved that the unit worked as advertised, in case she had somehow been followed up by someone less welcome than Dieter. A different reply would have brought building security up within seconds. She had never had to use the security system, except the one time she was very sick and needed to go to the hospital, but knew plenty of people who had, even in this secure apartment building.

It's been a hell of a long time since a real man was in here last, Karolena reminded herself, as she breathed deeply and looked around her empty apartment. It was too damn long, and now, her loneliness was fueled by the warmth of alcohol and too many disappointments. Her expectations took control of her reason, and as she looked at the muscular, ruggedly handsome Dieter, she knew for certain that this was no Blütfink and no Larry.

Dieter and Karolena sat down together on the floor in front of a low glass table off to the side of the simulated fireplace. Renata paced back and forth in his nearby cage, but uncharacteristically remained silent. Karolena found Renata at that moment to be distracting, and had the AllSee turn his program off.

Dieter smiled warmly at Karolena, and his strong hand soon found its way around her shoulder, embracing her and pulling her toward his solid body. Slowly, he moved his lips down to the nape of her neck, kissed her lightly and spoke to her softly, lovingly in German, both of which Blütfink was capable of doing but never did.

Her body ablaze with desire, it took every bit of self-control she could summon to not climax at that instant. She turned toward Dieter, receptive and warm, and he moved her even closer, placing her legs on the sides of his hip, riding her skirt revealingly up her hip. It was presumptuous, it was bold, and it was exciting and raised a level of arousal she found almost too intense to handle. It was as if an electrical contact was made which activated her sensuality, for soon, they kissed long and deep, passionate kisses that seemed half dreams. She felt on the verge of fainting.

With half of her face aglow from the fire, Karolena stopped kissing Dieter long enough to slide a piece of RetroGum slowly along the glass tabletop toward Dieter. She had picked it up from the lobby store before dinner, a common touch she had long since grown accustomed to. They savored the taste and chewed with a sensual pleasure that revealed their dreams, before finally showing each other the reassuring green color.

Dieter reached down and touched Karolena's inner thigh with his palm. His skin felt rough and his grip was firm, and Karolena found herself unable to resist. Her groin burned and felt simultaneously a tense firmness and hot liquid and seemed to move rhythmically back and forth on its own. She sucked a mouthful of air into her lungs, then couldn't exhale, the muscles of her chest paralyzed by his touch. Karolena didn't even try to move away, her body seemed to melt and to freeze solid in his grasp simultaneously, and never would have obeyed such a conscious command.

Sensing the opportunity, Dieter's hand slid forward under Karolena's dress and moved up, deep into her hot middle area. As Karolena turned toward Dieter and wrapped her arms around his neck, her legs separated slightly and she moaned a deep, throaty moan. Karolena's strong feminine scent filled the entire room, and Dieter smelled the heady, warm, sensuous female vapor, like a hunter to his prey, and pressed his advantage and with deliberate action advanced his hand.

She let out another needful groan, and could feel herself rapidly losing control. She whispered into Dieter's ear, "Oh, Dieter. Not so fast, please," as she hungrily kissed his neck. There was urgency in her breath. "I, I want to talk a little more first." She could feel her heart racing, pounding in her chest and into her throat, choking her, making her feel light headed. She knew an insatiable hunger had taken control of her reason and she was along for the ride, but not as the driver.

Dieter backed off and looked puzzled and hurt, his stare melting into her partially exposed breasts. "Of course. Then what would you like to talk about?"

Karolena anxiously ran her hands up and down his back as she sensuously kissed him full in his mouth, deep, long kisses, playing her tongue against his. '*Talk'* she asked herself, and then softly shook her head NO. As she reached down and touch his zipper with one hand, with the other she deftly slid an antiviral effervescent tablet into her moist vagina.

Karolena held Dieter tight, then smiled sadly.

"Is something the matter?" Dieter asked.

"Yes, no, no nothing's the matter." She paused, then explained, "It's just that sometimes I think men talk to women only to get to sleep with them."

Karolena was taught to wonder from years of disappointing experience if that were what he wanted, too.

"And women?" Dieter asked, his hand busy stroking her inner thigh. "Why do they do what they do?"

Karolena listened to her own rhythmic, deep breathing. She felt Dieter inch her dress up and slide his hands around her back and down into her panty. He grabbing both her buttocks and roughly pulling her around, and the sensation was intoxicating, overpowering, and she felt as if she would faint. She knew she was going to faint. But she fought against that. She was definitely intoxicated, on Dieter. Never having experienced foreplay as intense and pleasurable as this, she thought she might actually totally lose control from sheer excitement. She also feared precipitously reaching a sexual climax -- one that would undoubtedly be exquisitely intense -- at that very moment, but she fought against prematurity, not now, not here, not with him. No No No. No, she screamed at herself as she fought her own body for control. No, that would be too soon to suit her, and definitely too soon to satisfy her parched desert. Karolena desperately attempted to control her body; her emotions, yet she knew they were already lost, and she could care less.

"And women, ah yes," Karolena replied softly, contemplatively, adjusting herself slightly in the clumsy position she found herself in. "Well, I think that sometimes women sleep with men just to be able to talk to them." Karolena nestled her face deeper into Dieter's neck to hide her tears, and wondered if that was her motivation tonight. She certainly hoped not.

Chapter 29

The next morning, Karolena awoke with a start. Frightened, she rapidly glanced around the room, then quickly jumped out of bed and pulled a robe on. She had fallen asleep totally naked, which was unusual for her, leaving her feeling vulnerable and open. Her heart raced and her still damp skin enveloped her aching body, totally and joyfully exhausted. Karolena remembered being pulled awake from a terrifying dream; she remembered in her dream how someone was following her, trying to attack her. She ran to her car and drove off, but somehow, whoever was after her caught up to her, grabbed her by the arm and wouldn't let go. She fought back without any effect, but, before she could get away, she woke up. Now she struggled to remember more details, and most of all to remember his face.

Minutes after gaining her orientation, Karolena still felt terrified. She remembered last night, how close and how intense the sex was, and unlike all the others, totally without any pain whatsoever. She looked around for Dieter, but was disappointed but not too surprised to find that Dieter had already left. "Typical, just typical," she muttered to herself, as she also remembered how she felt both physically attracted and still slightly nervous in his presence. Then, her vision began to shift, making her wonder if her nerve growth factor was wearing off, and it was time for another dose. The borders of objects became indistinct, her concentration shifted elsewhere, and she felt her sight being pulled to another place, powerful, irresistible, as if another conscience had taken hold of her will to separately exist, and she saw . . .

. . . The logic system in her car warned, "Five minutes of driving time left. Please stop to recharge." She knew that she was Penny now, yes Penny, her graft donor. She felt uncomfortably aware that, with all the additional driving and acceleration she had been forced to make to escape from the van that was menacingly following her, her car's batteries must have been near depletion. Unfortunately, she would need to stop very soon, and remembered that there was a quick recharge station at a liquor store across from a field she was driving parallel to. After carefully looking around one last time to be certain she wasn't being followed, it seemed prudent to take a shortcut and she cut across a connecting road. First checking her mirror, she was relieved to see that she was still clear, and made the turn toward safety.

The sudden and unexpected rear-end impact was as massive as it was unforeseen, the brutal force slamming her face forward into the instrument panel against an air bag, and stunned her. Her car ran off the road like a toy and bounced roughly several times before finally landing in a ditch. The front glass cracked and the rough smell of machine oil filled her passenger compartment.

After the initial shock of impact wore off, Penny

noticed a sharp pain running up her neck, a pain accentuated by pressure from the airbag which had inflated a few milliseconds ago. Karolena could still feel that intense pain in her own neck right now, even awake. As Penny, in her dream she tried to move her fingers, then her hands, then her feet, and was relieved to find that they still responded to her, but were painful. Behind her, she heard the rough grinding of metal against metal.

With her eyes barely able to focus from the shock and with rivulets of blood running down her face, Penny, the young woman of her dream, perhaps the woman in all her recent horrifying dreams, struggled to look in the rear view mirror, and saw that another car had rear-ended hers. A stocky blond man in his early thirties had just left the other car and hurried over to hers -- the man who had been watching her back at the University. His face was pale and expressionless and his movements intense and purposeful.

A chill ran down her back, then her whole body shivered; she coughed, then gagged on some blood that was running down the back of her throat. Struggling against an urge to faint, she knew she needed to get out and run from him, but had trouble even moving her head to the side.

Gathering all her remaining strength, she opened her car door and prepared to run as fast as she could. Above her, she was startled to see entire flock of blood red birds suddenly taking off into the air, screeching as the sky began to swim. Alarmed, she desperately tried to get back in the car and slam the door shut.

The man who had rear-ended her car grabbed the door handle and forced it open further, reached in, grabbed the young woman by her coat collar and quickly aimed an ExploDart unit at her forehead. A ruby red pinpoint of light appeared on her right temple, and she heard a very faint clicking sound, followed instantly by darkness.

With the last of her strength, the young woman grabbed her assailant's arm and plunged her nails deep through his skin, scraping down almost to the very bone, her death grip boosted in force and purpose by the pain searing through her body as she collapsed.

With his forearm bleeding, the attacker dragged the young woman onto the street, took her purse, got back in his car and drove off. In less than fifteen unwitnessed seconds, her life as she had known it, and all its hopes and dreams for the future, was totally and completely over.

In her last moments of consciousness, the pain and the shock no longer a consideration, she remembered a very peaceful psalm she had once read:

"For you alone, my soul in silence waits."

A moment later, she entered a very long dream, and slowly drifted away. . .

Karolena snapped out of her day dream with a start, shocked by what she had just remembered, and immediately addressed her AllSee." Apartment security status, please." Her dream was so vivid and threatening, she felt it was she that was now in danger,

"All entrances secure, two persons present - Karolena Kreisler and one unknown."

Hearing that there was a second person in her apartment, Karolena panicked and immediately had the AllSee call security. As she waited by her open front door for the security team to arrive, she remembered more details from her dream than she had ever remembered before. She remembered the attack, the pain of being shot, digging her hand into her assailant's arm, and most of all, she now remembered his face. Penny's attacker was unmistakably .... Dieter. Yes. In her dream it certainly was Dieter.

Security arrived at her door in less than a minute. Testing her AllSee, it persisted in wrongly identifying one more person besides Karolena in the apartment, but could not give a location. After searching her apartment, the security team determined that Karolena was indeed alone. An explosives detector-bot passed near Karolena. It went wild as it neared the bathroom, awakening anyone still asleep in the entire building with its ear-piercing alarm. The apartment guard grabbed Karolena from behind. "Okay, stop right there. What are you hiding?"

"What the hell are you doing? You can't treat me like this, I'm a German citizen." Karolena protested.

"I really don't give a damn who the hell you are. The sensor detected explosives. That's all I need to know."

"Explosives? You must be kidding. You know me. I live here," she protested, hardly able to believe this was happening to her.

"That don't make no difference," the guard shot back, suspiciously eyeing Karolena from a distance.

"I'm hiding nothing. NOTHING. Look, your scanner must be broken." Karolena felt trapped and desperate; explosives were a serious issue, and terrorists weren't treated kindly. She was not a terrorist, and needed to get that fact across to the security guard.

By this time, other apartment security guards had arrived and congregated menacingly around Karolena. The detector-bot continued to roam her apartment, and stopped near her bathroom cabinets. A weak positive for plastic explosives displayed on its holograph, with a red arrow pointing to the bottom cabinet. Karolena was sure that Dieter must have used her bathroom while she was still sleeping, before he left.

The mention of Dieter triggered conflicting memories in her mind, but instead of sexually exciting memories, they were dragged screaming directly from the dream / nightmare she had just experienced. Returning her thoughts to the present, Karolena started to open the cabinet drawer, and looked inside. "Wait. Don't pull out any towels." the guard yelled out. She noted that the towels seemed a little out of place. One of the guards reached inside, and immediately yelled out, "It's beginning to feel hot." Panicking, Karolena dove backwards into the apartment lobby, with the guard quickly following her out of the bathroom.

The blast from the bomb gutted the bathroom, damaging the connecting wall and part of the ceiling. Plumbing burst and immediately released streams of hot and cold water, and sections of floor ripped away.

The shock echoed through the apartment, knocking over the gathering of security guards.

The lead guard was the first back up on her feet. Dazed, but uninjured, she yelled out, "Don't anyone else come in yet." "There may be more bombs and after-explosions."

By that time the city police and paramilitary had arrived, responding to the initial alarm given by the security scanner via its AllSee hookup.

Karolena, in near hysterics, was treated by the paramedics in her apartment building lobby for some surface cuts and bruises, then given a sedative skin patch. She collapsed, and slept in the hallway for almost an hour, until a police investigator named Blum arrived. Blum questioned Karolena, starting with whether she had any idea who had planted a bomb in such an unusual place, and why. Checking his notes, he said, "The apartment log shows you had a visit last night -- a Mr. Dieter Müeller."

"Yes, I did. Why?" she replied, trying to ignore the disapproval written over his face.

"Let's just say I'm familiar with him." Blum started to tell her something else, then stopped short.

Remembrances of her disturbing nightmare now flooded her mind, triggering a deep sense of panic and, more to the point, regret. Dieter was the man she had seen in the dream, and apparently, if her dream could be trusted, Dieter was the man who killed that woman. But, that was only a dream, not reality, and why was she having that nightmare? "Go ahead, tell me what's on your mind," she asked Det. Blum. Her concentration was elsewhere, on the woman dying in her dreams, and on Dieter. Was the dream a message to her, perhaps a warning, she wondered? She could her thoughts as they seemed to race away from her, and reminded herself that she was a logical person, one trained in the sciences, not a mystic.

"It's just that, if I were you, I'd choose the people I associate with very carefully. That's all."

"I do," Karolena insisted. "Look, Mr. Blum, Dieter's presence here last night was purely social. There was not, I can assure you, any anger or resentment involved on either of our parts when he left."

Blum's face was expressionless, but Karolena could see that something else was on his mind.

"I think you're making a mistake about Dieter Müeller," she insisted. She realized that trying to share her own doubts and suspicions of Dieter, based only on a dream she remembered, would sound totally ridiculous. She herself would never give credence if someone else told her that, no matter how much she knew and respected that person. "Someone else could very well have done this to me here, and I suggest you continue trying to locate who that person could be." She disliked Blum's insinuations about the man she slept with last night, and the implication to her personal qualities and standards, and was fairly certain that Blum already knew it. Still, given the frightening content of her dream, and its dangerous implications, she had to wonder whether Dieter could have done something so horrible to her. But why, she kept asking herself, why? And why have a nice dinner together, sleep together, go thru all that trouble, and then leave a bomb? It just didn't make any sense.

"We are actively looking for that person, Ms. Kreisler. Dieter, however, was here last night, not someone else. Your own personal emotional reasoning aside, he is our prime suspect at this point. And I mean you no disrespect." Blum shrugged. "I want you to set your personal feelings for this man Müeller aside for the moment. There are unsavory things about his past that you're not aware of. He is most capable of doing this to you, both technically and emotionally, of that I can assure you."

"But, Dieter would have no reason to do this, none at all." Karolena protested, almost breaking down and crying again. Still, Blum's words had a haunting compelling logic in her thoughts. What did she not know about him? Surely, almost everything. How could she be so reckless, so easily deceived? And if it was Dieter, then anything was possible, given just how little she really knew about anyone, these days. The stress of surviving an attempt on her life was almost enough to send her over the edge, and, looking at Blum, she realized she would be well advised to believe him.

"Let's assume that this Dieter had placed explosives in your cabinet," Blum continued. "I've been around a long time, Karolena, but I've never heard of putting plastic explosives in a stack of towels. And I don't understand why he would want to do that; after all, you two had, well I mean you probably were lovers, weren't you?" he added, almost matter-of-factly.

"Yes, sort of. We had sex," she said definitively. She guessed that much was fairly obvious, and was relieved when Blum didn't offer any criticism or commentary, the state of current mores aside. Then Karolena went on to explain why she still doubted, or wanted to doubt that Dieter was responsible.

"Do you recall any special conversation or perhaps a line of questioning Dieter took with you?"

"No. I don't think he really wanted information from me." Karolena winced, knowing that it was not information that he wanted, and regretting that she had been so easy.

"I see what you mean," Blum suppressed a judgmental smirk. "I think we had better look around your apartment, just to be sure there aren't any other explosive devices present. By the way, could Dieter have taken anything or looked at any of your papers or purse, or left anything else?"

"No, I don't think so," Karolena said, ignoring Blum's slimy insinuation for now.

She next took Blum upstairs, to what was left of her apartment, and, once they were inside, examined the contents of each room, piece by piece. Karolena found nothing unexpected, but Blum nevertheless examined each item of her property scrupulously, on his own.

Soon, building security returned, bringing a special "sniffer" unit into her apartment, with the programming and capability to identify plastic explosives, and certain chemical and biological agents. The security agents also methodically went room to room, examining all of Karolena's possessions. Her bags, makeup case, briefcase, purses, pocket AllSee, even her optical book collection all were thoroughly examined for explosives; fortunately, no additional ones were found. One by one they passed every object through thc sniffer unit, waiting for a telltale sign, any indication that Dieter or anyone else had left something behind. Only then were they and Blum satisfied that no other explosives were left. Shortly thereafter, the police left.

With maintenance not scheduled to begin repair work on her apartment until the morning, the apartment manager helped Karolena clean up the mess, and let her stay in an empty, furnished unit. Still finding it difficult to believe Blum's insinuation that it was Dieter who had just tried to kill her, Karolena attempted to call Dieter and ask him herself. Still, she had a difficult time planning exactly how she would ask someone she had just been intimate with such an accusatory question. As he had neglected to leave his AllSee number, she asked her AllSee to contact Dieter via his name, but curiously no corresponding number was located, and, physically exhausted, she soon drifted toward sleep. Her last conscious thoughts were of her last dream, how she had been awakened frightened, and how, shortly after, the bomb had been discovered, and then the pieces started coming together. She had been dreaming of Penny, and, in some mysterious way, she began to realize that it was Penny who was crying out from the grave to warn her, warning her of the presence of the bomb. Although she was no more convinced of the bomb's origin than she was earlier, Karolena now realized that she owed her life to Penny. Whether it was Dieter or someone else that had tried to kill her, in many ways she felt that perhaps she should recognize the dreams for what they really were – messages, warnings. She vowed to work with Penny via her messages, speaking thru her dreams, rather than trying to close her off.

Chapter 30

All the next morning, Karolena had an uncomfortable feeling she still missed critical facts concerning her own transplants, but she was uncertain where to look. She now knew more than ever that Penny's words could be true: maybe she was living off another's death -- Penny Forest. But how could this have happened? Karolena had not and never would have asked anyone to kill Penny, or anyone, in her behalf. Nor was anyone she knew capable of so horrific an act.

Between the violence she had managed to survive and the terrifying visions she was forced to experience, Karolena felt she would soon go mad. Above all else, she had to find a way to protect herself. In the past, Karolena had depended on her father, and later on to Blütfink to help her, but now, with her recovery, and after their recent attempt at reawakening their past close relationship, Blütfink's personal attention and his assistance was welcomed, albeit not too dependable.

Karolena had gone to Brighton to try and learn whatever she could about her donor, and at that time was unaware of a possible relationship between her needing a graft and a donor becoming available. Especially so quickly. Now, circumstances certainly had changed.

Karolena had overheard while at a visit with her transplant doctor of another transplant recipient, this one to a technician at FirsThought named Sentinal Southern, a person she had known, albeit only barely. According to some inside conversations she discretely had, the organ became available soon after his desperate family had personally come to see Bob Wilder. Although Karolena knew that this person's medical condition was none of her business, she had an unexplainable curiosity over subtle similarities to her own graft which drew her to discretely inquire a little further.

Searching for a pattern, Karolena queried Sentinal's medical records, but as she was not the treating physician, she could not easily access them, without a reason. Although the computer apparently was unable to supply the information to her, Karolena thought she knew where she might turn from within The Winston.

When Karolena asked Susan Wilder out for lunch, Susan was thrilled that Karolena was still recovering well, and quickly agreed. Susan had heard of the explosion at Karolena's apartment, and had called soon thereafter, offering any help she could, and was longing to learn more of what had happened. They arranged to meet at *The Natural Disaster,* later the same day. She immediately told Susan all about her fateful dream and the explosion which had followed.

After Susan got over her initial shock, Karolena brought up the subject that had prompted her to ask Susan for a meeting.

"Susan, do you know of a man named Sentinal

Southern, a former patient at The Winston?" She watched Susan's face for a sign of reaction. Susan appeared surprised, uncomfortable, and flustered.

"No, I can't say I recognize the name. Sorry."

Karolena could sense the evasion; Susan was no better a liar than was she. "Sentinal Southern was a patient in The Winston recently, for a transplant, and I thought the name might be familiar to you." She could see it obviously was.

"No, he's not someone I know of. Why, was there a problem?" Susan looked around at the other tables, at the window, at the mechanical waiter-bots serving food to other tables. She activated a sim-cig, offered one to Karolena, and took a deep drag.

"No, there wasn't really a problem." Karolena smiled back, trying to sound disinterested. "Sentinal, Mr. Southern, is a co-worker at FirsThought. We see each other occasionally."

"Oh?" Susan gave Karolena a knowing smile.

"No, Susan, it's nothing like that, really," Karolena smiled. "Sentinal is just an acquaintance, and his name came up recently when I was speaking to some people about my transplant. Susan, do you remember how you helped me deal better with my transplant surgery by telling me that my donor came from England, from Brighton, England and that her name was P. Forest?"

"Yes," she blurted, "but that was a special favor, Karolena. Only we two know about that. No one else," she emphasized. "And not something I've ever done before."

"Yes, and I appreciate your helping me, Susan.

Sentinal too is very interested in his procedure, which was similar to mine. You know, in many ways, getting an organ transplant is like having an adoption. Some adoptees want to know their parents."

"And others don't," she added. Susan began tapping her foot against the chair, then shifted around uncomfortably.

Seeing that Susan was getting a little edgy, Karolena added, "Oh, of course neither of us is interested in contacting our donors. After all, they're dead, aren't they?"

"Yeah, I guess so." As soon as she said it, Susan blushed and held her hand to her mouth.

So, Sentinel's donor died also, Karolena thought. "Well, here's how you can help," she persisted.

"But I never said I would help, Karolena," Susan objected.

Ignoring what she had just heard, Karolena pushed her point. "Sentinal would just like to know a little about his donor, enough background information to ease his curiosity. Please Susan, could you help just one more time?"

"Karolena, I'd really like to, but I can't. Yours was a special case, one-of-a-kind, because we're acquaintances, friends," Susan added for emphasis. "It was a very atypical situation. We just don't give out that kind of information, normally, I'm sorry. If Mr. Southern really wants to know more information about his organ donor, perhaps he could contact the UNITED ORGAN NETWORK."

Karolena listened, disappointed, but couldn't see

any advantage in pressuring Susan further. She wondered if the recently transplant coordinator had been replaced, if now, she could ask her if Susan wouldn't help.

"I could give Mr. Southern the address and AllSee number of UNITED ORGAN NETWORK if he'll call me. But I doubt that they would help him either. You see, it's very much like you described it, like an adoption; it's very private."

Later that day, as Karolena opened the AllSee in her purse to make a call, the message notification was flashing. She entered her encryption key, and saw:

To: Karolena Kreisler wncus212-22-36543x
From: Susan Wilder
Private and Secure Channel.
Subject: Donor for Southern
Text: I can't say for sure who the actual donor was, but apparently the organ came from Vienna, Greater Germany. I hope this satisfies Mr. Southern's curiosity. Next time, though, have the patient contact the transplant office. See you for lunch soon; it's your turn to pay.
Regards, Susan.

Karolena thought how grateful she was to Susan, and called on the AllSee to thank her.

Susan was as gracious as ever. She didn't directly mention she had not told her husband about this, but they both knew that this was a given.

Bob, however, already suspected his wife of leaking information: facts that might give the wrong impression, facts which might hurt The Winston or, worse yet, might harm him. Susan associated with Karolena much too much to suit him, and, because of that, Bob had the Information Sciences Department at The Winston install a special neural network program on the hospital's computer. This program could screen all calls coming in or going out of The Winston and his home, looking for key words such as "UNITED ORGAN NETWORK," "Transplant," "Karolena" and "Organ."

The computer program recognized and saved this last message from Susan to Karolena and sent a copy to Bob Wilder via the 'Personal' option on voice mail. He already knew Susan's encryption key, as he and Susan shared the same one out of simplicity. Bob's face darkened as he read Susan's meddlesome message to Karolena. Angry, Bob decided that his only option was to call his 'problem fixer.' Reluctantly, he picked up his AllSee.

"Hi, this is Bob Wilder. Look, we've got another problem, and I'm afraid that it is getting more bothersome every day. I'm forwarding a phone message via encrypted voice mail sent earlier today. It's from my naive wife to that ungrateful, frigid, meddling little bitch Karolena Kreisler. Listen to it and call me with suggestions. This has got to end. And this time, no mistakes."

Bob hung up the AllSee. What more could be

said? Hearing Susan again break his confidence, despite his clear warnings, made this a very sad day for him.

Later that day, Karolena finally received a message on her AllSee about the database search she had run on Sentinal. The holograph face display informed her that there were forty-one persons in North America who had a greater than 95 percent compatible Biotype to Sentinal Southern, and asked if she wanted a printout. When Karolena displayed the information on the first ten persons, she saw immediately by the red outline of the last names that most were *Retro* positive, explaining why Sentinal had such difficulty obtaining a donor.

Karolena requested that the search be expanded to include Europe. The computer responded that the estimated search time would be six hours, including two hours of Interconnect Central Processing Unit time, and asked for billing confirmation. Karolena gave her go-ahead, forwarding charges to her personal department code at FirsThought. Then, having second thoughts, she restricted the expanded search to include only *Retro-negative* donors within 100 kilometers of Vienna.

That evening, a hologram began flashing a colored pattern over her table in her living room:

"AllSee Message for You,"

with a beautiful computer-generated Bach fugue playing in the background. She turned toward the

AllSee. "This is Karolena. Play the message for me."

"It is in table form. You will need to see it, or have a printout."

"Okay, okay," she sighed. "Visual projection." She faced the wall opposite the window, the only one nearly free of paintings.

Computer Database Search Output.
Filter Specifications:
1) Biotype >95 percent compatibility with
H A557B3522C835445D145
and
2) Living in North America or Europe
and
3) *Retro-negative*

There are no persons fulfilling the search criteria.
Do you wish to change search criteria? Y N?

Karolena said 'No,' and signed off, disappointed that her hunch hadn't worked out.

She walked slowly into the kitchen area, asked her AutoBev for a glass of Orange Juice and took the glass into the living room to plan her next move. On her way out, she noticed a repair note from the building manager taped on the refrigerator door. The note informed her that a replacement toxin filter had finally been installed in her water system. "That sure took a long time," she sighed, grateful it was finally in.

As she passed a wall mirror she looked at her reflection and thought, 'Karolena, you look positively dead.' She vowed to spend more time fixing herself up this morning. Starting for the bathroom, shc frozc. "I look positively dead." she repeated out loud, a sense of realization sweeping her. "Why, the donor for Sentinal was dead." She turned quickly to the wall AllSee unit. "AllSee. Recall last communication."

"Working." There was a short pause. "Database search output. Continue?"

"Yes. Modify search criteria on Sentinal Southern to include persons who have died in the two months before today. Run. Redirect output to my AllSee. End."

Later that evening, another AllSee message arrived. "Display," Karolena said to the wall unit.

Computer Database Search Output.
Filter Specifications:
1) Biotype >95 percent compatibility with
H A557B3522C835445D145
and
2) Living in North America or Europe
and
3) *Retro-negative*
and
4) includes persons who died in the 12 months before today.

Display output? Y/N ?

Good, she thought. At least this time there's output. "Yes, display."

Last Name First Age *Retro* State
Klaus Luther 27 neg. Frankfurt, Gr Germany
Salerno Jimmy 77 neg. Florida
Salzburg Mistislav 20 neg. Austria Sector, Gr Germany
Sussa Tarcin 13 neg. Brazil
Tarinten Richard 37 neg. Arizona

Do you request additional information? Y/N?

Karolena looked over the list. She remembered that Susan had mentioned that Sentinel's organ originated in Vienna, Greater Germany. Mistislav Salzburg was *Retro-negative*, and his home of record was in Vienna, in the Austrian Sector of Greater Germany. Karolena considered that this was near an airport able to accommodate an SST if she wanted to visit, having remembered how Greater Germany had lengthened the runway shortly after merging with the economically devastated Austrian state about ten years ago.

Karolena keyed in 'Yes' for additional information, and was shown a screen of options:

Press 1 for Birth Certificate
2 for Death Certificate
3 for Credit Information
4 other

Karolena pressed "2", requesting the death certificate of Mistislav Salzburg, then logged off the computer. She next called Susan at work and made an appointment for lunch. There were coincidences to discuss: about her, and about others.

Chapter 31

Karolena met Susan for lunch at *The Natural Disaster*. They talked for half an hour before finally ordering, then asked for two coffees. Susan talked very little, preferring to stare out of the window.

"What's the problem, Susan?" Karolena asked. "You seem kind of nervous today."

"Bob and I had a big argument last night," Susan admitted. "Somehow, and I don't know how, he knew that I gave you information on Sentinel's donor, and he was VERY angry. I had to promise not to do it again. He doesn't even want me to see you socially again."

"I'm so sorry." Karolena exclaimed. She could see the fear in Susan's eyes, and asked her, "Are you afraid Bob will hurt you, Susan?" Abusive spouses, both male and female, were not unheard of at all these days.

"No, of course not. Don't be ridiculous," Susan said, looking around nervously at one of the security guards Bob had shadowing her -- for her own protection, he told her.

"Everything's okay, just forget it." Susan looked down at her coffee cup for a long time, silent, then said to Karolena, "Look, I really have to go now. I never should have come in the first place. If Bob finds out I was here . . . If that security guard mentions it . . . " Susan shuddered visibly, then got up and left without saying good-bye.

Concerned, Karolena paid the bill and left, but

couldn't see in which direction Susan had gone.

While driving home for dinner that evening, Karolena received a message announcement on her car dash. "Receive. Output: Voice," she said.

"Impossible. Output is Document."

"Then print." A laser printer output slid out from under her dash.

"24 July, 8 p.m.: Death certificate of Mistislav Salzburg, the donor of the transplant organ for Sentinal Southern." Karolena read that the cause of death was accidental, that his age was twenty years, his former address, and the names and address of his parents. She was relieved that at least Sentinel's organ donor wasn't murdered.

"AllSee," Karolena said. "Place a call to my office."

After a few seconds, FirsThought's automated scheduling system picked up the line. "FirsThought Scientific. Ms. Kreisler's Office."

"Hello, this is Karolena Kreisler. I need to make an unscheduled business trip to Vienna, Greater Germany, for tomorrow or whenever there's a flight that will get me in on a business day."

"Purpose?"

"Yes, purpose, . . . " Karolena had to pause a second. "Yes, well the purpose is to investigate a possible investment in a new biotech firm for FirsThought," she fabricated.

"Working," the logic system said. "Result: Ukraine

Air, Departs 0800 hours tomorrow morning. Adequate?"

"Yes, that will be fine. Link the tickets to my wrist ID."

Chapter 32

The next day, a highly suspicious Bob Wilder called Karolena's office, and told her sim-secretary, "This is Mr. Robert Wilder. I'm the hospital administrator at The Winston. Can I speak with Dr. Kreisler please?"

"I'm sorry, Mr. Wilder. Dr. Kreisler isn't in," the program responded. "Can I take a message?"

"Well, I don't think so. You see, I'm calling about some time-sensitive information on a biotech company that Dr. Kreisler asked me for. I'm afraid that if she doesn't get the information soon, it will be useless, and it could hurt a major client of FirsThought. Perhaps I could send it as an attachment to Dr. Kreisler."

"That might be possible. Let me get the AllSee number of the hotel she'll be staying at for you."

"Thank you," he replied civilly, fuming as he heard the word ‘hotel'. Bob quickly entered the number given him into his fax unit, and got the bounce-back location: "Reich Hotel, Vienna." That meddling bitch, Bob thought as he pounded his table angrily. He knew right away that Karolena must be trying to find out more about another donor's death. She had already pumped his secretary and his wife for as much as she could find out, and now this, he thought. If he could be in some way implicated, if he could be incriminated, his career would be ruined, all he worked for at The Winston, and his plans to commercialize on the nerve growth factor would be totally destroyed.

Bob's mind reeled as he considered the easily misinterpreted trail of circumstantial evidence that remained: the calls on his AllSee, the donor list he had constructed, just to name a few.

Bob felt sick to his stomach as he picked up the AllSee again, and hit a pre-coded sequence. "Dieter? This is Bob. Guess who's going to Vienna?"

Dieter paused for a moment, then asked, "Can you get her airline information for me?"

"I think so. This time, you better make it definitive."

"Right. Definitive."

Vienna prospered, as did most heavily debt-burdened cities in the formerly independent German speaking countries in that region, once it acquiesced and joined the Greater German State. Its airport was Vienna's crowning achievement, a wonder for the whole world. Called an AeroMall, for it truly was, it could just as easily have been a giant amusement park with an attached airport. Each part, airport and shopping, areas for living and working, entertainment, was equally important, and it only really mattered why you went there: shop or fly, fly or shop. Or both.

The Vienna AeroMall was one of the largest continuous buildings in Europe, security was relatively lax and the flow of people was considerable. The management and shop owners of the seven story mall that was directly attached to the four terminals insisted on loose access by the shopping and traveling public, and they usually got what they wanted. This made terrorist control difficult. Still, everyone underwent the customary thorough wrist ID verification before entering.

Dieter landed at the less secure Bonn airport three hours earlier than Karolena's flight, then took a magni-train to Vienna. He wanted to settle Karolena before she got into the city. As he expected, security for all Ukraine Air facilities was tight, as usual. Yet, it would actually be easier for him to achieve his objective right there at the Vienna AeroMall and still get out alive, he reasoned.

Dieter knew he might need hostages to escape. He also was aware that, in Greater Germany, hostages were often shot without regard, as long as the goal of killing more of the growing band of terrorists was achieved. And Dieter knew that Bob was worried, that much he could sense from Bob's voice. Bob wouldn't want Karolena finding out something that could incriminate him, and neither did Dieter. He could almost sense the fear in Bob's voice.

Dieter didn't plan to be as subtle or inventive this time as he had tried to be back at Karolena's apartment. Nothing interesting, nothing bizarre, only definitive. The deaths did not bother him, that he had gotten used to long ago, and he learned to profit from death, to be sure.

After parking his rented Nissan-NWO outside the Vienna AeroMall, Dieter headed for the half mile moving staircase leading inside. Just before entering, he put on his newly obtained wrist ID, still warm from the body that had been wearing it only minutes earlier.

A few minutes later, he calmly left the outer barricade area and approached the last checkpoint that would allow him to gain entry to the AeroMall. Here, a paramilitary soldier poked the barrel of his rifle in Dieter's chest and gruffly asked for his airline ticket or shopping permit.

"Guten tag. Das ist mein Fahrkarte," Dieter replied politely. He expected to be able to pass, but always awaited the worst.

Finally, the guard motioned Dieter to pass through the electric doors and enter the security scanner. Dieter had read that a new scanner capability had been added recently that could detect composite ceramic weapons, and he was carrying several.

As he passed through, uncontested, Dieter knew at once that the scanners either didn't exist or weren't functioning properly, and was greatly relieved. So much for new and better, he thought. He told a guard that his Ukraine Air bag was to be a carry-on, and picked it up after it too had passed through the scanner. Calmly swinging the bag over his shoulder, Dieter passed through the electric doors as they opened, and entered the mall.

"That was easy enough," he muttered to himself.

It seemed to Dieter that there were way too many guards everywhere today, and their presence made him very nervous. There were not just the usual AeroMall security, with their gray and red bullet proof jumpsuits, shoulder pistols and helmets. The more heavily armed soldiers of the central security forces were also present. They stood out in their telecommunications helmets, bulletproof flak jackets, and air-cooled machine guns - big heavy guns that took two hands to hold and could cut a car in half without trouble.

He entered through the AeroMall shopping entrance, knowing this would be easier than entering via the airport entrance itself. Later, Dieter intended on using stolen airline tickets to gain entry into the terminal. The place was mobbed as usual and the stolen wrist ID again worked perfectly, allowing him to pass through the crowded outer entrance. The flood of people put at least a 30-minute delay in holographic image ID verification, and by then he hoped to be long gone.

Going into the Vienna AeroMall was like entering one of the great shopping malls anchored just offshore. For Dieter it was an easy place to make a hit.

Dieter sat for coffee at a small circular glass table in one of the Food Courts, ordered cafe crème and a sandwich, and took some time to collect his thoughts and go over his actual plans for execution one more time before Karolena arrived. A diversion, probably a fire alarm, would be best, he thought, and he planned for it to go off as soon as he saw Karolena exit the aircraft. At that point, he would use the loud background noise to quietly kill that annoying Karolena, then escape in the milling throngs and the confusion. The plan was extraordinarily simple, and it ought to work. His failure last time was an embarrassment for him, and more than an annoyance for his contractor. Satisfied, Dieter rose and sauntered down the corridor.

Chapter 33

Karolena had arrived at her gate over an hour before her schedule, having decided to catch an earlier flight after a vivid dream of an aircraft accident prompted her to change her plans. Although she couldn't decide whether this was a free-floating anxiety about flying, which she had suffered from for many years, or whether the dream was perhaps a subconscious communication from her graft donor, and she still wasn't certain if that really was possible, she decided on it being an anxiety reaction. There was nothing about a young donor in her dream, so it seemed to her to not be relevant, but when the opening for an earlier flight arose, she took it. True, she acknowledged that directing her actions based upon dreams was the most ridiculous, superstitious and unscientific act she had ever taken. Still, after her life was spared from the explosion in her apartment, she had decided to search more attentively for meaning to her dream's content more carefully. Maybe, she wondered, although even Karolena had to admit it was a real stretch of the imagination, just maybe Penny was trying to communicate with her. After all, she did carry around a section of Penny's brain inside her skull.

Unlike her arrivals in the states, in Vienna it took only a few minutes for Karolena, a citizen of Greater Germany, to scan her wrist IDent and disembark from the plane. Once in the AeroMall, she paused at the bottom of the security carousel. Something was wrong; she could feel it. She couldn't say exactly what it was, but she sensed she was in danger just standing there, and had the urge to move away from the area quickly.

An AeroMall security guard watched as she stopped and looked around. After a minute, he came forward to ask her if there was a problem.

"No, I don't think so," Karolena said, a puzzled look on her face. "I just felt a little funny on getting off that plane, that's all." She scanned the arrival area briefly, still not willing to move forward. "I'll be all right. Just give me a minute," she smiled.

The security guard stared questioningly at Karolena, waiting for her to move, then firmly told her, "Lady, you're going to have to walk along, okay?" He reached for his AllSee as if about to notify his supervisor.

Karolena took a deep breath, tried to relax and stepped into the terminal. The last thing she wanted was being detained by AeroMall security. Although her strong feeling of uneasiness persisted, she could see nothing wrong, and forced herself to begin the long walk toward the baggage area. There, she instructed the baggage security ‘bot to have her luggage forwarded to her hotel, then went for a visit in the shopping side of the AeroMall.

Karolena found it reassuring to see so many people dressed in the simple, functional fashion trend in Greater Germany these last few years. She owned clothing like this, but since wearing it in Winston County would only call more attention to her, she rarely put them on. Halfway down the escalator she decided that she had enough time to go to the literature court to see what new hologram books were available. There she could browse and wait for her limo and guard, and she hoped that being there would get her mind off the strange, insecure feeling she still felt.

As Karolena walked down the corridor, she used her AllSee to call the FirsThought contact number and verify her pickup arrangements. Then, she turned the corner toward the book stalls, bumping her way against the crowds of people walking against her.

Karolena stopped in front of an AeroMall book store, and looked at the selection of holograph books displayed in the window glass. The reflections of people walking behind her and on the other side of the open center of the mall played upon the shiny book diskette covers and the circular surfaces, like schools of fish swimming in an aquarium. Suddenly, the image of one person in particular caught her attention, forcing her to hold her breath and almost making her faint.

Karolena barely heard the man standing only a few feet in back of her as he spoke in excellent German to a hall kiosk vendor. There was too much noise from all the other people around for Karolena to hear what he was saying. Then, he seemed to move away toward the terminal gates.

Breathless, Karolena quickly ducked into the book store, crouched behind a rack, and nervously peered around. She pretended to look at a book for a few moments, then turned back and stared. When Karolena finally got a better look, she was shocked to recognize the man many suspected had once tried to kill her at her apartment -- Dieter Müeller himself, standing here just a few feet in back of her. She realized now that this was no coincidence and that he must have been the source of her strange feeling of danger a few moments earlier.

A thousand thoughts flashed through Karolena's panic-stricken mind all at once as she crouched down on the floor, then collapsed into simple fear. Her heart raced as she tried to make sense of his presence, and tried to deny the obvious -- he was here for her. She forced herself not to panic, but nearly screamed out when a hand touched her shoulders.

"Can I help you, Miss?" a clerk-bot from the bookstore asked Karolena.

"Yes, no, I think so. I, I . . . lost something and I have to go now. Thanks." Karolena knew she sounded terrified as she blurted out the words, and she certainly felt that way. She tried to regain her composure as she stood up.

Dieter had quickly disappeared amid a crowd of shoppers, and was gone before Karolena could fully turn round. Karolena wasn't sure if he had heard her or seen her. Frantically she ran out of the store, and hurried in the other direction. Several times she thought she saw Dieter and turned to go the other way. Once, Karolena thought she saw Dieter head toward the gates to her right. As she turned around, she found her movements hampered by the many guards with their barking dog-bots She hated dogs, ever since being bitten on the face by one as a child. Karolena started to walk away when she felt a hand on her shoulder. Startled, she suppressed a screamed and quickly turned around.

"Can I help you, Miss?" a mall guard asked. "You appear to be looking for something?" His dog-bot growled menacingly at her. Its AI sensed everything about her by reading her wrist ID and scanning the expression on her face. And it sensed her fear.

Karolena feared that Dieter would come for her, would try to kill her again and this time be successful. Hurriedly, she explained to the guard that a man had tried to kill her, and described Dieter to him.

The guard looked at Karolena strangely, scanned her wrist ID to check, then called in her story to AeroMall security. His dog-bot barked and jumped menacingly at Karolena while they stood there, waiting for directions. The AeroMall guard had to jerk the dog's leash back more than once to keep it far enough from Karolena so it couldn't bite her.

Having confirmed her story, and receiving directions to "pursue," the AeroMall guard, followed by Karolena, walked rapidly along the shop corridors, frantically but unsuccessfully searching for Dieter. At the same time, a holographic reconstruction from Karolena's description of Dieter, along with a holographic "Wanted" poster, was sent to AllSee displays all over the AeroMall.

Oblivious to Karolena's presence in the AeroMall, Dieter calmly strolled into a nearby men's room. He bumped into a uniformed security agent on the way in, simply smiled, apologized and continued in. Once alone in a stall, Dieter carefully looked around before closing the door and rechecking its closure. While on the commode seat, he quickly assembled an all-composite submachine gun and placed it under his coat.

A monitor camera in the one-way mirror in the men's room caught all of the actions of this man who matched the description just given by Karolena, and the AeroMall anti-terrorist team was instantly alerted. From the moment Dieter left the men's room he was constantly in the sight of a rifle.

Leaving the bathroom, Dieter calmly and slowly walked in the direction of the ReichStaff Bank. His animal instinct, however, almost instantly made him aware of several uniformed soldiers following him, as he smelled the scent of being hunted. He reasoned that somehow he had been discovered, that he was now the prey and not Karolena, and grasped for a last chance evasion.

Seeing security police running toward him, Dieter grabbed a ReichStaff bank clerk from behind her desk. Holding her as a shield between himself and the police, he yelled at them to back off. Trying to remain cool even under these circumstances, Dieter desperately looked for the nearest exit.

Dieter inched toward the AeroMall exit, the bank clerk held like a shield before him. Only feet from the door, a bank customer suddenly panicked and stood up to run. Dieter quickly tried to see if he should try to shoot the customer or drop his own shield and make a run for it, but before he could decide, a shot rang out from a security guard. The burning hot lead missile slammed into Dieter's bulletproof vest, the force of impact knocked both him and his hostage down. Dieter turned, got his laser dot on what he thought might be a concealed spot in the upper walkway, and fired. The explosive bullet shattered the ceiling, causing several security agents to fall screaming to the ground.

The piercing noise of the terrorist alarm suddenly filled the entire terminal, causing everyone to run for safety. Shit, Dieter thought, I'm a dead man now.

At the AeroMall firehouse, sirens blared as a group of special anti-terrorist trucks shot out of their caves. The massive crowds panicked, with hoards of people racing toward doors, any doors, as long as they seemed a way out. Karolena heard the terrifying screams, the crash of falling glass, the bursts of automatic weapons fire, and the sirens of the security forces, and ran for her life out of the mall along with the panicking crowd. Miraculously, she escaped any injury and quickly moved safely away from the hell she had just landed in.

A trail of gunfire forced Dieter toward the nearest exit. He still held onto the bank clerk by the neck, realizing that without her, he was dead. Dieter turned and fired another shot toward the ceiling where he could see antiterrorist units training their lasers at him through protected slots. He missed them and hit the glass ringing the upper area, showering fragments down upon everyone, including himself. One razor thin shard pierced the protective tunic he wore, and, although the cut wasn't deep, blood spurted onto the wall and floor. Dieter stumbled through the electric doors, regained his balance by leaning on the bank clerk, and leapt forward.

Dieter continued to grip the bank clerk tightly, aiming his weapon at her head, and stared down the security forces who swelled around him. He knew they were willing to kill both him and the hostage. It was accepted, known, and he waited for his death, then wondered, when nothing happened, why.

An armored personnel carrier arrived, and troops poured out. "Back off and let me on the carrier or the hostage gets killed." Dieter yelled.

The Chief of Airport Security motioned for the security forces to let the terrorist through with his hostage. They now knew who this terrorist was, and had explicit directions from several other security agencies who wanted to talk to him, alive, if possible.

Dieter suspected a trap, but was short on options. He motioned the clerk to get into the passenger side of the impregnable carrier, jumped into the driver's seat and sped off. Behind him, he could see helicopters and police cars following, but didn't have time to be deterred or distracted.

Dieter raced into the underground tunnel connecting traffic from the AeroMall to downtown, quickly pulled over, took the hostage and put her in the driver's seat. He got out and yelled "drive," and as the carrier roared off, Dieter ran behind a holographic image of the tunnel surface. When the police escort howled past, he walked the other way, and in a few minutes he passed a cutoff under a bridge and disappeared into obscurity.

Chapter 34

Karolena stopped running when she reached a street corner about a mile away from the AeroMall. There, she looked on in disbelief at the NWO News Network coverage of the carnage displayed on a public flat screen covering the side of a building.

Quite shaken, she took a cab to her hotel and checked in. Karolena knew deep inside that she was the actual target of the attack and that Dieter was the terrorist. Following her premonition, or perhaps it was Penny's warnings, had again paid off, and had saved her life. Although she never would have believed it before, perhaps her transplant donor was, in some strange, bizarre way, trying to communicate with her, and help her. But why? That, she absolutely had to determine. At the very least, if she died, the transplant, that last living part of the donor, died with her.

Karolena checked in to her hotel, a masterpiece of last century architecture in the old city center of Vienna. Upon arriving in her room, she was pleased to discover that hotel security had already received, searched - a necessary annoyance, and unpacked her bags. Sitting on the side of her bed, she placed a call to the parents of Mistislav Salzburg. Unfortunately for her they spoke only Hungarian, and although she spoke several languages reasonably well, Hungarian wasn't one of them. Occasionally she wore her smart contacts, able to read and translate languages, display messages, and to some extent amplify images. They were often an annoyance, not totally comfortable to wear, and she hadn't brought them with on this trip. Instead, she pressed the help key on the AllSee, selected Translation services from the menu that appeared on the flat panel display, and slowly began to speak again.

Karolena heard her voice leave her throat in her native German but was amazed when she heard Hungarian echo to the other end, although she found the mixing of languages made it a little difficult to concentrate. "Hello; my name is Karolena Kreisler." She marveled at the way the translation computer mimicked her voice's tonal qualities and even her vocal intonations to some extent.

"Yes, what can we do for you, Fräulein?"

"You're the parents of a young man, Mistislav Salzburg, who passed away recently?" She stared at the holographic images of two sad faces, and wondered what types of persons they were, or had become after their son's death.

Silence.

Undaunted, she continued. "I'm an acquaintance of Sentinal Southern, a man living in the United States. He was severely injured a few months ago, and required a kidney transplant. We think that your son donated the kidney and we would like to express our gratitude."

Silence.

"We would like to express our gratitude in

person." She could see they understood her intentions quite well, but were reluctant to comply.

Silence.

"Hello. can you hear me?" Karolena asked.

"As you can expect, your call takes us quite by surprisc," Mr. Salzburg replied. "But we don't want to discuss this further with you. Please, leave us alone with the memories of our son. It is all we have left," Mr. Salzburg said, as he abruptly ended the conversation by disconnecting.

Not one to be put off, Karolena took a cab to the Salzburg's apartment complex, accompanied by a pocket voice translation unit supplied by the hotel. The cab dropped her off next to a reserved underground lot. The Salzburgs lived in an older brick industrial unit that had been converted to housing. It was built years ago, before the breakup of what had been the Russian Federation. Various vagrants, individuals and some families, were living on the streets nearby, and in the alley ways. A collection of bodies piled up on one street corner, which reminded her of a similar scene in her own Neuse. Several paramilitary units slowly patrolled in pickup units nearby.

Once inside the building, Karolena was relieved to note very comfortable carpeting covering the floor, a variety of paintings decorated the walls in the lobby and halls, and a rather human-like hologram greeted her. Karolena spoke into the translator unit and asked the hologram to call up to the Salzburg apartment.

Mr. Salzburg appeared on the flat screen, and when he found out what the visitor wanted, reached up to turn off the screen. Mrs. Salzburg, however, gently took his wrist, and said, "It's all right. Why not let her come for a few minutes?"

The door unlocked soon thereafter, and Karolena went inside. Once in the modestly furnished apartment, it was obvious to Karolena that both Salzburgs had been recently crying. Karolena immediately put her arm around Mrs. Salzburg's shoulder, and gently told her, "I know how much your son's death hurts you, and I really don't want to make you unhappy by coming here. The man who received Mistislav's kidney is truly grateful to you for making it available. He is so very grateful and asked me to tell you so, and to find out what I could about your son."

Mrs. Salzburg nodded that she understood, and spoke first. "On the day Mistislav died, I called my son several times to join us for lunch. When he didn't reply, I reversed the flat screen from our living room into his room. I could see that he appeared to have fallen asleep while reading on his bed, which was not unusual for him. Mistislav had been up late the previous night preparing for exams; he was very studious. I left him alone to rest." Mrs. Salzburg paused to wipe away another tear. "Several hours later, I again called him for dinner. When he continued to sleep, I tried to wake him."

Her voice broke, and Mr. Salzburg had to continue for his wife. "I found Mistislav unconscious; he was laying face down with a book open on the floor next to his bed. We still thought he was sleeping. Mistislav was breathing, but when he couldn't be aroused, I became alarmed and called an ambulance to take him to the hospital. In the emergency room the doctors said he had suffered a heart attack."

"Oh. But he was very young for that, wasn't he?" Karolena asked.

"Yes, we thought so too. The doctors said the heart attack was brought on by a bad heart rhythm, although they couldn't explain why this occurred." Mr. Salzburg stopped talking and stared out the window.

"The doctors told us that, although Mistislav's body was in excellent shape, and the part of his brain controlling breathing had survived, his higher brain had been severely damaged by lack of oxygen," Mrs. Salzburg explained. "Mistislav languished for a week at the hospital, but it became clear to us that the Mistislav we knew wouldn't recover. He was . . . gone," she choked, and looked down at the floor. Her husband took her hand. After a moment, she continued. "Eventually we agreed to allow the donation of his organs to other needy persons, to make his death meaningful, in a way."

"Do you remember any tests performed at the hospital? A CT scan perhaps, a nuclear medicine scan, or blood tests?"

"We were with him always. I can tell you that only the best specialists saw him. He received the finest of care and had many tests, but none could help restore him to us."

"Did he smoke cigarettes or take any medications?"

"No, he didn't smoke real tobacco or take

medications of any kind. We were asked that by the doctors at the hospital several different times."

"And did anyone in your families ever have such a thing happen to them?"

"No, not that we're aware of." Pausing, Mrs. Salzburg looked questioningly at Karolena and said, "You are German, aren't you?" Her visage immediately changed to suspicion.

"Yes, but I live and work in the United States," Karolena explained.

"I see. So, why are you asking us this many questions?"

"Just to tell my friend more about your son, that's all." Karolena could sense their anti-German sentiments, which was typical for refugees from recently incorporated states, and knew she had only a few minutes of qualified welcome left. "Did the doctors at the hospital give any opinion about why this may have occurred?"

"No, they couldn't explain it, but they said that although lethal heart rhythms in young persons are very rare, they can happen."

"Please, I know how difficult this must be for you, and you have been so understanding and kind, but would it be possible for me to visit Mistislav's room, just for a moment?"

The Salzburgs were very reluctant, but after much gentle pleading, they finally took Karolena in there. There she noted found several types of stringed instruments still hanging from pegs on the wall, including a Spanish style guitar and a viola. An electronic keyboard with assorted synthesis equipment stood against the wall, flat screen displays still showed music, and posters for concerts that Mistislav had attended or participated in dotted the walls.

Karolena looked around, commented on what a fine musician he must have been, then shc rcmarkcd, "The police must have thoroughly examined the room, I suppose."

"No, of course not." Mr. Salzburg turned away, appeared irritated, then asked Karolena sharply, "Why would they? Do you suspect something? This was obviously an act of God, it was a heart attack, not a crime."

"He wasn't involved in illegal activities or drugs. There was no reason for the police to investigate," Mrs. Salzburg added, defensively.

Karolena simply nodded instead of answering, then she 'accidentally' knocked over a lamp with her purse. She whirled about as it fell and watched it roll by the window side of the bed. Apologizing, she bent down to pick the lamp up and, while doing so, placed her palms out flat and pushed forward on her knees. "There is the lamp, near the bedpost," she announced for them to hear. Reaching for the small light unit, her palm snagged on a fine wire that had stuck into the carpet fabric. Karolena quickly twisted the wire around her hand and wrist, carefully looked around one more time, then grabbed the lamp and got up.

"Sorry about the lamp. I hope it isn't damaged."

"Never mind," Mrs. Salzburg said quickly. "Will that be all?" a pained and stern look covering her face.

"Yes. Thanks very much for your kind help under these most difficult of circumstances. I'm sure that your son must have given you much pleasure, and I hope that your grieving will be short and merciful. I'll relay what I know to his organ recipient, whom I'm sure will feel much better knowing what a fine young man Mistislav was."

On her way out of Mistislav's room, Karolena paused before a flat panel display, still showing some sheet music. "What was this?"

"Mistislav was active in the local Universalist fellowship, and was scheduled to perform the music you see: Psalm 130," Mrs. Salzburg said.

"It looks difficult."

"Yes, it is. He was always interested in new and interesting things, and was looking into chanting as a way to raise consciousness. He played the melody, and everyone repeated the phrase:

"For you alone my soul in silence waits,"

as a chant."

"It must have been very . . . ah, how shall I say . . . very repetitive," Karolena commented, noting that the psalm had a vague familiarity to it. She thought for a moment that she would lose her composure and cry at the utter tragic meaninglessness of his death, and began to wonder if this young man had died because Sentinal wanted to live, just as she had wanted to live.

"That's the point of a chant," Mrs. Salzburg said. "Anyway, Mistislav said that the people there found it relaxing."

"Good. Well, thanks for your help, both of you.

You have been very kind. I hope that you'll get on after this."

"Get on? Why, yes, I suppose we shall. Get on, but not forget," the Salzburgs said in a touching unison, holding hands.

Chapter 35

While on the short SST trip back to North Carolina, Karolena was surprised to receive a AllSee message from Daisy at the Medical Records Department at Brighton Hospital. The message simply read: "I changed my mind."

Daisy had probably done a little reexamination of her liquid assets, Karolena thought, and smiled. She quickly replied to Daisy that she also was still interested. Karolena repeated the terms of her offer, which included money, a great deal of money when taken from Daisy's perspective, and absolute privacy on both their parts. Daisy accepted, assuring Karolena that the documents would be sent by electronic mail once the transfer of cash was complete.

By the time Karolena returned home, she had already received the complete medical record, the surgical and operative records, the UNITED ORGAN NETWORK donor forms, and the Forensic Laboratory report for Penny Forest. To drive home her point that her donor's death was probably not simply coincidental, and for safe-keeping, Karolena forwarded a copy to Blum at the Neuse police.

The UNITED ORGAN NETWORK form didn't show the intended recipients of the organs, although at that point it might not have been known. The donor report also didn't list brain tissue as among the organs being utilized, but the operative report did mention a craniotomy with biopsy. A biopsy of brain tissue could have been used in Penny's surgical care, or to help the police investigation, or to get tissue for donation, as in her case, Karolena reasoned. But, although brain tissue was removed, there was no indication that any tissues had been sent to the Pathology Lab, and there were no pathology slips describing results.

The forensic lab report on blood samples taken from under the fingernails of Penny Forest was most interesting :

Report on Sample Submitted:

Penny Forest
UN Identity: F A314B514C753244D613
Criminal Case # A314B514C753244D613-1
Age: 19 years old
Citizen: England
Place of Death: Brighton, England
Criminal Code: Homicide

The sample submitted consisted of a single micro vial of dried blood; the source is from under surface of deceased right third and fourth fingernails. An additional sample consists of cell scraping from under surface of second and third digits right hand. These samples are submitted for UN ID.

Blood sample is *Retro-negative*. Two populations of white blood cells are identified, one belonging to a female, whose UN Identity matches that of the deceased.

The second population of white blood cells has a UN Identity biotype of:

M A271B224C121776D653.

This biotype does not match with known past or present male persons.

Cell scraping from under deceased fingernails

consists of squamous epithelial cells. Genetic analysis shows the source to be identical to that of the second population of white blood cells. The presence of blood and cell scraping is consistent with probable traumatic origin of samples.

Signed: Howard Deadtree, MD
Chief, GBPD, Genetic ID Unit

Karolena fed this information into a **UN ID** database at the transplant research lab at FirsThought, intending to then correlate the results with a public locator file that was available via AllSee. Running the program in reverse, Karolena entering the second biotype, and looked for a UN Identity. Unfortunately it only confirmed the forensic lab report: there wasn't a match for anyone living in North, Central or South America, or in Greater Europe and North Africa. An error detection subroutine in the program, however, suggested that the biotype might have contained a recording mistake. Its artificial intelligence suggested the source tissue be reexamined. Karolena reflected angrily that, of course, this would be impossible, since the source wasn't known.

Karolena knew that there had to be someone with this biotype, and that person had probably killed Penny Forest. Why else the scraped skin and blood on Penny's hand, much as had occurred in her last dream? And if there was such a person, could he have evaded getting a **UN ID**? She doubted it, as it was completely impossible to function in society without one. More likely the information was wrong, or someone was wearing an altered biotype.

Shortly after returning to North Carolina, Karolena stopped in to see Blum at his office. It was an appointment mutually arranged, and they had a lot to talk about.

"I'm glad to see you're alive," he smiled, shaking her hand. "I heard about the attack at the Vienna AeroMall."

"How did you know that?" Although mildly surprised, she was glad he was very aware of the danger she was in, and took it as a demonstration of his efficiency and his interest in her welfare. She liked that in him.

"That's what I get paid so much for," he grumbled. "Next time though, let's work a little more closely together, okay?"

Karolena smiled and nodded.

"And thanks for the forensic information on Penny Forest. It's most interesting."

"Good," she replied. Karolena took an envelope out of her purse and handed it to Blum, who carefully opened it, took out the thin wire strand, and started to examine it under a magnifying glass.

"Does this wire have any particular meaning to you?" It was the only thing she had found in Mistislav's room that she thought might be helpful.

Blum nodded thoughtfully. "What were the circumstances under which you found it?"

"It was lying on the carpet by the side of a bed

upon which a previously healthy young man, twenty years old, died of a heart attack."

Blum looked interested, opened the side drawer of his desk and took out an oblong black stone wristwatch and matching ceramic band. "Do you know what this is?" he asked, showing the band to her.

"A watch? A bracelet?"

"No, not exactly. Did you ever hear of a stun gun?"

Karolena looked puzzled. "I think I read of it once."

"Well, this is what they sometimes look like. It's not much of a gun, but it can be concealed pretty well. It can fire up to twenty feet of a hair-like carbonite cable that carries a powerful electric charge, and it can frighten away a street bum harassing you. It can also depolarize a large heart or induce a seizure, depending on the frequency and voltage selected."

"Like the young man whose bed I found it next to."

"Right. And like an ExploDart, it comes with a laser sight." He pointed the unit toward the wall, turned down the lights, showed Karolena where the red targeting dot was, and fired the unit.

Karolena never heard the charge go off and she never saw the unit hit the wall. "It looks like nothing happened."

Blum motioned her to the wall, and with the use of a hand-held magnifying glass, showed her the burn marks in the paint where the wires hit the wall. "And there are your wires."

Karolena whistled. "Are you saying that man may have been the unlucky recipient of this wire?"

"Exactly."

"But how could this have been used without the police noticing?" Karolena wondered. Then she remembered that there had been no police investigation. "There was a fire escape right outside Mistislav's window. Maybe someone climbed up it and shot Mistislav with a Stun Gun through the open window to induce unconsciousness."

"There's an art and science to all things, Karolena, both on the assailant's part and on the investigator's part. Let me see what I can do with this," Blum told her reassuringly.

The next day after her visit to Blum, Karolena went to The Winston for a routine follow-up blood test. She returned to The Winston less frequently now as he healing progressed, but knew she still needed to carefully monitor the progress of her transplant. Karolena felt stronger and more healthy now than she had in years; her mind seemed more rested and clear and her total outlook on life had turned completely around. Still, she remembered the words of the woman reporter at the awards banquet and lived with the guilt. Karolena wondered if she really was a vulture, sucking sustenance off someone else's life blood.

While sitting in the phlebotomy chair, a device which probably hadn't changed in design in over a hundred years, she began to feel dizzy, then noted her vision shifting, and her concentration waning.

. . . Karolena thought she saw a momentary glimpse of a repairman leaving one hospital room for another. She moved forward cautiously down the empty hall . . . Her heels clicked on the tile floor, and despite her trying to walk very softly, she couldn't muffle the sound.

A Nurse Aide passed Karolena in the hall, pushing a medication cart. "Are you looking for something?" the aide barked.

"Yes, I'm a patient here, and I thought I saw a repairman go into a room up the hall," Karolena said. "I want him to fix something in my room."

"The proper procedure is to call your nurse; the nurse will put in a repair request. You must return to your room, NOW." The nurse pointed a large red Stun Gun at Karolena's face and used the gun to motion Karolena back to her room. "Move, faster."

"Really, that's okay. If I could just find the person . . . "

"This area is closed. You must return to your room, IMMEDIATELY."

"Okay, okay," Karolena said, then darted off down the hall, ignoring the Nurse aide's calls from behind her. She heard the hiss of the Stun Gun fire from behind her and saw a sear form in the wall a few inches just to her side where it barely missed her. Rounding the end of the corridor, Karolena passed a room and ran in. It contained four empty beds without bedclothes, the usual flat screen monitors, but no light panels and no pictures on the walls. There was little

opportunity for her to hide, but it appeared the nurse was no longer after her. Karolena walked over to the curtain and inched it open. A small blood stain blotted a corner of the curtain, faded by age and exposure to sunlight.

An old style paper book lay open on top of an older wooden bedside table. Karolena had not seen a non-e-book in a long time, and walked over. She placed her finger on the page to mark it, then momentarily closed the book to see who the author was: "Mark Twain." Karolena opened the book again and saw one sentence underlined in red ink:

"Everyone is a moon, and has a dark side which he never shows to anybody."

Suddenly, a hand reached tightly around her throat, choking her and pulling her backward. Although unable to scream, she thrashed around trying to fight off the attacker and managed to turn slightly. "Wait; I know you." She tried again to scream, even to breathe, but no life-sustaining air could enter and no sounds could leave her chest. Her attacker pulled a long butcher knife from his pocket, put it to Karolena's throat and . . .

Karolena, drowning in a sea of fear, completely disoriented, lashed out violently with her arms until she was finally restrained by a lab technician, who grabbed her hands, and asked, "Lady, lady, are you all right? Are you having a dream or something?"

Karolena shook her head, confused, until, recognizing where she actually really was, seated in the hospital laboratory. She took a few moments to regain her composure, then breathlessly apologized. Although she now realized that no one was attacking her, nevertheless, she also knew the truth of what she had just seen, and experienced. This had been too real to be simply a daydream. Was she hallucinating, she feared, or was she even losing her mind?

After leaving the hospital lab, Karolena walked back to what she thought might have been the room that she had seen the repairman enter in her 'dream.' Although it might have been possible that she had passed by there during her long hospitalization, she was fairly certain that she had not been inside. Turning on the overhead fluorescent lamp, she now found herself in a large equipment storage room. Inside were various medical equipment units, some labeled 'Organ Transport Support.' Otherwise, the room was empty. Whomever she thought she had seen in her vision wasn't there now. Full of doubts, she wondered if perhaps she had imagined the whole thing. After all, she had 'seen' things in the past, both before and after her VAA transplant.

Worries about the meaning of the violent "daydream" she had just experienced clouded her mind. Would these dreams persist forever, and what would it take to stop them? Was her problem related to the graft, the medication she was on, or to some supernatural possession now residing inside her skull, with her, perhaps, forever? Certainly, being such a visual dream, it must have, she reasoned, involved the optical area of her brain.

In an attempt to get to the bottom of these bizarre visual disturbances, and to put an end to them, Karolena called Dr. Nabula Fromposi's office for an appointment. If she could discuss these problems with Fromposi, perhaps an etiology and a treatment might be developed that could help her. When asked for a reason for the appointment, Karolena simply told the receptionist that she needed to have a follow-up visit, and that she had a few questions to ask.

"Fortunately, Dr. Fromposi has no surgery scheduled today," the holographic receptionist replied. "She does have an open appointment for this afternoon. Could you come in around two?"

Karolena immediately took the opportunity, and started to collect her thoughts.

Chapter 36

"Dr. Fromposi, thanks for agreeing to speak with me on such short notice," Karolena said. She considered just how reluctant she had been to make this office visit to discuss potential problems with her transplant, and apprehensive at what the findings might really be. "I hope you remember me, although I don't remember seeing you when I was a patient." Karolena stopped for a moment to reflect on how odd this sounded, then continued, "What I meant was, I was very ill at the time of the surgery, and I don't recall your visit."

"Why, yes I do remember you, Ms. Kreisler, Dr. Kreisler," she added gratuitously. "I'm glad that you appear so much better." She motioned for Karolena to sit in a chair across from her in the examining room. "How is your vision?" Fromposi asked, never looking directly at Karolena, preferring instead to make notations on a nearby stack of patient charts.

"Much better, thanks. I have no problems with knowing what I'm seeing, and I'm experiencing no problems with clarity, so, in that regard, everything seems okay." Karolena gratefully reflected on how her recovery from the experimental surgery on the vision area of her brain was much more remarkable, rapid, thorough and uncomplicated than she could ever have hoped for, and she had often since reflected on how truly fortunate she really was.

"Good. I think you can thank the visual graft

transplant for that. Now, what brought you here today?" Dr. Fromposi reached over to the hand-held ophthalmoscope plugged into the recharging base, anticipating the need to perform an exam. "Are you having problems with blurred vision, double vision, fuzzy vision?"

"No, none of that. As I said, I can see just fine." Getting more anxious about explaining the strange visual dreams she had been experiencing, Karolena said, "Look, I had an experience earlier today where I thought I saw something that probably wasn't there."

"Did you see spots, floating lines, halos, changes in colors, . . . "

"No." Karolena interrupted, wondering if Fromposi was even listening to her. She seemed to rattle off questions like a machine, like a out of control AllSee unit. "I thought I saw someone who was trying to KILL me." Karolena stared straight ahead, her face emotionless and pale. "And I've had this vision, if you will, several times before."

Fromposi raised an eyebrow, but said nothing, but it was quite apparent to Karolena that Fromposi had thought of something which disturbed her.

After a tense few minutes, Fromposi said only, "I see." Apparently unwilling to reveal her thoughts, she instead directed Karolena to look straight ahead and not move her eyes, and performed a basic ophthalmologic exam. After another few minutes, Fromposi said, "Everything seems normal, Karolena."

"Good. Thank you. I feel reassured. But, let's get back to what I thought I experienced, Dr. Fromposi. Of course, I don't really think anyone was trying to harm me. Not really. But, believe me, it LOOKED very real, so very physically real, that I was actually living through it. I sweated, my heart raced, I felt terrified." She knew in her heart that the dreams had probably saved her life, but to claim so to Fromposi would have destroyed her credibility.

"I'm afraid this isn't any sort of ophthalmologic abnormality that I can help you with," Fromposi said, appearing uncomfortable with the line of questioning. "If you really think it was simply a daydream, than I think you can be assured that there isn't anything physically wrong with you. I think many of us have them. But, on the other hand, if you think it was a visual hallucination, perhaps you need to be seen by a neuro-psychiatrist."

"No, I guess it's not a physiologic abnormality," Karolena sighed. "But could this be a side-effect from the ocular cortex graft, perhaps some unusual perceptive derangement?"

Fromposi laughed. "You have got to be kidding. I don't see how it could happen. . . . And, it would require . . . " Fromposi considered this for a long time, then shook her head as if dismissing her thoughts as preposterous. "Anyway, I've never heard of this happening before. However, visual transplants are a new procedure, and just an experimental one at that. There just haven't been enough cases to build a very good experience base from."

Karolena began to feel like a fool for bringing her abnormal experience, frightening as it was to her, to

Fromposi's attention. "Well, that's all I wanted to know. Thank you for your time," she said. Struggling against feeling even more ridiculous, Karolena turned to say good-bye, then added, "If you ever learn anything more about this, would you please give me a call?"

"Yes, I will," Frumposi reassured her. "Thank you for coming, and I'm glad that otherwise you're doing so well."

After Karolena left, Fromposi sat in silence in her office for a long time, staring at her desk. "Could I have transplanted memory, visual memory from the donor?" Fromposi asked herself. "What if it was a visual record of the donor's life, and of her death? Oh God, what if it's true? What have I done?"

Chapter 37

The next morning Karolena drove to FirsThought and spent some time slowly moving back to her office, and integrating into her old job. Although she had not yet decided in what capacity she could resume working, she did strongly believe in the importance of the discovery she played a part in -- the application of the nerve growth factor. While at FirsThought, she stopped in to visit an acquaintance in the human genetics department, Dr. Isaku Udone. "Dr. Udone," she began, "I want to ask you for some technical information about transplants. Can you help me?"

"Please call me Isaku," he smiled. "Yes, of course I'd be delighted to help you in any way I can."

"Okay, Isaku," she smiled, reflecting that he was one of the few physicians she had ever had respect for as a person; clearly he wasn't phony or self-centered. "What are the odds of finding a biotype in the UN Identity Database that has no matching **UN ID**?"

"Nearly impossible," he scoffed. "Think what you're saying, Karolena. If it's available to be entered into the database, then it can't be unknown."

Karolena showed Udone the biotype from the unknown male's blood found on Penny's hands. She explaining that a search of the **UN ID** database had not found a matching person, but that she had thought this very unlikely.

Udone examined the biotype carefully, jotted

down some notes, made some lists on a sheet of paper, referred to a few log type books, and his computer several times. "Yes, I agree with the computer that there must have been an error. There's something wrong with this biotype. The numbers themselves appear incompatible," he said, holding up some numbers for Karolena to see. "More than likely, though, only one digit is off." Looking at the numbers again, he added, "It's probably the 3rd digit on the 3rd locus, rather than the 4th from last number that the computer scan identified as in error, although I could also accept that explanation."

Karolena considered this for a moment, then asked, "If only one digit is off, like you suggest, does that mean that if I run all combinations of the last digit that I might see the correct biotype?"

"Better than that," Dr. Udone smiled. "I think that you could simply ask a database for all known variants of the last digit to see what's available."

"Thanks very much for your time, Isaku," Karolena said. She couldn't wait to get to her AllSee and try this out.

Returning to her office, Karolena had her research computer run all possible known combinations of the 3rd digit on 3rd locus of the unknown biotype. The next day, the computer produced a list of six acceptable and known combinations, with the potential list of 45,756 persons possessing these biotype combinations. Overwhelmed, Karolena then asked the computer how many of these persons lived in Winston County. There were five. She then queried about how many lived near Brighton, England, and the answer came back as seven.

Karolena thought that she was looking at an interesting vein, but was still not quite there. She was frustrated, knowing that she had yet to find the appropriate question to ask. Karolena wished she could ask the computer if any of those on the list in Winston County had been in Brighton, England in the last year, but knew that the computer couldn't determine that. The information needed for this wasn't yet in any database that she knew of. Reasoning that Blum's computer might be able to query about credit purchases, she forwarded the names to him, asking him to search if any of those on the Winston County list had passports.

Several hours later, Blum replied to her that eleven had passports. She then returned his message, asking him to see if any of those eleven had made airline purchases around the ten days before Penny Forest had died.

When Karolena arrived home, the message light was on her AllSee. She logged into the AllSee, and looked on with surprise at the list Blum had sent her:

AllSee Electronic Mail

To: Karolena Kreisler wncus212-22-36543x

Message: Concerning your search request on 3rd digit combinations and international travel reservations purchases around the specified dates, only one person

meets the search specifications:
Dieter Müeller:
UN ID:45345-SDG-3452354dlfk
Biotype: M **A**271**B**224**C**121776D654
Current Location: Winston County, North Carolina

"By the way," Blum's message continued, "Dieter had traveled to Vienna the day of the attack at the AeroMall. I'm sure you're not any more surprised than I am."

"Although we want to speak with him about the bombing at your apartment, as far as "organ-legging", or organ trafficking, which I think you are suggesting, you've got no hard evidence, no motive. All you got is coincidence and circumstantial material. And anyway, the database says that the biotype found on Penny Forest isn't Dieter's biotype. Dieter only matched up on a slightly different sequence." Not hearing a reply, even an objection from Karolena, Blum explained a bit more. "Karolena, how many murders do you think occur in Winston County on an average week?"

"One?" she replied, timidly, knowing that this probably was just wishful thinking.

"Try ten," he laughed sardonically. "Do you think the police have time for your amateur detective work? Look, I'm not trying to belittle your efforts, but if you called, they would just hang up on you."

Although frustrated, Karolena could nevertheless understand how random combinations of numbers didn't add up to a conviction, let alone an arrest warrant. Resigned for the moment to think things through a little more, she thanked Blum and ended the call.

Although feeling fine, or perhaps to keep feeling that way, Karolena made an appointment for noon the next day for a routine follow-up visit with her transplant team. She had been putting this off for weeks, but now it gave her the excuse she needed to go to The Winston. While waiting there to see the '*Transplant Surgeon Of The Day'* -Karolena thought that she would never get used to that term - she ran into an acquaintance of hers, Robilyn Carter.

Karolena met Robilyn during her stay when they were both awaiting transplants. They had developed a casual friendship, then saw each other only occasionally until now.

Robilyn had been unfortunate to have contracted liver failure, even at her young age. Unlike Karolena chronically stable liver disease, Robilyn had contracted her liver problem from heavy metal poisoning, the toxic spill occurring last year while she was visiting Sao Paulo. Robilyn's liver failure had, fortunately, abated and she had not yet progressed to needing a liver transplant. Judging from her appearance - Karolena thought Robilyn had aged considerably, gotten heavier and puffier, and was mildly jaundiced - it wouldn't be much longer. Karolena had a lot to talk to Robilyn about, and arranged to meet her for tea later that day.

She and Robilyn went for tea at the Sans Bolero

Cafe later that day. Even though the police had reassured her that Dieter was nowhere to be found, Karolena still wanted to maintain every possible distance.

Very soon the conversation drifted to things that troubled both of them: liver disease and transplants. Robilyn commented that she had been undergoing intensive treatments that had held off her liver failure. Lately, though, the therapy had not been working as well as Robilyn would have wanted, and she was being scheduled for elective surgery, once a suitable liver became available. Timely access was always the caveat. Robilyn had already been waiting for some time for a transplant, and hoped to get one soon. A server 'bot brought their cappuccinos and biscotti, and they paused to partake.

As was common for any two people in their particular situation, their conversation soon turned to their medical problems. Robilyn had been experiencing nausea and fatigue ever since she had started to show signs of liver failure, and they were symptoms Karolena too had occasional problems with. Fortunately, her own liver had, up to now, been strong enough to resist needing a transplant, a situation she hoped would continue. For Robilyn, the symptoms came and went in cycles and today, fortunately, was one of her better days, hence her moderate appetite.

"Robilyn, are you having any problems seeing?" Karolena asked, wondering if her problems were related to the transplantation process in general, rather than to the type of graft she received. It was a hopelessly unlikely question, and Karolena realized that.

Robilyn looked up, surprised, and asked, "What are you referring to?"

"Not just trouble seeing well, but not recognizing things you see and should know." She remembered very well experiencing those exact symptoms, and how it had led to an experimental visual transplant. Fortunately for her, the graft seemed to be functioning well, at least as far as visual recognition was concerned, although she wasn't certain she or her doctors understood why.

"No, and I sure hope I never do. I'm having problems with my eyes being too dry to use my contact lenses, though," she noted.

It was obvious to Karolena that Robilyn hadn't been having the same visual problems, and she decided not to discuss it any further. The conversation returned to small talk about personalities at the transplantation clinic at The Winston. Soon, their bill came, Karolena paid for them both, and they walked to the door together, then went their separate ways.

On her way back to her office at FirsThought later that day, Karolena's thoughts took a rather morbid and sinister turn. She came to realize how, if she could use a database to locate potential donors for someone, Sentinal or Robilyn, for example, or even for herself, then, she could use that same database to learn if a particular potential donor were alive or dead, and if dead, how they died.

Killing someone and using their body parts for transplantation was not a novel idea, having been around before the end of last century, and killing someone was exactly what she was speaking of here. The pressure to kill people for organs was even greater now than in years past, with toxic pollution relentlessly destroying organs and the plague of retroviruses making more and more people unsuitable as organ donors. She had once read of the "commercialization" of this illegal form of donor organ acquisition, although not in Neuse, and of course not involving The Winston. Yet Karolena did know that the donor of her own transplant was murdered, although she had yet to determine that Penny Forest was killed specifically to donate graft tissue. Karolena still felt that Penny's death, although tragic, was simply coincidental. From what she had learned on her recent trip to Vienna, the organ donor for her acquaintance Sentinel had also not been a volunteer donor or a for-price donor, but had also died unexpectedly. Although perhaps there was a tie, it was very unlikely.

Acting on a suspicion, Karolena went to her office, and looked up Robilyn Carter via a credit database on a public computer bulletin board. In years past, obtaining this information might have been considered an invasion of privacy, but, with the proliferation of commercial computer databases, guarding these personal facts was practically impossible. With time, and little recourse, the populace long ago had become accustomed.

Once having located Robilyn's **UN ID**, Karolena

then transferred the numbers to the **Bio-Infinity Database,** a marketing research oriented database which also listed biotypes, and was helpful in medical marketing-related searches. Karolena had used **Bio-Infinity** once to compile for Rickhard a list of local persons genetically susceptible to both arthritis and diabetes. The search request she now entered was for a list of potential donors with over 95 percent compatibility with Robilyn's biotype. Karolena then logged off, to give the computer the necessary time to complete the search and forward a copy of the report to her AllSee.

Chapter 38

Several hours later, Karolena's AllSee notified her of the receipt of a message. As expected, it was the results of the search on the Bio-Infinity database. Karolena carefully examined the names on the printout for a long time, then fixed on the second to last name:

Last Name	**First**	**Age**	***Retro***	**State**
Lorentaine	Lanette	27	neg.	Manitoba United States

According to the supplemental information provided, this woman was *retro-negative,* single, had no children, possessed A+++ credit, owned a house and a late model car, belonged to a ski time-sharing club, traveled frequently, preferred fine wines and cheeses, and remotely belonged to the Cagnawaga Indian tribe. Lanette was the essence of a SINK -- Single Income No Kids. Wow, she lives a lot better than I do., Karolena marveled.

Her exercise in computer searches had demonstrated how, with very little effort, it would have been relatively easy for almost anyone to locate a list of suitable transplant matches. The fact that Lanette lived near an SST-capable airport made transport of a donor organ convenient. Maybe, Karolena wondered jokingly, I should consider giving Lanette a call, especially while she's still around.

As she was about to log off, Karolena had a most strange thought, a thought that perhaps she didn't want to have answered.

"Computer, can you tell me if this is a common search request?"

"Working . . . 210 searches of biotype compatibility last month, average 232 per month for this year."

"Are all these for hospitals or were any for biotechnology companies?" she asked.

"All but three were for hospitals."

"Can you tell me what searches were run from hospitals in North Carolina?"

"Working . . . That request will take several days to complete. Do you want to continue?"

"Yes," she said, then disconnected. She wondered if she even really wanted to know the results, and have perhaps her worst fears confirmed.

At first, she thought about letting Blum know what she had found out, and what she was planning to do about it. Then, she remembered how much he had disapproved of her visiting Mistislav's family. Even though that trip had almost ended in her getting killed, she was certain that would never happen in Manitoba. Instead of a call, she left Blum a message after the fact.

Karolena had to admit, it was a big gamble. Nevertheless, Karolena immediately booked the next SST to Manitoba. On the way, she called Lanette Lorentaine from the aircraft and introduced herself as an author writing a book on the Cagnawaga Indian tribe of Manitoba. Lanette was more than obliging when Karolena asked for an interview and invited Karolena to meet her after work.

After arriving at Manitoba International AeroMall, Karolena took a Magni-Train to the central city business district. There she located the offices of Fujimura Electronics and went inside. The 80-story building in this regional business capital of America's fifty third and northern most state was new, massively built, and very spacious, with unusually high ceilings. Karolena was impressed with the modern French-Canadian art work on the walls, combined with lithographs of assorted French Impressionist and neo-impressionist works. Various pieces of clay sculpture tastefully lined the lobbies and outer offices.

A fountain bubbled jets of colored water skyward in the main entrance to Fujimura Electronics. Karolena went up to the nearby reception desk and introduced herself to the holographic receptionist. "My name is Karolena Kreisler, and I have an appointment with Lanette Lorentaine."

The neural network program detected Karolena's wrist ID way in advance, as she approached, verified her appointment, but instead of directing her in, the hologram replied, "I'm sorry, Ms. Lorentaine just left for the day. Perhaps you're mistaken?"

"No, no," Karolena insisted, incredulous that such a misunderstanding could have occurred after having so carefully arranging for the meeting. "This is very important. I had an appointment. I flew here from

North Carolina just to meet with her."

A solid-looking older woman with a no-nonsense facade quickly strutted up to the desk. "Hello. I'm the regional manager," she said in a loud and firm voice. "Perhaps I can be of assistance."

"Yes," Karolena said, apprehension and urgency in her voice. "I just arrived for a previously arranged interview with Ms. Lorentaine. Do you know where she might have gone? We just made the appointment earlier today, and I'm sure she hasn't forgotten."

The regional manager scanned the building's personnel movement log, then said, "Ms. Lorentaine left less than five minutes ago. I was near her desk when she got a call just before leaving. I thought I heard her say that she would meet someone at the Queen Victoria Restaurant, in the lobby of our building. Could she have been talking to you?"

Sensing a problem, Karolena didn't reply. Hurrying over to the lobby, she anxiously asked the hostess at the Queen Victoria if Lanette was waiting.

"Yes, but she just left," the hostess said. "She met a man here. I think I heard the lady tell him she was expecting to meet with an author, a Karolena something. The man seemed surprised, said that he was with the same publishing house, and that he suspected the author had been delayed. A few minutes later, they told me they were going to get something from a car and would be right back, and to save the table."

Karolena turned away from the restaurant, then, unable to believe what she had just seen, nearly froze. Slowly turning around, she faced what appeared to be the English Tea house she visited in her dreams. But Karolena was certain she had never been at this restaurant before, had never even been in this city before, never, that is, except in her dreams. A sick feeling crept through her body and up her spine, and she felt like screaming and running away. She now recognized exactly what the source of terror almost surely was, and nearly spit out the word, "Dieter."

At that instant, Karolena suddenly knew what she had to do. She quickly took directions to the parking lot, and asked the hostess to call the police. Then she tore down the stairs, not wanting to wait for the elevator.

A massive parking structure attached to the Fujimura Building, with several floors connected by sloping concrete ramps, all looking alike. Each of them could be hiding a secret. Karolena ran down the first ramp, but saw no one in the aisles or in the cars that resembled the person she had spoken with earlier by AllSee.

Abruptly she stopped cold in her tracks, uncertain if she were dreaming or hallucinating. Ahead of her she could see two images, superimposed. One was the view of the parking lot exactly as she had just seen it, but on top of this was a second image. She could see a woman in a parked car, a woman Karolena suspected of being in great danger. A man was approaching the driver's door of her car and Karolena could sense that he intended to hurt her. Abruptly the dual images vanished, and Karolena ran even faster to warn Lanette.

Nearly out of breath, Karolena hurried up to the second level. A Parking security guard, who had been alerted by the restaurant receptionist, pulled up to her in an electric golf cart. "Is there a problem, Lady?" he asked sarcastically, annoyed by all the break-ins he constantly had to deal with.

Karolena hurriedly explained that someone who worked in the building was about to be attacked in the parking lot. The security agent's sarcasm vanished, and he quickly told Karolena, "Get in."

On the third Parking level Karolena and the parking guard could see a man and a woman standing by the driver's side of a parked car, talking. Hoping that they were the people she so desperately searched for, they raced their cart forward. For a moment, she thought she heard Penny's voice whispering to her, "I've got this."

Dieter tightened his fingers around the trigger of the stun gun attached out of site on his right wrist. Smiling, he handed Lanette a small brown package, and told her, "I hope you like this gift from Ms. Kreisler. It was so unfortunate that she was unable to come. At least we can still complete the interview."

Dieter was distracted suddenly by the appearance of a large red bird with a crooked black beak perched in a crevice along a beam in the ceiling. He struggled to deny his distinct impression that the bird was watching him. Trying to focus, he turned back toward Lanette, looking for the hand in which she held her keys so that he could make a smooth transition to driving once he shot her and pushed her over into her car.

. . . Karolena closed her eyes and in her mind leapt out of the cart and ran forward. Sensing something terribly wrong, she stretched out her arms, much as she remembered doing before, in her dreams. Shocked, she looked on as a set of powerful wings unfolded from her sides and forcibly grabbed the air. Karolena lifted off smoothly and purposefully, searching with hunter's eyes for prey to attack, . . .

Slowly and gracefully, the large bird dropped down from its perch near the ceiling and flew toward Dieter, its harsh caw echoing hauntingly off the bare concrete garage walls.

The sound of flapping of strong wings filled the garage. Dieter reached out to fire his stun gun at Lanette; he aimed, began to squeeze the trigger, then screamed out in pain. Excruciating pain gripped his hand, as if someone were driving an ice pick deep into his flesh. Looking down, he cried out in anguish as he saw the bird's beak embedded in his wrist, wildly pulling out his tissues by the mouthful, twisting and pulling at tendons and muscles and blood vessels like he were road kill for the taking.

Dieter yelled out, terrified as blood spurted from the impaled artery in his wrist. He desperately tried to pull the bird off him, but couldn't shake free from the claws digging into his skin and the beak that feasted hungrily on his wrist.

Still screaming and flapping his arm to shake the

bird off, Dieter took off toward his own car. He soon found that his way was partially blocked by a parking lot security cart careening down the ramp toward him. Dieter jumped aside as the cart passed him, bruising his shoulder as it slammed against the cart's side. The bird was thrown against the windshield of the cart, then deflected upward. Turning sharply, the bird circled back and dove at Dieter repeatedly.

"No." Dieter yelled. As he turned to run, his eyes fell briefly on Karolena. "You bitch." he yelled out, as his car ran into a retaining wall, knocking him unconscious.

Lanette ran over to the parking guard, screaming hysterically for help. Karolena got out quickly and put her arm around Lanette's shoulder.

The parking guard quickly handcuffed Dieter, then called the police on his AllSee.

"Are you all right?" the guard asked Lanette.

Lanette stood up, and said, "I'll be okay, thanks to this lady," as she looked appreciatively at Karolena."

Seeing that Lanette had no idea who she was, Karolena extended her hand and said, "My name is Karolena Kreisler. I was to have an interview with you just now."

""Oh yes, that man," she indicated disdainfully in Dieter's direction, "told me that you'd be late, and he was to meet me instead. Was he working with you, and how did he know that?"

"No, we're not at all working together. He lied about that, and I'm sure he has lied about a number of things. I'm not sure how he knew I was to meet with you, but I think he tried to kill me in my apartment a few months ago. I'm certain the North Carolina police will want to be speaking with him.'"'She looked around at them all standing in the middle of a parking garage, then over at Dieter, and suggested, "Perhaps we'd be better off waiting at the restaurant in the lobby." When Lanette agreed, she led Lanette back to the Queen Victoria Restaurant.

"Look, you're hurt," Lanette told Karolena once they were back at the restaurant. She took a napkin and wiped a corner of Karolena's cheek, which was scuffed from a superficial abrasion.

Karolena looked confused, and brushed her hand along her cheek, not remembering having injured it. A light streak of blood pooled near the corner of her mouth. "I'll survive. And you will too, thankfully."

"Whoever that crazy man was, he was going to shoot me with some kind of gun. Then a bird suddenly attacked him. What was that all about?"

Karolena had no remembrance of what had happened while she was in the parking lot, or how Dieter had been injured and then captured. Her arms hurt, and she had a salty taste in her mouth. Her fingers felt sore and tight, as if she had been gripping something.

"I think I know why he was going to shoot you, although I have no idea why the bird attacked him."

"Didn't you see it?" Lanette asked.

Karolena shook her head NO, then talked fast, explaining to Lanette as much of the background as she could. Karolena had a basic distrust of the authorities at this point and was wary of staying around to answer questions under interrogation.

Still in a state of near shock and confused, Lanette could only think Karolena to be as crazy as her assailant. Nevertheless, she listened attentively, admiring Karolena's strength and determination, realizing that as crazy as Karolena might seem right now, she just had saved her life.

The police inspectors arrived shortly to take notes and ask their usual questions. Disgusted and indifferent, after interrogating Dieter, they indicated that they were going to treat this attack as a standard purse-snatching attempt. Karolena wisely didn't tell them all that she thought had happened. What could she say, after all? That she had gotten Lanette's name from a database search of biotypes, that she had a "vision" of the attack while coming to find Lanette, that this had been a premeditated hit to get Lanette's organs for transplantation? No, she thought, I'll keep this to myself. I have other ways to handle this. Now she could see the association between contract organ procurement and Dieter. She suspected that there was a connection to the Winston's transplant program, as the presumed recipient was in their program. She would send a note to Blum, although she suspected that he was way ahead of her on all this. At least, with Dieter finally apprehended, the constant threat of death finally was lifted from her life.

Chapter 39

Once the SST landed back in Winston County, an exhausted Karolena could hardly wait to return to her apartment. With all that had happened, she needed time to think things out and formulate a plan. Above all else, she would need to contact Blum and get his feedback. She was sure that Blum already was aware of Dieter's apprehension. Blum needed to contact the Manitoba police and have them hold Dieter for further questioning, rather than treat him as a petty criminal and release him.

After passing through the outer security net, Karolena was allowed to disembark from the plane and enter the terminal. Karolena wristed at the airlock, then wristed again as she stepped off the ramp by the airline counter.

A line had formed in front of the inner security net that didn't seem to be moving at all. Everything was taking too long today, she thought impatiently. The airport screening seemed to take forever, with more than the usual complement of armed guards stopping, detaining and searching. The line looked like it might last well over an hour, snaking around the terminal waiting room.

"Ms. Kreisler?" A large airport sentry in flak dress, carrying a semiautomatic assault rifle, finally addressed her.

Relieved to be nearing the end of this waiting

ordeal, Karolena nodded "Yes," and waited. She was accustomed in the States to feeling different. Her style of clothes, and of course her slight accent always set her apart.

"Ms. Kreisler, step this way," the security agent said sternly. He didn't say "please," didn't look as though he had forgotten to, and pointed her toward the containment area. Inside, they were joined by a female security agent carrying a magnetic wand. He spoke again. "Ms. Kreisler, where have you been?"

"Manitoba." She concentrated on simple, direct answers, trying not to display her impatience. The plane clearly came from Manitoba, and she had obviously just come off that nonstop flight. It shouldn't be hard, she thought, for this genius to come to that conclusion.

"What was the purpose of your trip?"

"Why? What is the matter?" Karolena replied, suddenly getting defensive. "Are you looking for something? Am I being accused of anything? If so, I want to see my attorney." Calm down, Karolena, she thought, or this will take even longer.

"We can stay here a long time if need be," the guard replied, an ironic grin on his face. "And that attorney crap ended years ago. You know that. Now, let's see how well you can answer a simple question. What was the purpose of your trip?" He spoke each word slowly and with a mocking tone to his voice.

"Business and personal, mixed."

"Can you provide names to verify?"

"Yes, of course." But if she did, then there would

be the messy police report about Dieter's attempted murder of Lanette that would need explaining.

"Would you agree to a search of your property?"

"Of course. But I've already been through several levels of security going into and out of airports." Stay cool, Karolena. Don't get rattled, she thought.

The female security agent searched her outer body with several scanner loops. Of course, nothing unexpected showed. "May I touch your body?" the agent asked.

"What?" Karolena asked, caught off guard. Everything seemed to be happening too quickly.

Without waiting for a reply, the female and the male guard stepped menacingly forward and gave Karolena a thorough frisking, patting down her legs, her upper body, examining each piece of jewelry. The male guard ran his hand high up into her groin, felt around quite a bit unnecessarily in her opinion, ran his hand up her front, grabbed a feel of her breasts, then roughly shoved her forward, laughing.

"Hey, you dirty creep, keep your hands to yourself." Karolena yelled out.

The guards ignored her and brought up her baggage next.

"Who packed your baggage, gorgeous?" the male guard sneered.

"I did," she said, readjusting her clothes, feeling totally humiliated, and violated.

"Did anyone give you any packages to take along?"

"No." And even if they did, I wouldn't be stupid

enough to take them, she thought. She tried to get the male guard's name off his badge to report him, but was angered to see that he wasn't wearing one. Typical, just typical, she fumed.

"Were you with your bags always after packing them?"

"Yes." They definitely are looking for something, she thought. The male guard started to move toward her, and she slowly backed away.

The airport security agents looked at each other and exchanged some unspoken communication. Karolena's wrist ID scan results finally came back after an unusually long delay. The data verified that she was *Retro-negative*, and had a negative criminal history. "You can go now, gorgeous," the male guard told her.

As Karolena got up to leave, the first agent said, "We're looking for a middle-aged female, possible English accent, purportedly carrying a weapon. If you know of anything or see anyone fitting this description, call us immediately."

Shaken, Karolena promised to call and then left the airport lobby, quickly heading toward the parking area. She was more than a little insulted to think that they would stop her because she looked "middle-aged," and she definitely did not have a horrible English accent. Karolena paused and looked at her reflection in the glass outer automatic doors. Did she really look that old? Karolena wondered just how many years her surgeries had added to her appearance. She nervously brushed her hair back and stood up straighter.

As she stared into the glass doors, she suddenly

noticed the reflection of a red dot in the glass off from her right side. Quickly, she dove off to her left and down a short stairway, hurting her shoulder as she tumbled down. Behind her, Karolena heard the impact explosion as the door shattered into thousands of pieces of glass. Some splinters landed in her hair and on her face as she lay on the floor. Terrified, Karolena got up and ran without looking back, ignoring the screams of the crowd behind her.

Reaching the parking lot, nearly breathless, Karolena keyed the code to her car door and jumped in when the door up with a hiss. In one continuous movement she switched on the electric motor, hit the disconnect lever to release the charging cable, and took off toward home. As she sped away from the airport she could hear the sounds of ambulances and police cars racing in the other direction. Maybe there really had been a person on board her flight with a weapon, she wondered, although, with what the public was constantly told was the state of security at airports, that seemed very unlikely. Now that Dieter was finally apprehended, she should have been free from this kind of danger. But, a woman?

Welcome back to Winston County, Karolena thought grimly, as she drove home, shaken and fearful. At every corner, at every window and mirror she awaited the red light of death, and was ready to run and hide once again.

Chapter 40

On her way home from the airport, Karolena remembered to stop at the hospital Pharmacy to pick up her weekly dose of recombinant growth factors. She called ahead from her car, and upon arriving, used the special drive-through window reserved for immune suppressed patients. Karolena wristed at the window, and then waited in her car while her medication was prepared. After being called on her car AllSee by the pharmacy computer, a small 'bot brought her package and she left.

Karolena hurriedly took her doses of growth factors while still in her car driving, and waited impatiently to feel their strength flowing into her body. This time, though, she felt no beneficial effect at all, although she attributed that to all the additional stress she was under.

Entering the safety of her apartment, Karolena first checked the security status indicator before taking off her coat and feeling a little more secure. This time, the AllSee showed only one person in the apartment: her, and all security devices indicated ready. She felt good that the management had gotten around to repairing the identity sensor.

First, Karolena thought, I need to assemble the appropriate tools to calm down and think about all this. She addressed her AutoBev and said, "cappuccino." Cappuccino wasn't really an addiction, she thought, just a passion. It was one of the few pleasures she allowed herself, and so far one she had not tired of and one that didn't hurt her. Settling back in her couch, she set the temperature to forty degrees centigrade, started the ripple effect, and considered her options. Picking up her AllSee, she called Blum.

"Hi, Karolena. Welcome back. Did you have a good trip?"

Sensing a hint of anger and annoyance in his voice, she asked, "I must admit I'm surprised that you keep track of my travel plans, but, yes, I did. And I got a lot done too."

"It would be a lot easier if you discussed these things with me first, you know, before going off on your own" Blum scolded her.

She paused a second, then told him, "You wouldn't have approved, would you have?"

"No, and would you have blamed me?"

"No, I guess not. Look, let's not argue. I have some ideas that I want to bounce off you. Okay?"

"Sure, Karolena. Shoot."

"Bad choice of words," she chided. "I had some trouble at the airport today when I arrived."

"Sorry. You can't continue to be a target too much longer before your luck runs out. Tell me what happened on your trip."

"Are you saying that I was the target?"

"Not at all, just that maybe you attract problems. But now that Dieter Müeller is out of the picture, I am hoping that both our lives will be more peaceful."

"I think you know why I sent to Manitoba. I was

simply trying to look at everything in reverse. I wanted to see if I could predict who would make a good donor for someone high on the transplant list, and I wanted to see if that person would become a donor."

"Is that what you think happened in your case?"

"I don't really know, but I'd like to find out. Robilyn Carrier, a woman that I know at The Winston, is awaiting a transplant, and I ran her biotype on a database at work."

"I'm following you," Blum said.

"I wanted to look for compatible donors, and voilà, the name Lanette Lorentaine came up." Karolena looked at Blum's image in the AllSee screen; he didn't seem too surprised. "Are you listening?"

"Yes, I am. I think your approach is very interesting. I did know a little of what you were up to, though."

"Can I ask how much you knew?"

"Don't ask," Blum smiled.

"I see. When I went looking for Lanette, to try to warn her about the possibility of an attempt on her life, Dieter showed up. Fortunately, he was caught before he could harm her."

"So I heard. We're requesting his being extradited back here for interrogation."

"Good. From what I learned, I must have been right, there was some sort of an "organ-legging" operation, and apparently Dieter was the hit man."

Reading the look on her face, Blum apologetically said, "I congratulate you on following through with your idea. You certainly were correct, but who do you think is running this ring you speak of? Someone at WCMC? I doubt it was Dieter."

"I see your point." She had not considered whether others than Dieter were involved. Now that she thought about it, though, several names came to mind. Bob Wilder, in his position as hospital administrator, could have enough access to the key players, and she knew Susan was terribly afraid of him, although she didn't know why. After telling her thoughts to Blum, she asked, "Who do you think it is?

"Oh, I've got my suspicions, but, for now, it's best if you leave police work to the police. Interference can mess things up for us, and could result in your getting hurt."

"Maybe I need some extra protection," she interrupted, then smiled. "I must say though now that Dieter is out of the picture I do feel a whole lot safer. For now, I'm getting very tired." Karolena stretched and yawned.

"Sure, I'm not surprised after all you've been through."

"No, no, it's more than that. Even with all the excitement of the last few days, and all the traveling I've done, I feel more tired than I ought to be." Karolena walked over to her AutoBev unit while talking, and started to key in for another cup of cappuccino, paused, then changed her selection to a cup of hot tea and a scone. She knew that washed-out feeling all too well. Although she rarely complained of fatigue, this seemed a little bit out of the ordinary.

After ending her conversation with Blum, she

finished her cappuccino, then started to read a magazine on the flat panel display. Her attention lasted only a few minutes before she fell sound asleep.

Chapter 41

When Karolena awoke from an exhausted and restless sleep nearly twelve hours later, she felt no less fatigued, and now had taken on a slight feeling of nausea. Concerned that her transplant might be "acting up," she reached for her purse to take some nerve growth factor from her newly dispensed containers. Since returning home from her transplant surgery, whenever Karolena became very tired, she used the medication almost as a tonic, although the instructions didn't provide for this. She looked inside her purse, anxiously pushing the contents to one side and then back the other until she found the bottle, then took another dose. Unexpectedly, after another hour, she felt no better, and really noticed no change whatsoever.

Wondering if there could be something wrong with her refill, she went to her frig and located her previous bottle. Although it was almost a month old, according to the label, the few doses that were left weren't yet out of date. Karolena quickly took a gelatin capsule from the bottle and wedged it under her lower lip next to her gum. The capsule adhered almost immediately and began to release its growth factor into her blood. Strangely, Karolena noticed over just the next few hours that welcome and recognizable sensation of well-being she was accustomed to but had not experienced when she had taken her new refill of medication.

Scanning into her AllSee's memory the product numbers from her last bottle so she could make a comparison, she found that the product number was the same as on her refill, which probably meant that they were made from the same batch.

Karolena took the package insert micro tab, a commonly used memory device resembling a contact lens, from the medication box and slid it into the AllSee. The literature was full of technical information describing the use of the medications and proper storage conditions. Karolena was always careful, and she was certain she had never exposed the bottles to heat. Besides, she observed, the temperature exposure indicator strips on the side of the bottles were still green.

The nerve growth factor was produced by Genetic Generics, a separate and autonomous division of FirsThought Scientific, located in nearby Durham, North Carolina, in the old North Carolina Biotech Ring. Karolena had understood that Bob Wilder was one of the founders.

"AllSee, call Genetic Generics," Karolena instructed. The AllSee was particularly slow today, and while the unit analyzed her voice command and looked for the number on the package insert diskette, she went into her study area and pulled out some reference documents on Genetic Generics that she kept.

Within minutes, the synthesized voice notified her, "Genetic Generics is on the line."

"Welcome to Genetic Generics," the voice on the

AllSee said. "If you have a question about our product, please say 'QUESTION' now."

"QUESTION," Karolena replied.

After a short pause, she was connected to the Medical Department. "Thanks for calling. This is Dr. Hans Guntrerman, of the Medical Safety Division. Can I help you?"

"Hello, this is Dr. Karolena Kreisler from Winston County, North Carolina." On occasions like this, she found it helpful to use her professional title. "I am a research physician and I'm taking your growth factor product. I have a question. Usually I can tell right after I use the medication that it's having a beneficial effect. I generally feel much better, and can see colors better."

"Thank you for using our product. It's not often that I speak with a physician that also is taking our medication. But, did you say you see colors better?" Guntrerman asked.

"Yes, and yesterday after I took a dose from a new bottle there was no such effect. I then tried some older medicine that I still had in my frig, and I got the characteristic good response I'm used to. What do you think about that?"

"I don't know yet. First, you said you see colors better. What do you mean by that? Our growth factors are not indicated for problems with color vision."

"I know that, but I had an experimental optical cortex graft, and my transplant doctor told me to use it for that."

"Maybe so, but it's off-indication use. Did you store the bottles properly in a refrigerator?"

"Yes, or in my purse, but never in the heat."

"And the temperature strips?"

"They had a good color," Karolena told him. "Is there any way to check for potency? Could there be something wrong with the medication, or should I go see my physician? Maybe my grafts arc causing a problem."

"It could be that the medication isn't the problem, and you should visit your physician," Dr. Guntrerman agreed. "But, just in case, why don't you return the bottle to your pharmacist and exchange it for a new bottle?"

"Can you test it for potency if you need to? I'd think that you would want to get that bottle into your lab, just in case there was a manufacturing or storage problem you need to know about and correct." She knew that it was a new product, and one with only a preliminary release.

"Yes, we run potency tests daily. Could you place the package insert lens into your AllSee, please?"

Karolena had already slipped the memory lens in.

"Well, this medication certainly hasn't expired," Guntrerman said with some relief. We've scanned the manufacturing lot number and note no similar complaints."

"Nevertheless I can't help thinking it's a bad bottle. I live nearby. Could I drop it off myself? I really don't want to raise a problem at the pharmacy."

"If you insist. All pharmacies are accustomed to medication returns, though; we fully reimburse them. However, we could run the assay today, and call you with the results."

Propelled by the fear that her graft might be failing, Karolena made the two hours trip back to Neuse in record time. She dropped off the medication along with her personal holocard and home AllSee address for a reply, and then returned home. Karolena was given courtesy bottles of growth factors as she left, with a thank-you for using Genetic Generics, and reassurance of their highest quality.

Even before arriving back at her apartment, she received a call on her car AllSee.

"Ms. Kreisler, this is Dr. Guntrerman at Genetic Generics. About the bottle of nerve growth factor that you brought in earlier. Curiously, all the protein in your bottle had precipitated out, coagulated, as if they had been exposed to heat. We'll be notifying the hospital pharmacy where you purchased this bottle, so that they can return all their remaining stock, warn their clients, and check their storage conditions."

"Thanks very much, Dr. Guntrerman," Karolena said. "I knew something was wrong with the medications."

Knowing that she had her bottles in her possession or in her apartment always after she bought them, that meant that the only time they were apart from her and potentially exposed to heat was before she received them from the pharmacy.

An angry Karolena immediately drove to The Winston and marched into the pharmacy, demanding to speak with Nadish Pahklirvari, the Director of Pharmacy Services, whose name appeared on her prescription bottles. When Pahklirvadi came out to the waiting lobby, Karolena introduced herself.

"I purchased some growth factors here recently and I have reason to think there's a problem with the medicine," Karolena forcefully told him. She was getting better at extracting information from others under pressure, and made sure that she spoke loud enough to move Pahklirvadi to the defensive in front of everyone waiting in the lobby. The fact that she could have been put in danger, either by a stupid accident or, worse yet, intentionally, made her furious.

All the color drained from Pahklirvadi" face, as he said, "Dr. Kreisler, I think we can discuss this better in my office. Don't you? Please, this way," he said, nervously gesturing her toward the hallway in the back of the waiting room.

Noting that he appeared more nervous than annoyed, Karolena told him, "Okay, but only if you leave the door open." She tried to imagine exactly how Blum would handle this, were he here, and tried to emulate him as best she could.

Once inside his office, he motioned for Karolena to have a seat, then, visibly rattled, asked, "What do you want to see me about?"

"I just have a few questions about the medicine I picked up here earlier, that's all," Karolena explained. "It seems it was bad. Taking them could have hurt me, and I wouldn't like that at all. You wouldn't know anything about that, would you?" she asked, getting up and walking menacingly near to where he stood. She could sense his evasiveness and it made her more suspicious and more distrusting of anything he actually told her.

"Oh? I am sorry to hear that. Sometimes when drugs approach their expiration date . . . " he started, searching uncomfortably for words.

"This was fresh medication," Karolena persisted, jabbing her finger sharply into Pahklirvadi's chest.

Pahklirvadi swallowed hard, his eyes darted around his small office nervously, but didn't reply.

"When I took the medicine to the manufacturers, Genetic Generics, they tested the bottle and found that all the protein had coagulated, like it had been microwaved. Now what do you think about that, little buddy?" Karolena saw that Pahklirvadi was getting more annoyed with repeatedly being called that, and played on the line some more. "Why would only ONE PARTICULAR BOTTLE of medication given to me be bad? Huh, why?" Something in his evasive face made her ask, "Maybe someone doesn't like me?"

"I, I uh think that I better not say anymore. I . . . uh . . . want to talk to the hospital attorney," Pahklirvadi stammered, no longer looking directly at her.

"The hospital attorney? That's funny," Karolena laughed.

"Why?" Pahklirvadi asked.

"Oh, I don't think that will be possible," Karolena replied, trying to sound sympathetic. "Especially if he's as much an accessory to this crime as you are. Maybe you'll share a jail cell with him, if you're lucky. Maybe you two will become REAL intimate friends, if you know what I mean," Karolena winked at him, flashing him an odd smile. "Who knows?"

"Crime, what crime?"

"Look, Pahklirvadi, take it from me," Karolena said, trying to sound sympathetic. "Attempted murder and malpractice of your pharmacy license are bad things, very bad, but, things might go a lot better for you if you were to cooperate?" Karolena said, innocently.

Pahklirvadi swallowed hard, and simply stared at her as if he had suddenly lost his ability to think or to speak.

"So, what do you say, Pahklirvadi? You don't want to become someone's boy friend, now, do you?" Taking out her AllSee, Karolena added, "You know, I can summon the police here faster than you can get a lawyer. And you realize, don't you, the effect of the recent Supreme Court decisions striking down right to legal counsel before talking to the police? Why, I'll bet they can get you to be helpful real quick, don't you agree? So what will it be, Pahklirvadi?"

Not surprisingly, it didn't take long for Pahklirvadi to tell Karolena everything he knew. What happened to Karolena's medication wasn't very complicated, and it certainly was nothing that he hadn't done as a "special service" before. The information Pahklirvadi supplied was limited, but in Karolena's mind it was more than enough to implicate Bob Wilder.

According to Pahklirvadi, Bob had requested that Karolena's medication be adulterated, although he had no idea why, and neither did Karolena. Pahklirvadi had complied, simply and unquestioningly, and Karolena could only believe him. Karolena found both Bob's 's and Pahklirvadi's actions totally reprehensible and incredibly unbelievable. Yet, they were true. But why would Bob want to harm her? After all, he was behind the effort to commercialize the nerve growth factor and he would be harmed too.

Karolena shook her head in disbelief. "You could have killed me," she yelled at Pahklirvadi, as he glumly sank into his chair, then she used her AllSee to relay what she knew on to Blum. Karolena knew that she had to get this information to Blum as soon as she could. Not only was The Winston trying to harm her, but others might be in danger as well.

Just as Karolena was about to call Blum, her AllSee notified her of an incoming message. It was the results of her last database search, giving the number of Bio-Infinity searches comparing transplant donors to potential recipients which were run from hospitals in North Carolina? Apparently, there were seven, and all were to the account of Bob Wilder, at WCMC.

Karolena was almost paralyzed, unable to speak. After a few minutes she regained her composure. "Date of these searches relative to my transplant operation?"

"One was four days prior."

Her voice trembled as she said, "Print out the search contents."

The computer knew that she worked with the initiator of the search, and replied, "Retrieving. This request will take approximately five minutes. Do you wish to wait?"

"Yes." Karolena busied herself with speculation on why Bob had wanted to search for this information, afraid to have the computer tell her what she could easily guess. Hospitals needed this data, she tried to rationalize, although she had presumed that UNITED ORGAN NETWORK would have provided it for him without his needing to bother performing the search himself. A few minutes later, the results came through on the AllSee's screen:

Computer Database Search Output.
Filter Specifications:
1) Biotype >95 percent compatibility with
F A658**B**333**C**983475D243
and
2) Living in North America or Europe
and
3) *Retro-negative*

Karolena scanned the list as it printed out. There were fifteen names in total, none familiar to her at first. Looking closer, she was astonished to see printed out:

Last Name	**First**	**Age**	***Retro***	**State**
Forest	Penny	19	neg.	Brighton, England

Of course Penny Forest was on the list, Karolena rationalized. Her heart was racing and she felt dizzy and disgusted, as she attempted to sort out rationalization from analysis, and found it almost impossible to do.

Yes, Penny was bio-compatible, and yes, Karolena had needed a donor and Penny was one of the few who could have donated. Surely there was no relationship other than this, she tried to rationalize. There could be no definite cause-and-effect link, she tried to reassure herself. But she couldn't help believing otherwise. The realization that Bob had known of Penny's existence before Penny died, that he had sought out this information, horrified Karolena. What terrible act had Bob done with this list? And on whose behalf?

Chapter 42

Armed with the information she had obtained in the hospital pharmacy and by her AllSee, Karolena took off toward the main hospital area. Karolena felt certain that she would find Bob at The Winston this time of the day. She needed to speak to Bob immediately, she felt betrayed and deceived, and she intended to demand some serious answers to some hard questions.

Karolena got off the WCMC elevator near the Executive Offices, and approached the holographic receptionist outside Bob's office and stated her name. Marveling for a moment at how incredibly lifelike this hologram appeared, she asked, "Is Mr. Wilder in?"

The holographic program had already picked up Karolena's identity from her wrist ID as she entered the room. "No, I'm afraid he's not," the hologram said. As it spoke, the neural network automatically searched its computer banks for any particular replies to be used for Karolena Kreisler. It noticed that Administrator Bob had wanted to be notified whenever Karolena visited The Winston, and to have hospital security notified as well. Bob had also instructed the system to delay Karolena until hospital security could respond.

The receptionist hologram continued, "Mr. Wilder isn't scheduled to be here now.

"I see."

"Do you have an appointment? Could someone else help you?"

"No thanks. Can you tell me where Dr. Blütfink is?" realizing that Blütfink might have Bob with him, or at least knew where Bob was.

The hologram took a long time to process its response, making Karolena suspicious. She turned to leave, but the receptionist said, "Wait. Do not leave yet."

"Why not?" Karolena asked the hologram.

Not being programmed to deceive or lie, it replied, "Because Hospital Security wants to talk to you."

Hearing that was enough to make her run out of the office, before hospital security would be able to hold her. She could just imagine herself a prisoner of Bob in some dark O.R. As she started to run, her vision shifted suddenly and dramatically, until …

. . . The walls in front of her melted away, and Karolena suddenly had a vision of an operating room, a scene so terrifyingly real that she momentarily forgot where she was. Only this time she didn't think it was here at The Winston. No, she thought, it looked more like the experimental surgery area at FirsThought Scientific. Rickhard Blütfink was standing over the body of a patient lying on the operating table. He grasped a scalpel blade in one gloved hand and a surgical retractor in the other. Traces of fresh blood coated the gloves. Blütfink looked her way, but either didn't see her or was indifferent.

Approaching the operating table, Karolena looked down at the patient and recognized Mr. Bob Wilder himself, unconscious, an endotracheal tube protruding from his mouth. Bob's eyes suddenly popped open, startling Karolena. He smiled menacingly up at her, then reached out and tightly grabbed her arm, pulling her toward the operating table, dragging her down toward him, . . .

"No." she shrieked out. Shaking her head, Karolena retreated a step, and instantly her sight switched back to the reality of the hall she stood in. She took one look around, then broke into a fretful run toward the O.R. suite, taking a clue from Penny.

Karolena took an open elevator down to the surgical suite level. Because she was still considered an employee at FirsThought and occasionally needed access to the surgical suite along with Dr. Blütfink, her wrist ID provided her access past the electric door.

Outside the O.R. area, Karolena hit the concealed plate on the molding as she had seen the nurses do on her way to the O.R. ages ago. The doors swung open, revealing an empty hall area. The O.R. receptionist was absent, but Karolena could see several lights on at the end of the hall leading into the O.R. offices.

Karolena hurried through the O.R. entrance way, where the scanner picked up her wrist IDs, and another computer-generated warning was sent to WCMC security.

Karolena stopped around the corner from the entrance, donned a mask and paper hat as an attempt at disguise to surprise Blütfink, then put on some paper bootie covers and a loose scrub cover. She passed the supply room, thought better of it, then backtracked and went inside. Karolena quickly searched the shelves for something to use for defense, just in case she needed protection from Blütfink. Near a top shelf she found a box of individually wrapped surgical scalpel blades mounted on green plastic handles. Karolena took a handful and stuffed them into her scrub jacket pocket. She had never used a weapon in her life, but was certainly prepared to in defense of her own life now.

Exiting the supply room, Karolena crept close against the wall as she cautiously went down the hall. Soon she could hear the unmistakably irritating voice of Rickhard Blütfink coming from inside an office. Looking in, she saw Blütfink seated at his desk in full O.R. scrubs with a face mask draped low over his jaw and covering his throat. Blood droplets spattered the sleeve of his light green O.R. jacket, leading Karolena to wonder if he had just finished an operation. He was giving instructions and orders to an AllSee when he looked up and saw Karolena come in.

"Call you back later, babe. Got to go now," he gruffly said, a scowl forming on his face, and he quickly hung up. Blütfink turned toward Karolena, his annoyance evident. "This is a restricted sterile area. What gives you the right to come in here?"

"Why, Rickhard, I just want to talk to you. Aren't you glad to see me?" She despised him more now than she ever had, and went out of her way to lay on a heavy dose of the sarcasm he hated so.

"I don't recall ever being glad to see you, and if you don't leave immediately, I'll call Security and have you removed forcibly."

"Oh, go ahead, call security," Karolena taunted. "I wish you would. I think they'll be very interested to hear about your involvement in murder, medical malpractice, ethical misconduct, *et cetera, et cetera.* You squirrelly little bastard, you'll be the one who goes to jail, and probably to hell after that for all you've done," she screamed, her face flushed scarlet, angry remembrances of what it was like to live with that egotistical creep flooding her mind.

Blütfink sprang up and yelled, "How dare you talk to me like that? I'm your doctor."

"You were my doctor. Now you're nobody's doctor. In fact, why, you're NO doctor at all, Rickhard. You're a murderer."

Enraged, Blütfink moved forward suddenly and slapped Karolena across her face. "You can't threaten me, you little bitch. I saved your life, don't you ever forget that." As he spoke, he slid his right hand into the pocket of his O.R. jacket and got a firm grip on a Stun Gun he kept for protection. "Thanks to me you have a functioning visual center and can see again."

"Yeah, with a piece of brain from a girl named Penny Forest, in Brighton, England. A girl who is dead."

"Sure, your donor was deceased," Blütfink shot back. "What else would you expect? Healthy people don't donate, and sick people aren't acceptable donors, especially if its brain tissue. But that isn't any reason to accuse a medical professional of criminal conduct."

"According to the police report, Penny Forest was murdered."

"I'm sorry, but I know nothing about that."

"Oh, I think you know something about everything that happens here," she countered.

"This isn't my hospital, Karolena. I just work here. I'm only an independent contractor. I'm not responsible for donor graft procurement. And I certainly don't know anything about any criminal activity committed by other persons at the hospital." Blütfink reached down and reactivated the alarm signal on the outside of his AllSee. "You know, Karolena, I'm sure this is going to surprise you, but . . . " he laughed nervously, " . . . you will want to know this. When you were very ill, your father would constantly call to threaten and attempt to intimidate both the hospital administrator and me. He kept pressuring me, he offered bribes, he wouldn't let the donor identification process take its own course. No, he was so concerned about you that he had to have a donor available instantly. He had no idea how hard we were trying, first to stabilize you in any way we could, and avoid a transplant, and then to find a healthy donor when only a transplant would save you."

"I know that. I realize that my father can be pushy, but he was under incredible pressure and worried constantly about my health."

"Oh yeah? Well, then maybe you didn't know this. Your father offered Bob and me over a million DM to locate a donor for you. That's a pretty strong incentive, if you ask me. Somehow, and believe me, I don't know how he did it, your father managed to find out about a potential donor list that Mr. Wilder had obtained."

Karolena could see where Blütfink was going with his accusations, and didn't want to listen.

"Your father demanded that Bob give him the list, but Bob refused, and wisely so. Nevertheless, a donor appeared shortly after that. Now, what conclusions do you draw from that?"

"I know about the list, although I had no idea my father requested it," Karolena snapped. "My father probably only wanted it to see how long I might have to wait for a donor. Besides, Penny Forest was killed by Dieter Müeller, not by my father."

Apparently, by the shocked look on his face, Blütfink didn't know, nor did he doubt her. "Okay, then what makes you think I'm involved? UNITED ORGAN NETWORK notified us that the needed organs were available after Penny Forest died, and we accepted them. That's all we did. That doesn't make us murderers. I'll tell you this much, Karolena. **WE** didn't kill this Penny Forest and **WE** sure as hell didn't ask Dieter Müeller or anyone to kill her for us."

"Then who did? Just what are you implying?" Karolena shouted at Blütfink.

"Your father knew about Penny Forest, and your father is a reckless and impulsive person. You know that. He loved you so much he would do anything to keep you alive. You know that too, Karolena. It's entirely possible that your illness forced him to have Penny killed, and, in that case, ultimately, it's really you and he who are responsible for her death."

"No way." Karolena replied, defensively. She violently shook her head as if the action would both deny the accusation and throw the thought from her mind. "My father would never do that," she insisted, although in some deep recess of her consciousness she had already suspected just that possibility, ugly as it was. "I think you and Bob had her killed, and you used Dieter to do your dirty work. Dieter killed Penny for you, and he probably killed some others, too. And now the police have him, and I'm sure that, after speaking with Dieter, they'll be coming over here to talk to you too." Despite Blütfink's vehement protestations otherwise, she said, "I'm going to the police about this. You know, I can't believe I ever had any feelings for you. Just thinking about it makes me sick. You're finished, Rickhard. FINISHED."

As Karolena reached into her pocket for her AllSee, Blütfink pulled a Stun Gun out of his pocket and lunged at Karolena. Seeing him charging at her, she dodged out of the way and ran through the door, dropping her AllSee unit and spilling some scalpel blades from her pocket along the way. Expecting to be hit by the stun gun any second, she frantically looked around for any space to hide in.

Blütfink chased Karolena around the empty O.R. control desk and back into the hall, waving his Stun Gun wildly and slashed and stabbed at her with one of the scalpel blades Karolena had dropped. Karolena screamed, her desperate voice echoing furtively off the tile walls of the empty corridor. She pushed a gurney at

Blütfink, making him trip and fall to the floor, then, while he was down, quickly toppled an IV pole down on top of him, hitting his head with a large fluid pump unit.

Karolena turned and ran into an open operating room and closed the door behind her. She cursed when she saw that there was no inside lock, and no other way out. She had no idea just how much she had hurt Blütfink, but wanted to get safely away in case he would still be after her. There was nothing to grab but a metal bed pan as a weapon, and she turned out the light and crouched down in the corner.

Momentarily stunned, Blütfink managed to grab the IV pole from the gurney and struggled to use it as a crutch to get up off the floor. Picking up his stun gun, he followed Karolena into the operating room. Even with the light out, he saw her immediately and fired his stun gun.

The blast hit near her head, but fortunately missed her by several inches. Angered even more, Blütfink stabbed at her violently with the pole. Bleeding from a gash on her shoulder, Karolena fell exhausted against the wall. Blütfink lifted the IV pole high in the air over Karolena's head like a triumphant warrior, the light from the hall highlighting him from behind, making him appear to Karolena like the monster he actually was.

"This is my life, my career, and I'll not let you destroy it." he screamed. "I saved your life, but that wasn't good enough for you, and now I'll take it back."

"You and Bob were killing people to get transplant

organs, and for what? Just to make some money, you greedy bastard. You never have enough, you're never satisfied," Karolena yelled. "But what about what I wanted? You never asked **me**. I never wanted to live at someone's expense. Can't you understand that?"

"I never killed anyone. I never had anything to do with it. It was Bob Wilder, and your father too. I never knew until the end, when it was all too obvious. But I'll not let you destroy my years of work. I've always hated you."

With the IV pole held high, Blütfink moved closer and swung it down at Karolena's head, but she dodged, and the pole dug cruelly in her shoulder.

Karolena screamed out in anguish, and managed to kick Blütfink solidly in the groin and pushed him back against the wall. He cried out in pain, and rolled down on the floor, gripping his crotch.

Karolena placed her palm tightly over the cut on her shoulder, applying pressure to stop the bleeding. The cut looked deep, and the bleeding was slow to stop. She knew she would need to go the ER for sutures to close a laceration that severe. The wound stung terribly and the rest of her arm felt numb.

Karolena started crawling toward the door, when, in disbelief, she saw Blütfink slowly get up. "Stay away from me, you crazy bastard," she yelled out, but, when her warning went unheeded, she wondered what she could do now to stay alive. Grabbing the pole he had just swung at her, she stood up and hit him hard over his head, dropping him back to his knees.

Exhausted, Blütfink stopped moving after this last

hit, and wasn't for the moment a threat to Karolena. Trying to use the opportunity to find out as much as she could, to try to disprove the terrible things he had just accused her and her father of, she asked him, "Are you telling me that you functioned merely as a technician to place the organs in?" Blütfink had no response to give, at least none that would make him appear innocent.

Karolena saw that the gash on her shoulder had stopped bleeding, but it still hurt like hell, and she had a terrible headache. Bits of paint and plaster covered her clothes, and her face and hair smelled of burnt smoke from the stun gun's discharge.

"Yeah. Absolutely," Blütfink cried out. "I was only the middleman. Dieter was the supplier; Bob Wilder was the one who placed the first order. And your father did it all for you."

"Even if he did ask Dieter to help me, I don't see how my father could have been involved in the deaths of all the other donors for the patients at The Winston." Besides, she remembered, her father hasn't visited her in almost a year.

Blütfink stayed coiled up on the floor, covered with blood and debris, moaning and slowly rocking back and forth.

"You kept track of who on the transplant list wasn't moving," she seemed to be restating the obvious. "You knew who had the most critical need for an organ, and which ones were unlikely to be met. It had to have been you and Bob who sent Dieter to find the donors and that came after Penny." Blütfink wasn't replying or denying, but his silence, the way he looked away, the lying look on his face that she knew all too well, that said it all.

Blütfink glanced pleadingly at Karolena, but tellingly didn't dispute what she was accusing him of. "But your father started this mess, and he gave Bob Wilder and Dieter the goddamn idea." Blütfink protested.

"Why did Dieter ever get involved in this?" Karolena demanded. "Was it for money?"

"For the most part. Once Bob figured out what Dieter was willing to do at your father's request, he forced Dieter into solving other '*difficult*' donor situations. And he also got Dieter to help with some sticky personal problems."

"Like me?" Karolena demanded. "Did Bob tell Dieter to kill me?"

Blütfink shook his head. "I don't know, I really don't," he moaned, although it was obvious to Karolena he really did. He looked at Karolena and started coughing a choking sound and crying. "Why don't you ask Bob?" Blütfink asked her, looking up at Karolena, his face a tearful mass of confusion. "I really don't know anything more. Please, believe me."

As Blütfink pleaded, Karolena could see that he probably was telling the truth for once. She felt only revulsion and hatred for the man, without any pity or understanding at all, and she knew that whatever relationship they had once had was gone forever. She really didn't know him anymore, and had no desire to even try. His evil sucked the very life out of her, she could feel that and wanted to get as far from him as possible.

Chapter 43

After seeing Karolena, the woman she blamed for her daughter's death, run by in the hospital lobby, Barbara Forest entered the surgical suite to catch her. Walking down the empty corridor, Barbara noticed the disarray that was everywhere and assumed there had been a fight. Pulling out her ceramic stun gun and listening carefully, the first sounds were a male voice moaning, which led her to a room where she found Blütfink.

"What happened to you?" Barbara asked.

"Who are you?" Blütfink asked while looking in her direction, trying his best to focus.

"I'm Penny Forest's mother, and I am here to avenge her death. I loved her very very much." Looking beyond his face, staring into his very soul, she asked, "Are you the one that killed my daughter?"

"No, not me, not me. I am a doctor. But I know who did." Seeing he had her attention, and thereby a moment of relative safety, he continued, "Karolena Kreisler killed your daughter. Yes, it was her. And she was just here, and she attacked me because I tried to stop her from hurting more people. Please, help me get to the ER for some help."

Ignoring Blütfink's wounds, Barbara asked, "Do you know where she went?"

As she walked down the first floor hall of The Winston, looking for a way to contact the city police,

Karolena was astonished when she saw Blütfink, who had struggled after her from the O.R. She realized that hospital security must be here, in this very building, and they would be looking for her.

She ran toward Blütfink, angrily calling out his name as he hobbled toward the ER doors.

Blütfink turned to see a screaming Karolena chasing after him, and yelled out for the hospital security guards to help him.

Karolena desperately grabbed at Blütfink's coat and pulled him around.

"What the hell do you want?" Blütfink sneered at Karolena. "Didn't you do enough to me? You'll pay for all this, believe me you will."

As soon as Barbara left the stairwell, she saw Blütfink walk by, chased by the very person she had been pursuing for so long. Barbara's pulse raced as anger swelled up in her chest. There's the son of a bitch who got Penny's brain, she thought. We want our revenge, NOW.

As she moved toward them, Barbara watched Karolena and Blütfink stop momentarily to argue, before Blütfink proceeded toward the ER. The conversation between them got hotter by the minute, Blütfink grabbed Karolena's coat, and threw her down on the ground. As he lifted his foot and prepared to kick her, Barbara pointed her ExploDart at them both and yelled out for him to not move.

"It's because of you that my daughter died, and now you deserve to die," Barbara yelled out to Karolena.

Karolena realized that this woman was Penny's mother, and surmised why she was here. "I know your daughter died, and I'm truly sorry for that, believe me, but I had nothing to do with it." Pointing over at Blütfink, Karolena said, "He arranged to transplant part of your daughter into me, and for that, I'm alive. I have no idea how she died or why, but you must believe me that I had no part in it. If I ever thought I could only live if someone else died, I would rather have died too."

Turning the ExploDart toward Blütfink, Barbara asked, "What do you have to say to that?"

Nervously eyeing the ExploDart, Blütfink pleaded, "I don't have any idea what she's talking about," but as soon as Barbara directed her attention back to Karolena, Blütfink ran for the door.

The ExploDart moved faster that Blütfink, and tore into his upper back between his shoulder blades, inches below his skull. As soon as he was hit, fins in the ExploDart caught in his shirt before detonating. The explosion, sounding like no more than a dull thud to Karolena as she ran next to Blütfink, smashed him to the floor and into unconsciousness. Karolena panicked, now aware that she too was under attack. She threw herself onto the floor and looked around for a safe place to hide. That time Blütfink, not her, was the intended target, but her turn was next.

Karolena's desperate screams for help drew several nurses and a Surgical Resident out of the ER and into the crowded confusion. Karolena was soon pushed aside by the growing crowd of medical personnel, and she took advantage of the confusion and used the crowd as a shield while she moved quickly away from the scene of carnage, a scene she felt certain could have been her.

One of the paramedics from hospital security ran out of the ER entrance when she heard the screams. After examining Blütfink's back wound briefly and appreciating the magnitude of damage, she looked up at the nurses. "Please, call a Code. And get the Trauma Team over here." Almost immediately the overhead speakers announced, "Code Blue, Administrative Corridor 1 South."

The paramedic tried to shield Blütfink from further harm as she helplessly looked around for his assailant. Then, she saw some unusual movement out in the courtyard. An older woman with a large handbag pushed her way into a line outside the bookstore. Other people in the line were complaining and shoving back. The woman looked strangely unfamiliar, disheveled, and definitely out of place. Sensing something terribly wrong, security desperately ran after the elderly woman. Bolting out into the courtyard, shoving people out of her way, she angrily pulled her pistol out from its holster. She grabbed the older woman and swung her around.

Barbara Forest, realizing she was recognized, fought to get hold of her ExploDart. "Penny, help me, please." she screamed.

Seeing Barbara's hands move, the woman from security forcefully drove her knee into Barbara's chest, then gave her a spinning side kick into the face. The force of the blow sent Barbara shattering through the plate glass window of the bookstore.

Hospital security walked up to where Barbara was lying, bleeding from several glass cuts, and unconscious on a bed of glass shards. She handcuffed Barbara, and then helped the trauma team load her onto a gurney.

Chapter 44

Blütfink struggled to awake in the Surgical Intensive Care Unit hours later. Through a fog of pain, he recognized Malawassi's familiar face, discussing his case with some other people in hushed and worried tones off to the side of his bed. The halo of a Magnetic Resonance Imaging unit purred away over his bed. Blütfink tried to move, but the pain crushed him back. He groaned at the sensation of a hot iron burning deep between his shoulders, a constant, severe, gnawing pain. He saw Malawassi speak to a person from hospital security, shake his head angrily, then leave the room.

"What happened?" Blütfink struggled to call out, having barely regained consciousness, "what happened?" He found it hard to speak with a suction tube in his nose and down the back of his throat, and gagged and coughed intermittently.

Malawassi came over to his bedside and said, "Please try to be still and don't more, Rickhard. Someone shot you with an ExploDart. You're lucky not to be dead."

"Maybe I would be better off that way. Please, tell me the truth. How bad am I hurt? Will I be all right?"

"We'll see," Malawassi told him, his voice cracking under the stress of the violence as he fought to remain calm.

Blütfink tried to recall what had happened, then yelled out in his anguish, "It was Karolena. She was with me. She tried to kill me, didn't she?"

"No, it wasn't her," security told him. "I found out who it was, and you won't believe it."

"Try me," Blütfink groaned.

"It was that woman reporter from England. You remember the weird one the police have been looking for. The one whose daughter was an organ donor."

Blütfink looked up at Garcia with confused disbelief. "Why her?" he choked.

"We don't know right now. The police are trying to help us. But, well we just don't know."

"Will I be all right?" Blütfink pleaded again to Malawassi.

"We don't know for sure. It's too early to say; we have to run a lot more tests, but, well I'm afraid it doesn't look very good," Malawassi said. "You suffered some very severe injuries."

"What do you mean? What kind of injuries?" Blütfink cried out. "Tell me. I want to know the truth, I want to know how bad I'm hurt, damn it." Tears formed in Blütfink's eyes.

"You should rest now, Rickhard. You're going to need all your strength for later." Malawassi turned away and continued his discussion. Blütfink coughed, then said groggily, "Can't you tell me? How could this happen to me?

"Oh, Dr. Blütfink, I'm really sorry," the woman from security apologized, reaching under the covers and holding his hand tightly.

Blütfink muttered a soft, "Yeah," before lapsing back into unconsciousness.

Later that evening, the Surgical ICU nurse brought two trays of food to Blütfink's room, known to WCMC insiders as the "Green Room." A special suite on the top floor of the hospital, it was reserved for VIP patients and their guests. A green plush rug covered the floor, totally inappropriate considering the types of fluids that inevitably spilled upon it. The stark hospital decor was softened with a light green curtain tied with a blue sash, and simulated mahogany furniture. A wall-size flat-screen display with a special sound system, and green and gold bed covers finished the room. Green and gold towels accentuated the attached bathroom.

The security representative took one of the trays from the bedside cart for her own use, and rested the other on Blütfink's legs, and started to prepare the food for him. The noise awoke Blütfink, who opened his eyes and then tried to reach up to scratch his nose. His eyes widened as he asked, "Where are my hands? I can't feel my goddamn hands," he yelled out

"Easy, Dr. Blütfink. Your hands are there," she reassured him.

Blütfink looked puzzled. "But I can't feel them."

"I guess they didn't tell you," she stammered.

"Tell me what?" Looking down at the tray lying across his legs, Blütfink realized suddenly that he also couldn't feel either the tray nor his feet. He tried moving his feet, but again felt nothing and saw no movement. "What's going on here?"

"Let me call Dr. Malawassi. He's really the best one to explain everything," she stumbled, as she quickly slipped away.

Malawassi wasn't able to return to Blütfink's room for several more hours. Finally, he rushed into the outer Green room, apologizing to the nurse about his delay in visiting Blütfink. Flashing his wrist **UN ID** to the security guard assigned to the Green room, he tried to look calm at the guard dog-bot that growled when he passed into the inner Green room.

Blütfink's eyes were closed so Malawassi addressed the private duty nurse assigned to him. "How is he doing?" Malawassi looked at the numbers flashing on the monitors and glanced at Blütfink's chart.

"The same," the nurse said. "He complains of loss of motor and sensory function in his lower extremities, and is in a lot of pain. The wounds on his hand and forehead are stable."

"Is he awake?" Malawassi asked the nurse.

"Hell, yes, I'm awake," Blütfink grumbled, opening his eyes. "All I want to know is one thing."

"Dr. Blütfink, I'm truly sorry for what happened and . . . "

Blütfink cut him off. "So am I, but your sorrow doesn't help things any. Can you fix it?"

Malawassi gave a nervous chuckle. "Fix it? I'm afraid it's not that easy. You can't simply 'fix' a transected spinal cord, . . . "

"A transected spinal cord." Blütfink exclaimed. "Nobody told me I had a . . . "

". . . not to mention all the ancillary tissue damage," Malawassi finished. "I mean, it just can't be done. You're lucky that you're even alive. If you hadn't been in a hospital at the time, . . . "

"Yeah, I'm real fortunate," Blütfink grumbled.

"I'm afraid, Dr. Blütfink, that you don't fully comprehend or perhaps aren't ready to accept the extent of your injury just yet," Malawassi said.

"Actually, I know it all too well, doctor. Well, so much for my dream of immortality." Blütfink interrupted, tears filling his eyes. "I'd rather die than live the rest of my life like this. SHIT."

Malawassi asked the private duty nurse to leave, then turned back to Blütfink. "I don't know about philosophical issues of life and immortality, but I think the situation isn't entirely hopeless. Not yet, that is."

"What do you mean? It looks pretty damned grim to me. I certainly don't want to live the rest of my life as a helpless quadriplegic, strapped to a motorized wheel chair, with an aide feeding me with a spoon and wiping my butt for me."

"It's certainly better than being dead, Dr. Blütfink."

"That's strictly a matter of opinion and perspective," Blütfink retorted. Then his face changed as he appeared to be pondering something deeply inspirational and encouraging. "We could try those nerve growth factors that can repair cut spinal cords, couldn't we?" Blütfink suggested to Malawassi. He was desperate, and reached for desperate measures.

"Yes, we certainly could. They work well on lower animals, but not so well on humans yet, especially with your extent of tissue damage. He paused a moment, then asked, "Do you remember the experimental surgery we performed on Karolena Kreisler?"

"Of course I do." The mention of Karolena's name irritated and pained him, as he recalled all the injury she had caused him. "What's that awful person got to do with reversing all this?" Blütfink demanded.

"Karolena received a transplant of the visual association area, a very limited type of experimental graft. Of course, no one has ever received an entire 'brain' graft."

"Sure, because that's not technically possible. It isn't possible, is it?"

"No, not as far as I know. Even the thought is unheard of," Malawassi told Blütfink.

"Than what has Karolena's optical cortex transplant to do with my condition?" Blütfink asked.

"Listen to this, please. Long after her operation, Ms. Kreisler came to see Dr. Fromposi about some troubling visual disturbances she was having," Malawassi continued. "At first, after Dr. Fromposi related this to me, I discounted it as a weird paranormal type of experience. I always thought Karolena was a little strange anyway."

"Yeah, she is," Blütfink agreed.

"But her strange visions, or whatever she was having persisted, and after a while they apparently took on a special meaning," Malawassi said.

"Like what special meaning?" Blütfink asked.

"Well, I think that at least some of her violent visions might have been attributed to the optical transplant she received." Malawassi said, looking uncomfortably away.

Blütfink was stunned, but was too surprised and shocked to say anything.

Malawassi looked dead serious, then continued in a low voice, "Maybe we actually transplanted visual memory from another person."

"You're joking," Blütfink nearly choked out, then asked, "You are joking, aren't you?" When Malawassi didn't back down, Blütfink asked, "Do you really think it's possible for Karolena to see what her donor did, even the events surrounding her death?"

"I don't know about that," Malawassi said, uncomfortable with this whole line of conversation. "There's very little experience to go on here, as optical transplants are such a new procedure. But we looked into it further, and another optical graft recipient reported similar visual aberrations. At first, I thought it was weird and impossible, but we ran some tests, and now I'm not so sure."

"But what does all this have to do with me?" Blütfink asked, drained from the effort of listening.

"Just this," Malawassi said, leaning over Blütfink's bed. "You really have few options here with the amount of damage you've sustained."

"So, you're telling me there's nothing you can do for me, is that it?"

"No, perhaps I'm telling you the opposite, Dr.

Blütfink. Most of the neural matter in the human brain is responsible for lower activity, like controlling muscle movement, processing sensation, breathing, regulating heart rate and temperature. Basic activities like that, except for some severed motor pathways, they're still unharmed and working for you now. But higher thoughts, memory, feelings, emotion, what makes you '*you*,' are located in the cerebral hemispheres. We think, that is my colleagues and I think . . . "

Blütfink could only stare in total disbelief at Malawassi, unsure if he correctly understood where this discussion was going.

"What I'm trying to get at, Dr. Blütfink, is that we propose taking those higher parts of your brain that carry your consciousness and personality and memory and transplanting them into an intact, uninjured body. Perhaps even into a younger, stronger body," Malawassi said.

Totally stunned at the magnitude of what Malawassi was proposing, Blütfink considered the ramifications for a long time before replying. He had a hard time taking Malawassi seriously, but managed to ask, "And even if I agreed to such an absurd idea, just where would you plan to find this other body?"

Malawassi looked questioningly over at hospital security.

"I think we can take care of the details," security said calmly. "But you're the only one who can give the go-ahead."

"I understand the alternatives," Blütfink told them,

directing his gaze back to Malawassi. "But, what are the risks?" As he stared pleadingly into Malawassi's face, he could already see the evasion forming. Under dissimilar circumstances, Blütfink would have been a great deal more demanding, forceful and insistent. Now, hopelessly trapped, he seemed to himself almost docile, and loathed the helpless quadriplegic he was fast becoming. His options were all too painfully narrow and limited.

"We can say with certainty that this has never been done before. You'll be breaking new ground," Malawassi said, his reticent voice devoid of reassurance.

"Great," Blütfink said, sarcastically. "That's what I'm afraid of." He looked around, puzzled.

"I'm afraid you have little choice. No guts, no glory, they say," Malawassi forced a smile. Malawassi impatiently waited for Blütfink to absorb what was happening, then said, "In terms of what might go wrong," he persisted, "well obviously, you could die, . . . "

"Yeah, thanks," Blütfink interjected. "Spare me the specifics, please."

". . . the transplant might not take, our theory might be wrong and your 'essence' might not be transplantable," Malawassi persisted. "A million other things could happen, but think of the benefits, Dr. Blütfink. You could get another sixty plus years of life, a new body, and escape from whoever was trying to kill you. And, you won't have to live the life, if you can call it that, of a quadriplegic."

Blütfink could scarcely imagine the fame, the money, the immortality that even attempting such a procedure would give him, whether successful or not. "Just think," he said to Malawassi, "just ten years ago you couldn't even get permission to try something as totally outlandish as this. But, today . . . " Blütfink became more excited by the minute. In some ways this possibility felt better, more exciting, than even a sexual climax, and he was finally, truly enjoying himself in the potential of a new, younger life.

"What do you say, Dr. Blütfink? The sooner we move on this, the better."

"Where would you perform this complex a neurosurgical operation?" Blütfink nervously asked, still highly skeptical, despite his being short on options. "Here?"

"No, not here. At FirsThought, in their experimental neurosurgery unit," Malawassi told him. "So, what's it going to be," he gestured to the shell of a body, "yes to immortality or no and live like this?"

Chapter 45

Karolena quickly escaped from The Winston, drove over to her apartment, and immediately called Blum. After explaining what had happened a few minutes ago, he instructed her to remain in her apartment, and under no circumstances was she to leave.

As soon as Blum had hung up, the vision of Penny appeared, even without Karolena being in a dream-like state. "Come with me," Penny moaned, motioning with her arm.

"I wouldn't like that, Penny," Karolena insisted, suppressing her own terror and fighting to speak softly to the apparition. She felt an uncontrollable urge to run and save her own life now. Still, she knew she had to maintain some hand in the events, some semblance of control, not yielding everything to Penny, least she suffer the same gruesome fate as Blütfink. "I belong here, Penny, and you need to go back," Karolena said.

Penny gently took hold of Karolena's wrist and tried to draw her into the kitchen.

Karolena looked into Penny's translucent eyes and firmly told her, "I belong here. I fought so hard to live, to get well. Please, I want to stay. Let me stay and live. And you can live too, thru me."

Penny stared at Karolena for a long time without speaking. She held onto Karolena's hand, and again insistently tried to lead Karolena out, not forcefully, just firmly. *"Karolena, there's something I have to find before dinner. Let's look together. Please."*

"Okay," Karolena said, seeing she had little choice, "but just for a short time. But then I'm staying here at my home."

Penny nodded, walking into the kitchen. She held a piece of fresh liver in one hand, dripping a trail of blood along the way, and Karolena's hand in the other.

As they passed next to a mirror, Karolena saw her own reflection but not Penny's, and she felt a chill, causing her to utter, "Die Frau Ohne Schatten." Karolena felt as if she was going to faint, and leaned momentarily against the wall for support as she walked. In silence, they continued slowly moving down the hall, together but dimensions apart.

Penny stopped in the middle of the kitchen, only now it had morphed into an operating room. On the kitchen wall, a sign announced,

> **EXPERIMENTAL SURGERY**
> O.R. Room #7. Organ Donation. Sterile.
> Entry Restricted.
> Use Containment and Scrub Room #7A."

He's in here, Karolena," Penny whispered, her words almost a moan.

"Who's in here?" Karolena asked, already numb with fear at the physical transformation she was witnessing.

Penny didn't reply, but motioned her forward.

Karolena tried the door to the kitchen but found it was locked. Determined, she went around the corner looking for another way in to what was now, apparently, the O.R. The door to the outer scrub room was unlocked and she quickly entered. In the subdued light Karolena moved cautiously, feeling her way past various wash basins with faucets activated by knee movement, and packets of sterilizing soap and brushes stacked nearby. From here, Karolena tried to open the door leading into the inner room, but still found it locked. Frustrated, she turned to leave.

Just then, the outer scrub room door through which Karolena had entered finally closed against the back pressure of its hydraulic lifters. There was a soft click and instantly a green light came on. This directed them to an exit door from the scrub room into the O.R. itself. The light indicated that the door interlock had engaged. Quickly, Karolena hurried through the hissing of air blast curtains and the ultraviolet barrier and into the operating room.

Under the subdued greenish lights Karolena saw what appeared to be a body lying on the operating table, covered completely with a green sheet. Her heart pounding, Karolena moved closer. As she accidentally brushed against the body, a hand fell over the side, swinging back and forth like a pendulum. Gingerly, Karolena picked up the wrist and read the name "Blütfink, R." on the wrist **UN ID**. She steadied her nerve, then slowly drew back the sheet. She had to know for certain.

Blütfink faced upward, his appearance an ashen

gray. Drained of life, his chest no longer rose and fell with the breath of live. Karolena looked down at Blütfink in disbelief and checked for a pulse to be certain that he really was dead. "You bastard," she cursed under her breath. She picked up the O.R. record attached to the clipboard lying on his chest and read, "Cause of Death: ExploDart wound to the upper back. Expired during emergency surgery."

The body disposition log noted that Blütfink was scheduled for cremation in the hospital incinerator at The Winston in the morning, after a short ceremony in the hospital auditorium.

He's dead, Karolena," Penny said. She took Blütfink's death record from Karolena and crumbled it in her hands. *"It's all over now. Let's go home."*

"I am home, Penny. Please, let me stay," Karolena pleaded. As Karolena walked out the O.R. doors and back into her apartment's kitchen, she was relieved to see Penny slowly move up through the ceiling and merge into the nothingness from whence she had arrived. *Good-by, Penny*, she thought, then slowly turned her gaze away.

Chapter 46

Auditorium, Winston County Medical Center

The next day, a ceremony honoring Doctor Rickhard Blütfink, former surgeon at the Winston County Medical Center, took place in the hospital auditorium. In silence, a few mourners filed out after the short presentation. Once the auditorium was empty, two hospital workers moved Blütfink's flower-covered body from the display coffin and moved it onto a metal tray for transfer to the crematorium. Unexpectedly, one of the men lost his grip on the transfer tray, allowing Blütfink's corpse to drop three feet onto the floor with a loud crash.

"Wow, what a mess. Help me lift the stiff back on," he yelled.

"Take it easy," said the other man. "I don't think anyone will notice, least of all this guy." They both laughed. As they flopped the body back onto the cart, the right side of Blütfink's head seemed to come loose, and his skull opened up like a coconut.

"Hey, look at this," the first man said, pointing to the inside of Blütfink's skull, which was completely empty. "Well, it sure backs up what I always thought about him," he added and chuckled.

"I wonder where the insides went?" his companion asked.

The first man shrugged without answering, a look

of uncomfortable confusion on his face.

A few minutes later, the hospital workers reached the incinerator area. A sickly dry chalky odor permeated the small concrete room. The workers lay one end of the heavy body tray on the outer edge of the incinerator door and tipped the other end up. Blütfink's corpse slid silently into the flesh-destroying inferno. Heat and smoke from the furnace blew out and into their faces, forcing them back, coughing.

The lifeless body of Rickhard Blütfink M.D. with the essence of a recently killed street urchin - a kilogram of semisolid brain - instantly became unrecognizable ash on its fiery journey to oblivion. Stuffed into Blütfink's pants pocket, burning along with his mangled body, was the essence of his former identity, his wrist ID bracelet.

Ethics Essays of Donald H. Marks

Jonas Salk, Polio Vaccine and Vaccinating Against Hate. Thoughts on treating hate as an infectious disease.
https://dhmarks.blogspot.com/2018/10/jonas-salk-polio-vaccine-and.html

Einstein, Relativity and Relative Ethics. Considerations on whether ethical decisions can be situational.
https://dhmarks.blogspot.com/2018/10/einstein-relativity-and-relative-ethics.html

What I Have Not Told My Family About The Meaning of Time. Personal reflections on mortality.
https://dhmarks.blogspot.com/2018/10/what-i-have-not-told-my-family-about.html

Available on search engines and on the author's blog https://dhmarks.blogspot.com

Made in United States
North Haven, CT
12 November 2024

59797156R00286